THE
MANGROVE
COAST

ALSO BY RANDY WAYNE WHITE

Fiction
Sanibel Flats
The Heat Islands
The Man Who Invented Florida
Captiva
North of Havana

Nonfiction
Batfishing in the Rainforest

THE MANGROVE COAST

Randy Wayne White

G. P. Putnam's Sons
New York

G. P. Putnam's Sons
Publishers Since 1838
a member of
Penguin Putnam Inc.
375 Hudson Street
New York, NY 10014

Library of Congress Cataloging-in-Publication Data

White, Randy Wayne.
The Mangrove Coast / by Randy Wayne White.
p.   cm.
ISBN 0-399-14372-6 (acid-free paper)
I. Title.
PS3573.H47473M38   1998   98-22243 CIP
813'.54—dc21

Printed in the United States of America

1   3   5   7   9   10   8   6   4   2

This book is printed on acid-free paper. ∞

BOOK DESIGN BY RENATO STANISIC

Author's Note

✳

The portions of this novel set in Panama and the former Panama Canal Zone could not have been written without the advice and patient guidance of men and women who know the area far better than I. For this I thank: T-Bird Tom Pattison, Captain Bob Dollar and Mindy, Queen of the Chilibre Hill Gang; Taj Mahal advocate Jay Sieleman, *la chinita linda* Priscilla Hernandez, Legendary Vernon Scholey, Renate Jope, Mimi and Lucho Azcarraga, and my friend Teresa Martinez. Not only did these kind people introduce me to sunsets at Panama's Balboa Yacht Club; they also added much in terms of detail and texture about life in the former Canal Zone. However, the portrayal of what is now happening in Panama, while factually accurate, has been filtered through my eyes and my eyes only. Any errors or misrepresentations of fact in this novel are entirely my fault, or of my own creation, as are all claims, insights or opinions implicit or otherwise that might be considered political or controversial.

I would also like to remind readers of the many thousands of Americans past and present who were proudly and justly called Zonians. Without complaint or excuse, these extraordinary people kept the canal open and running every hour of every day flawlessly and without pause for nearly nine decades.

The entire world owes them a debt of gratitude.

I also thank Lee and Debbie White for their steadfast support, as well as my friends in Cartagena, Colombia, for their help and unfailing hospitality: Alvaro Sierra, Norm Bennett, plus George Baker and Jorge Araujo of Comexa Co. They really do make one of the best and most fragrant hot sauces in the world: Fiery Green Amazona.

Finally, I thank Rogan White for his assistance, and Dr. Roy Crabtree and Lewis Bullock for allowing Doc Ford to help with their grouper research.

For . . .

Dr. Floyd L. White, a good man. The great Totch Brown who did not share Tuck's negative qualities. Mark Bryant, Larry Burke and all the fine editors at Outside *magazine who kept me on the road. And the Panamaniacs.*

To educate a man in mind and not in morals is
to educate a menace to society.
—THEODORE ROOSEVELT,
SHORTLY AFTER THE COMPLETION OF THE PANAMA CANAL

E-mail is not to be used to pass on factual information or
important data. It is for departmental use only.
—DIRECTIVE TO FEDERAL EMPLOYEES FROM
A CLINTON APPOINTEE (FOUND ON THE INTERNET)

Our ends are the same. We can do somethin' big or we can
play it safe. Either way, our ends are the same.
—ERVIN T. ROUSE,
COMPOSER OF "THE ORANGE BLOSSOM SPECIAL,"
IN CONVERSATION AT THE GATOR HOOK BAR, THE EVERGLADES

Prologue

It was Tomlinson who suggested that I write about Panama; that I review on paper what happened and how it happened. He told me, "It might be good for your soul, man. Kind of a purge deal. Your tummy's upset, you pop a couple of Alka-Seltzers, right? Maybe eat some stewed prunes, get rid of the bad stuff. Same thing. Put it down on paper and it's gone."

I was on the deck of my stilthouse at the time, Dinkin's Bay Marina, Sanibel Island, southwest coast of Florida.

I'd been doing pull-ups.

Lately, I'd been doing lots and lots of pull-ups.

Thinking about Panama brought back specific unrelated images: black rain, banana leaves fauceting water, lunar halos, small precise breasts, a woman's eyes diminished by uncertainty, wood fires, a mangrove shore . . .

I told Tomlinson that my soul was doing just fine, thank you very much.

It was a lie.

✳

Three days later, I said to Tomlinson: "Write it all down, huh?"

He was momentarily confused, but then he was right there with me. It is, perhaps, because Tomlinson is always lost that he is also endlessly empathetic. He said, "Just a suggestion. I got to tell you, Doc, you haven't exactly been yourself. When you look inward, man, your eyes actually change color. What used to be your Gulf Stream stare? Kicked back, friendly, drifting? It is now gray, dude, seriously gray. I mean like boiled beef. Not a pretty sight. Or maybe get some counseling. We catch a virus, we go to the doctor, no big deal. So we get an emotional virus, what's wrong with getting a little psychiatric help? Christ, I spent a year making wallets and signing my letters, 'Sincerely as a fucking loon.' And look how together I am now."

I said, "Right. Your stability is . . . well . . . right out there for anyone to see." Then I said, "Like a kind of intellectual exercise." I was still discussing the prospect of writing.

"An exercise, sure. That's one way of approaching it."

The difference between patronization and kindness is intent. I was being treated kindly. Still . . . it struck me as having interesting potential.

The human animal is accurately named. And I am, after all, a biologist.

✳

Here's what I'd been wrestling with ever since returning from Central America: What quirk of experience or genetic coding compelled certain men to isolate vulnerable women and then to prey upon them?

That kind of behavior certainly did not benefit the species, so why were their devices so commonplace . . . and so successful?

The problem had bothered me since Panama. How can one protect all good and delicate people, all the children and wounded ladies, who are potential targets?

Perhaps it is more accurate to say that the problem haunted me.

For Tomlinson, I condensed the dilemma: "Not all sexual predators are killers or serial rapists. The most successful of them live well within the boundaries of the law and they're probably more common than we'd like to believe. See . . . the problem is identifying the bastards. They are not social anomalies; they are social deviants."

He said, "I'm with you, man. The difference is subtle but specific."

I said, "Exactly. So what's that mean? What it means is, to succeed they must give the appearance of living socially acceptable lives. They must construct a believable facade so that their secret motives go unsuspected. Like camouflage, understand? They live a lie their entire lives . . . which means they become superb liars and actors."

Tomlinson was nodding, following along, indulging me. "You're talking about that guy. Merlot? Jackie Merlot."

Just hearing the name keyed the gag reflex in me . . . and something else, too: dread.

I said, "Yeah. Pedophiles, voyeurs, wife beaters, the back-alley freaks. Ted Bundy—he's another textbook example. But that's an extreme case. More commonly, only their victims know who these people are and what they really are. No, I'll amend that. The truly successful predators are probably so adept at manipulation that their victims never realize they've been used."

Tomlinson was listening sympathetically, not analytically. I found that irritating. Did he really believe that I was so adolescent that I needed that kind of friend?

He said, "You've got a lot of anger built up. The subject makes you furious. I can see it."

I winced. "You're missing the entire damn point. I'm talking about difficulties of assessment. Pathology, not emotion."

"Sure. I relate entirely! It's exactly the kind of stuff you need to be writing. Get it out of your system. You know another reason it might be good to get it down on paper? If the feds decide to take up the case again, call you in to testify, you can always refer to your notes. Tell them, hey, this is the way it all went down. I mean, if they decide the guy didn't exactly disappear on purpose, they might come around again and ask more questions."

I was nodding; smiling just a little. I said, "Yeah, a written record. I see what you mean. Accurate notes of what went on, plus it might help me deal with losing what I lost."

But I was thinking: *No matter how many questions they ask, they'll never find out what happened to Jackie Merlot. . . .*

The Mangrove Coast

Certain odors key the synapse electrodes, and there is no alternative but to return to the precise time and place in memory with which those odors are associated.

Why is the linear memory so much easier to discipline than memories that are sensory?

It's like one of Tomlinson's favorite little paradoxes: *I have no choice but to believe in free will.*

If there is such a thing as free will, how is it that one can have no choice?

What I am avoiding discussing, I guess, is how I happened to return to Panama. What I'm avoiding discussing is how it all began and what happened afterward.

It would make an interesting research paper: "The Olfactory Senses as Conduit to Recall . . ."

Yes. Odors . . .

The barrier islands of Florida's west coast have their own odor, their own feel. It's a fabric of strata and weight: seawater, sulfur muck, white sand, Gulf Stream allusions and a wind that blows salt-heavy out of the Yucatan and Cuba.

Think about hot coconut oil. Add a few drops of lime, then a drop or two of iodine. Dilute it with icebergs melted by ocean current: even if you've never been to Florida, reconstitute that mixture and you will know how the air feels and smells on the mangrove coast. You'll also know something about a pretty little village there called Boca Grande.

Boca Grande is on the barrier island of Gasparilla. It is one of the isolated, moneyed enclaves south of Tampa, north of Naples—way, way off Florida's asphalt network of theme parks and tacky roadside attractions.

It's a place that I associate with quiet dinner parties, Sunday tennis, tarpon fishing and bird-watching . . . not with violent death.

That's one of Florida's charms: Places like Boca Grande still exist. They are always full of surprises.

The first thing I noticed upon entering Frank J. Calloway's secluded beach house was that there was something disturbing about the composition of the air. Less an odor, really, than an adverse density.

It was as if oxygen molecules had been weighted with water plus unknown organic particles, then compressed and compressed again in the silence of a process so newly completed that something—illness? decay?—had only recently begun.

It was a piscine acidity. It had an oily tinge. . . .

I noticed the odor as I passed through the living room—What's unusual about the air in this place?—which was just before I stepped into the kitchen and found the body of a man lying belly-down on glazed Mexican tiles.

I stopped, took a step back and said, "Hey . . . are you okay?" Then I said, "Hello . . . ?" and stood listening in the heavy air.

I'm ashamed to admit how often I say idiotic things and ask dumb questions. This was one of my dumber questions. The guy definitely wasn't okay.

But it was a startling scene to discover: A stranger's clay gray face wedged against custom cabinetry . . . copper pots and skillets suspended from hooks above rows of stainless burners . . . a mottled black swash of blood on the cupboard which marked where flesh and bone had impacted marble countertop, then wood.

The man was wearing green swim shorts, no shirt or thongs.

He had fallen heavily. Big men in their forties always do.

Standing there looking at the body, I could hear Frank Calloway's stepdaughter, Amanda, tell me, "Frank loves to cook. He studies it, like a gourmet. If he invited you over and he likes you, he'll probably want to make dinner. If his ditzy new wife—he calls her 'Skipper,' for God's sake. If Skipper will let him."

But there was nothing cooking on the stove. Nothing to account for the weightiness of atmosphere . . .

I stood beneath the cathedral ceiling, aware of a silence amplified by the sound of skittish palm fronds outside and the slow collapse of waves on sand. A little-known fact: Waves do not move horizontally; only the disturbance that creates them does. Like fog in a breeze, water only illustrates energy.

Even so, on this summer-bright afternoon in April, the Gulf of Mexico seemed a gelatinous membrane that was part of a greater respiratory system. I could look through the kitchen, through the shattered sliding glass door and beyond the pool and patio furniture to the beach: Wave after low jade wave sailed shoreward . . . one long exhalation followed by another . . . another . . . another.

The waves made a hissing sound that gathered volume then deteriorated, gasped in the spring heat, gasped again and collapsed.

Just one more dazzling beachfront day in the village of Boca Grande. Yet the sound of waves underlined something else that I had noticed: The man on the floor did not appear to be breathing. . . .

※

In movies, blood and a body cause the fainthearted to scream and the brave hearted to rush to the fallen's assistance.

That hasn't been my experience.

Nope. The more common reaction is a mixture of atavistic dread and a reluctance to get involved.

Most people do exactly what I did: we look, take a step back, then look again. Basically, we act like dopes.

Maybe there's a reason. It is in the milliseconds of shock that the brain has time to charge the flight-or-fight instinct with adrenaline, preparing to take control. Are we in danger? Has the predator struck and run? Or has the predator lingered?

Then we stare; a stare interrupted with quick animal-glances over our shoulders and to our unprotected flanks. We draw closer, still staring. Is this death? Is this the thing we fear above all else in life?

For most, death is a spiritual concept, not a chemical process, and the flesh-and-fluid reality of it cleaves a hole, a momentary hole, in our illusions.

Death must be approached cautiously like an abyss . . . or like disease.

I am not fainthearted, but neither am I brave. I stood for a moment, alert to the possibility that I was not alone in this stranger's house. My eyes reconfirmed that the sliding glass door which opened to the pool had been knocked off its tracks and shattered.

It was a big door. Lots of wrought iron and storm glass. It had required some animal force to tear it free of its casing. Calloway was big enough to do it. But why would he have done it?

I noted the beach towel dropped in a heap on the kitchen floor. It appeared to be dry; no blood. There was a deliquescent sheen of water on the copper-red Mexican tiles.

I turned my head enough to see the high-beamed great room behind me and a winding staircase that spiraled to a beach loft. Stained-glass windows—bottle-nosed dolphins leaping—allowed tubular blue sunlight through the hipped roof.

In the living room below were islands of white leather furniture on an acre of white carpet.

About her stepfather, I remembered Amanda telling me, "When my mom married Frank, he was a clinical psychologist. *Her* psychologist after my real dad was killed; that's how they got together. Financially, I guess he did okay, but then he began to invest in land. Money, money, money, if you're smart enough. And Frank's pretty damn smart when he's not thinking with his testicles.

"Finally, he gave up his practice completely to organize Florida land syndicates. He had a knack for knowing what people wanted before they actually wanted it. It must have been the shrink in him. He got really rich just in time to divorce my mom and marry his secretary. Jesus, Skipper. Can you believe he calls her that?"

Sure, I could believe it.

What was a little harder to accept was that I would be the one to find Frank Calloway, the former psychologist who'd made all the money even though he occasionally thought with his testicles, but who was now lying in the glaze of his own blood, dead on the floor of the kitchen where he might have cooked me a gourmet dinner had he decided he liked me.

❉

The type of house in which I stood is becoming a fixture on Florida's west coast: a passive totem of wealth reconstituted as imitation Old Florida architecture. It had the obligatory tin roof, the Prohibition-era lines, the driftwood coloring.

Inside, though, it was diorama-neat, a model of interior design, a place through which to tour admiring guests. Note the terra-cotta tiles, the polyester and acrylic fabrics, the recessed lighting and beveled glass, the breakfast room in red cedar, the Monticello tubs and gold faucets, the saxony cut carpet, the imitation pecky cypress made of some kind of Du Pont synthetic.

It was not a home. It was an emblem in which to live.

Not even that anymore for Frank Calloway.

I crossed the kitchen and knelt, cupping my hand around the man's wrist: skin cooler than the tile beneath me, no pulse.

I changed my position, considered the dried blood on the man's face and neck. Something else: Streaking along the jugular area were two parallel red lines.

What could have caused something like that? Had he somehow scratched his own neck as he fell?

I gave it a few seconds before I touched fingers to the carotid area: coated hair bristles, skin dry as a mushroom, still no pulse.

What I felt was relief. He was dead. Yeah, he was dead.

Not a very admirable reaction. But I am seldom as admirable as I would like to be. Still, personal ethics are the measure of one's own self-image, one's own self-respect. Had I noticed normal body warmth, a hint of heartbeat, I would have done what was required. I would have rolled him over, checked to make sure his airway was clear and then performed the required CPR. Two breaths to five chest compressions.

So, yes, I felt relief. But some regret, too: Death may be solitary, but it reverberates. In a few hours, somewhere, someplace, unknown people—probably good people—would be in shock, crying, perhaps shattered with loss.

As Tomlinson says, and quite accurately, all life forms are symbiotic. Each life is interlaced.

I pictured Amanda: the skinny, mousy woman and her New Age tough-guy feminist attitude. Was she too aloof to shed tears for her stepfather?

It was something I would have to find out. . . .

I'd never met Calloway, but I'd spoken with him a couple of times on the telephone and Amanda had sent me a photograph. Black curly hair, styled neat. Nose and narrow chin that suggested Italian antecedents. Jowly middle-aged face, bright, aggressive brown eyes behind oval-rimmed designer glasses that made a calculated statement: taste, intellect, money—powerful but in tune; youthful.

He wasn't wearing the glasses, but this was Calloway on the floor. And, yes, he was dead; had been dead for . . . how long? I'm a marine biologist not a medical examiner, but it wasn't difficult to make an educated guess. How long would it take for a pool of water to evaporate off tile on a balmy, April afternoon? How long did it take for blood to coagulate and dry? An hour? Two hours?

Not long. He hadn't been here long.

I placed my hand beneath Calloway's shoulder, lifted and turned him slightly. No blood on chest or bloated stomach . . . perhaps a hint of priapism.

Did that suggest death by head wound? Maybe. I wasn't sure.

I let the body settle on the tile; tried to ignore the rumble of internal gases. Crossed to the kitchen sink and washed my hands—a compulsion I would not have felt had a living Calloway and I shaken hands or whacked each other on the shoulders while trading jokes over beer.

Stood there knowing that my next logical move was to pick up the telephone and dial the police. Maybe Calloway had come wet from his swimming pool, slipped and taken a bad fall.

It happens.

Or maybe, just maybe, I had stumbled onto a crime scene. Either way, dutiful private citizens turn such matters over to the authorities.

But I did not behave as a dutiful citizen should.

There were reasons. Maybe they weren't great reasons but they were my reasons. One reason is that I had made a promise to a determined woman. Another reason was an implied promise to a long gone friend, a guy named Bobby Richardson. The fact that Bobby had been dead for nearly twenty years seemed to matter less and less.

A promise is a promise. Right?

❉

The promises I'd made created a couple of problems. For one thing, I hadn't exactly been invited into Calloway's house. I'd been invited TO his house. We were supposed to meet for drinks promptly at six. On the phone, he'd said, "But if you're like a lot of these islanders, always late, tell me now. I'll just keep working till you surprise me."

Meaning I'd better be on time.

My reply had been a bit more terse than he'd expected: "Geez, Frank, I've got nothing better to do than bounce around doing favors for your family. Your ex-family, I mean. So, yeah, make it six. I'll try real hard."

One of the oddities of living on a coast bordered by islands is that it is often faster—and a hell of a lot less nerve-wracking—to travel by boat. Because of the configuration of roads and because it was close to peak tourist season, it would have taken me more than two and a half, maybe three, hours to drive from Sanibel Island to Boca Grande. Bad traffic and toll bridges. Lots of stoplights. Many intersections with Kmarts and Burger Kings, busy 7-Elevens and city-sized malls, their parking lots jammed with Winnebago clones and midwestern license plates. Acres of asphalt, drifting exhaust fumes and metal baking in the April heat.

In my fast Hewes flats skiff, though, on a calm day, the trip was forty minutes of open water and good scenery.

Not a tough choice to make.

I left my piling house in Dinkin's Bay on Sanibel Island at precisely 4:30 P.M.—plenty of lag time in case I saw something interesting and wanted to dawdle. I am, by profession, a marine biologist. I make my living collecting sea specimens, which I then sell to research labs and educational facilities. The name of my company is Sanibel Biological Supply. I am sole owner and lone employee. This means that dawdling—and the right to dawdle while on the water—is part of my job description.

It's one of the perks of working for myself.

So I got in my skiff and I ran the inshore flats past Chino Island, Demere Key and Pineland, then cut northwest toward the blue convexity that is Charlotte Harbor. The bays and water passages of Florida's west coast resemble lakes more than they resemble seacoast. It's because they are hedged by mangroves. The mangrove is a rugged, wind-stunted tree that elevates itself above swamp on monkey-bar roots. Because the tree employs its arched roots to creep and expand, it is called the 'tree that walks'; the name itself alluding to qualities of silence that hint at dark groves of speechless men.

These roots grow so densely that mangrove forests not only protect; they also isolate. You can't walk through a mangrove forest; you must climb. Which is why the most inhospitable sections of the world's most inhospitable tropical regions are always, always marked by an expanse of mangroves. And yet, as seen from a distance, mangroves give the misimpression of lushness and shadow that one associates with fresh water.

It's an illusion. Mangroves denote harsh sunlight, salt and sulfur. When it comes to dependence on the chemical processes of the tropics, mangroves are as basic as lightning or ozone. Coconut palms are trees of tradewinds and ocean currents. Mangroves are creatures of muck and equatorial heat. Because of the primeval conditions in which they thrive, they are trees that seem more intimately related to the basic procedures of cellular life. It is one of the reasons that I am an admirer of mangroves.

I am not troubled by illusions that I understand.

So I headed north through long lakes created by mangrove islands.

The Mangrove Coast

It was a good day for it. Lots of sun and very little wind. The starboard beverage locker was packed with crushed ice, bottled water and a couple of bottles of Bud Light. In the port locker, I had stashed swim shorts, towel, a mask, snorkel and my trusted old Rocket fins just in case I got the urge to get in the water. The bottom of my Hewes had been recently pressure-washed and I'd just had my 200 Mariner serviced and tuned, so the throttle handle was sensitive to the touch; a tempting energy conduit that, if pressed to sudden speed, seemed to dilute gravity as it created velocity.

Just turning the key caused the fiberglass hull beneath me to oscillate like the skin of a nervous horse.

I like that feeling: the feeling of being alone on open water in a fast boat. It's more than recreation, it's more than transportation. It is a chunk of the scaffolding upon which I hang my life. Going alone on water is an act that, at once, insulates and defines.

It feels like freedom. It is freedom.

Which is the way I felt on this hot, hot April afternoon, a Thursday. Heat radiating off the water created distant mirages that, as I approached at speed, dissipated into panels of quaking light. I flushed cormorants and wading birds. I left a billion swimming, crawling, oozing life forms—the living, breeding, breathing body of the tropic littoral—in my indifferent wake.

April is also the front edge of tarpon season, and Boca Grande Pass is one of the most famous tarpon fisheries in the world. For two months out of each year, the water space between the islands of Gasparilla and Cayo Costa becomes a fiberglass municipality; a night-bright and morning-light city with its own rules and laws and procedures.

It is a city that drifts with the tide while its members, running beam-to-beam, jockey and leapfrog and shout and swear, all fighting to maintain strategic position over the pass's deep ambush holes.

With time to kill, I idled through and watched several hundred boats—from mega-yachts to Boston Whalers—moving in patterns that were no less strange than the deeply coded patterns of pelagic fish beneath. Sat there in my skiff riding the outgoing tide, taking it all in and enjoying myself. Boca Grande Pass during tarpon season is equal parts drama and slapstick comedy: a hundred million dollars' worth of high-tech equipage designed and purchased so as to more effectively hook a chromium, six-foot fish that is primeval, unchanged, so primitive that it can breathe surface air, not unlike the first sea creatures that crawled landward out of the slime.

I appreciated the irony of that. Plus, it's a nice thing to sit on open water and watch pods of tarpon roll past.

In hindsight, I should have stayed right there and fished. Could have pieced together my Loomis 12-weight fly rod, headed out to Johnson's Shoals and casted to passing schools of daisy-chaining tarpon. Weeks later . . . months later, I would think of that moment, me floating there open and alone in the pass, and I would regret my decision to keep the appointment with Frank Calloway.

It is an irony that I also appreciate but makes me forever uneasy: nearly all life's passages, tranquil or tragic, hinge on a random intersecting of events, a chance meeting, or on some seemingly insignificant decision.

Free will or not, none of us seems to have much control. . . .

❋

By 5:30 P.M. I was tied up at Whidden's Marina, south of Miller's Marina near the waterside golf fairways of the Gasparilla Inn.

Calloway had given me directions to his home. Very detailed, precise directions, too. Not that they needed to be. Boca Grande is a tiny little New England–sized village with tree-lined streets. Not a very complicated place.

I took a slow, lazy walk across the island so that, at five-till-six, I was ringing the bell at Calloway's house, a gray hulk built on stilts on the Gulf side, just off Gilchrist Avenue, set back behind a low brick wall and hidden in the shadows of casuarinas and palms and hedges of sea grape.

No answer.

Rang the bell a couple of more times. Same thing. Finally, I rapped on the door . . . and the door swung open.

That was my first surprise. Why would Calloway, a punctual man and, by all accounts, a details freak, fail to be at home at the time of our appointment? And why would he not only leave the door unlocked but open?

A very pretty friend of mine, who also happens to be very wise, once told me that the reason I prefer to live alone is because I abhor confusion. "With you, Ford, everything has to be orderly and understandable."

My pretty friend was caricaturizing with way too broad a brush. Yeah, I'm rational. Or try to be. But the reason I'm uncomfortable with confusion is because I realize that I don't possess the peculiar genius required to arrive at intuitive but accurate conclusions.

Tomlinson does. I know a few others who have the same kind of superior intellect.

But not me. I'm the slow, steady, methodical type. I've got to think things out, take it step by step. I am a chronic neatener and straightener. In the lab and in the field, I'm compulsive about understanding behavior and interrelationships. Every action and reaction is sensible once the observer understands motivation and makes sense of the objectives.

Calloway's absence and the open door did not make sense.

Which is why I pushed the door open a little wider . . . and why I took the first few tentative steps into the living room, calling Calloway's name the whole time . . . and how I happened to end up in the kitchen, uninvited, kneeling over a corpse.

It put me in a delicate position. Individuals who find bodies while trespassing in a stranger's house must necessarily spend lots and lots of time answering questions from edgy cops.

It was not a major dilemma, but it was something I preferred to avoid.

The second problem was trickier. The reason I'd boated all the way to Boca Grande was not just to speak with Calloway in person, but also because he'd promised to show me something: a manila folder with a sheaf of papers therein.

He'd been very protective, very closemouthed about what was in that folder. "The guy I hired to put this report together," he'd told me, "took some . . . let's say unusual steps to get the information I wanted.

So, no, I'm not going to mail it, and, no, I'm not going to make copies and, yes, it is very confidential."

I wanted that folder.

I wanted that folder because I'd already promised Calloway's step-daughter, Amanda, that I would look through it and help her if I could.

It's another quirk of mine: I take personal promises very, very seriously.

If the cops arrived, though, the house would be sealed. I wouldn't get the folder. It wouldn't matter if Calloway had died a violent death or from natural causes. I would have to leave empty-handed.

Still standing at the sink in Calloway's gourmet kitchen, I looked again at the man's body; stood there feeling the weight of adverse air and the twittering, skittish afternoon silence. Finally, I reached for a dish towel.

It was yellow with green embroidered dolphins. Bottle-nosed dolphins were, apparently, a domestic theme.

I used the towel to wipe clean the faucet I had touched, then continued to use it to wipe away fingerprints as I methodically searched the drawers of Calloway's bedroom, then his study.

I thought to myself: *Christ, I speak with Tucker for the first time in years and, next thing I know, I'm burgling a dead man's house.*

Meaning Tucker Gatrell, my late mother's only brother and so my only living relative.

Which, in truth, is how the whole business in Boca Grande, and then in Panama, started.

All because I made the mistake of listening to Tuck . . .

Tuck called me during the last minutes of a breezeless, moonless Saturday night, April 19, in a spring remembered for the Comet Hale-Bopp.

For more than a month, I'd had a great view of the comet: a foggy contrail in the western sky that resembled a fragment of some far-off navigational beam. Shift your eyes one way, there was Mars, a bright pellet of rust colored ice. Move your eyes another way and there was Venus, solitary and blue. Turn your head a little farther, and there were the lights of Dinkin's Bay Marina casting yellow pathways across the black water.

Each evening, I'd walk out onto the porch, stand peering over the mangrove fringe of Dinkin's Bay, then wander back inside. It got so I was working later and later just to take advantage of the nice diversion.

I was still working the night Tuck called, even though it was nearly midnight. I normally wouldn't have answered the phone, but I have a short list of longtime friends who sometimes suffer the beery blahs or late-night panics and who are welcome to call at any time, from any place in the world. Midnight on the Gulf Coast of Florida could be a troubled lunch hour in Brisbane or a desperate morning in Kota Kinabalu. So at the first electronic warble, I left the grouper I was dissecting, trotted across the open-air walkway of my stilthouse and pushed open the screen door to the little cabin that is my home.

I was wiping my hands on a towel when I heard, "Duke? Jesus, it used to be easier calling Truman than gettin' holt of you. Back when I was guiding, I mean."

I recognized the voice immediately . . . which is why I was immediately sorry that I'd answered the phone.

The voice said, "As in *Harry* Truman—you maybe heard the name? Which, a'course, was when both us was still alive and fishing the islands down off the 'Glades." There was a pause before he added, "Him being the dead one, of course. Me being still full of ginger."

"Your fishing buddy, the president," I replied. "Yeah, I think you mentioned him a couple of times before."

I then heard the sound of a belch, part gas, part grunt, followed by: "Whew! Little bastard snuck right out the front hatch. Well . . . they say beer's got body so it's sure as shit got soul, and that was the sound of a six-pack headed south. *¡Vaya con Dios, mi amigo!* The beer, I'm talkin' about, Duke." Then he belched again.

So the man was drunk. No surprise there.

Into the phone, I said, "Look . . . about that name—you can call me anything you want. Ford or Doc or even Marion. But not Duke. You say it, I look around, like, 'Who's he mean?' I don't know who the hell you're talking about."

He said, "You serious? Goddamn, you are serious."

"It's a small thing to ask," I said.

"But, hell, I thought up that nickname my own self."

I told him, "I think we've discussed that a couple of times, too." Said it nicely.

Why had I spent so much of my life trying to be nice to the man?

❋

Tucker Gatrell: line up a thousand men and he's the one you'd vote most likely to die in a trailer fire or while replacing the shocks on some beat-up half-ton Ford.

He was more than a decade older than my late mother. He looked seventy when I was fifteen. By the time I was thirty, he still looked seventy and he still wore skinny-legged Levi's and pearl-buttoned shirts. Cowboy clothes, because he owned a mud-and-mangrove ranch in a backwater called Mango; little tiny fishing village south of Marco Island where he kept a horse and a few cows.

Journalists loved the guy; saw him as an Authentic Everglades Voice. That he claimed to have guided a lengthy list of rich and famous sportsmen added fabric. More than one writer said Tuck resembled an older Robert Mitchum, but that had more to do with his attitude than his looks. He had the Jack Daniel's swagger, the polar blue eyes, the shoulders and scrawny hips, but he lacked the style. Not that any journalist ever nailed down the man's deficits.

No. They saw in him whatever they wanted to see. That was an indicator of Tucker's one true gift: He had the qualities of a mirror. That he lacked depth was part of the deal. Not that anyone, except for me, of course, was critical enough to notice.

There were reasons I didn't like or trust Tuck. Several very good reasons, indeed.

So now he'd called, I'd answered, and I'd have to listen to him . . . but that didn't mean I had to stand there wasting time when there were fish waiting to be dissected in my lab.

I said to him, "Did you telephone just to see if I got your messages? Or is there actually a reason?"

"So the boys at the marina told you I've been callin'."

"They stick my messages on the board just like everyone else's. But you never said what you wanted."

He seemed momentarily miffed. "God dang! I got to have a reason to call my own nephew?"

"At midnight? Yeah, you need a reason. It doesn't have to be a great reason, but a reason. I was trying to sleep."

Another lie. The man brought out the very worst in me. Which he seemed to realize . . . and it delighted him.

"That right? You don't sound the least bit sleepy. 'Fact, you sound chipper as can be."

His way of demonstrating that he had good instincts for what was true, what wasn't. Infuriating.

I said, "I was getting ready to go to bed. That's what I meant. I've been working in the lab."

"Ah."

"I've got a lot of things going on right now. Some of us have obligations."

Jesus—he had a knack for making me sound like a pious little geek.

Tuck replied, "You were always the busiest kid I ever seen. Lotsa people get shit stacked on 'em, but you'd always grab a shovel and dig your way towards the bottom of the pile. Couldn't tell if it was 'cause you got a bad sense of direction or just loved being alone.

"A man who can't find time to have a little fun, I always kinda wondered about."

Before I could reply to the implications of that, he asked, "Still studying them baby tarpon?"

This was another part of his ritual, talking about tarpon.

Knowing what was coming, I listened to him say, "Still putting them under microscopes and stuff just to figure out where they spawn? I coulda solved that one for you years ago, saved all you busy biologists the trouble. You want me to tell you where tarpon spawn?"

He was going to tell me anyway, so I said, "I'm all ears."

He said, "The tarpon, they come shallow to spawn, which is why you find so many baby tarpon up the creeks in the Ten Thousand Islands. All you got to do is go out and look with your own eyes. I know places way up in the sawgrass the water's so fresh they's gar and bass and bullfrogs. But there're plenty of them baby tarpon, too. Why else? 'Cause the males and big cows migrate shallow to spawn, just loaded with milt and roe."

He was right about finding immature tarpon in fresh water, but he was wrong about everything else.

Typical Gatrell.

More than once, I'd patiently explained the facts to him: despite the folklore, research indicated that tarpon spawned in deep water . . . but I wasn't going to waste my time going through it again.

I said, "Yeah, tarpon. I'm still working on tarpon."

Another lie.

Truth was, for the last couple of months, I'd been helping doctors Roy Crabtree and Lewis Bullock of the Florida Marine Research Institute on a study they were doing on the age, growth and reproduction of black grouper in Florida waters.

I found the subject fascinating.

Tucker Gatrell would not.

So I did not tell him that, for the last many weeks, I'd spent my time in the lab preparing thin sections of otolith—ear bone—taken from grouper I'd caught, then counting annuli, or growth rings, using my powerful Wolfe compound microscope.

One ring equaled a year's growth, just as with many trees.

And I did not tell him that I'd spent the last several days offshore with two Useppa Island friends and part-time treasure salvers, Harry and Jane Robb, aboard their forty-two-foot Shay, catching more grouper to bring back and dissect for a broader sample. Which is why I had only recently received his phone messages . . . not that I would have called him anyway.

Why bother? In Tucker Gatrell's vision of existence, all fellow life-forms were treated as props and sundries to better stage his own little forays against boredom and normalcy. He had no interest in what I was doing. More to the point, he had no interest in a process that could be weighed and measured and proven to be true.

We were, in short, exact opposites. And, unlike some opposites, we repelled rather than attracted.

Which is why I pressed the lie, continuing, "Yeah, the tarpon studies have been moving pretty well. And now that you explained to me where it is tarpon go to spawn, I should be able to wrap up the whole business in another day or two. After that, I'll take a couple of weeks off. Kick back and relax."

There. Show him I could have as much fun as the next guy. . . .

Which I thought was cynical and witty and rejoining until Tucker said, "Only a day or two? Perfect."

Jesus, he believed me.

I said, "Yeah, two days at the most, I should have the whole tarpon puzzle solved. . . ." But then I caught myself and said, "Perfect? Why's that perfect?"

"Because that's what I was hoping for."

The way he said that, I felt a little chill; as if I'd stepped on a false floor of bamboo—a punji pit—and could feel the bottom falling away.

※

I listened to him say, "Reason is, I got a favor to ask and I felt bad about it. You being usually too busy and all."

I hated the feeling that gave me, of being so stupid. The old bastard seemed to have the ability to anticipate my thoughts, my moves, and neatly manipulate my reactions, just as he had once manipulated herds of his damn wormy cattle.

I said, "Favor?"

He said, "Yeah. Now that I know you got the time, it shouldn't be a problem." Then he added quickly, "It's not for me, understand. It's for a woman. Pretty little woman, by the sound of her voice."

Thinking, *Is he drunk or insane?* I said, "By the sound of her voice? You call me at midnight to ask me to do a favor for a woman you've never even met?"

"Oh, I met her. I met her on the phone when she called huntin' you. It's just that I never seen her. You ain't, either. Or so she says."

Was any of this supposed to make sense?

I said, "What the hell are you talking about?"

"Ain't you listening? The woman who called me, the one I'm bringin' to your house tomorrow morning. Well . . . actually, I'm driving my pickup and she's gonna follow me in her own car. Unless I can talk her into ridin' with me . . . which I damn sure hope to do. She says she needs to talk to you, but the only address she had was from back in the days when you had mail sent to my ranch. So she had to track me down first. Amanda Calloway. That name don't ring a bell?"

I said, "I don't know anyone named Amanda Calloway." I mulled it over a few more seconds before I said, "Nope . . . I've never heard of anyone by that name. So, with all the work I have to do, I don't have time to meet her or anyone else—"

He cut me off, saying, "Wait, I don't mean Calloway. That's her what-a-you-call-it . . . her adopted name, the name she goes by now. The name she gave me, the one she said you'd know is Richardson. Amanda Richardson. That's who she used to be."

"Same thing. I don't know any Amandas—"

"And she said to mention Bobby Richardson."

It stopped me cold.

Bobby Richardson . . . ?

I hadn't heard his name spoken aloud in fifteen, maybe sixteen years. Not that I had forgotten him. No. Men like Bobby Richardson, you don't forget.

I said, "Amanda is Bobby's widow? . . . wait a minute. That doesn't sound right. His wife's name wasn't Amanda. Her name was . . ."

I couldn't remember. What the hell was the name of Bobby's wife? He'd talked about her often enough during those long, soggy nights in the rain forests of Asia. It was stored somewhere in my memory, but I was having trouble bringing it to the surface.

Tucker said, "The girl says her mamma's name is Gail—"

Gail. That was the wife's name. Gail Richardson.

"—but this is his daughter; she's the one I'm talking about. Amanda. She's the one who wants to see you, this man's little girl. Or was the man's little girl, I guess. She said he died when she was, what, less than five years old?"

I said, "Bobby died when his daughter was a child. That's right."

"Then she's the one. The one who called me trying to find you and that I'm bringing with me to Sanibel tomorrow . . . now that you said you're not too busy. 'Cause she wants to talk to you and needs to ask a favor."

Bobby's daughter? Just hearing the man's name brought back memories of a time in my life and of a style of life that now seemed as remote as the far side of the Earth or as distant as a comet's bright contrail.

The girl was wrong about one thing, though. I *had* seen her before. I'd seen her in a photograph, long, long ago. . . .

❊

When I hung up the phone, I wandered around the lab putting things away, getting dissecting table and instruments clean and neat so I could start fresh the next day. But I was operating on autopilot. My routine in the lab is so entrenched that it takes no conscious effort. Good thing, too, because my mind had locked onto the task of digging out and dusting off memories that were nearly two decades old.

The photograph . . . I could still see the photograph of a little girl named Amanda Richardson in fairly precise detail . . . probably because Bobby had pulled it out and showed it to me so many times.

It was one of those quick-print Polaroid shots, Easter-egg bright colors, that someone back in the States had had the good sense to have laminated before sending it to our APO address in Bangkok.

There's lots and lots of rain in the jungles of Southeast Asia. Metal rusts. Cloth rots. Paper turns to paste. But, because it was laminated, the photo survived our months there.

Unfortunately, Bobby had not.

Here's what I could reconstruct of the photo: a tiny girl with hair the color of freshly sheared copper wearing a frilly yellow dress, as if ready for a birthday party.

That was it: the photo had been taken on Amanda's birthday. Third birthday or fourth, I couldn't remember.

And . . . the girl wore plastic-rimmed, nerdish glasses . . . and gloves. Yes, gloves. Her small hands folded.

Nothing very distinctive about that, but what I remembered better than the glasses was that the child's left eye was turned slightly inward, a malady that I knew to be strabismus, or lazy eye, as it is sometimes called. Bobby said they'd have it fixed when the girl was old enough, not that he was worried about it. And buy her some more stylish glasses, too.

To me, her wandering eye, that slight imperfection, implied a depth of character . . . or of vulnerability . . . that made the child's face distinctive, lovely to look upon, and I told the proud father that he should think twice before getting the thing fixed. It was harmless flattery that he took seriously.

"Doc," he'd told me, "the only reason you say that is because you know absolutely nothing about the intrinsic vanity of women. Or about women at all for that matter."

True enough . . . but this from a man with a film-star face, a quarterback's body, who was a little bit vain himself.

No, not a little bit vain. Bobby was one of the sharpest, toughest and most dependable men I'd ever met, but that did not alter the truth that he was vain; very, very vain indeed. . . .

It was strange thinking about him after all the years that had passed. It was strange and unexpected and oddly, oddly unsettling, too.

I am not a nostalgia buff. I do not prefer to haunt a past softened and brightened by imagination. The past is constructed of memory, the future of expectation. I live most comfortably in the present, because that, in truth, is the only reality. It is all a reasonable person has.

Besides, my memories of Bobby and Asia weren't all that rosy. And I certainly hadn't planned to stay up long past midnight thinking about old friends, old battles and long gone losses. . . .

❋

No, what I had planned was a quiet night alone at home. . . .

I was looking forward to it: just me and the microscope in my lab, sea specimens arranged neatly and in order over the stainless-steel dissecting table . . . gooseneck lamp adding precise illumination . . . music on the stereo, if I wanted, or maybe the portable shortwave radio.

I'd rigged an external antenna off the wooden water cistern outside, so I could pull in programs from Hanoi or Jakarta or Beijing, even Australia Broadcasting out of Perth, no problem at all.

And there was, of course, the comet.

When I needed a break from the microscope, it was a nice thing to walk outside and look into littoral darkness, still listening to some solitary radio voice that was ricocheting off stars from the other side of the globe. The electronic connexus is deceptively personal. It seemed to flow down out of space and directly into my remodeled fish shack which is built on stilts over water.

So no, I didn't expect or want to hear from Tucker Gatrell, and I certainly didn't want to be drawn into a revisitation of my former life, my former occupation.

Absolutely not. Lately, in fact, I had been restricting all my socializing to the guides and the liveaboards at Dinkin's Bay Marina.

Just wasn't in the mood for outsiders.

There was a reason, a very specific reason.

My friend Tomlinson said it was because I had entered a reclusive period. The man is part savant, part goat, so he is usually at least half right about everything he says. An example: "Unrequited love, man. What a serious green weenie that is. Remember: love is what goes out of us, not what we take in. It's the union of two solitudes, yeah. Two solitudes willing to protect and trust. But just 'cause it didn't work out doesn't mean that you have to spend all your time alone."

Tomlinson talks like that; he really does. He says it is because he has evolved spiritually after years and years of study and meditation. I think it's because his thought processes have been chemically altered during years and years of abusing marijuana and hallucinogenics.

But it was also Tomlinson who, after cracking a cold bottle of Hatuey, told me, "Amigo, if it's got tits or tires, you're sure to have trouble with it down the road. Face it, man, she's committed to Central America. Nothing you can do is gonna change that. So, the way I see it, it's time for us to find you a new ride."

He was talking about a woman I knew, a woman I shared history with, a woman named Pilar. Pilar was a former lover.

I had to keep reminding myself of that: Pilar was my *former* lover.

It was not an easy truth to acknowledge.

So, yeah, I'd entered a reclusive period. For weeks, I worked in the lab. I listened to my shortwave radio. I lived alone in my little sea-cabin house. At night, I'd sit on the porch listening to the mountain-stream gurgle of tide rivering past the pilings beneath me. I'd listen to the snap-crackle-pop of pistol shrimp and the *bee-whah* groan of catfish.

I looked at the comet.

Daytime was different. When the sun's out, it seems reasonable to pursue goals. I defined mine by writing them each and every day in one of my notebooks. They were simple goals.

Twice a day, seven days a week, I rededicate myself to getting back into shape. It was none too soon. I'd let myself go over the last several months, and in that very short time I'd gained maybe fifteen pounds. I felt soft and slow and grainy. I felt as if age and gravity were vines that were working their way up my legs, taking control. I was eating too much, drinking too many beers, sleeping way too much.

So the rules were simple: beer on Fridays and Saturdays only. Absolutely no food of any kind after 8:00 P.M.

It was time to take charge of my own life once again.

Every year, getting into shape seems to be a tougher, slower, more painful process.

Each year, my knees and shoulders and ankles seem to hurt a little more.

Tough physical work was exactly what I needed. Pain is good. Extreme pain is extremely good. I punished myself with it and then I used it as a purge.

I lost the fifteen pounds of fat, and then I lost five more for good measure. I spent so much time running up and down the beaches of Sanibel that I began to recognize the condo owners and individual vacationers at resorts such as Sundial, Casa Ybel, Sand Castles and Sonesta.

They'd wave; I'd wave back.

Gradually, I began to come out of my shell a little.

❊

On one of my runs, I was passed by a lean blonde with a ball nose and the thighs of a high hurdler. She had a good grin; a kind of jaunty we're-both-distance-junkies attitude.

I caught up and introduced myself. Her name was Maggie. She was married; lived in Tampa, but she and her husband were having problems. She'd taken a place at Breakers West for the week to be alone and think things over.

We had a nice run. Same thing the next day and the next. She appreciated the insights of an objective man. I appreciated her humor and her strength. We became friends. We agreed that, considering her circumstance, it had to be a nonphysical friendship . . . which took all the pressure off both of us.

We stayed in touch after Maggie returned to her life in Tampa. We decided that, as friends, we should meet a couple of times a week in some neutral place and work out together.

She chose Pass-a-Grille, an off-the-track beach village south of St. Pete that, with its Mexican tile and palm-lined streets, reminded me of the best parts of southern California. Pass-a-Grille was a small town with history and humor and texture. People there were amused by their own isolation. It made them easy to meet. Maggie and I would run four or five miles, swim a mile along the beach, then we'd eat shrimp or crab at the Seahorse Restaurant. Sit there talking to Gary the bartender while we ate, then walk up the street to Shadrack's and have a beer with Big Al, the owner.

Big Al also owned Harleys.

I was surprised to hear that Maggie the housewife had always wanted a motorcycle.

It gave them something to talk about.

Maggie and Pass-a-Grille were a good break for me. Getting away from Dinkin's Bay and Sanibel reminded me that there was a big wide world out there. Other lives were going on whether I was reclusive or not. I have been in love only twice in my life and have gradually come to the conclusion that love is not a condition, it is a dilemma. Love, I believe, is chemically induced; created and maintained by the little-understood and complex chemistry of the brain. How we target and connect with our partners is anyone's guess, but the resultant response has more in common with addiction than with rosy emotion.

Realizing that helped me feel better, too. Chemistry is something I understand. It is chartable, predictable. Withdrawal from a chemical dependence would take time, but the chemical's hold must necessarily grow weaker day by day by day.

It made sense that the same would be true of Pilar's hold on me.

So slowly, surely, I began to resume my old life at Dinkin's Bay as well as my old role as willing confidant, sunset cocktail buddy, dependable big brother, dispenser of cold beer and heartfelt advice and of confidential favors.

In short, I was making the return to the quiet and peaceful life I've always wanted.

Which is when Tucker Gatrell called. . . .

3

The thing that first surprised me about Amanda Calloway (Amanda Richardson, as she told me to call her) was that she looked so unlike her father.

Didn't have Bobby's perfect features, that's for sure.

No, he'd been tall and golden haired; of a type you sometimes hear women say, "He's *too* good looking," as if, by dismissing him, they could distance themselves from a man who was probably beyond their wildest hopes anyway.

Bobby knew it, too. Was very, very careful about his hair and his clothes. On R&R in Singapore or Bangkok, he had his favorite barbers, his favorite masseuses, his own personal tailors.

Vain, yes. But a womanizer, no. He was committed to Gail, his wife. We spent four months together in Asia; he'd been there a couple of months before I arrived and there was not a single lapse. Not that he ever mentioned to me. No joking around about being "separated," no locker-room winks and nudges. The man loved and was dedicated to the woman with whom he'd already had one child and hoped to have more. And half a year is a long time to be alone in a region we called the Back of Beyond.

So it wasn't women. No . . . Bobby just liked it; liked being healthy and handsome; the expensive life. The same way some men and women enjoy bodybuilding, he took pleasure in the details of an elevated lifestyle and the way he looked.

"This is why I need to make lots and lots of money," he'd tell me. Or: "Man, I was born to be rich. I got no other choice." He might be modeling some silk suit; looking at himself in the mirror, being critical and enjoying it. "There's no way I can afford this kind of stuff—a tailored Armani? Even a copy like this. Are you kidding? Not back in the States on what I make. I need to get the hell out of this work and start my own business. Or maybe the movies. What'a you think?"

I told him he'd made a very strange choice, getting involved with Naval Intelligence and Naval Special Warfare, if he had aspirations of being a film star.

He'd said that he couldn't help himself. He was hooked, out of control or something like that—which was bullshit. He was playing a standard role, Mr. Adventurer, for standard reasons: "I'm a dead-on adrenaline junkie and where else can I get paid to sky-dive, scuba dive and sneak around at night wearing tac-paint while bad guys try to pop me? Carry a weapon, allowed to *kill* people? Jesus, anyplace else, what I do'd be illegal."

No argument there.

It was that way with most men who were involved in that peculiar and dangerous line of work. They had talent, brains—name a field, they would have probably excelled in it. And Bobby seemed to have more going for him than most. He had looks, taste, style . . . and that peculiar light that one associates with certain politicians who have the knack of inspiring affection rather than creating envy.

Bobby Richardson had it all; seemed to have been born under a lucky guardian star. Until one night, 100 klicks north of Phnom Penh, he was vaporized by a mortar round and was sent back to the States in a sack not much bigger than a cigar box which contained a hand, a foot, bits and pieces of hair and bone, with no space at all left over for ego or hopes or vanity. . . .

❋

Bobby's only child, however, was very plain in comparison to the way he had looked. . . .

I was on the lower deck of my stilthouse working on the fish tank when they arrived. Felt the familiar wooden tremor that told me someone had mounted the walkway that connects my house to the mainland.

Looked up to see a woman wearing pleated white shorts and baggy gray-blue T-shirt striding toward me, the female variation of the Generation X look. It was a style that implied limited body-piercing, maybe a small tattoo or two, an affection for MTV. The anachronism, Tucker Gatrell, walked behind, western hat in hand . . . clomping along in cowboy boots, for God's sake. A man who was always on stage, always in costume.

Saw that the woman was a rust-blonde redhead with one of those boxy haircuts so that her large brown eyes looked out at me from beneath a shield of bangs, hair squared heavily over hunched bookworm shoulders.

The way she walked, the way she carried herself, she reminded me of that: the type who escaped into books. Athletic-looking; she had a rangy, cattish quality, but also bookish. Or maybe it was computers these days. The studious variety of loner, isolated by self, maybe a little self-conscious, judging from the way she moved, knowing I was watching her; aware of it and not comfortable being the center of attention.

It tightened her movements. Added a mechanical stiffness. She had the gauntness, that hollowed quality, of the ultra-long-distance runner.

But no glasses. Not like the little girl I'd seen in the photograph. And . . . as she drew closer, I could see that the wandering eye had been straightened.

The disappointment I felt was surprising. I'd liked the face on that child from long ago.

Had Bobby's eyes been brown? I couldn't remember . . . more likely, I'd never paid enough attention to know. But there was something familiar in her eyes . . . could see it as we shook hands—"It's nice of you to meet with me, Dr. Ford"—as she held my face with her gaze, then allowed it to wander.

Got a glimpse of something tougher than suggested by her averted eyes. A little bit of Bobby in there peering out. Then could hear that toughness in her voice when she said, "You're the man in my father's letters, right? You knew my father."

I thought, *Letters?* but answered her by saying, "Years ago, I knew a man named Bobby Richardson. If he was your father, then you have a lot to be proud of. He was a fine man."

Her expression softened momentarily. "Then I'm glad I found you. I don't know if you can . . . can help me. But I know it's what my father would have wanted. My real father. Talking to you, I mean. It's what he told me to do in his letters, so that's why I'm here."

Letters again.

Turning to Tucker, she added, "So, if it's okay with you, Mr. Gatrell, I won't waste any more of your time. I can talk to your nephew alone."

Not asking permission, but telling both of us where she stood, just what she wanted.

But she obviously didn't know Tuck very well. Not if she expected to get rid of him so easily. He touched his hand to her back, steering her onto the deck and then up the stairs toward my house, saying, "Miz Richardson, I come this far with you, I kinda hate to let you sail solo now. Besides, Duke here's not the quickest on the draw, if you know what I mean. I'm not talking 'bout brain power, understand. Let's just say he's not the type to let sympathy get in the way." Maybe joking but maybe not; hard to tell from his tone. Then he replied to the look I gave him as he brushed past me, saying, "Excuse me. I meant Marion."

Wearing Levi's and a rodeo shirt, he smelled of rank hay and whiskey and chewing tobacco. Like horse, too. An old horse.

The man did not change.

※

I watched Amanda watching Tuck as he rambled on and on, dominating space and conversation as he always did, Tuck and the woman sitting with glasses of iced tea at the galley booth, me leaning against the door frame in the small room, taking it in.

The night before, on the phone, Tuck had tried to tell me what her problem was, but he had it so convoluted, so confused, that I'd finally told him to keep quiet, let her tell me and I'd judge for myself.

The Mangrove Coast

So now I stood there listening, waiting, looking at her. What I was thinking was: Not attractive, yet something solid about her and . . . troubled. Yes, a troubled young woman.

It gave me a pang. How would it make Bobby feel, seeing that his little girl had apparently grown up to be gawky, lacking confidence and seemed to be unhappy?

She was what? Twenty-four, maybe twenty-five years old. About the same age as Bobby when I knew him. But gaunt as she was, she did not have the look of health, only endurance. Had dull, brittle-looking hair—it didn't get much attention—and long wading-bird legs with calves traced by varicose veins. Runner's legs. And the way she dressed: everything baggy; clothes that were chosen not to look good but because she could hide in them. Shirt and shorts were feminine and casual like "Who cares?" but also vaguely defensive, with maybe a hint of aggressiveness. A T-shirt that read: *Thirty-Second Rule Strictly Enforced.*

What the hell did that mean?

But a good face. Strong nose, but a little too much of it; solid jawline but flat cheeks that made her lips seem thin, pale. Bits and pieces of her mother and father bonded together, no doubt about it, but the proportions were just a tad off. It was hard to believe that two people as attractive as Bobby and Gail Richardson had produced someone as plain as this girl who now sat in my house. Gail was Latina by birth, mother and father both from . . . South America? Maybe Mexico or Central America, I couldn't remember. Bobby had bragged to me more than once that his wife was a direct descendant of pure Castilian royalty. Her great beauty, he claimed, had been handed down through the blood.

There didn't seem to be a hint of Latin blood in Amanda. Well . . . perhaps a touch in her dark eyes. No place else, though. But the vagaries of genetics are ever-surprising and cannot be predicted.

Or maybe . . . maybe it's just the way that Amanda Richardson chose to look.

Some makeup, maybe. A decent haircut. Some clothes chosen to set off her lean lines; better posture.

I wondered. . . .

Every now and again she'd glance up and catch my eye—a searching look of appraisal—then return her attention to Tuck.

Tuck had been talking about his years shipping and working cattle in Central America with his old partner Joseph Egret: "But the Indian bastard up and got hit by a car. Killed him deader than two smoked hams, which taught me once and for all, no more Injuns for partners. The poor fools got no brain for modern times. Took me fifty years with Joe to learn that an Injun can't be trusted, but I finally did. These days, ma'am, I work strictly alone."

Which is when I finally made a move toward the table, planning to tell Tuck, enough, for God's sake, take a walk so the woman and I could talk.

But Amanda intercepted me. First, it was with a look—*Don't hurt his feelings*—and then by touching her fingers to the back of my hand— *Let him talk for a little longer.*

So I did. Listened to the old man ramble for another fifteen or twenty minutes before she finally cut him off. Asked him for half an hour alone with me so she could share the contents of a letter—"It's confidential," she explained—and Tuck left as meekly and amenably as I had ever seen him, charmed by her or manipulated by her, it was difficult to say which.

I studied the girl's face, thinking maybe she wasn't as troubled or as defenseless as I'd believed.

※

"The rule has to do with this idea some friends and I came up with. The thirty-second rule. The way it goes is, a guy comes up—this is usually at a bar, a concert maybe, someplace like that. Nothing to do with business, but like at a party or something. So a guy comes up and he's got exactly thirty seconds to prove he's not plastic or full of crap or a fake. If he doesn't say something honest or worthwhile in thirty seconds, what's the sense of wasting your time?"

Trying to keep things relaxed, trying to ease her into what she'd come to talk about, I'd asked her about her T-shirt: *Thirty-Second Rule Strictly Enforced.*

I said, "And the guys know there's this time limit? It's a new thing now . . . or—?"

"You mean do a lot of women use it?"

I was nodding. "Yeah, that's what I'm asking." There were enough years between us that this might have been some generational fad. If it's not on shortwave radio or on the VHF weather stations, I have no way of keeping up.

She said, "I just told you, some friends and I, it's our idea. But yeah, it's getting around. Like the university towns. Gainesville, Tallahassee, Miami. I heard some girls down on spring break took it back to Michigan, University of Iowa. Some other places, too. But it was all our idea."

Proud of that.

I had taken Tucker's seat at the galley booth facing her until she scooched a little closer to the wall to create an extra couple of inches of distance between us. That slight movement stirred the air enough so that she left a few scent molecules lingering. Body powder. Shampoo. Woman.

The thirty-second rule, I guessed, was like her baggy clothes, her hair: a place of her own creation in which to hide.

I said, "I've been talking to you for a couple of minutes and I don't feel like I know very much at all about you. A lot longer than thirty seconds, but I wouldn't presume to make any judgments."

"But this isn't social. So the rule doesn't apply, see?"

I said, "It's not business either, though. Or is it?"

Amanda was sipping her tea, hands very steady, eyes and eyebrows showing just above the rim of her glass. "It's neither," she said. "What it is is personal."

✵

She had handed me a sheaf of letters, all of them getting brittle and yellow, they were that old. Written on airmail onion-skin paper, so they were slightly brittle to begin with.

As I leafed through them, she said, "He wrote my mom almost every day. That's how much in love they were. The whole time he was in Asia or wherever he was. Those APO return addresses, you've got no way of knowing. But he mentioned Bangkok quite a bit, so that's what Mom figured. And he mentioned you. Your name's in there a lot." Amanda looked at me, let her eyes linger for a moment, then looked away before adding, "One of the reasons I wanted to talk with you was so you could maybe tell me more about my dad. About where you two were when he was killed, what you were doing. It's weird, but, my own father, I know almost nothing about him"

I said, "I'll tell you what I can."

"I'd appreciate that. Maybe more than you realize."

"My pleasure. And Tuck said something about you having a problem. Maybe a favor to ask."

"That's why I brought the letters, because I wanted you to see how I came to know about you. So . . . what I'd like you to do now is read this—" She carefully unfolded another letter, placed it in front of me and tapped a paragraph midway down, knowing the letter so well she didn't have to read it again because she knew where the paragraph was. "This will tell you why I'm imposing on you. Why I went to the trouble of finding you. Because, well, I *had* to. It was like it was an order from my father or something. Go ahead, take the letter and you'll understand."

It was very strange reading words written by a friend who had been dead for nearly twenty years. About the dead we often say that their spirit remains in our hearts. But that's seldom true. Not really. We abandon the dead as quickly as our emotions will allow, and Bobby had been dead for a long, long time. Now here he was speaking to me from paper that his hands had touched, through ink that was a direct conduit to what he had been thinking and feeling at that time.

I could picture him hunched beneath a gas lantern, jungle moths fluttering around, writing. I'd probably been there when he'd put it on paper. Yeah, I probably had. Now his words created a voice that resonated as if it came from his own mouth:

> . . . Gail, darling, there's something else that's been on my mind. I don't know why, but it's something I've been thinking about. I've mentioned my buddy Doc a couple of times in these crazy letters of mine, but what I want you to have is his

whole name and how to get in touch with him just in case.
I've been asking him for a week, but the stubborn bastard
only just now told me where he can be contacted back there
in the world. Here it is, I think it's the phone number and address of some relative—

What followed was the address of Tucker Gatrell, Mango, Florida,
just south of Marco.

I looked up from the letter and turned to Amanda, who was staring
at me, watching me read. "I remember your father bugging me about it
now. He wanted a permanent address. A hometown address, he called
it. So he could always get in touch. I'd completely forgotten that he'd
asked. This is really weird."

"Keep reading," she said. "It'll seem weirder."

. . . Don't go getting superstitious on me, babe. That's not
why I'm telling you about Doc. I'm not going to die over here.
I don't know why I'm so sure, but I am.

But what I'm thinking is what happens if you or Mandy
ever get in trouble when I'm not around? Like you always say,
I'm a worrier. But that's why I want you to know about Doc.
This letter makes it official. You get in trouble, Doc's the guy
to call. I'm talking about the kind of trouble where the police
or a lawyer can't or won't get involved. Like a spot where
someone's giving you problems or scaring you or taking advantage of you—something I'd normally handle. Or maybe
someone's trying to take advantage of Mandy, like some asshole boy. That's when I want you to contact Doc.

Maybe I'm being silly, but you two are the only girls I got,
and I always want someone nearby you can count on. So no
screwing around, you talk to him. You can trust him, take my
word for it. Let's just say the man has special skills. If he can't
handle it, then he'll know someone who can. And when Little
Miss Mandy's old enough, I want you to tell her the same
thing. It doesn't matter how many years have passed, not to

guys like Doc and me. After what we've been through, a couple of decades or so don't mean a damn thing. . . .

I removed my glasses, cleaned them with a paper napkin, then fitted them back over my nose. "I see what you mean," I said.

She was leaning toward me, voice lower, intense. "It's like he knows. Like he's talking to us. I found these letters not quite two weeks ago, and that's just the way it seemed. Like he knew exactly what was going on."

"He called you Mandy. A nickname."

"I guess. I don't know. I don't remember anything about him. I used to pretend I did; made stuff up, but it's because I wanted to believe I'd known him at least for a little bit. Daddy."

"It's been nearly two decades," I said.

"That's why it's so weird."

"Because he mentions it in the letter—that time won't make any difference to me? Or because you're in some kind of trouble?"

Amanda thought for a moment, not looking at me before she said, "All of the above."

✵

"The problem is, I think something's happened to my mother. She took off with a guy and now she's disappeared."

I said, "What?"

"Gail, the woman in my father's letters, my mom. She's been gone for nearly three months."

"Do you mean that she went away on a trip and you haven't heard from her? Or do you mean she's vanished?"

"I'm not sure. That's why I came looking for you. Maybe both."

"Then you should be talking to police, not me. Or the FBI."

"I already have."

"Then you *are* serious."

"Of course I'm serious. Why would I say such a thing? I haven't seen her or spoken with her since early February. And it's been more than a month since I got a postcard from her. My mom would never do that. She wouldn't drop out of sight like that unless something was really wrong. When I explain it you'll understand. Coming to you is about the only thing I haven't tried. I mean, who else am I going to ask?"

After I'd listened for a while, I thought: *Who else, indeed?*

Amanda had trouble telling a story sequentially—most people do— so I interrupted occasionally to keep her on track or nudge her off lengthy asides. Mostly, though, I just listened. You have to let people tell stories in their own way. Take all the pieces apart, rearrange them neatly, and here's what happened: After Bobby's death, Gail Richardson was so devastated by grief that she sought professional counseling. "This was in Lauderdale," Amanda explained, "and Mom had to find a counselor that was approved by the VA. They'll only pay for certain ones and Mom ended up with Frank Calloway. I was so young at the time I really don't know for sure what happened, but what they told me later was that Frank treated her for the next year or so . . . nearly two years, I think, and he gradually fell in love with her. When he realized his interest in Mom wasn't just professional, he sat her down to explain why, ethically, he could no longer be her psychologist, but ended up asking her to marry him instead."

Gail, widow and the mother of a very young daughter, did not accept right away. But Frank persisted and, slightly more than two years after the death of her husband, Gail became Mrs. Frank Calloway. Within months after that, Amanda was legally adopted.

"I don't think that Mom was ever in love with Frank. Not like she'd been in love with my real father, anyway. Read the letters and you'll see the kind of passion they had for each other. That's pretty rare." Amanda allowed a reflective, cynical beat before adding, "These days, in fact, it's almost nonexistent. But I think my mom's a realist. She knew how tough it'd be raising me on her own, and I think she came to feel real affection for Frank. She certainly came to be dependent on him. She looked to Frank for everything. Financial security, emotional approval, the whole works. With some men, I think they'd rather have that than love."

"It sounds like you're not a big fan of your stepfather."

"He's not my stepfather anymore. He's my mother's ex-husband."

"You don't like him."

"I respect Frank. At times I even find him likable and entertaining. But he never pretended to be my real father. No, with Frank and me, it was . . . it was more like a business arrangement. I think we both knew we had to accept each other or risk hurting my mother. Even when I was very little I can remember thinking that. It was the only way to keep my mom happy, and we both loved my mother very much." She paused for a moment, remembering how it was, before she added, "You said my dad, my real dad, had a picture of me. Did he ever show you a picture of my mom?"

I nodded. He had. Yes, he certainly had.

✳

Bobby had carried a couple of photos of Gail. One, I couldn't remember much about . . . a busty teenage Latina girl in shorts and a T-shirt? Yeah . . . posed in front of some kind of fast car. A GTO, maybe or a 442. One of the popular muscle cars of the day. Essence of the American male from that period: dream car, dream girl, a bank loan and marital obligations implied.

But the picture of Gail I remembered best was a glamour shot apparently taken by a professional photographer: haunting eyes, high cheekbones that created their own shadows in tricky lighting, long black hair with auburn overtones brushed as bright and smooth as a candle's flame. It was the face of a starlet; one of the classic beauties from the forties. Imagine Rita Hayworth, but with Veronica Lake's sleepy, secretive eyes, and you'd come pretty close to Gail Richardson.

Bobby had called it his "'Twelfth of Never' photograph." Which made no sense until one night, as I boiled coffee over a can of Sterno, tropic rain drumming down, he explained: "It's because of the way she looks. Her face, her hair, the way her eyes look right into mine. It reminds me of the song "The Twelfth of Never." It's our song, Gail's and mine."

I said, "Huh?"

"What'a'ya mean, 'huh?'"

"I mean 'The Twelfth of Never.' I don't know what you're talking about."

At first, he thought I was kidding. Then he realized that I wasn't. "Doc, you're telling me you've never heard it? Not even on the radio? The Johnny Mathis song, for Christ's sake!"

"Nope. But it's been a couple of years since I've been back to the States. Nearly four years, actually."

His expression was pained. "You'd have to live on the frigging moon not to have heard that song."

I was boiling the coffee, listening to the rain, looking at the blue flame of my miniature chemical fire: Sterno in the jungle. "The moon," I said. "For the last few years, yeah. The moon, that pretty nearly describes the places I've been."

He said, "You're serious. You're really serious. Okay . . . you want to know what the song's like? Look at my wife. The way her face is, that's exactly what the song sounds like. Too beautiful even to describe. A thousand years ago, she coulda been an Aztec princess or she could be Miss Latin America today. You know what you can't tell from that photograph? Her eyes; Gail's got the most unusual eyes you've ever seen. Her right eye's bright blue. Powder blue like those stones the Navaho Indians wear. Those stones . . . turquoise, that's what they call it. But her left eye is green. Really deep green, jungle green. I look at her eyes and I know that there'll never be anyone else for me but Gail. Like until the twelfth of never, get it? I mean forever."

Later, much later, when I finally heard the song, Bobby had been dead for, what, six months? Maybe a year. But listening to it, I'd thought about how right the man was. In his life, there had been only one true love. Gail. One blue eye, one green eye. And probably his toddler daughter, as well. Another girl with unusual eyes.

Back then, I'd thought of them as Bobby's girls.

The only loves he would ever have. Just like he'd said: forever.

✳

To Amanda, I now said, "I never met your mother, but I remember the photos. She was a very beautiful woman."

"She still is. She's in her forties, but the men—when she walks into a room?—men still stop what they're doing and stare. She has that . . . I don't know what you'd call it. That grace or something, it's almost like an odor. When the two of us go into a restaurant or a lounge, she's the one who gets the attention. But if I try to joke about it, like, Hey, Mom, they think I'm your younger plain-Jane sister, she gets this really hurt look in her eyes. Because she loves me, understand, and I think she's always felt bad that she's so much prettier than I am."

When I started to speak, Amanda held up her palm, shushing me. "I'm not fishing for compliments here, so you don't need to offer any. I'm trying to make you see how it was with Frank and my mom. He wanted to possess her, and that's exactly what he did. He possessed her, treated her like some kind of treasure. Which sounds great until you realize that treasure is nothing more than property with a specific value. There's a Hindu saying that a woman's face is shaped by her heart. My mother's face is soft and kind and caring, but it's not very strong. She let it happen, which isn't uncommon for women of her generation. But she's still the one who allowed herself to become completely dependent on Frank. And that's why she was so unprepared for what happened last year."

What happened, according to Amanda, was a woman named Capricia and then a man named Jackie Merlot.

In terms of male behavior, the story of the Calloways is so unfortunately commonplace that you have to wonder about the validity of the human male as a lifetime mate. When Frank gave up his psychology practice, his land syndicate business blossomed, then it boomed. He kept his old secretary, a woman named Betty Marsh, and hired a second secretary to handle the growing workload. She was a twenty-seven-year-old former art student by the name of Capricia Worthington, "Cappy" for short, which Frank allowed a nautical interpretation, and so his name of endearment for her became Skipper.

"I don't know when the affair started," Amanda told me. "I didn't see much of Mom and Frank before the split up because my job keeps me so busy. I'm district manager for Vita Tech, a medical supply company. We're based outside Pompano Beach, just south of Deerfield, and I'm almost always on the road. That, plus I share a condo with a girlfriend—a pretty nice place north of Lauderdale called Sea Ranch Lakes—so it's not like I got by their house much.

"But I remember this one time I was over there for dinner and Frank had this moony, distracted look. Like he had to really force himself to pay attention to what my mom or me said. Something else is, he gave Mom a couple of very pointed, well-disguised cuts about weight she'd gained and something about the way her skin looked, wrinkles, I think. My mom loves to lay out in the sun.

"He's very good at stuff like that, making criticism sound like it's some harmless observation or a joke, but he really means it, and he knows how to make it hurt, too."

I asked, "Was it unusual for him to criticize your mother?"

"About her actual physical appearance, yeah. She's so beautiful, that's what he loved about her. In every other way, though, he was a very demanding person. The way she dressed, the way she spoke, the way she hosted a dinner party. Frank was always in control, and he let her know it.

"He was never loud or vicious, but just sharp enough to make his point stick. Oh yeah—that night, he made some remark about her being too old to do something. Learn to play tennis, I think, but he gave it a sexual connotation, as if to imply she was letting him down in the romance department. I didn't say anything, but I felt like smacking him. My mom's so damn sensitive, I knew she'd spend the next couple of weeks eating nothing but lettuce and carrots and fretting about the way she looked. Yeah, she'd gained a little weight. She was forty-four years old, for God's sake. But Frank didn't like it, so he had to let her know it and, at the time, I remember thinking, *Uh-oh, this marriage is in trouble.*"

It was indeed.

Frank moved out and rented a penthouse beach condo just across from Bahia Mar Marina, Lauderdale. Capricia Worthington moved in.

"I met Skipper three or four months after the divorce was final. Frank was having a house built for her at Boca Grande. New life, new home, new ocean, that was the thinking, I guess. Frank was being very modern and civilized about it all, so he and his young bride invited me to dinner. I accepted out of curiosity more than anything else. What did this woman have that made Frank act like such a complete dumbass? That's what I wanted to find out.

"So I found out. She has the body, she has the looks, but in an . . . artificial mall-girl kind of way. Implants and fitness classes, that kind of body. Meet her and you get the feeling that, if stores sold women, she'd be in the front window of Dillards. Something else, she's totally New

Age, but the Junior League variety, the kind that takes money to maintain. She said things like 'The reason I prefer crystals instead of magnets when there's a full moon is, I'm an Aries, but with Scorpio rising, so my needs and my sensitivity change just like the tides.' The details may be off, but that's the kind of stuff she'd say. Or she'd say, 'I hope to do a couple of seminars in Sedona, Arizona, over the ski season and learn exactly why I'm lunar-sensitive more than solar-active.' Buzz phrases. She uses all the newest buzz phrases. A real ditz."

"Sedona?" I said. "I have a friend who says Sedona is a major refueling spot for alien spaceships."

Amanda mistook the comment for sarcasm. "Seriously, Sedona's a real place. She wants to go there and take a seminar or take a sweat lodge, one of the two. Frank, he just sat there smiling, accepting it like a complete idiot. He told me that's what she offered him, a new way of looking at life. She'd awakened a new spirituality in him. Something like that. They'd known each other in a previous karma—Jesus, it was all I could do not to bust out laughing—and that, together, they'd discovered a mystic link to certain elements in the sea. Bottle-nosed dolphins. They are very, very big on dolphins."

I liked the way she said that. I liked her hard-nosed rationality; was beginning to see Amanda Richardson more and more as an individual and less and less as the daughter of a long-dead friend.

She was still talking about the new wife; didn't like her, but I also got the impression that part of it, maybe a lot of it, was jealousy. "My God, listening to Skipper, it really was a struggle to keep a straight face. But Frank, this guy I'd always known to be damn near cold-blooded when it came to logic or business or anything like that, was sitting there sipping a fine cabernet telling me he and his new squeeze had been talking to Flipper. The way he was behaving, it was like aliens had come down from Mars and taken over his body or something."

I said, "When people go through big changes, they sometimes stop thinking rationally."

"It sounds like you speak from experience."

"I do my share of dumb things. I've gone through periods where I seem to specialize in the behavior. But I'm usually rational."

"There was a time when I could say the same thing about my step-father."

"Then I don't understand it."

"Yeah, well, you haven't met Skipper. Frank was thinking with his testicles, trust me." She paused for a moment; gave me an amused look. "Tell me something, Dr. Ford. You're a biologist, one of those solid, mild-mannered, up-front guys. It's practically stenciled on your fore-head. And Frank can't be more than seven or eight years older than you. So why is it that middle-aged men confuse immaturity with youth? Or is it just that an aging brain starts shrinking before the rest of a man's body?"

She gave it a light touch, but there was some anger down in there deep, the same place her thirty-second rule came from.

Thinking, *Me? Mild-mannered?* I said, "So your stepfather's not the only one in the family who knows how to make cutting remarks."

"It wasn't aimed at you, just an overall observation."

"Men in general, huh?"

"They do seem to be fairly predictable. Not all, but most. Don't get me wrong. I'm not gay, if that's what you're wondering."

"I wasn't wondering. I was commenting on your attitude." When I saw her expression condense, I added quickly, "Not criticizing. Just commenting."

"You didn't see how devastated my mom was when Frank left. Like I told you, she was dependent on him. I'd moved out, then he moved out. So there she is, forty-some years old, overweight and a dud in bed according to the husband who abandoned her, living all alone. This beautiful woman, probably the kindest person I've ever met, and I'm not saying that just because I'm her daughter. She was hurt, disillu-sioned, she was depressed and vulnerable as hell. A perfect target for any wandering asshole who wanted to take advantage of her. You ex-pect me to be happy about that?"

"Are you talking about the guy she disappeared with or someone else?"

Amanda said, "I'm talking about him, yeah, that's exactly the guy I'm describing. Jackie Merlot, the one I'm telling you about."

According to Amanda, Gail had met Merlot years ago. She pronounced it "MUR-lowe," similar to the pronunciation of the wine. At about the same time, Gail also started seeing Calloway as her psychologist. "Apparently, Mom knew Merlot back when the two of us still lived alone. I say apparently because I can't remember ever seeing the guy until about eleven months ago. When I did meet him, just looking at him, something about his face, those eyes, it gave me the creeps. Jesus, talking about him gives me goosebumps right now. See?"

I looked at the freckled arm extended toward me. When I touched my fingers to her forearm—there were, indeed, goosebumps—she flinched slightly, saying, "Merlot was supposedly one of Frank's earliest land syndicate investors. I think he and my mom met through Frank at some party or something, got to be friends, but once she started to date Frank, Merlot vanished from the picture."

Nearly twenty years later, Merlot had reappeared.

"I don't know how he heard about the divorce. Maybe he read it in the paper or something, but only a couple of weeks after the thing was final, Merlot was back on the scene. Mom had been living by herself for more than a year by that time. Frank and his soulmate bimbo were a public item, not even trying to hide the fact they were living together. He'd even gone to the trouble of making a full confession to my mom about his affair. About why he'd outgrown the relationship and why he hoped they'd be friends, but their life as husband and wife were over, because he needed space to grow and he'd met an old spirit probably from another lifetime, meaning Skipper. Can you imagine someone as nice as my mom sitting there listening to this bullshit? Also that he wished her well, but that she had to go on and find a new life. Nice guy, huh?"

"Kind of surprising behavior for a psychologist."

"Yeah, it's like little Skipper had actually screwed the man's brains loose. But you know what gets me most of all? Frank really is a pretty nice guy. That's one of the reasons it hurt my mom so much. She wasn't just dependent on him, she liked him. He took care of her, he made her laugh. About a month after Frank left, she told me the whole story. The both of us just sat there holding each other and crying."

I was sitting at the galley table, drinking iced tea, listening. I could look across the water to the row of guide slips, each with its own ornate wooden sign. Name of captain, name of skiff. At the end of the T-dock was Janet Mueller's bright blue houseboat moored snugly among the more expensive sailboats, Aquasports, Makos and fiberglass party cruisers. Curled up on the stern deck of Janet's boat was the marina's black cat, Crunch & Des. His tail was slapping rhythmically in sunlight. He looked as predatory and as bored as some of the big lions I'd seen years ago while working in Mozambique.

Thinking about Mozambique, the way its jungle rose as a green bluff out of the mud of the Zambezi River, caused me to think about the small Central American nation of Masagua. Similar jungle, similar earth odors, similar rust-red rivers. It also caused me to think about Pilar Balserio.

I said to Amanda, "I've read that losing a lover is like having someone die. Someone you care about. When a relationship ends, they say you have to go through a mourning period."

"Well . . . my mom certainly did that. She's a very sensitive person. If there's a commercial on television that uses a dog or a baby, she gets teary eyed. It used to drive me nuts, but that's just the way she is. When I was growing up, all my girlfriends absolutely loved her. Same with the boyfriend I had in high school. The two of them still stay in touch. At least, they stayed in touch before she met Merlot. See, I'm telling you about the kind of person my mother is. She's very caring and extremely thoughtful. You need to understand that to understand why I'm positive she's in some kind of trouble."

According to Amanda, Merlot began by telephoning her mother regularly, checking on her, then dropping by to bring her books or little presents. Gail Richardson was lonely, depressed, and she welcomed the friendship.

"This was after they'd spent quite a bit of time getting reacquainted on the Internet."

I said, "What?"

"You know, the Internet, the America Online thing. You don't have a computer?"

"No."

"I thought everyone had a PC. But you know how it works, right?"

I nodded. Tomlinson had told me about it.

"Mom and Merlot did a bunch of E-mailing, visiting the same chat rooms, that sort of stuff. Conversations through cyberspace. Merlot in his house, Mom in our old place, which is why it always seems so safe having on-line friends. I guess the two of them spent a lot of time getting reacquainted, just typing away.

"After a while, they had their own Internet friends, their own little circle, people she'd never met. This was early on she told me about the Internet stuff, back when she was still open about her relationship with Merlot. Like I told you, the Internet stuff always seems so harmless."

"Your mother's good with computers?"

"No. You don't have to be good with computers to work the Internet. She was just lonely, that's all. She'd be on-line almost every night. I know, 'cause I'd always get a busy signal when I tried to call. Finally, I talked her into getting a second line."

"She spent that much time."

"Yeah. What else did she have to do?"

"And always with Merlot?"

"Not at first. I spend my share of time on-line. I've got E-mail friends all over the world, so Mom and I used to jabber away to each other. For some reason . . . it's hard to explain . . . but there are certain subjects that are easier to write about than talk about. So that's what we'd do. Write notes back and forth about all kinds of stuff. She'd write about the way it was between her and my real dad, and I'd write about . . . well, private stuff, the way I felt about things."

"So what happened?"

"What happened was she got involved with a different group of E-mail friends. I wasn't a part of it. And I think she had an on-line crush on some guy from California. She never told me that, but if my mom mentions a guy more than twice, I know she has some feelings for him. I warned her about telling strangers too much about herself. I mean, no one really knows who anyone else is on the Internet. Right?"

I didn't reply. I had never been on the Internet. I had a phone. Sanibel's good little library and the post office were just down the shell road. What did I need with the Internet?

She was still talking about it. "Like the guy she was E-mailing, the guy who she said was from California. He could have been anyone. Like a ninety-year-old man from Jamaica. Or maybe not a man at all, but a woman. Or maybe some kinky teenager who lived two houses away. People can say anything about themselves. And there's no way of knowing."

"Did she say how Merlot found her on-line?"

"No. Just that she'd been E-mailing an old friend who'd been very kind and helpful to her. Her saying that, I think it was her way of telling me that she was going to start dating again. Mom and Frank were couples people. The only people they socialized with were married couples, so Merlot was one of the few single men in the picture. But every time I asked about him, my mom insisted that she had no romantic interest. Just that he was very kind to her, someone to talk to. So I figured, fine, that's exactly what she needs. A friend."

But Amanda's opinion changed when she finally met Merlot. "I stopped by Mom's house one afternoon. I hadn't called ahead and he was there, the two of them sitting out by the pool. Have you ever surprised someone doing something they shouldn't be doing? That's the way Merlot reacted. I could see his expression change when I walked in, surprised like he was ready to jump up and hide. I couldn't figure out why. They were both fully dressed, they weren't even sitting that close together, but I still had the feeling I'd interrupted something. Not from my mom. She was happy to see me, perfectly at ease. But from him, he was very nervous, lots of shifting around in his chair and the kind of eye contact where someone's searching your face for a reaction.

"He recovered pretty fast, though. After that, he was as nice and charming as he could be. He'd been saving a couple of presents for me. A hat and a T-shirt from some rock group he claimed to be associated with. And he made sure that I was the focus of conversation. But even if he'd have reacted differently when I walked in, I don't think I'd have trusted the guy. He's got all the social skills and he's very, very smooth. Too smooth. He's a hugger and a cheek-kisser, one of those feel-good people who's great at a wedding or a dinner party, but there was something odd about him. Just looking at him made me feel . . . dirty? No, that's a little strong. But creepy, yeah. Something about Jackie Merlot . . . just wasn't right."

Amanda said she didn't tell her mother about her negative reaction to Merlot because she didn't think it was necessary. Gail Richardson insisted that Merlot just wanted to be friends and that she had absolutely no romantic interest in the man.

"I believed her. Up to that point, I don't think she'd ever lied to me in her life. She needed friends and I wasn't about to interfere. Besides, I never in a million years imagined that someone who looked like Merlot could get to first base with my mom. The man is more than just unattractive, he's actually kind of disgusting."

I said, "Oh?"

"Picture a mound of mashed potatoes or a very large marshmallow with the face of a teenage boy attached. Hairless and cheeky, that kind of face. Add one of those tiny, round mouths you sometimes see; one of those rosebud Irish mouths, then stick a blond toupee on top and razor-cut it smooth. You know, a disco haircut from the seventies. I don't know why it's blond, because he looks like he might have a little bit of something else in him. Asian? I don't know, *something*. Eastern European maybe. But that's Jackie Merlot. And he's big. Huge, actually. One of those really freakish oversized men.

"But the way he moves, the way he looks, he seems far more feminine than masculine. When he walks, he takes small, quick steps, almost like he's dancing, and he has the kind of high, gravelly voice that I associate with large women who smoke a lot or who are very overweight." She paused for a moment, thinking about it before she added, "So make it two reasons I didn't think Merlot had a chance with my mom. Physically, he was way too unappealing, plus I also figured he was gay. He seemed so . . . safe.

"Turns out," she said, "he wasn't."

※

By the time it was obvious that Gail Calloway and Merlot were involved in a physical relationship, it was too late for Amanda to tell her mother about her gut reaction to the man. Not that she didn't try to tell her.

She did.

But it was too late to carry much influence. Merlot had a hold on her by then.

"It's the only way I can describe it," Amanda told me. "He had a powerful hold on her that just kept getting stronger and stronger. When I asked her why she was interested in Merlot, her answer actually gave me chills. Her exact words were, 'Because he thinks I'm pretty. He buys me presents and he says the nicest things to me.'

"Doc, my mother is not a shallow person. Besides, she's a fairly wealthy woman on her own. Frank and the courts saw to that. The way she said it, 'He buys me presents,' her voice had this robot kind of little-girl quality that scared the hell out of me. 'He thinks I'm pretty.' My God, like all the confidence she'd once had had been destroyed when Frank split.

"I'm no spoiled little brat. I don't have to approve of the man my mother dates, but there was something . . . weird? . . . yeah, something weird about this guy. It really bothered me. Another thing was, the more she saw of Merlot, the more distant she became toward me. Same with her closest women friends, and she had quite a few. We almost never heard from her. That sense that something sneaky was going on—the same thing I saw in Jackie Merlot's face the day I surprised them—I now began to hear and see in my mother. It wasn't like her. I knew then what I'm now positive of: Merlot had control of her and, whether she knew it or not, my mom was in trouble."

Gail Richardson began to spend weekends at Merlot's home. Then she spent whole weeks at a time; increasingly long periods when Gail seldom made an attempt to communicate with her daughter or her friends. Amanda had the strong impression that Merlot discouraged outside contact. She saw her mother briefly in September, then again around Halloween. More than a month of silence followed before Gail finally replied to one of Amanda's many phone messages to Merlot's house. A few days later, Merlot had his telephone number changed.

"It was getting pretty close to Christmas by then," Amanda said. "I didn't know what in the world to do, so I finally broke down, called Frank and I'd told him what was going on. What scared me most of all was the sound of Frank's voice when I told him. He recognized Merlot's name right away and I realized that maybe, just maybe, Merlot had been a patient of Frank's instead of an early investor like Mom had told me."

"You say that just because of the way your stepfather reacted?"

She was nodding, very matter-of-fact. Her expression said: *You'd have to know the guy to understand.* "The way Frank reacts, that's the only way you'd ever know anything from his shrink days. He takes the ethics of his old profession very seriously. It's the only thing that explained why he sounded so damn worried."

"When you mentioned Jackie Merlot."

"Exactly. When I told him, what he said was, 'Jesus Christ, no wonder your mother didn't tell me.' And a little bit later, he said, 'I thought Jackie Merlot would be in a facility by now,' and then he clammed up quick, like it had just sort of slipped out. But he was worried enough to hire a professional to have Merlot investigated, and he also offered to go with me to Merlot's house and insist that we be allowed to speak with Mom."

Which is just what they did.

※

Confronting Merlot while briefly reuniting with her mother had created an awkward, emotional scene. Amanda had a tough time telling me about it. People who shield themselves with a hard outer core do it for reasons of protection. Her voice broke several times. She drifted between tears and rage, but each time fought her way back under control.

Merlot had a rental in one of the older canal-front subdivisions off A1A, Lauderdale. That he apparently had a live-in male roommate was unexpected. Amanda described the roommate as tall, muscular, not really black but not really white, with some kind of heavy accent, maybe French or Creole.

The roommate intercepted them and refused to let them speak with Merlot or Gail Calloway. Then Merlot appeared, saying he would call the police if they didn't leave. Frank asked to speak with Gail alone, just to confirm that she was all right. No deal. Then he asked to speak with Merlot alone. Same thing, and Merlot again threatened to call the police.

"It was the first time that I can say Frank ever really let my mother and me down. The son-of-a-bitch was ready to walk away, saying it was a legal matter or time to call a lawyer, something like that. Not that angry, just frustrated and maybe a little pissed off because we were imposing on his new life. I wouldn't budge, though, so the police finally did come, but at least they made Merlot bring my mom to the door.

"Doc, I hardly recognized her. In the six or seven weeks since I'd seen her, she'd lost maybe fifteen pounds. She looked pale and gaunt, all eyes and hair and cheekbones. Her eyes, she's got the most unusual eyes you've ever seen. One green, one blue, and I know she's sick when her eyes get this milky, glassy look. Well, that's just the way her eyes looked. Glassy, like she wasn't well. She even sounded different when she spoke. What's that word—mesmerized? That's the way she sounded, but more like she was dazed. She came out, gave me a big hug and kiss right there in front of the cops. Then she told Frank and me that we had to stop saying all the bad things we'd been saying about Merlot."

I interrupted and told her to explain that in a little more detail.

"My mom told us that we had to stop spreading lies about her friend Jackie."

"She was convinced that you two had been lying about the guy?"

"Exactly."

"Did she seem paranoid? Or as if the guy might have her on drugs or something?"

"No. She just seemed absolutely confident that Frank and I had been spreading lies about her boyfriend. She said that she knew what we'd been saying and that we had to stop because we were making ourselves look silly."

"Had you and Frank said anything to anyone about Merlot?"

"Nothing. Yeah, we'd talked between ourselves, but we hadn't said a damn thing to anyone else. Then she told us that she'd never been happier."

"Judging from her voice, did she mean it?"

"I don't think anyone was forcing her to say it. But she didn't sound normal, either. Not like she was drunk or anything, but, like I told you, kind of in a daze. Or like she was trying real hard to show Merlot that she was a hundred percent on his side. That she was protecting him. You know the way people behave when they're trying to let someone know they care? Like that. She said that she was living with Jackie now and they'd soon be going on a trip."

"Did she say where?"

"I asked her, but Merlot cut her off before she could answer. As we were leaving, she kind of blurted out that it might be a while before she'd be able to call me on the phone. Because they'd be sailing and some of the ports were remote."

"The police were still there, they heard that exchange."

"Yeah, and it was . . . awful," Amanda said. "It was like one of those nasty little scenes you see on television cop shows. Lights flashing, neighbors staring out their windows, trashy white people arguing on the sidewalk. That's the way I felt, trashy. And helpless. Helpless because of the way my mother was behaving. You know what the worst thing was? Mom, my own mother, she believed Merlot, not me. That business about Frank and me spreading lies. It was like she'd been brainwashed or something. He'd been telling her that crap. Why? I mean, why go to the trouble? Christ, I wanted to scream I was so frustrated.

"So then the cops tell us we've got to leave, stop harassing the happy couple. What choice did I have? I told Mom to please call me. I couldn't make her believe that I couldn't call her. She didn't even know Merlot's number'd been changed. So Frank and I go get in the car. Mom's standing there behind the cops. Merlot, the fat ass, he's got his arm around Mom, his Creole roommate standing there still looking pissed off, ready to fight. You know what Merlot does then?"

"What."

"He flashes me this smug little smile as we're pulling away. A very private smile, him looking right into my eyes, just him and me. It was kind of like he was telling me, yeah, you're *right* about the kind of person I am. But your mother doesn't know it and no one else will ever believe it, so screw you."

The way Amanda described it, I could picture it: the man's eyes boring into hers, making her hate him even more, wanting her to hate him because he was enjoying it.

Slightly more than two weeks later, Amanda received a card from her mother postmarked Cartagena, Colombia. All it said was that they were aboard a forty-eight-foot sailboat and having a wonderful time. Over the following two months, she received three more cards, all of them postmarked Cartagena, all of them pleasant and very brief. They offered no return address and gave no more information than the first.

"She might have been writing to a stranger," Amanda said. "They were that impersonal, that cold. And there wasn't a clue about what their plans were, where they were headed."

✸

Amanda received the last of the three cards nearly a month before she tracked me down on Sanibel. Increasingly concerned about her mother's well-being, she contacted the Broward County Sheriff's Department and then the FBI. Both agencies were attentive and sympathetic, but how could they list Gail Calloway as a missing person when an official police report quoted the woman as saying that she was staying voluntarily with Jackie Merlot? Not only that, but Gail had volunteered that the two of them expected to be out of touch for a while while traveling.

"It's quite a predicament," I said.

"Yeah. Now you see what I mean when I say the police can't help. And the private investigator Frank hired, he's not going to travel out of the country to try to bring Mom back. He'd be risking his license."

I thought about it for a moment before saying, "I'm going to tell you something that you may not want to hear. You're assuming that your mother wants to be rescued. You need to face the possibility that your mother really is happy, that she meant exactly what she told you. She's a grown woman. Merlot may be a bad guy, maybe the scum shyster of the earth, but it doesn't much matter what we think. She may be doing exactly what she wants to do."

"No, nope, I don't think so. I know my mom. She's in trouble. She may not know it yet, but she is." Amanda gave it a couple of beats, looking at me before she added, "And you think so, too."

I said, "I do?" amused by her confidence; sat there letting her know I was waiting for an explanation

"I've been watching your expression, Ford, the way your eyes changed. While you were listening, I could almost see the wheels turning. You're a smart man. You've been around and you're good enough at reading people to figure I'm not the kind of person to exaggerate or to panic or go all freaky just because I don't get my way. I'm not exactly the all-American girl, but I'm no ditz, either. And I'm not one of those adult children who can't leave their parents. For the last five years, I've lived very happily on my own, thank you.

"But what I told you about my mom, it got to you. It made you mad. I could tell. There's something very . . . unhealthy about Merlot's behavior, and you know it. You and my real father were once very close friends, and the woman that he loved is in trouble. Guys like you—and I may be wrong here, but it's the way I read it—guys like you, the straight shooters, you're throwbacks. You take friendship seriously, and what I just told you really pisses you off. Not you personally, but in a way that offends your sense of loyalty. I may be way off base but, hey, I hope I'm right because there aren't many people left, male or female, a person can count on. So, the question is, do you have any ideas how to find her and pry her loose from that fat bastard?"

So, along with her other good qualities, give the lady low marks for her generous, hopeful assessment of my character, but high marks for the way she read my reaction to her story.

She was right. Even though I had never met Gail Richardson Calloway, I felt fraternal and protective toward the woman to an emotional degree that I found surprising. I was also surprised to realize that Amanda's story had filled me with an irrational dislike of a man I'd never seen, spoken with or met: Jackie Merlot. It had to do with an image that lingered in my imagination: a fat man with a boy's face flashing a private smile at a tough, introverted girl with stringy strawberry blond tomboy hair; a man who took perverse joy in driving a wedge between a mother and a daughter.

But I was wary of my own reaction because I am wary of emotion as a motivator. Emotion is energy without structure, without reason. Emotion can be a dangerous indulgence.

I finished the last of my tea; rattled the ice cubes in my glass as I said, "What you want me to do is go to Colombia and try to find your mother. That's the point of all this, isn't it?"

Amanda was shaking her head. "I won't say I didn't come here hoping you'd offer. Yeah, that's what I was hoping. I really was. But the main reason I came is because of the letters I found, my dad's letters. It's like he knew what was going to happen and he was giving me directions what to do. But I don't expect you to try to help, Doc. Not now. Not after meeting you."

What the hell did that mean? I said, "You just lost me."

The girl stirred from her seat, stood away from the table and tugged at the T-shirt with its terse warning message. Through the window, near mangroves at the back entrance to the marina office, I could see Mack at the fish-cleaning table filleting a couple of pompano. Tucker Gatrell watched, yammering away. Suspended from the porch overhead was a cast net. It looked like a gigantic spider's web. Jeth was enmeshed in the thing, carefully inspecting its elemental network, using a spool of fishing line to mend holes.

Amanda swiped a wisp of copper hair from her eyes and said, "I hoped you'd volunteer to go help my mom because of the way my dad described you. But the thing is, I pictured a . . . well, let's just say I pictured a more adventurous type of guy."

"More adventurous?" I said. "Is that right?"

"What was that line in my dad's letter? 'The man's got special skills.' He was talking about you, so I pictured one of the soldier-of-fortune types. One of the tough guys you see in films. But not somebody like you, Doc. As big as you are, I didn't picture somebody who looks like they spend all their time reading books and looking through a microscope."

"I like books," I said agreeably. "And it's true that my work requires a microscope."

"Don't take that the wrong way. It's not a cut. I don't like the macho types. Not at all, so no offense. Really."

Listening to Amanda's story, her tone, her tough logic, I could hear the faintest echo of a good man who was lost long ago and far away. It was a frail thin chord that was the voice of an old friend. I fought the urge to allow myself an ironic smile as I replied, "Gee, no offense taken, Amanda. Really."

"But any advice you have to offer," she added, "it could be very helpful."

"Advice, sure. If I can help, you bet I'll try."

"I'll give you my number in Lauderdale. If you have any ideas, you can give me a call. I figure what I'll have to do is just fly down there— Colombia, I mean, maybe get a friend to go with me—and have a look around." The smile she then allowed me was one of those bright, meaningless smiles of dismissal; the kind of smile we all use when we are dealing with people who are attempting to sell us something we do not want, or who have not met our initial expectations.

I hoped my own bright smile mirrored hers. "Give you a call in Lauderdale, Amanda, you can count on it. Boy oh boy, I'll give it some thought, too. Maybe try to figure out a way to locate your mom and the guy she's traveling with. What was his name again?" Said it with false gusto, as if I hadn't been paying attention.

"His name? You mean after listening to the whole story, you've already forgotten—" She stopped and eyed me closely, thinking it over.

I said, "Isn't it handy to be able to take one look at a person and know what he's like? And you're so right! I'm the big, gawky, absent-minded-professor type. My brain's so jammed with research material I just can't seem to remember that guy's name. The big fellow you described. Boy do I feel like a dope."

I watched her expression: Is this an act? Then her face narrowed: Yep, it was definitely an act . . . but why?

"His name's Merlot," she said slowly.

"*Merlot.* That's right. You know, something that may account for my bad memory is when your dad and I were living over there in the jungles of Cambodia? It was almost *too* darn stressful. About half the time these little black-haired people were sneaking around trying to kill us. Well . . . I say 'kill us,' but what the Khmer really wanted to do was cut our heads off and carry them around on a pole. Know why?"

Her expression changed, but she didn't answer.

"The reason they wanted to cut our heads off is because they believe a man remains conscious for nearly a minute after his head's been severed. Which makes sense if you stop and think about it. Sure, you can't breathe, you can't walk, but your eyes and your brain are in the same place, right? To them, it's like the perfect punishment. They'd cut off our heads and then position us in such a way so that the last thing we saw before we died was our own headless corpse. You talk about having a bad memory? The strain of worrying about that probably killed off some my brain cells."

Her expression changed again. "Oh my *God*. You're not exaggerating, are you?"

"Wish I was. So, yeah, I can understand why you wouldn't trust someone like me to deal with a guy who might be taking advantage of your mother. This . . . what's his name again?"

Reevaluation time: Maybe I wasn't such a bookish, nerdish type after all. "Jackie," she said. "Jackie Merlot."

I was still smiling when I said, "Gee, a guy like that, I'd just love to meet."

I got a fresh notebook from the lab and, in my small, blocky print, jotted down all the useful phone numbers and addresses that Amanda could provide.

Someday, if the notebook became important, I would attach a label, give it a file name, then lock the notebook away with the others I'd kept and saved over the years. There were some interesting titles in that fireproof box:

Coast of Bengal
Borneo/Sandakan
Nicaragua/Politics/Baseball
Havana I. Havana II
Ox-Eyed Tarpon/South China Sea
Masagua's Ridley Turtles and the Magnetic Mountain
Singapore to Kota Baharu (with 3rd Gurkhas)

There were others.

All contained the carefully kept details of a lifetime spent traveling alone through the Third World tropics; necessarily duplicitous years spent doing clandestine work, as well as the work I still care passionately about: marine biology.

The notebooks added order. They allowed me a sense of purpose, even though much of what I've done in my life now seems absurd, nearly existential because of the violence to which I've contributed.

Tomlinson knows a little bit about it. Not much, but enough to attempt to comfort me one beery evening when he said, "You're not the Lone Ranger, Doc. Take the seventies, for instance. It wasn't a decade, man. It was a damn crime scene. And you worry about the little bit of political stuff you were involved in?"

As I said, Tomlinson doesn't know much about it.

So Bobby Richardson's ladies were allotted their own notebook.

When I'd finished with phone numbers and addresses, I asked Amanda if she'd thought to bring the four postcards she'd received from her mother. She had. They were in the envelope that contained her father's letters. She paced around studying my overloaded shelves of books while I studied the postcards.

All the cards were postmarked Cartagena, Colombia, and onto each was pasted a hundred-peso stamp that paid tribute to emeralds, the gem for which the country's jungles are famous. Cartagena is an ancient seaport city built like a fortress during the 1500s, when conquistadors shipped gold and silver to Madrid. I'd been there a number of times, but that had been years ago.

Three of the cards were photographs of sites I recognized as Cartagena tourist attractions: the clock tower entrance to the old walled city; a busy street vendor scene; a small Spanish garrison (stone walls with gunports overlooking Cartagena Harbor) that was now a restaurant, according to the card, called Club de Pesca.

Had I once eaten at that restaurant? It was possible. There was a little marina close to that old Spanish garrison. I'd maybe stopped at the marina for a beer, but I couldn't remember the name of the place.

Who could I check with to find out? I'd have to think about it.

The fourth postcard showed a roomful of polished ship's bells— "a magnificent nautical museum," according to florid Spanish on the back of the card. The place was apparently a private museum near Cartagena called CoMarCa.

The cards were not dated, but they were postmarked: 6 January, 12 January, 16 February and 20 March, respectively.

On the back of each postcard, in flowing, ovoid script, were typical tourist inanities: "Everything is so different here!" . . . "The weather is very warm because we are so close to the equator!" . . . "Miss you, wish you were here!"

They contained nothing more personal than that.

There was no mention of Jackie Merlot, of where they were staying, or of where they planned to travel.

Each card was written in black ink from what might have been the same rollerpoint pen. I also noticed that each of the last three cards had suffered a few water smears, as if the wet ink had been splattered with random raindrops . . . or maybe beads of sweat.

I found that very odd. But still . . . there was a benign explanation. Wasn't there?

I said to Amanda, "Are you absolutely certain this is your mother's handwriting?"

"I've seen enough of it to know, yeah. Everything about her is so beautiful; even her letters are rounded and neat and perfect. It's definitely my mom's writing."

"You mind if I hang on to these, maybe give them a closer look later?"

The woman shrugged. "They're not exactly what you'd call private and personal. She could have been writing to a stranger instead of her daughter."

"It's one of the things that bothers me."

That stopped her. She glanced up from the book she was leafing through. "Which tells me there are other things about them that bother you."

I said, "Maybe. I'm not sure."

"What's that supposed to mean?"

I smiled. "It means I'm not sure. Relax. I'm on your side. I'm not hiding anything. But give me some time to think about it."

She wanted to talk some more—I could tell, but she was also getting restless. Maybe she was uncomfortable in the close quarters of my little ship's cabin cottage. The spartan furnishings and the near-absence of decoration make some women uneasy. Tomlinson says that it is because my lack of creativity strips away all pretense and therefore reduces sexuality to its most basic and unromantic components.

Personally, I think the soft but constant gurgle of the many aquarium pumps keys a urinary restlessness.

While I was questioning her, she happened to mention that she liked boats; hoped to one day buy a sailboat and do some cruising through the islands. So I said boats? She liked boats? Then how about the two of us go roam around the docks, do some window-shopping?

Dinkin's Bay is among the last of Florida's old-time fish camp marinas: wobbly docks, bait tanks, tackle shop, fish market, some deep-water dockage on the bay side and lots of shallow water slips along the mangrove shoals. Everything built of wood, everything sun-leached gray. It was a Sunday in April: busy day with lots of Sanibel day-trippers roaming around, lots of cars coming and going in the shell parking lot. And all the slips were full.

People with the boat bug—and it was apparent that Amanda had a bad case of it—are never happier than when they are poking around marinas, fantasizing about owning other people's boats. It's a disease that costs more to cure than any other single common learning disability.

So we crossed the walkway to shore, skirted the hedge of mangroves and the two-story marina office, where we saw Jeth walking down the steps from his apartment. Heard him call to me, "Your uncle Tuh-tuh-tuck . . . he's inside speaking with Mack."

I waved him off—let Mack deal with the neurotic old fool—and steered Amanda past the Red Pelican clothing shop and down the long main dock so that she could look at sailboats to her heart's content. I stopped only briefly to say hello to a couple of the fishing guides who were in for lunch, and then to introduce Amanda to JoAnn Smallwood, who lives aboard the soggy old Chris-Craft, *Tiger Lily*. Stood there listening to the two of them talk, then, as we parted, JoAnn gave me a little wink—a private sign among our small marina community that indicates approval of an outsider.

It spoke well of Amanda . . . and it also said quite a bit about the quick assessment process common to women in general and to the ladies of *Tiger Lily* specifically. JoAnn had inspected, interviewed and evaluated Amanda as quickly, as efficiently, perhaps as accurately, as two dogs unexpectedly met on a sand road. It is something most of us pretend that we don't do. But the ladies of the *Tiger Lily* do not posture. They are precisely what they seem to be. Not that I pretend to understand their own particular reality. They are honest women; they speak their minds. It is a rare thing and enough for me.

As we moved off by ourselves, Amanda said, "I like her. There's something very . . . solid? Yeah, solid about her."

I said, "I'm glad to hear that. JoAnn and Rhonda—Rhonda Lister, that's her roommate—they're two of my closest friends."

"Do you mean roommate as in someone who shares the rent? Or as in 'Roommate'?"

"The former. Not that I'd ever impose by asking."

"I wasn't being judgmental. Just curious. In fact, I'm surprised it even crossed my mind."

"From the signals they give out, they're happy, healthy heterosexuals. A nice change in this day and age, huh? Mostly they're nice people . . . good ladies. Men come around sometimes. If the guides approve of them, sometimes the men even spend the night. I've watched a couple of those guys leave. The smile on their face, it's hard to describe. Do people still use the word *dreamy*?"

She seemed amused. "People your age probably do."

"Thanks a lot."

"I didn't mean to offend. It's what I was thinking."

"Well, it's an eloquent word, *dreamy,* and it fits. What goes on when Rhonda and JoAnn don't have men guests is none of my business."

"The tone of your voice, I can tell you're protective. You look after the both of them."

"More like the other way around. They treat me like their slow-witted brother. And for good reason."

"You strike me as being anything but slow-witted. But what I meant was, you guys take care of each other. I've got friends like that. Not many but, yeah, I've got them. That's why she was giving me the eye, trying to figure out what my intentions are toward you."

"This is a very small marina, and it is a very large and dangerous world outside the marina gate. We're careful about who we let in."

Amanda said, "A safe place, that's good."

I said, "Yeah. They're getting harder and harder to find."

✴

I could tell that she'd been thinking about it, how to get me back on the subject of her father. Looking at her, seeing the intensity—being so careful about how to bring it up—it crossed my mind that her unanswered questions about Bobby were nearly as important as telling me about Jackie Merlot.

I listened to her soften me up before risking the subject: "It explains a lot," she said, "meeting you. I can see now why you and my dad were buddies. About why he said to come to you if I needed help. It tells me a little. I look at you, his friend, and I think, okay, that's the kind of man he was. *This* is the kind of man he was."

"I guess I'm flattered," I said.

"It's been strange thinking about him so much lately. I mean, I'm an adult now, close to the same age he was when he died, and finding these old love letters to my mother, it's like he's become a real person. It's like meeting the man for the first time."

"He was a good one."

Me saying that, it meant something. I could see it in her face.

"You wouldn't lie about a thing like that, would you?"

I thought for a moment before I said, "Yeah, I would. A guy I knew nearly twenty years ago? His daughter shows up out of nowhere and she asks me what he was like? Yeah, he could be the biggest jerk of all time and I'd tell her he was a nice man. But Bobby was something special. He was a friend. And a good man. A very good man. I don't say that lightly."

She was nodding, letting the subject build its own momentum. "We've got a lot of unanswered questions about him. My mom and I,

The Mangrove Coast

65

we used to talk about it. Not much and not very often. She married Frank, started a whole new life, plus it hurt her, remembering him, because they were so much in love. But the times we did talk, she didn't know a lot. About what happened, I mean. My father never said what he was doing or where he was doing it, and the Navy never gave us much of an explanation."

I waited for her to ask and she finally did: "So . . . maybe you know. At least you have to know more than they told us. You were there. You were the military guy he was closest to when he was killed."

Feeling increasingly uneasy, I said, "It's a minor point, but I wasn't in the military."

"You weren't? But he wrote about you. You had to have been there with him—"

"I was there. Yeah, we were together a lot. All I'm saying is, I was over there for a different reason."

"See? I don't even know where 'over there' is. It's with little things like that you can help. Fill in some of the holes if you don't mind talking about it. Bobby Richardson was killed in an explosion during a training exercise, that's all my mom was told. A couple of times in his letters he mentioned Thailand, so we assume it was in Asia. She wrote and made phone calls, but never got another speck of information. Something else she said was that she tried to get in touch with an old buddy of his. She musta meant you. Who else? But that she never heard back."

I was shaking my head. "I wrote your mother a letter after it happened. Whether she got it, I don't know. I never received any calls or letters from her. That doesn't mean she didn't try. More likely, I was out of the country, on the road, no way for me to receive mail or messages. That was pretty common in those days."

"I don't get it. You weren't in the military but you were that far out of touch?"

I said, "I was talking about the area your father and I were in. Primitive, that's the point I'm making. You want me to answer questions about your father, I'll answer as best I can. Ask me anything you want. But I'd rather deal with the present than talk about the past."

A change of subject, that would be nice.

She wouldn't be put off, though. "I'm his daughter, his only child. I think I have every right to know what happened to my own father, Doc. You don't know what it's like growing up without a real dad."

Didn't I? She could ask Tucker Gatrell about that. Not that Gatrell had ever been known to treat that subject with much honesty.

I stood there saying nothing. Listened to her say, "Tell me what you know. That's all I'm asking. I've come a long way. And I've waited one hell of a long time."

That kind of stubbornness. Her father had been like that. . . .

✵

I was looking at her face, her hands, learning what I could about her: she'd once had braces, had had an eye surgery, was right-handed, a nonsmoker, had a pencil callus on the inside of her middle finger— probably meant that she was an artist or wrote in a journal. She kept her nails short, polished, too . . . but it had been a while. No dates recently. No one to look nice for, maintain all the little hygienic details.

Maybe the woman had little emotional shelters for every occasion.

So what choice did I have? I told Amanda that I would share what I knew. By which I meant that I would tell her all that I was allowed to tell her about our time in Southeast Asia . . . and maybe hedge a little bit by telling her more than I was allowed to tell. But not much more.

I explained to her that, in the years following the Vietnam war, the United States maintained a military presence in places such as the Philippines, South Korea, places in Indonesia and Malaysia, so it wasn't so unusual for her father to be pulling operations in places like Thailand. I didn't mention that Thailand abuts Cambodia and I did not mention that an ethnic and political component of that nation, the Khmer Rouge, was slaughtering millions of its countrymen in nightly raids and in some hellishly one-sided firefights.

Let her look at a map, read some history if she wanted to put the pieces together. It was all there; plenty of photographs of all those skulls piled up. How many millions had died?

Something else I did not mention was that some very savvy and competent American intelligence officers—Bobby Richardson being one of them—were investigating the possibility that at least a few and, perhaps, several dozen, American servicemen listed as missing in action after Vietnam were actually being held in prison camps in the eastern regions of Cambodia.

Bobby and his team didn't necessarily believe it, but they were investigating: MIA guys too deeply hidden to fuel the rumors, but they were there, just across the border of Vietnam.

Or so a few powerful people seemed to suspect. . . .

The MIA guys, that was Bobby's pet project. I was never much involved, simply because I doubted that such camps actually existed. Why would the Cambodians or the Vietnamese invest sizable amounts of time and money to secretly maintain American POW camps? There was no political leverage to be gained, no monetary profit. The premise sailed all the familiar red flags that I associate with conspiracy theories, and I do not believe in large-scale conspiracies. If I ever meet more than three or four people who can actually keep a secret, then maybe I'll reconsider.

So . . . Bobby and I were both working in Cambodia. Along with his MIA project, he was assigned to train and lead guerrilla groups made up of a mountain people known as the Phmong. I was assigned to gather intelligence relating to the support or lack of support among Cambodian academicians for Pol Pot, leader of the CPK, the Communist Party of Kampuchea.

That Bobby and I would be thrown together and work some of the same missions wasn't in our official orders, but it was something that two Americans, alone and in Asia, would naturally do. It was a brutal, brutal time in a fascinating area, and had anyone discovered what we were doing and why we were doing it, there was no doubt about how we would have been dealt with.

The story I had told Amanda about decapitation was true.

And there were other scenarios. Worse things to fear . . .

So, yeah, I watched Bobby's back and he watched mine, and after just a few months we were buddies and confidants to a degree experienced only by those who have shared the uric-fear of being isolated and under fire in a foreign land.

His letter home was quite correct: After what we'd gone through, a couple of decades changed nothing.

❄

I told Amanda Richardson, "Your father didn't die in Thailand."

We'd found a quiet spot off by ourselves at the very end of the dock complex. She'd plopped down on the boards and sat with her legs dangling over the water like a kid sitting on a bridge.

Now, as I spoke, she sat back a little and said, "Oh," listening very closely.

I pressed ahead. "Bobby . . . your dad . . . was killed in the mountains of Cambodia. It wasn't on a training mission and it wasn't because he was screwed up, made a mistake and stepped on a mine. He was a high-level intelligence officer—some said brilliant—who knew exactly what he was doing . . . who knew the risks involved. He died fighting for what he believed was a . . ." I paused. How to say it honestly? Bobby was a patriot in his way, but he was no toy soldier, he wasn't naive. He didn't believe in noble causes or that war was a contest between good and evil. Bobby was a pragmatist; a professional. Finally, I said, "He died fighting for what he believed was reasonable and . . . *right*. Few men have that honesty of conviction. As his daughter, you should be proud of that; be proud of him and the work he did. Something else is . . . what I hope is . . . that you'll respect the code of silence that his work required. And still requires." Looking at her across the table, I added, "Do you understand what I'm saying, Amanda? What I'm asking?"

She didn't respond for several seconds. Finally: "His death was no accident?" Shocked, but very calm about it.

"No. Not more than any other death in war is accidental . . . random."

"Then how?"

"He was working as an advisor . . . no, that's not true. Your dad was in command of a group of Phmong guerrillas who were on a mission to blow up—"

She interrupted: "What guerrillas?"

"The Phmong. It's a generic term; not a very nice one, really. But the actual name of a tribe—well, there were two tribes—the Saochs and Brao from the Elephant Mountains and near the Laotian border. I don't know why I remember that, but I do. Your dad was leading a group of Phmong men on a strike against a munitions storage dump. Or some village that had stockpiled a lot of weaponry. I'm not sure; he wasn't specific when he talked about it. But somehow the government forces were tipped off and nailed your dad's group with a mortar strike. It wasn't a mine and it wasn't a training mission. That's how your dad died."

"And this was after the Vietnam war ended."

"Yeah. Way later."

"But why? Were we ever at war with Cambodia? I'm no historian, but I can't remember—"

"We weren't at war with Cambodia. Not officially. There was this Communist army, the Khmer Rouge, that took over the country right after the U.S. pulled out of Vietnam. It was led by an electronics student, Saloth Sar, but he called himself Pol Pot. The Khmer slaughtered anyone who got in their way. So it was like a war. Maybe worse."

"But why?"

"You want the truth? Sar's army was made up of many thousands of teenaged boys who were pissed off about having their farms and fields and families bombed during the Vietnam war. They were uneducated and they hated anyone who was educated. They had the weapons and they had permission. So they started killing and kept killing. That's what your father was trying to stop."

"Then what you're asking me, the thing you just mentioned, that's why: a code of silence. Confidentiality is what you're asking for. You don't want me to repeat what you've just said."

"That wouldn't be reasonable to ask, so I won't ask it. What I'm saying is, be very picky about who you tell. Your mother, she should know. She deserves to hear the truth."

"When we find her, I'll let you tell her."

I liked the way she said that. The confidence in her voice.

I said, "And your children, they should know about their grandfather. Maybe your husband when you marry. But if you leave here in a huff and run to the newspapers crying about how your government lied to you about the death of your father, then I'll disappear from the picture. That's the silence I'm asking you to respect."

Another long, thoughtful pause. "You're sure about this? Were you there when my father was killed?"

"No. I learned of it two, maybe three, days later. Some of the Phmong told me, the mountain warriors. They had tremendous respect for your father."

"They're the ones who brought back his body?"

I could have said, "What was left of it." Instead, I said, "He was killed in a mortar attack. Yes. They were there and brought him back. It happened not too far from our camp."

"If you weren't there, then how do you know what they said is true?"

I could have said that I saw the hand, the foot, the flesh detritus of what remained. Instead, I said, "They would have lied to protect your father, but they had no reason to lie. With your father gone, they had no one they needed to protect. So why make up stories?"

She was asking some pretty good questions. Not suspicious, but careful—checking up on this and that to let me know she was keeping track.

"Something else you said, it bothers me. Not that I don't believe what you're saying, I'm just trying to be clear. The business about his being an intelligence officer. In every picture of him, he's wearing a Navy uniform, but now you're telling me he was like some kind of CIA person. What were you guys, spies?"

"I was what I am now, a marine biologist. Your father was with Naval Special Warfare, the SEALs, and attached to Naval Intelligence. He was a very gifted man. We became close friends quickly. Bobby was smart, funny, tough . . . a good person; a good guy. He had a photograph of you, a Polaroid, that he loved. At night, just sitting, talking, he'd bring out this picture and pass it around. We had Coleman lanterns for light. It was you in a yellow party dress."

I thought that would please her. Instead she seemed momentarily flustered. "You mean a picture of when I was an infant."

"Uh-uh. You were four, maybe five, years old. There were a couple of people in the background, maybe your mother."

"Oh, that old." She had her face turned away, looking out the window. Then I realized what the problem was: seeing the photograph meant that I had seen her before a surgeon had straightened her wandering eye. I knew what she had once looked like . . . probably what, in her own mind, she was supposed to look like . . . and the fact that I knew made her uneasy.

So I decided to confront the subject: "I remember telling your father that you had a wonderfully wise face. I loved your eyes."

"You said that?"

"I did."

Which earned me a snort of cynical laughter. "You're telling me . . . you're saying that you liked the fact that I was cross-eyed? I'm supposed to believe that? Maybe you have us confused. My mom's the one with the gorgeous eyes."

"Nope, I liked yours. A lot."

"I'm supposed to believe that, just like I'm supposed to believe that the reason you were with my dad in Cambodia was because you were a marine biologist? Jesus."

"Both true."

"I'm sure." Her tone said: bullshit.

"Cambodia's on the Gulf of Thailand. There's a species of fish there, the ox-eye tarpon that I was studying. There are only two species of tarpon on earth. And there are some interesting islands off a place called Saom Bay. Rain forest and thatched huts built on poles. Every afternoon at sunset, these giant fruit bats would drop down out of the high trees. When they extended their wings, you'd hear a popping sound, like parachutes opening. That's how big they were."

"You sound so reasonable."

"I try to be. I was associated with a thing called the Studies and Observations Group."

"I bet."

"That happens to be the truth, too."

"Oh yeah? So, if you worked near the ocean, then how did my father happen to be in the mountains when he was killed in a mortar attack? You said it didn't happen too far from camp. You remember saying that?"

Smart woman. Not looking around at the boats now; was looking right at me, showing me with her expression that she wasn't a child and she wasn't a fool. Not angry, but stony; chilly and a little judgmental.

I said, "Not all mountains are inland. Some rise out of the sea."

"And that's where you're saying your camp was."

I thought about it a moment before I replied. "I guess if you were applying the thirty-second rule I'd be in big trouble, huh?"

"Unless you come up with something convincing in the next five or ten seconds. But yeah, it would have to happen pretty quick."

"What I told you . . . it's true, like I said. Factual, anyway. But it's not entirely honest."

"There's a difference?"

"Fact only requires accuracy. Honesty requires disclosure."

"Now we're getting somewhere."

"Except the part about the Studies and Observations Group. And your eyes. The way you looked in that photograph, very wise for a little girl. I really did like your eyes. And they weren't crossed, just off center."

She said, "Uh-huh, a thing of beauty," her tone saying once again: bullshit.

✳

Her little white Honda Civic was parked in the feather-duster shade of a coconut palm. She said it got great mileage and had a decent sound system.

Two necessities of Generation X: music and considerations of mobility.

As I escorted her across the dusty parking lot, I told her to give me a few days; time to check with some people, think it over, maybe come up with a simple and productive course of action.

"What we might have to do is hop on a plane, fly to Cartagena and have a look around," I said, "but let's hope I can fit a few pieces together and narrow down the options."

My saying it—we may have to fly to Cartagena—seemed to make the prospect real, and I could tell that it set her back a little. "Colombia," she said, her tone a little less vivid. "That's like one of the drug countries, right? Do you know anything about the place?"

"Some," I said. "A little."

The less she knew about my years in Central and South America, the better.

Something else I told her to keep in mind was, If we did find her mom, and if Gail still refused to leave Merlot, there was absolutely nothing we could do about it.

"I know, I know," she replied. "All I want is a chance to get her alone and talk some sense into her. If we go, I can cover our expenses. I've got some money in savings and there're some bonds I can cash in. Plus, Frank's offered to kick in if things get expensive. The big spender, he's so damn worried. *Right.*" She let that settle before she added, "The point being, I'm not asking you to pay your own way."

I told Amanda that her offer was premature. What I didn't tell her was that, if we could find Merlot's sailboat, I didn't think I'd have much trouble prying her mother free. Not if it seemed like the right thing to do.

Probably wouldn't have to do much more than scare Merlot a little. Get the guy off alone for an hour or so, tell him some tough-guy story about Gail having family ties to the mob. Or maybe say she had ties to some drug cartel; that would make more sense. And how she doesn't even know it, but she's under the personal protection of some honcho with an Italian or Latino name. Watch the guy, Merlot, turn white and start shaking, then sit back and wait while he raced off to tell Gail to leave him alone, get the hell out of his life forever. Sneaky predatory types are also usually very predictable cowards.

The problem was, finding a lone sailboat with all that coastline, all that water.

But I didn't go into any of that. Instead, I gave the girl a job to do. I asked her to visit her mother's house, gather all the mail from the neighbor who was collecting it, then open and read it, just to see if she found anything interesting. And while she was at it, I told her to try to find any old letters from Merlot or photographs of the guy just to give me a better handle on who I was dealing with.

The idea offended her. Open her mother's personal letters? She didn't think she could do that.

I said, "You had to hunt around to find your father's letters, didn't you?"

"Yeah, but they were put away in her hope chest. I'd been looking for old photographs, and I'd just about given up. For some reason, my mom had packed them all away."

"Old pictures of you?"

She made a snorting noise. "No way. Those were hidden away a long time ago, and I'm the one who did it. I'm talking about a picture of my mom with my real dad, that's what I wanted. But they were packed. Every single one of them, she's such a neatness freak. So I wasn't prying, it was more like researching family history."

I said, "What's the difference? Look, Amanda . . . if you're serious about locating your mother, we may have to do some stuff you wouldn't normally do. Behavior-wise, I mean. You used some kind of saying when you were describing your mother's face; some Hindu maxim. Well, there's a truism that your father and I came up with while we were in Asia. One of the Great Laws, we called it. Just for the hell of it, we wrote it on a piece of paper and passed it back and forth, each of us trying to take out or replace words. Like editors, see? We were trying to make the law just as simple and precise as we could. You care to hear what we ended up with?"

I waited for the girl to nod before I continued. I had no trouble remembering: "Okay, here it is: 'In any conflict, the boundaries of behavior are defined by the party that cares least about morality.'"

She thought about it for a moment before she spoke. "Repeat that one more time."

I did.

"My father, he thought of that?"

"We batted it around for a week or so. We were bored as hell during the daytime. I remember we spent an hour debating whether the last word should be *morality* or *ethics*. Your dad won."

"He had to be a smart man. Very wise to put something so clearly."

"Yeah, he was. But what I'm saying is, if your judgment of Merlot is correct, we're going to have to adapt. Does he strike you as the type to play fair?"

"Of course not. I wouldn't be worried about my mom if he were."

"Then we have to play by his rules, not ours. If we don't, he's at a big advantage. But what I'm hoping is, we can track your mom down by phone. When she realizes how worried you are, she'll either fly home or agree to meet with you down there. Or better yet, you'll hear from her in the next day or two; get a phone call or a letter saying she's come to her senses and she's leaving the guy."

Amanda looked up at me with burrowing brown eyes; eyes that, in their reluctance to stand fast, illustrated the painful memory that she had once been different. Her eyes had once been unlike the eyes of other children and so were things of which to be ashamed.

But I liked those eyes. I liked them in a long-ago photograph seen in the waxy light of a military lantern, and I liked them now. The awareness of individuality is implicit in the face of anyone who, as a child, is forced to stand apart from the crowd. The reason doesn't much matter. It might be because of skin color, problems at home, clothing that doesn't come up to the expectations of peers, perceived differences in social worth, acne . . . or one wayward, lonely eye.

That strength was in Amanda's face.

Something else I liked was the attitude she'd brought with her to meet me, the stranger who had once been a friend of her late father. She was businesslike, tough, but she wasn't one of those women who plays the cast-iron role of feminist, thereby sacrificing her own personality along with her credibility as an individual. Nope, I liked her. A good woman; one of the private people who sat back, watched carefully and thought about things.

Standing beside her car, I listened to her say, "Doc, for the first time in about a month, I feel pretty good about the chances of helping my mom. My confidence, I'm talking about. Just talking to you, it's made me feel better."

I leaned to give her a quick hug good-bye—felt her body go tense as I did, so I did not prolong it—as I told her, "You have a safe drive across the Glades. And just to make a nerdish, middle-aged bookworm feel better, why don't you give me a call when you get to Lauderdale? Let me know you made it."

"Okay, okay, I guess I deserve that. I shouldn't have judged you so quickly. By the way you look. Me of all people, I mean . . ."

"Why not? I read lots of books and I'm kind of a nerd. Ask anybody."

Which earned me a sheepish smile, a quick little peek at the girl who lived behind the barriers.

Tuck's spackle-gray Dodge pickup, the one with the buckle-high tires and a bumper sticker that read A COWBOY'S WORK IS NEVER DONE, was still sitting in the heat of the marina parking lot as I watched Amanda exit through the gates onto Tarpon Bay Road, headed for the toll bridge and then Alligator Alley, Lauderdale bound.

The man was probably still regaling Mack and Jeth with stories about Old Florida; probably attracting an audience of tourists with his tales about fishing with Ike Eisenhower and teaching Ted Williams how to fly-cast in the early bonefish days, down on the Keys with Jimmy Albright and the other pioneer guides.

Or maybe he was using his Deep South voice to describe to listeners how he helped train Cuban troops on nearby Useppa Island for the Bay of Pigs invasion, or how it was him and Dick Pope, founder of Cypress Gardens, who took Uncle Walt Disney around and convinced him Florida was a can't-miss choice for a second Disneyland.

"Disney, he favored the east coast," Tucker liked to add, "all those hotels, all those built-in customers. But I says to him, I says, 'Walt, in the last twenty years, just how many hurricanes you figure has tore the east coast its own new asshole? And I'm not just talkin' about them official whirly-girls, neither. I'm talkin' about the no-name gales that you folks in California never hear about; the ones your fancy lawyers ain't gonna find in the record books. From Miami to Palm Beach, they get more heavy wind than a Puerto Rican chili parlor, so, you build her on the east coast, you better nail Mickey's ass to the deck 'cause Minny ain't gonna be the only bad blow job in town."

Tucker Gatrell's explanation of how he personally brought Disney World to Central Florida. It was a story I'd heard, didn't much believe and didn't care to hear again . . . so I walked along the periphery of mangroves, out of easy sight of the marina, back home.

※

Before Amanda left, she'd hurried off to say good-bye to the old fraud and returned to tell me how kind he'd been to her, what a gentleman he was, which proved that the girl was not foolproof when it came to strangers. Same with her mother, apparently.

Few of us are.

She said she hated to just go off and leave, because she felt sorry for him, after all he'd been through that week.

I said, "Huh?" but was thinking, *Now what?*

She said, "About his horse dying. He didn't tell you?"

I said, "Tucker's horse died? You mean Roscoe?"

"No, he didn't mention anyone named Roscoe. It was the morning I called him at his house. When he told me, he got so upset I thought he was going to start crying. He called the poor thing his cow pony. 'Just went out and found my cow pony laying dead in the stall.' You know the way he talks. 'My cow pony, he's hit the high trail.' Like that. Kind of tough, like nothing much bothers him, but he's really so sentimental."

For fifteen years or so, pretty close, Roscoe had been both horse and human to Tuck. Big gray appaloosa that Tucker treated like a house pet. Even when I was around, he maintained a running monologue with the animal. Rode him everywhere, strip malls, busy streets, drive-through banks, it didn't matter to Tuck. His way of showing off, of demonstrating who he was.

I told Amanda, "Roscoe, that was his name. The horse's name. But I wouldn't worry about it. He can always buy another horse."

Which didn't elevate the woman's opinion of me, no mistaking her reaction. But there it was. I had to listen to her say, "People can become very close to their pets, you know. Animals aren't like car tires or bad lightbulbs or something that can be easily replaced. He really cared about that horse. I could tell." A very chilly edge to her voice.

I said, "Yeah, the man wears his heart on his sleeve."

"Okay, okay. You two aren't exactly close. Like there's this constant friction. I can feel it. But he's an old man. All that talking he does, wanting attention, I think it's because he really is sensitive. So why not be nice to him?"

She was right.

I decided the nicest thing I could do for Tucker Gatrell—and myself—was avoid him. Save us both some wear and tear. Besides, it was a Sunday on Sanibel . . . which meant that I had better things to do than hang around my lab waiting to be cornered by my idiotic old uncle.

Of late, Sunday meant baseball, then chicken wings and beer.

So there was no reason to talk to the man . . . or even say good-bye.

※

I am not a baseball fan, but I am a fan of baseball. That's not the paradox it seems. I have never followed teams and box scores, but I love to play the game. Which is why I was not unhappy that Amanda had to leave early and get back to Lauderdale. I had a game that afternoon.

What a strange thing to remind myself of after all the years since I'd played competitively: *I have a game this afternoon.*

Actually, it was a doubleheader.

A month or so earlier, Tomlinson had signed us both up to play in a baseball league; the Roy Hobbs League it is called, a national organization named after the fictional hero in Bernard Malamud's valuable book *The Natural*. Not softball, baseball, a game where players steal bases and slide and wear helmets at the plate for a reason.

It was the real game. Rules required that players had to be over the ripe old age of thirty, and a solid baseball background was requisite. The league attracted a lot of former college players and a few ex-professionals, but mostly the teams were made up of an eclectic bunch of amateurs who, in their spare time, were attorneys, surgeons, plumbers and teachers or followed other vocations that were not as much fun as putting on spikes and playing nine.

Without asking my permission, Tomlinson signed us up because he said it would do the both of us good, getting off the island. No . . . what he actually said was, "It'll be good for our heads, man. Get out there between the lines where the karma is purer. Keep in mind, amigo, that the shape of a baseball diamond is nothing more than two pyramids joined at the base. And I suspect that you've read about the electromagnetic vibes generated by pyramids. Very powerful, man. A very heavy mojo."

Which was Tomlinson-speak that meant playing baseball would give us something to do that wasn't based on boats or water . . . a nice change that might help get my mind off such things as the sexual transformation of grouper and my own failed love affair with Pilar.

Maybe Tomlinson was right, because I'd come to look forward to playing baseball on Sundays. Sometimes on Thursday nights, too, under the lights. And I wasn't about to let Tucker Gatrell hold me up or make me late. So I hustled around my cabin, dressing myself in cup and supporter, stirrups over long white socks that were still known by the odd, antique name of "sanitaries." Pulled on gray stretch baseball pants that buttoned tightly where white pinstripe jersey bloused at my waist, then settled my team's ball cap on my head with no less care than knights of old who once added crowning balance to their personal armor-work.

Presto. Marion Ford, Ph.D. and purveyor of biological specimens, was now a simpler man of purer purpose. I was number 13, proud member of the West Florida Tropics, catcher and occasional relief pitcher. Dress a seventy-year-old man in a football uniform and he'll look idiotic. Put him in a baseball uniform, though, and he'll look like he can play nine and steal a base or two. That is one of the sport's mysterious qualities . . . so maybe Tomlinson deserves more credit than I give him when he speaks of baseball's nonlinear aspects.

※

The Mangrove Coast

Once dressed, I peeked out the window to make certain Tucker wasn't on his way. Then I picked up the VHF microphone and hailed Tomlinson on channel 12, our personal channel of contact, saying, "*No Más, No Más.* This is Sanibel Biological Supply, Whiskey Romeo X-ray six-seven-nine-six. Copy?"

Waited a few beats before I heard, "Got you good, Doc. I plan to drink a few beers after the game, so maybe you'd better drive."

Which was no surprise. I always drove to our Sunday games and Tomlinson always drank heavily afterwards. Besides, Tomlinson had no car.

Then he said, "But we've got to stop at my farm on the way home."

Tomlinson's farm: a small portion of rented lot off Casa Ybel Road where he was pouring a lot of time and energy into a new passion— growing chili peppers. Jalapeños, habaneros, Thai, Scotch bonnets, you name it. He grew them all. "The history of Anglo trade and corruption can be read in the pericarp of the humblest chili," he was fond of saying.

What that meant, I have no idea.

Another claim: "The world chili market is dominated by the same three species that Columbus brought back to Europe from his first couple of voyages." Talking like some first-rate ethnobotanist.

I found that interesting: three species of wild plant had been spread singularly, hand to hand and generation to generation, among all races and cultures. There were now, of course, hundreds of varieties, but nearly all were descended from those same three species of wild chilies that had probably evolved in the Amazon valley.

It was an unusual pastime for a man who'd spent most of his life at sea, but Tomlinson had apparently entered a back-to-the-earth phase; a revisitation, perhaps, of his commune days, when he lived on some California ranch with similarly long-haired kindreds who went by names like Moon Dance and Autumn. For a year or two, long ago, Tomlinson himself had assumed a name of choice. An "Earth name," as he described it. He'd gone by the name of Lono, he claimed, out of respect for some Polynesian god he admired.

He'd worked on the communal farm and now he'd been called

back to the earth, or so he said. He liked to get his hands and knees black with the commercial growing humus he trucked in because of Sanibel's poor, salty soil. Growing chilies suited a certain need in him, and I was beginning to find it interesting, too, because he had planted seeds from all over the world. Plus I love to eat chilies.

"We can stop at the farm," I radioed back. "I'm about out of jalapeños."

"Then after the game," he said, "we stop at Hooters for chicken wings and beer. Or hey—we can boat over to St. James City and listen to John Mooney play."

John Mooney, one of the great blues guitarists, lived on Pine Island. Every baseball Sunday, we always did that, too.

❋

On the way into town I told Tomlinson about my conversation with Amanda Richardson. Glancing from the road over to this strange vision: cattle rustler's face, hippie hair, goatherder sandals and baseball uniform.

He smelled of primo glove leather (he was breaking in a beautiful Wilson A2000 infielder's glove) and patchouli, the favorite perfume of dope smokers. Probably had a joint hidden somewhere on his person, too, for he had embraced some of his old habits. By unspoken agreement, he pretended not to know that I knew.

Yet, for all his weirdness and his flaky spiritualism, Tomlinson is an attentive listener and he possesses an intellect of the first magnitude. I wanted his assessment of the situation. In hindsight, I realize now that I was not as open-minded as I generally pretend to be. Yeah, I wanted Tomlinson's opinion, but I had already come to a conclusion about the so-called disappearance of Gail Calloway. My old buddy's widow was being taken advantage of by one of the common cast of chubby, middle-aged Casanovas that infest every Florida beach town from Jacksonville to Pensacola. True, there were a couple of elements in Amanda's story that I found unusual, even troubling. But the chances of Gail's being in genuine danger were very slim indeed.

Not that I wasn't interested and not that I wouldn't help. I'd do what I could, no questions asked. Bobby would have done the same for me. Besides, I liked his daughter a lot. Yeah . . . nice woman with an outsider's gift for observation and a no-nonsense intellect.

We all prioritize, and I had already put the problem on one of the middle burners: important but not so pressing that I needed to drop everything and go charging off to the rescue.

So, also in hindsight, make note of another screw-up by the kindly, well-intentioned dumbass, Doc Ford. Add one more M^2 to a growing list. M-squared as in double M—which stands for Major Miscalculation. It was not my first nor, unfortunately, will it be my last, for I seem to have a limitless gift for failing to heed my own instincts . . . particularly when the welfare of an innocent person is at stake.

Why that is true, I cannot fathom. It hurts me. It makes me furious. But the fact that I so seldom seem to meet my own expectations is probably the main reason why I hang in there and keep banging away, trying to get it right. I can forgive myself for being dumb or for lacking insight. I could never forgive myself for quitting.

So, in truth, all I wanted from Tomlinson was for him to validate my view by echoing my opinion. Isn't that what we ask most often from friends?

Tomlinson, however, is not your run-of-the-mill friend.

※

As I drove across the causeway, then north into Fort Myers, he listened patiently as I spoke. He grunted and humphed and made attentive listening sounds while he chewed at a strand of his scraggly blond hair, a nervous habit.

He questioned me closely about certain details of Amanda's story. At one point he asked, "Old photographs? Why was she going through her mom's stuff looking for old photographs?"

"Sentimental value? I don't know. She wanted a picture of her mom and real dad."

"You believe that?"

"Of course I do. Why shouldn't I?"

"Which she said she found in her mother's hope chest. The photographs. That was the only place?"

"No, what she said was, she was looking for old photographs and was about to give up. There's a difference. Her mother had apparently packed them all away. Amanda said she's a neatness freak."

Now Tomlinson was twisting his hair into a braid. "You don't find that odd? I find that very odd."

"You find it odd that a woman who's been a widow for nearly two decades has put away photos of her late husband?"

"And of her own daughter, too, apparently."

"The girl did that herself. Because she once had a crossed eye. A lazy eye and she's probably still ashamed of it."

"She told you that?"

"You drive me nuts sometimes, Tomlinson. You know that? *Yes,* she told me that she'd put the pictures away. Hid them, that's what she said. I'm guessing at the motive. But it's a reasonable assumption based on circumstantial evidence."

"Like you said, man, sentimental value. A guy like you, a guy who doesn't feel much emotion, it's something easy to miss. But to a spiritual headbanger like me, it stands out like a sore beezer."

I thought: *Jesus, you're weird, Tomlinson.*

A few minutes later, he asked: "You're absolutely sure this girl you're talking about—Amanda?—you're sure she's really the biological daughter of your old friend? Him and his wife, I mean. She wasn't maybe adopted or has a different father or something?"

"What difference would that make?"

"I'm just asking. The thing about the photographs bothers me."

The photographs again. What the hell was he talking about?

I said, "I would bet that she's the biological daughter of Bobby and Gail Richardson, yes. But no, I haven't asked for a DNA test to prove it. But I look in her face, I can see her dad. No doubt about that. Something about the eyes. And her mom—I've only seen photographs—but she's got her mom in her, too. I may not be an expert on sentiment, Tomlinson, but give me some credit for basic observation. Genetics aren't easy to disguise. We're necessarily bits and pieces of all the people who went before us. And don't forget: I saw a picture of Amanda as a little girl."

✳

There were other things that troubled him about the girl's story. I drove and looked at the scenery, listening a lot, answering occasionally.

We were driving into the heart of Fort Myers. Municipalities on Florida's Gulf Coast tend to expand in population, bulging southward and northward until they finally rupture and are absorbed by the concrete artery that is U.S. Highway 41, a strip-mall corridor that is a mile wide and more than a hundred miles long. U.S. 41, or the Tamiami Trail as it is called, connects the rolling oak pastures north of Tampa with the saw-grass hardpan of the Everglades. The city of Fort Myers lies just off that fast conduit, a kernel of old buildings built of brick and coquina rock, a tiny Old Florida town at the core of massive, modern growth.

Fort Myers is called the City of Palms. It is well named. Cuban royals lined the street. They are palms that look as if they had been made by squirting cement into a pillarous tube. The high fronds caught the spring sunlight. As Tomlinson talked, I watched the Sunday flow of joggers lope down the small town sidewalks. A girl with hair the tawny red of autumn leaves and honey-colored skin caught my eye. I watched her until she vanished from my rearview mirror.

You see one like that, a woman with the physical sensibilities of a deer, and you wonder if she is The One, The One you have been waiting all your life to meet.

You also worry that if you don't immediately stop, if you don't act on the strange urge to introduce yourself to a stranger, that you may have forever missed the chance. . . .

✳

We were headed toward the city's eastern border and an antique baseball complex named Terry Park. Since 1925, the diamonds there have been a hub of Grapefruit League spring-training activity. Terry Park is one of the reasons I didn't mind making the long drive into town. It is among the last fields of its kind in Florida: a precise space of grass and red clay to which baseball legends once arrived by steam engine and, decades later, left for Opening Day by charter jet. The main stadium is made of tin and wood, everything painted gazebo-green. It looks small and shaded, as if it comes from the time of straw hats and nickel beer. It does. That's why the modern major league teams have moved on to more sterile, twenty-first-century plants.

But the dugouts of Terry Park are still cool little caves with slabs of wood for benches; benches that are pitted by seven decades of wooden bats, Copenhagen cans and steel spikes. And the base paths are still the exacting conduits over which ran all the boys of summer from all the summers past. Name a player: Ruth, Cobb, Berra, Mantle, Maris, Clemente, Mays, Brett, Blyleven. Name ten thousand players. They sat on those same benches, they ran the same base paths. They all came to Terry Park to play a game called baseball, and the game is being played there still . . . often by wanna-bes like Tomlinson and me. Not that we felt any shame in that.

No indeed.

I was looking forward to the game. We were to face an ex–minor leaguer; a left-hander named Johnson who was pitching for some Minnesota team that was using men's baseball as an excuse to get the hell and gone out of the snow. Except for the snow, I could relate. The doubleheader was my mini-vacation away from the lab and island life.

But Tomlinson wouldn't let go of the Amanda Richardson story.

"I've got some very serious concerns about the mother," he said. "Children and middle-aged divorced women are the two most vulnerable groups on earth. Children, at least, are resilient. They're mobile in terms of life options. But a middle-aged woman, she's a sitting duck. Easiest target in the world."

I didn't want to hear it, because I'd already made up my mind about Gail Calloway.

"What worries me most," Tomlinson said, "is that business about Merlot changing his phone number. You don't catch the significance of that?"

I'd caught it—but I wanted to hear Tomlinson put it into words.

He said, "What I think he's trying to do is isolate her, man. Doesn't want the woman to speak to her own daughter. Keeps her too busy to see her old friends. That is a serious damn red flag. It sounds like obsession, but what I really think it is, it's the need for complete control. It's a form of murder, man. Total dominance." Tomlinson hunched toward me to make his point . . . then, still talking, he took out his billfold.

Why the hell did he need his billfold?

He said, "It's what cults and dictators do. To control a country, you must first isolate it. No shit, Hitler, 1938. A nation needs information from the outside to know the truth. Same with individuals. To control a person's future, all you have to do is cut off her past. That's exactly what certain asshole husbands do, the abusive ones. The pea-brained creeps with their frightened little wives. And the perverts. The sickies. And a few really bad corporate bosses. Total control. You know what else worries me about that story?"

I was listening more closely now. Baseball was still on my mind, but Tomlinson was impressing me, being uncharacteristically logical.

Tomlinson was into it, on a roll. So I said, "What?"

"The Stockholm Syndrome," he said, "that's what worries me. You know what I'm talking about? Back in the fifties, I think, this Swedish guy, a guy named Ofulsen, he robs a bank but gets cut off, so he takes hostages. Most of the hostages are women. By the end of the siege, every one of the women is madly in love with the asshole. I mean they're telling the cops don't hurt him, they love him, he's just misunderstood. Him in there with a gun, swinging it around, threatening to kill everybody if the cops charge. The guy you're talking about, this Jackie Merlot, if he really is a control freak, then the longer she's with him—Gail I'm talking about—then the harder it's going to be to pry her away."

I said, "The point I thought you were going to make had to do with the lying thing. Merlot telling Gail in advance that her own daughter was spreading lies. The daughter and the ex-husband both. It's a device. Kind of a sinister device but pretty common. If he convinces Gail that her daughter and Frank are telling lies about him, then Merlot's already diffused any damaging truth they might uncover. He can say, 'I warned you, I told you they were going to say that.' See what I mean?"

"Yeah, yeah, I missed that one. Jesus, what a jerk. Seriously." He had his billfold open . . . yes, he was removing a hard-wrapped joint. I watched him wet it between his lips as he patted his jersey mechanically, looking for a light. He said, "Another thing is, those postcards—"

Smoking dope in my truck? I interrupted: "What the hell do you think you're doing?"

His innocent expression asked, Who? ME? as he said, "I'm trying to relax, man. All this thinking has tightened my receptors. Christ! That woman's in trouble, mark my word. It worries me. Makes me tense. *You're* the one who always gets involved in this kind of shit, so don't give me that look. And how do you expect me to hit the curveball if I'm not relaxed? We want to WIN, don't we?"

As I watched him light the joint, I said, "If the cops stop us, I'll help them cuff you. I mean it. Maybe help them beat you if it comes to that."

"You would, too. You really would."

"I can't believe you still smoke that crap, Tomlinson."

"Try it just once, you'll understand. It's herbal, you know. Grows right up out of the ground." He took three more quick spasmodic inhalations, held his breath for several seconds before he added, "If it came from the ocean, oh man, you'd be all for it. Like if it was processed from a rare fish or something. But because it comes from the earth, you've got this, like, bias thing, man."

I said, "Jesus, Tomlinson."

"That's very unfair."

"Uh-huh."

He smoked intensely for a few blocks, everything focused inward, before he said, "*Ah-h-h-h, um-m-m-m,* yes . . . this is as natural as it gets. Very uplifting. Already I can feel the neurons returning to sync with certain rhythms. Earth rhythms, we used to call them. Yes, that was the precise terminology: Earth rhythms. Not that that would interest you. No sir, not mister big-shot marine biologist who hates anything that doesn't come from the sea."

I said, "You're hopeless."

"Uh-huh, keep thinking that. They said the same thing about the Edsel and look how much *those* things are worth. So I'm just biding my time, man. Biding my time till the big dogs start barkin.' Us strange ones, we keep getting closer and closer to the head of the line. Count on it. And remember that you heard it first from me."

I was shaking my head as he inhaled again and added, "Hey . . . wait a minute. I just flashed on something: Have you ever stopped to realize that a right-hander's curveball—picture it now. Follow along with what I'm saying. I'm saying that a right-hander's curveball spins in the same direction and with the approximate same degree of inclination as the Earth. Which is a very heavy dose of symmetry, if you dig where I'm headed with this. Squatting back there, Doc, looking through your catcher's mask, you ever notice the similarity? Watched a baseball spinning toward you like this quantum miniature of Planet Earth?"

I said, "What I've noticed is, the more you smoke, the weirder you sound."

"Really? Humph . . . Wait a minute, did I say 'symmetry'? I meant *redundancy*. Gad, no wonder I didn't make sense. It supports my Redundancy Theory. Remember my book, *No End in Sight*? The premise is that time and change are an illusion. Time is an invention. Change is a misperception. The proof is all tied to my Redundancy Theory, which states that all life is repetition of a solitary design. And that design has been inexplicably set in motion.

"Have you ever noticed that the six points of a snowflake precisely reproduce the design of a pine-tree bough? Or . . . you want something from the ocean? How about the polyps of a coral colony? They're the mirror image of neuron cells in the human brain. That's all the brain is—a colony, little synapse junctions, all interconnected just like coral. You *know* that.

"You want a simple example of my Redundancy Theory? An echo. Seriously, man, a simple echo. If you yell into a cave, the echo you hear is not a new sound. Right? Same with all life, man. We are shadows and echoes set in motion. Understand what I'm saying?"

No. I'd heard this theory before, but had never gotten it straight . . . or maybe it was just that Tomlinson's shaky memory recalled it differently each time. I said, "The stuff you're smoking, it affects you so quickly, is it laced with something? They soak it in some kind of chemical?"

"No-o-o-o, man. Just really good shit, that's all."

"It has that odor. Kind of sickening sweet."

"Yep. God aw'mighty how I love the smell of cannabis in the morning. This is a little bit of White Russian that some compadres of mine grow. I won't tell you where. All those buddies you got in the DEA, you might find it too tempting. No offense, Doc, your sense of righteousness is one of your best qualities, but it's also among your worst. And like I said, this is completely natural. Same with chili peppers."

This was too much. I said, "Don't even try to make a comparison."

"If I'm lyin' I'm dyin', man. The alkaloid that peppers contain—capsicum, the stuff that burns, I mean—it causes the brain to secrete endorphins. Same thing. People say they're bad for ulcers? Bullshit. That's an old wives' tale. Plus a chili's got more vitamin C than a whole grapefruit. They make you feel GOOD, man. That's why the more you eat, the more you want. Why else would the indigenous peoples keep eating them, even though—and let's face it—the little bastards make our assholes hurt."

I said, "Are you going to be too stoned to play ball?"

"Are you kidding? Back in high school, I woulda never been named All State if it wasn't for cannabis. Drugs give me the little extra edge that's so important in athletics. Jesus, I didn't even understand what baseball was really all about until I developed a personal relationship with the herb."

We were on Palm Beach Boulevard, headed east, and I could see the entrance to Terry Park just ahead: a convexity of oaks and palms beyond railroad tracks, a military surplus store, a boat dealership. I said, "You really think Gail Calloway is in trouble?"

He nodded reflectively as he inhaled.

"You started to say something about the postcards."

He was still nodding: "They were sent approximately one month apart."

"Yeah. That bothers me, too. Even if they're gunkholing, using Cartagena as a base, it's the rare cruise that only gets near a post office once a month."

"And you said the cards looked as if they were all written with the same pen."

"That, too."

"You see what I'm getting at?"

"Of course. That maybe the cards were all written at the same time and are being mailed periodically by someone other than Gail. But that's melodramatic. And unlikely."

"But it's possible."

"Sure."

Tomlinson looked at me, trying hard to focus. "In that case, there are serious discrepancies between datum and reasonable, healthy expectations of normal behavior. So, yeah, you bet. The lady, she's in trouble. Maybe more than you think, man. Fuckin' A."

That night, I telephoned Frank Calloway. He was in the middle of a dinner party, he said. Could I call back another time?

There was New Age music playing in the background. It sounded tribal: tom-toms and chanting and wind chimes only slightly softer than the conversational drone of people making polite conversation. I could picture them up there in wealthy Boca Grande, glasses in hand, windows showing no horizon, the Gulf of Mexico probably, through the sea grapes right outside.

I said, "I'll call you tomorrow at your office if you want, Frank. Or you can call me later this evening."

He said, "You say you're a friend of Amanda's?" As if he had no idea why I was calling; as if he'd never heard my name before.

Maybe he hadn't, but that was unlikely. According to Amanda, she'd told him that she and I were going to meet and that I might call to ask him some questions. But the big-money guys are necessarily suspicious, plus there is a behavioral dynamic that may well account for some of their success: They are very, very reluctant to give away information, or anything else, without getting something in return. To profit, they must get the upper hand. Gaining control of dialogue is a first step, a brand of gamesmanship for which I have zero tolerance or interest.

I told him, "I don't know Amanda well enough to claim her as a friend, Frank. If you doubt my motives, talk to her. Get her on the phone. When you're satisfied, she has my number. Call and we'll talk."

In an articulate baritone, the voice of a don't-screw-with-me CEO, he said, "There's no need to get indignant, Dr. Ford. I get a lot of calls from a lot of people. I want the best for my ex-wife, but I have to be careful. She has enough personal wealth to attract every third-rate con man for miles, thanks to our divorce settlement. Count on it, I'm protective. Without apology."

Yeah, Amanda had briefed him.

I said, "Did you start protecting Gail before she ran off with Jackie Merlot? Or was it after he managed to slip through your security?"

"Making moral judgments is an attractive trap. Personally, I'm trying to evolve beyond that."

"I don't have much interest in evolving, Frank. As a biologist, I know it takes more time than I've got. I called because Amanda's mother is apparently in trouble."

His thin laugh said he wasn't going to comment.

I said, "You have dinner guests to deal with. Check with Amanda, then give me a call."

He said, "When I can," and hung up.

※

I was up early, as always. Watched the sun push a mesa of gaseous pink light out of eastwardly mangroves. The circumference of the sun was precise, huge, orange as a Nebraska moon. It energized the shallow water of Dinkin's Bay; changed the color from gray to cobalt to purple to tangerine as wading birds glided on an air-foil of their own reflection.

The birds ascended, then banked away to feed.

I lit a propane burner on my little ship's stove, put coffee on and did my pull-ups while it perked. I did what we used to call a 'Chinese series.' I don't know why we called it that, but we did. You do ten pull-ups, then nine, then eight; work your way down to one in decreasing increments. On the last set, you do as many as you can. Result: You end up doing at least fifty-five pull-ups, but usually more.

Pretty good workout for arms and shoulders.

I checked all the delicate pumps and filters on my main fish tank and smaller aquaria while I drank coffee and munched on an English muffin upon which I'd slathered a healthy layer of Vegemite. Vegemite is an Australian concoction; a yeast spread that's as dense and meaty as bone marrow and once you get used to it (it takes awhile) the stuff is damn near addictive. Sat at a little table on the outside deck watching the morning and thinking about Gail Calloway. Decided that, if I hadn't heard from ex-hubby Frank by noon, I'd call his office.

Maybe Tomlinson was right. Maybe the lady was in more trouble than I suspected.

Thought about Gail some more as I jogged Tarpon Bay Road to the beach, then turned toward Captiva Island. Occasionally, my thoughts strayed to Maggie, my married friend from Tampa. I hadn't heard from her for a few days. Were we going to get together and work out this week?

I stayed on the harder sand near the surf line, running at a pretty good pace. The sun was behind me, gathering heat. A little-known but potentially useful fact: When children wander away from their parents while on a beach, they almost always go in a direction that puts the sun at their back.

Same with aging runners.

For some reason my thoughts shifted from Gail Calloway to the apparent difficulties of maintaining a marriage. Running promotes a random, free rein of thought, so it seemed a natural progression to end up thinking about my own failed relationship with a woman who was as impossible not to love as it was impossible to be her lover.

Pilar Fuentes Balserio, that's who I was thinking about. Pilar is the prominent chief executive of the small Central American nation of Masagua. I'd met her when she was the wife of the President of Masagua.

We became lovers nearly a year before her husband's term came to an end. Shortly thereafter, she gave birth to a son. It was also at about that time that she ascended to power.

I suspect I played more than a small role in her success, occupational and otherwise.

There were reasons, all political, why I'd been able to see Pilar only occasionally. It became clear to me that circumstances weren't going to change. How? Pilar had sat me down and told me in unambiguous terms.

A very strong woman.

Here's what she offered: We could have a few days at Christmas, perhaps. Maybe a week when the Masaguan National Assembly recessed for summer. Maybe a weekend if she could wrangle a few days in Miami for research. And secretly. Always, always secretly, arranged in ways so that absolutely no one could know.

But my feelings for Pilar are such that occasionally just wasn't enough. So, slightly more than two months ago, I'd taken a few weeks to think about it, another week or two to build up sufficient courage, and then I sent her a telegram.

The guy at Western Union seemed surprised by the request. In this age of E-mail, he did mostly money transfers, not messages.

But I liked the style of the thing. Stupidly, I pictured a kid with a weird little hat pedaling up on his bike to make this dramatic delivery: "Telegram for you, ma'am. . . ."

The telegram consisted of four words.

It was a proposal. The only one I've ever made.

Hopefully, it will be the last.

The first two words of the telegram began: *Will you . . . ?*

❄

Pilar's reply had come three thoughtful days later; the only time she'd ever risked telephoning me. She was tearful. She was resolute.

Her answer was no.

It had to be no, she said. She had no reasonable options.

Consider, she said, who I was: A North American; a gringo. How could that possibly be accepted by her people?

What she really meant was: *Think about who you once were, about the work you once did to hurt my country.*

I felt like an even bigger dope than usual. I pride myself on being reasonable, but I hadn't even taken the time to analyze her position. Of course she had to decline. She had no other choice. So why the hell had

I risked her refusal? It was out of character for me to put so much emotional currency on the line.

Tomlinson's assessment had been uncharacteristically blunt: "You'd have never asked her, Doc, if you thought for a minute she'd say yes. Most people live alone because they have to. But you . . . you live this way because you like it."

Was that true? I wondered about it as I ran along the beach.

No, I decided. It wasn't true. My proposal to Pilar had been genuine. I liked the idea of entering into a partnership with her . . . the woman and her handsome blond-haired son. That she could say no, that she had to refuse, still caused a jolt of disappointment in me that was as powerful as any physical pain I'd ever felt.

One thing was obvious: If I did not marry Pilar, I would ultimately lose her. And she would not allow me to marry her. . . .

That realization created in me a feeling of internal deflation that seemed to wither my perceptions about whatever future I hoped to have. That is not a dramatic assessment. For weeks after making the decision not to see Pilar again, I felt like crap. I mooned around like some adolescent idiot. I felt embarrassed by my inability to control my own thoughts and feelings. The only emotion I'd ever experienced that was as intense was when I'd lost another good woman, a powerful woman named Hannah Smith. Finally, I began to get mad. Mad at myself, no one else. And that's when I began the slow, slow process of recovery.

Pilar was out of my life.

Fine. I had my work, my routine, my fish tank, my boats.

And no more proposals. Not of that kind, anyway.

One night, when I had dumbly observed, "Love can be extraordinarily painful," Tomlinson had sagely replied, "No shit, Sherlock."

An insightful man.

But not me, I told him. Never again.

※

I tried Calloway a couple of times at his office on Monday, didn't get him. It was a Lauderdale area code. Apparently Frank did his work over the phone or by computer and probably made the occasional cross-state commute.

By car, Boca Grande to Lauderdale would have been two and a half, maybe three hours.

By chopper, maybe forty minutes.

I wondered if the efficient secretary who took my messages was the infamous Skipper. The wise thing to do when in doubt is to ask, so I finally asked.

No, indeed, I was told. I was speaking with Ms. Betty Marsh, Mr. Calloway's executive secretary. Without prompting, she added, "Ms. Worthington hasn't worked since she became Mrs. Calloway." Her tone carried the careful professional indifference that is designed to mask disapproval. I also noted the judgmental 'hasn't worked' instead of the more specific 'hasn't worked here.'

Calloway's longtime secretary clearly did not approve of her boss's new young wife.

I wondered how far she was willing to go with it. I said, "I was aware that Frank married her, but I didn't know she'd left the office."

"Well, she has. Hasn't worked here for nearly a year now."

I said, "Must be nice," with the slightly cynical, the-world-just-isn't-fair chuckle that always accompanies that phrase.

And that's when she closed the door just a little. "Who did you say you are?"

"Ford. First name Marion, middle initial D, which is why most people call me Doc. I'm a friend of Amanda's."

Her voice brightened. "You are? In that case, I'll save you another phone call: Mr. Calloway won't be available till tomorrow morning, maybe early afternoon. You try then, I'll put you right through if he's here in Lauderdale or give you the number where he'll be. She's one of the good ones, Amanda is. Enough character in there for two or three people. He's in meetings today with investors, the whole bunch of them working late. Over in Tampa."

So I went back to the lab where I'd spent much of the day carefully removing otoliths from grouper I'd collected.

It was exacting, painstaking work. First I used my Buehler low-speed saw to cut paper-thin sections, then Histomount to mount the sections of bone on a slide. Careful polishing was then required to make the annuli visible.

When I was done, the tiny white discs were as bright and delicate as cultured pearls. And so thin that a puff of wind could blow them around like autumn leaves.

If the annuli were readable (all too often, they weren't), then and only then was I able to count the rings through my compound microscope.

One ring equaled one year of growth.

Painstaking work, yeah. Sometimes frustrating, but it's the kind of work I enjoy. It requires precision and offers clarity.

So why was I spending so much time trying to figure out the age of a fish? Simple. The black grouper is no ordinary fish. It's a large, aggressive bottom dweller that inhabits coral reefs and rocky ledges from North Carolina to southern Brazil. It's a popular sport species as well as the most important commercial species of grouper in South Florida.

You see grouper on a restaurant menu, it's most likely black grouper. Translation: economically, it is a very, very valuable animal.

An interesting thing about the fish is that, like most grouper species, black grouper are hermaphrodites

That's right, hermaphrodites.

Protogynous hermaphrodites is the exact scientific term. What that means is, all grouper are born female and, at a certain stage of maturity, most (perhaps not all) make the transition to male.

The data compiled by doctors Crabtree and Bullock had already produced some interesting statistics. We'd examined 1,164 black grouper and found that approximately 50 percent of the female population had reached sexual maturity at an age of slightly more than 5 years. By the age of 15.5 years, half the sampling had transformed into males.

This was noteworthy because Florida imposes both recreational and commercial regulations on black grouper caught in state waters. To be killed, a grouper must be at least twenty inches in length—a fairly large fish.

In isolated regions of rock and reef, did this mean that the largest fish, all males, would be the first to be exterminated? And, if so, would grouper respond differently to fishing mortality than typical gonochoristic species?

In plain English: Would the depletion of male stock cause the species to adapt more quickly? Would smaller, younger females make the transition to male in order for the species to survive?

I found the question intriguing. Successful species have an extraordinary ability to adapt quickly to ensure procreation. In humankind, adaptability tends to be behavioral rather than physiological, but the ability is there because the mandate is so strong.

I wondered vaguely if Gail Calloway's strange behavior was symptomatic of some deep need to reacquire a full-time male partner.

From what Amanda had told me, her acceptance of Jackie Merlot had been so quick, so unquestioning that it had the flavor of panic. Maybe she was reacting to some powerful internal drive that was deeply coded. I'd heard the wartime stories of total strangers desperately copulating in bomb shelters. To be abandoned by a husband of many years had to be no less traumatic, no less terrifying than war.

Tomlinson was right. Divorced middle-aged women were easy targets indeed. I'd never given it much thought before, but I'd seen enough of them to know. And there is no shortage. More than half of America's marriages end up in divorce and, in a generation of Baby Boomers, it means there are a lot of forty-something women out there going it alone. By the dumb measure of generations past, too many of these women see themselves as failures because they failed to maintain a marriage and "keep their man."

What nonsense.

Women between thirty and fifty-five are at the height of their intellectual and physical powers. That they and their former mates have separated effectively obscures that fact. Nor are they necessarily victims. What these women illustrate is the changed dynamics of a changing society. Yet their sense of desperation proves that the self-image of modern women has yet to catch up with the realities of modern times. That's why they are so very vulnerable . . . and way, way too eager to reprove their worth.

Why else would a woman like Gail Calloway give herself to a man that her own daughter had described as a pile of mashed potatoes beneath a face that made her skin crawl?

Clearly, she was troubled, desperate. The question was, what kind of man was Jackie Merlot? And to what degree would he try to take advantage?

✻

Frank Calloway called me the next morning, Tuesday, talking at first on a speakerphone—the bad audio was distinctive—but picked up the handset when he realized that he had me on the line.

"Sorry I didn't get back to you yesterday, Dr. Ford. It's a busy time of year in my business."

In a state that attracts nearly a thousand new out-of-state residents a day, I wondered if there was such a thing as a slow time of year in the land syndicate business.

"No need for the prefix, Frank. I'm not a physician."

"Then is Ford okay?"

"Ford's just fine."

"In that case, Ford, I apologize for not getting back to you. I gather you're in a rush. I should have made time." Very easy, very congenial, not at all like when I interrupted his dinner party.

"Amanda's the one in a rush. I'm not so sure what my approach should be. You apparently know Jackie Merlot, so help me out: Should we be in a hurry to find your ex-wife?"

"Aside from a recent and unpleasant reintroduction, I haven't spoken to Mr. Merlot in fifteen years."

"Was he a patient of yours?"

"I really can't comment on that."

"Frank, I'm trying to help your stepdaughter and your ex-wife. If you won't answer the easy questions, what's going to happen when we get to the hard ones?"

"It's frustrating, yes, I understand that, but there are professional considerations here that I can't—and I'm talking about state and federal laws—that I can't breach. I'd tell you if I could. The law won't allow me. My professional conscience won't, either. When psychologists begin to breach the confidence of patients, psychology will no longer be a valid tool."

"Would it make a difference if we met privately, just you and I?"

"It would make no difference whatsoever."

"The inference is that, yes, Merlot was once a patient of yours."

"If that's what you infer, I won't argue. The thing I can and will talk about is business dealings I've had with Merlot in the past. That might be useful."

"He's in development and construction?"

"No . . . what he now does for a living, we can talk about later. But back then he sold real estate. That, and he was involved with making . . . souvenirs? Something like that. T-shirts and hats, maybe. Some kind of cheap tourism scam. This was more than fifteen years ago. Merlot signed a note to invest in one of the first land packages I ever put together. It wasn't for a lot of money. Five thousand. Not much. I let him in as a favor. He practically begged me to get involved."

I said, "It was that good."

"Yes, it really was. It was a beautiful little project. A kind of mini-gated community; half a dozen duplexes built with enough taste and sufficient screening to give the impression of total privacy. At the center was to be a courtyard: nice little pool, Jacuzzi, propane grills, a small workout room with weights and sauna. This was before the fitness craze. We'd lowballed a chunk of riverfront near Wauchula that abutted a small state park and couldn't really believe it when the sellers accepted.

"You ever hear of Highlands Hammock? Beautiful place and you can't find a nicer town than Wauchula. So we had immediate land equity, a built-in buffer, guaranteed appreciation on the land and plenty of eager investors. But believe me, even a project as small as that one, five thousand doesn't buy much of a piece. Like I said, I was trying to do the guy a favor."

"Because . . . ?"

"Because I felt it would be good for him. Good for his . . . well, let's just leave it at that. Even in those days I occasionally tried to be a nice guy."

"So what happened?"

"The gas shortage, that's what happened. Remember how it was? An ineffective president, interest rates were close to twenty percent, national confidence was nose diving. Then all of a sudden you had to get up at four A.M. and wait in line for an hour, sometimes more, just to get a tank of gas. No one knew how long it was going to last. Maybe a couple of months . . . or maybe the United States of America really was on its last legs and economic collapse was just around the corner.

"Panic is contagious and people panicked. The contractor we'd subbed to clear and grade the property was only a week or two from being done, but he had to stop because he couldn't get diesel. The construction guys had two of the units all framed and inspected, but they couldn't buy gas for their cars. Most of them lived near Sarasota, fifty, sixty miles from the job, so how were they going to get to work? Same with our potential buyers. We planned to draw the young, upwardly mobile types; professionals who wouldn't mind commuting twenty or thirty miles to work. Today, no problem. But back then, no way, not after a fuel panic like that. My investors got scared and the project died on the vine. We lost everything. The only project I ever did where my backers lost money. But it was good experience, a good lesson for me."

"How did Merlot take it?"

"That's what I'm getting at. Merlot didn't. He refused to make good on his note. He hemmed and hawed and finally said, hey, it was all my fault, I should have planned a little better, so why should he have to pay?"

"You're telling me the kind of guy he is."

"Exactly. I'm telling you the kind of guy he is. Or at least was."

Calloway went on. "I told Merlot that if he refused to honor his debt he could forget investing with me ever again or, for that matter, anyone else in Broward County. I also told him I was going to sue. Which I did. He didn't even bother fighting it, but I never collected a cent. Not that I expected to. Turned out he'd passed bad paper to other investment groups around the state, and my little suit pushed his reputation over the edge. The district attorney got after him, and I think Merlot actually spent some time in prison. Four or five months, not much. I was deposed but never actually testified."

"He blamed you for sending him to prison?"

"Probably me among others. But without good cause. My suit was one of many. I never spoke with him again after that. I didn't know he was still around until Amanda told me that he was involved with Gail."

"How'd you take it? When you heard that Merlot was dating your ex-wife?"

"Is that question pertinent to finding Gail?"

"It might help give me a clearer picture of how it was between you and Merlot."

"Before I answer that, I really need to ask: Have you done this sort of thing before? I mean, you say you're a biologist, so what's a biologist know about finding missing people? I appreciate your intentions, sure. You're an old Navy buddy of Gail's late husband. Military buddies stick together. Very noble, I'm sure. But if this is some kind of well-intended gesture, I don't see the point of us wasting our time."

I said, "I couldn't agree more, Frank. But Gail and this guy Merlot are apparently in South America. Right?"

"That's what Amanda says."

"And Amanda wants to find her."

"She wants to know that her mother's safe. Of course."

"Well, Frank, I've spent a lot of time in South America. I know a lot of people. So, yeah, it's possible that I can help. Let me ask you this: Your ex-wife, do you consider her a good person, a valuable person?"

"Of course I do. I've never doubted that. Gail is a good person."

"Is her well-being worth a minor emotional risk?"

"I'm not going to dignify that with an answer."

"Okay, so the question hasn't changed: How did you react when you found out about Merlot and your ex-wife?"

I waited and waited and finally he said, "Gail and Merlot together? I didn't like it worth a damn. It made me . . . it gave me a sick feeling. That's not easy to admit, by the way. I'm trying to broaden myself as a person. My wife and I are working very hard at enlightening ourselves, becoming wiser, kinder beings. But when I heard that Merlot was seeing Gail, I felt a kind of reflexive emotional revulsion. You've never met the man . . . and I really can't go into all the reasons why I felt the way I did. But, no, it hit me hard when I found out. Men, all of us, probably, tend to be more territorial about women than we'd like to admit. So that's part of it, too."

"When Merlot refused to pay off, did you two argue?"

"Years ago, you mean?"

"Yes."

"I wasn't very happy about it. No one likes to be cheated."

"It got personal."

"As in a shouting match? No. I . . . we had words, sure. But I'm a psychologist, remember. I don't lose my temper easily. Don't need to. I'm afraid I have a nasty gift for picking a person's soft spot and saying exactly what will hurt worst. That's something else not easy to admit, but I'm working on it."

"What did you say to hurt Merlot? What's his soft spot?"

"I'm not sure what I told him . . . and I don't see why it's pertinent. As I said, this was more than fifteen years ago."

"I think it's pertinent as hell."

"Dr. Ford, if I can't remember, I can't remember."

I said, "Look, there's a chance I may have to go hunting for this guy, Frank. I need to learn all I can about him."

"I appreciate that. I'm not trying to be difficult."

"Then tell me what you said to really piss him off."

There was a silence. "You know what we need to do? Maybe get together for a late lunch, you come up to Boca Grande. You asked if I believe we should be in a hurry to find Gail. The answer's maybe. I'm in a tough ethical spot. You can understand that. So what I did was hire a private investigator to put together a dossier on Merlot. If someone else generates data, then I'm not responsible for how that data was assembled, right? Not ethically, not legally."

"That's an interesting finesse, Frank. Very smart. You told the guy you hired where to look but not why."

"I didn't say that."

"But that would be the smart thing to do."

"Yes, I suppose it would. The guy's retired FBI; got an office off A1A in Delray Beach. Castillo, that's his name. He was very thorough, very competent. For what it cost me, he should have been. Yeah, I read the report, some of the stuff I already knew from a long time ago. Jackie Merlot has some problems. I knew that, too."

"How do you think he found out that you and Gail were divorced?"

"I don't have a clue. I hadn't thought about him for years. As you'll see when you read the report, he apparently spends most of his time outside the country."

"In Colombia?"

"Colombia and Panama City. Over the last ten years, according to the financial stuff Castillo dug up, Merlot has done a number of money transfers between Lauderdale and some of their offshore banks. And he does real estate down there. Sells little bits of paradise to gringos who want to live like kings and queens."

"Panama City, Panama."

"Central America, yeah. But to begin with, he was mostly in Costa Rica. That's what Castillo's report says. I guess he left Florida after getting out of jail. Costa Rica is a favorite of Americans who want to retire outside the country. No taxes and the dollar's worth three, maybe four, times what it's worth here. But he apparently had to leave Costa Rica, too. Castillo wasn't sure why."

"And he's got a place in Lauderdale, too."

"Just a rental. He paid month to month. It's in Coral Ridge. Not far from where Gail lived; the house where we all lived when Amanda was growing up. At least Merlot used to live there. He skipped without paying the last month's rent when he and Gail left. Something that's more interesting is, he started renting the place just a few weeks before he and Gail started seeing each other." Calloway paused. "That was a little less than a year ago."

"You think starting a relationship with Gail was a way for him to get back at you."

"That's exactly what I think. I think he realized that she was available and he targeted her. There's no way to prove it, but I would bet on it. People like Merlot—he's an example of a specific pathology, understand—people like Merlot can hold a grudge for decades."

"Gail met Merlot through you."

"No. He met her before she became my patient. Before I even knew she existed."

I was surprised to hear that. "How?"

"Somehow Merlot was associated with a group that was organized to help family members traumatized by unexpected death or injury. This was way back, right after Vietnam, when the country needed something like that. He didn't get paid for it, it was volunteer work. I think it was through some church. Scientologists? No, but it was a similar kind of thing. She was the newly aggrieved widow, he was the kindly social worker. It sounds like a noble calling, but . . . well, you learn a little more about him, you'll see how he might tap into an organization like that as a way of picking out . . . picking out people to take advantage of. People like him, they've got a real gift for knowing how to manipulate the emotionally damaged. A genius for it, actually."

"He's a con artist."

"Maybe. I don't know that he's capable of making ethical distinctions. I'm speaking as someone who's dealt with him in business, understand. Healthy normal children progress from a completely selfish quick-gratification view of life to a more mature understanding that it's necessary to give and take. I don't think Merlot ever made it through that developmental stage. At least he hadn't when I knew him."

"Do you think he's dangerous?"

"In a socially destructive sense? Yes. In a criminal sense, I doubt it. But it's possible. He had very good people skills—not unusual for his . . . particular type. And physically, he's huge. I mean massive. But he also struck me as being very tentative and sneaky and cowardly. A mama's boy. That's what we used to call people like him."

"He served time in prison, you said."

"That's right."

"How would a stint in prison affect someone like Merlot?"

Judging from Calloway's reaction, I got the impression he hadn't factored in that component. "Well . . . he was only in for a couple of months. At least, that's what I heard. I can't see it affecting him one way or another. But . . . maybe. Depends on how he was treated, what happened while he was there. I think there was something missing in him before he ever went to jail. Something very basic."

"How do you mean?"

"You need to read the report. That subject's covered, plus a lot of other details."

"Then have your secretary send me the file first thing tomorrow. Overnight it."

Calloway said nope, he couldn't do that, and explained why.

I said, "So I'll come to Boca Grande and take a look. Probably by boat. Is tomorrow okay?"

"I was planning on flying to Lauderdale, but I'll have my secretary check the calendar. Maybe tomorrow or Thursday at the latest."

"Betty Marsh," I said. "I spoke with her on the phone."

He said, "Smartest woman I've ever met. I don't know what I'd do without her."

8

I keep a P.O. address at the Sanibel Post Office, Box 486. But I also occasionally get mail at the marina, and that's where Amanda had the overnight package delivered: an envelope containing two photographs plus Xeroxes of several bank statements detailing activity on her mother's personal account. Amanda called me Tuesday just before noon to tell me to go look, maybe the priority package had already arrived.

"You are one very efficient lady," I told her.

There was a little frown in her voice this morning. Seemed distraught and a little impatient. "Damn right I'm efficient. What I sent you is a framed picture of Merlot I took from our house. Christ, Mom had it up on the mantelpiece over the fireplace. That face of his looking out like he owned everything around him. I'm sending it mostly to get rid of it. She doesn't like it, tough. And a picture of my mom and Frank together. When you see Frank, you can give it to him. If he wants it."

I said, "I think I'll leave the distribution of family photos to you."

"Okay, whatever. The bank statements, though. That's the big news. Pretty shitty news, as you'll see."

I said, "Oh?"

"Yeah. You know how glad I am you had me check the mail? Mrs.

Patterson, our poor neighbor lady, she couldn't wait to get rid of it. So I'm sitting home going through this stack of stuff and it starts dawning on me what I'm seeing. I mean, holy shit! I couldn't believe it. It almost made me sick."

What was she talking about?

"The bank statements," she said. "I didn't make myself clear? Take a look when they get there. They're self-explanatory. My mom, she's on this deposit, withdrawal deal where all her bills go directly to the bank and the bank makes direct transfers. Electric bills, charge card, taxes, the whole works all done through proxy. Frank probably set it up that way. Take care of the little ex-wife, make sure he's still in control of how things get done."

That bitterness again.

She said, "But the reason I'm sending the bank statements is you'll see she's transferred a bunch of money in the last few months in four big lumps. I have no idea why. Three withdrawals of forty thousand, then one for seventy-five thousand. Something else, back in December, almost every day for a month, she made the maximum daily withdrawal on her ATM card. That's like six hundred dollars times twenty-one, twenty-two withdrawals. Something like that. So the total's another thirteen thousand dollars plus the hundred and ninety-five thousand from the bank. Major bucks."

I said, "You need to call Frank right away and tell him."

"I already tried."

"You need to keep trying till you get him."

"Why?"

"He's the money guy in the family, right? The ex-family, anyway. I just talked to him, and he would have said something if he knew. All that money missing, yeah, he would have said something."

"I guess."

"He'd even hint about it to you: 'Your mom's been moving a lot of money?' Or: 'Your mom's acting a lot differently since her new boyfriend?' That's the sort of thing he might have said."

"No. Not a word."

"Then he doesn't know. Activity that heavy, you'd think the bank's computers would have flagged it and contacted your mom."

"They did. I found a letter from the bank saying that if they didn't hear personally from my mom, they would freeze her ATM card. Some of the earlier statements, they'd been opened before she left for Colombia. I found them in her office file. This letter, though, was among the unopened mail the neighbor'd collected. It was dated January seventh. After that, there were no more withdrawals from her ATM, so maybe they did freeze it."

"Were any of the withdrawals made before you last saw and spoke with your mother?"

"Yeah, almost all of them."

"So you have to assume that she knew. She was aware."

"I guess so."

"And the bank had no reason to contact Frank."

"Right. Because the money was drawn on my mom's personal accounts."

"Is there any money left?"

"Not much. The CD and money market accounts are all wiped out. In the savings, the balance is like thirteen-five, so she's got a little left. Look at the statements, see for yourself. I'm so pissed off, I can hardly even talk about it. When I was going through those bank statements, my hands were shaking like crazy. That asshole is robbing my mom blind."

"We don't know that yet."

"You have another explanation?"

"There are a couple of possibilities."

Several, really.

I thought of something. "Do you know if Frank is having any financial difficulties? Maybe he worked it so he still had access to your mom's accounts. Maybe that's why he never mentioned that he knew about all the activity."

""Geez, you really do have a suspicious mind."

"That's right. The question is, Do you think Frank is capable of doing something like that?"

"No way. Even if he wanted to, her money was completely separate. I remember Mom talking about how, for once, she was finally on her own. That was right after the courts and the lawyers got done. Plus, the last time I spoke to Frank, he told me that this was the worst April ever, because he'd made more money than he'd ever made in his life. Taxes, he was talking about. He had to pay out so much in taxes."

"Okay, so we eliminate Frank. That leaves Merlot. Wait till I get the papers, let's see what I can come up with." I thought of something else. "Did she get any cash advances on her credit card?"

"I don't know. I don't think so."

"Did she sell or cash in any stocks and bonds?"

"There was nothing in the mail about it. Jesus, I'm shaking again. More than two hundred thousand dollars, most of my mom's cash savings gone in less than four months." Her voice broke slightly, the transition from fear to anger. "The son-of-a-bitch. You don't think he took her off someplace to hurt her? Like get rid of her, I mean. The woman he stole all the money from and who witnessed what an asshole he is?"

I said, "Amanda, calm down. There's absolutely no reason to suspect something like that. Maybe she moved the money to another account she's set up. Maybe she was investing in stocks or more CDs."

"With cash from the ATM?"

"Yeah, I see your point. But there's no reason to get upset until we find out for sure what's going on. When you were going through your mother's stuff, did you find any letters, any notes from Merlot?"

"A card, that's all. It must have come with some flowers or something. It said, 'Not even these are as beautiful as you.' Can you think of a slimier line than that?"

I was puzzled. "Your mom has an eight- or nine-month relationship with this guy, but he didn't send her a single note? Nothing in writing?"

"Nothing that I found. Just the flower note."

"That doesn't make any sense at all."

"They were E-mail friends, I already told you. She'd be on the computer half the night with him. Where've you been? People don't write on paper anymore."

"Is the computer still at her house?"

"Yeah, but I didn't think to check it."

"You mean you could go back and check her old letters if you wanted to?"

"Maybe. Depends on if she saved them or not."

"But you'd have to know her password, right? Or some kind of entrance code?" Tomlinson had become obsessed with his little briefcase-sized portable. I'd picked up a little bit of information just hearing him talk about it.

"I already know her password. Mom, her memory's so bad, she uses the same pin number for all her cards, her message service, the electronic security system at home, everything. She uses the same three numbers as her password to get on-line. It's simple: two-seven-two. A-R-C on the phone dial, which stands for Amanda Richardson Calloway. My name. One day she'd forgotten something—to pick up her laundry, I think—and she was laughing about how absentminded she was, and that's when she told me. She said it was her way of honoring me."

Amanda's voice cracked again just a little when she added the last sentence. A daughter worried about her mother; trying to keep the emotions in check.

"Then check her computer, see what you can find. Is the phone still on at her house? The phone needs to be on, right?"

"It's on temporary disconnect. I'll have the phone company switch it on as soon as I can. Probably late this afternoon, if I get pushy about it. You want me to try to find letters that Merlot sent to her."

"Anything that has to do with him and your mom. Maybe there'll be some hint about where they are."

"Then I should forward what I find to your computer. So I'll need to know your E-mail address."

I reminded her that I didn't have a computer but I did have a telephone. If she found something, she could call me and read it to me.

"I keep forgetting, you're maybe one of the three or four people I know who doesn't have a computer."

I said, "A regular dinosaur, that's me. And, Amanda? Something else you need to do is call whoever you talked to at the Broward County Sheriff's Department. The FBI, too. Tell them you want to send them copies of the bank statements, it might get them interested. Tell them what you think: that your mother is being robbed. They're a lot better-equipped to handle stuff like this than we are. And don't forget to call Frank, tell him about the money."

"You think it'll make a difference?"

"With the cops? No. Not right away. But at least it will keep your mom's file open in case there really is something wrong."

Talking about Merlot, all that missing money, had upset her, so I tried to swing the conversation around before I said good-bye; give her a chance to calm down. Sat there with the phone wedged against my ear, looking out at the water, at small boats fishing the mangrove hedge, while I listened to her ask more questions about her father.

There was something oddly forlorn and touching in her tone. She was frightened for her mother's safety and deeply missed the father she had never met. She had no conscious recollection of ever seeing the man, of being held by him, but she was inexorably connected; seemed to know and understand him on a bone-marrow level. One thing I did not doubt: Amanda was the daughter of my old friend Bobby Richardson.

I answered her questions as best I could. Then she changed the subject on her own: told me she'd spoken with Tucker Gatrell a couple of times since she'd gotten home.

I said, "You mean he's been calling you?"

"No, I called him. I like him. He makes me laugh. And I think he's honestly worried about what's happened to my mom. So I told him I'd keep him updated on how it was going, what we were doing. He seems to know a lot about Central America. He was asking me all kinds of questions."

I said, "Central America. Yeah, he used to be in the import-export business down there. Just ask him, he's a real expert."

I'd never risked inquiring, but there wasn't much doubt that, along with dealing cattle from Managua to Colon, Tucker had dabbled in drug running during the wide-open, early years of dope smuggling. A Florida cowboy who'd somehow found his way to the jungle. He liked the women, the lawlessness of the place. Probably liked the way that a man with money could live like royalty. Something else I never asked was how he'd managed to piss all that easy money away.

Amanda said, "He wants to help. I told him that'd be fine with me."

I said, "Oh?"

"Why not? What could it hurt?"

All my life I've been baffled at how someone as transparently self-serving as my uncle can so quickly and completely earn the confidence and loyalty of otherwise-intelligent strangers. Tucker was a rare, rare being in that you had to know him well before you could distrust and dislike him.

I said, "Just don't loan him any money. And don't let him get you alone in a room."

"You've got to be kidding. An old man like that?"

"Look, I know what I'm talking about. You don't . . . okay, let me tell you a story. I listened to a TV reporter interview him; this attractive woman not much older than you. This was a couple of years ago. Tuck was trying to get rich selling swamp water, saying it was from the Fountain of Youth. The way you just laughed, you don't think I'm serious, but I am. That's exactly the con he was trying to pull.

"So this woman's interviewing him, talking to him like he's the Old Man of the Everglades, which is a role he loves to play. And she asks him, 'Mr. Gatrell, at what age does a man stop thinking about his own needs and start thinking about more spiritual things?' Tuck didn't miss a beat. He said, 'Sweetheart, if you're talking about sex, you're gonna have to ask someone a hell of a lot older than me. You want, I'll prove my point.'"

Amanda was laughing. "But he was joking."

"No. No, he wasn't joking. It was one of the few honest things I've ever heard him say."

"Hey, come on, Doc, it isn't my place to tell you, but . . . okay, you seem like the nicest guy, a very reasonable man until you start talking about your uncle. Why? It doesn't make any sense."

I told Amanda, "Believe me, it makes sense. I know him. You don't."

"Is it the way he acts? He likes to be the center of attention, there's no doubt about that. Or was it something he did?"

I said, "It's both. But mostly it was something he did."

We talked for a while longer after I'd said, yeah, maybe someday I'd tell her about it.

✳

So, slightly after noon, when I was finished with my morning's work in the lab, I wandered over to the marina to see if Amanda's package had arrived. Stopped on the dock and talked to Mack for a little bit. Mack is stocky and rumpled, smokes expensive cigars and wears cheap flipflops. Mack's a displaced Kiwi who came to the U.S. where, as he is fond of saying, "Free enterprise is just a little free-er." He owns Dinkin's Bay Marina. Most of it, at least. And he is the marina's devoted advocate, peacemaker, judge, host of Friday-night beer bashes, boat trader, wheeler-dealer, fish cleaner and collector of clowns, both real and clowns painted on canvas. Mack normally maintains an attitude of predatory amusement that he shields with a professional coolness not uncommon among those who must deal day-in, day-out with the marina-going public. But on this hot April afternoon, Mack was anything but cool. He was, in fact, in a fiery mood.

"The goddamn bureaucrats," he told me. "The goddamn bureau-RATS . . . there, that's more like it. They were snooping around the marina this morning, acting like they owned the place, telling me how to run things. They were telling me I had to do this, I had to fix that or they'd shut me down, and you know what? Those tight-assed little bastards don't have a clue what it's like to run a business. They've never made a payroll in their life. They've never gambled their own savings on a business of any kind, let alone a ballbuster like a marina. And they've never lain awake all night worrying that they wouldn't take in enough cash the next day to make a mortgage payment that's due by four P.M. And they're judging me? They're telling me how to run MY business?"

I said, "One of the inspectors find a snake in the restaurant again?"

A year or so before, that's exactly what had happened. While looking behind one of the refrigerators, a woman from some esoteric state agency had come eyeball to eyeball with a very large and very territorial rat snake. How long the snake had lived there, Joyce, the fry cook, could not guess, but the woman's reaction had coupled hysteria with a mobile incontinence that darkened a fast trail between the restaurant and the parking lot.

After that incident, Mack had had to shut down the takeout's fry vats and the grill for more than a week. It cost him several hundred dollars, plus the snake disappeared and no one got a chance to admire the thing or even reward it.

Now he said, "I wish to hell it'd been a bloody rattlesnake. Or . . . one of those tiger snakes from Oz. One of the deadliest snakes in the Outback. See how they deal with somethin' that's real instead of their tight-assed little rules and regulations. Those people live in a bloody fantasy land. The way they act is, we work for them. Like they're doing us a favor just to let us stay in business. Mark my word, when bureau-crats refuse to respect private enterprise, this country's in big trouble! And ninety percent of the inspectors they send 'round, I wouldn't hire as dock help. They got attitude without brains. Cadillac dingoes. They remind me of bloody Cadillac dingoes!"

When Mack said Cadillac dingoes, he meant poodles. When he said Oz, he meant Australia.

Yes, he was definitely in a mood. And since I count among my good and trusted friends several of the "goddamn bureau-rats" to whom he referred, I decided to leave him to his anger. For many years, it was car salesmen and insurance salesmen who drew the generalized contempt of a judgmental public. Then it was attorneys. These days, it's govern-ment employees. I have known too many first-rate men and women who happened to be car salesmen or attorneys, or worked for county or state governments, to fall into that easy and unfair trap. Want a tough job? Try selling Oldsmobiles, whole-life or anything else for a living. Try dealing with red tape and outraged citizens all day long. But I have noticed that the contempt reserved for bureaucrats seems more fervent than that aimed at other groups. Why? Mack is a good and fair busi-nessman, and I trust his judgment and his intellect. And he is quite right: There is something desperately amiss when government and pri-vate enterprise are at philosophical odds.

The whole gradual shift in attitude suggests an unhealthy antago-nism: the government cadre (count teachers and union workers among them) versus businesses large and small, as well as any self-reliant indi-vidual who chooses to live independently by his or her own wits. There is no doubt that the cadre's membership is dominated by talented, rea-sonable professionals. Unfortunately, it is the cadre's least-gifted mem-bers who tend to be the nosiest. It is this group that the Macks of the world find infuriating because these members project an attitude of intellectual elitism that is, in truth, the kind of adolescent stupidity that nearly destroyed China. It now threatens Westernized powers, Mack's New Zealand among them.

These dopes loathe the public and anything that the public embraces. It is this stunted, snobby minority that generates genuine hatred from the "bourgeois." That a few of them have their hands near the reins of power is a frightening thing indeed.

Mack's anger was real. One or more of the stunted ones had, apparently, visited the marina and my friend's reaction was both protective and illustrative.

As I walked away, Mack called to me, "The guy who was the worst of them, I told him I'd run his ass off if he ever came back to the marina again. Took up two solid hours of my time with absolute bullshit. You know—just to prove he was in control; making sure I understood that I might pay all the bills and taxes, but he was the one in charge. Know what he said when I threatened to run him off? He said 'Try it.' My property, all the work I've put into this place, and his exact words were: 'Try it.'"

※

From my lab, I'd telephoned in an order for a fried conch sandwich, coleslaw and iced tea, which Joyce served to me in a brown-paper sack with a stack of napkins. As I left, she said, "In case you haven't heard, stay out of Mack's way. He's on the warpath."

I said, "Too bad the snake didn't make an appearance. That would have made him happy."

"Oh yeah, the snake. What I'm still worried about is that drunk we had as a part-time cook—Laurie?—that Laurie cooked the thing and served it. The snake I'm talking about. When I was away on vacation, she have any specials with Italian sausage? Bratwurst, anything like that?"

I was smiling. "I usually stick to the conch or the grouper."

"Playing it safe, I don't blame you. Just the same, it worries me. And I meant it about Mack."

I said, "I know, I know," and carried my lunch, along with Amanda's envelope, out onto the docks.

The fishing guides were just returning from the morning charters, and I watched them tie up their skiffs as I took a seat at the picnic table which was beside the big bait tank between the Red Pelican gift shop and the water. Jeth Nicholes was now running an eighteen-foot Hewes, BUSHMASTER painted in red script on port and starboard sides. Big Felix Blane—all six feet, five inches and 250 pounds of him—was backing his twenty-four-foot Parker, *Osprey*, into its slip, and Nelson Esterline was hunkered down in the live well of his Lake & Bay, transferring fish into a bucket, getting ready to head to the cleaning table.

The guides always drew an audience, which they not only knew, but enjoyed, each of them handling the attention with a kind of jaunty, wind-weary cheerfulness that put their audience at ease and, more importantly, attracted new clients.

If you meet an aloof, self-important fishing guide, he probably isn't a very experienced guide.

I watched a crowd of tourists collect around Nels as he carried the bucket toward the filet table—a couple of big redfish judging from the tails protruding, and several trout. A half dozen pelicans waddled along in pursuit, while an umbrella of gulls and terns circled above. There was lots of noisy squawking and screaming; tourists moving in a hurry now, trying to get a good spot to watch. Then Jeth came behind with three large tripletail—a strange fish that resembles a massive leaf because the dorsal and anal fins are situated far to the rear: effective mimicry, which allows the animal to float suspended on its side and ambush smaller fish that come to it seeking shade or protection. These fish looked as if they ranged between ten and fifteen pounds. Nice tripletail.

The docks were a good place to have lunch at the marina. There was always something interesting to watch while you ate.

As I munched my sandwich, I called to Felix, "You tarpon-fishing today?" speaking loudly above the noise of the birds.

He flashed me an appreciative look: Good, let the tourists know why he wasn't standing at the cleaning table with the other guides. "My angler, Mr. Palmona, he wanted to see what it was like to fish Boca Grande. Left before sunrise, we just got back. You ever see so many boats in your life, Mr. Palmona?"

Felix's client was a lean, dark-haired man who had the articulate, easygoing look of old money. He stood on the dock packing his gear into a little duffel, getting ready to leave while Felix cleaned his boat. "I thought Felix was exaggerating. A show like that, I wouldn't have missed for the world. All of those attractive women in the bikinis, he told me what it would be like, but . . ." The man gave a bemused shrug.

In crowded Boca Grande Pass, the largest and most expensive of the fishing yachts were invariably bedecked with lounging, sun-lazy, beach-browned women who were proud of their improbable bodies—living, breathing symbols of wealth whom the guides appreciated as interesting adjuncts to the great tarpon-fishing. Emboldened by the built-in anonymity that boats provide, it was not unusual for some of these women to sunbathe topless. The guides always made running commentary on the VHF of what they saw, and since I hadn't spoken to Felix by radio that day, he updated me while I ate.

"One of the Futch boys was running some big corporate boat, had five or six girls topside, out there on the bow all oiled up and baking. Frank Davis had him an even bigger boat and more women above deck. The swimsuits now, they come in these bright colors like pieces of Easter candy. That's the way the girls looked. Sweet as candy out there. Two of them had just their bottoms on and both seemed to like Mr. Palmona. They waved a lot."

Felix's client had a dreamy, reflective expression on his face.

Yeah, he'd enjoyed his morning fishing in Boca.

I glanced around to see if any of the marina's female liveaboards were nearby. I don't have much patience for the hardcore politically correct. It's the newest form of Fascism. But living on a boat requires a certain drive and independent spirit that, for good reason, would not allow our marina women to tolerate their kindred being discussed as mindless confections. JoAnn Smallwood, pretty Donna Legges of the sailboat *Bowhard,* and Janet Mueller were aboard *Tiger Lily,* sitting in deck chairs and locked in animated conversation. But they were close, well within listening distance, so I decided to change the subject. "You catch any fish?"

"We jumped four tarpon, landed one. About a hundred-pounder, wasn't he, Mr. Palmona? One of those juiced-up males, Doc, that's harder than hell to get to the boat."

Felix's client was still wearing the bemused expression. He wasn't following the conversation. "The girl in the apple-green bikini," he said, "she really did seem to be waving at me. There was eye contact, I'm absolutely certain. Looked right at me and *kept* looking at me. I'd swear to it, I really would." He seemed to be talking to himself.

Felix said, "Or the fish could've gone maybe one-ten. Pretty good-sized tarpon, Doc, but one of the kind that doesn't want to jump. We had to chase him through the whole fleet, then follow him halfway to Siesta Key. He was a beauty, huh, Mr. Palmona?"

I smiled at Felix when the man said, "Beauty? Oh, she was absolutely gorgeous. Her hair, that kind of cinnamon-colored hair, it's my favorite. The green suit, the red hair. And the way she singled me out and waved at me. I found that very flattering. It was a wonderful day on the water. An absolutely wonderful day. Wish I didn't have to fly home to Chicago, Felix, or I'd book another trip. Maybe two or three trips. But if I work things right, get one of our younger partners to cover for me, it's possible, just possible, I can be back in a couple of weeks. Will the big boats still be fishing Boca Grande Pass?"

Felix was smiling back at me. Guides made their living on repeat business, and Mr. Palmona clearly planned to be a regular. "You bet, Mr. Palmona. Fishing will actually get better, plus there'll probably be lots more big boats carrying pretty girls." Then, as he finished swabbing out his boat, Felix said to me, "Hey, I forgot to ask. How'd you and Tomlinson do in your baseball game Sunday?"

I had opened Amanda's manila envelope and was shuffling through the contents. There were several bank statements, to which I gave a quick look and then set aside, as I answered Felix: "We lost, six to four. Pretty good team from Minnesota. Their pitcher had a nasty slider."

"You catch?"

More bank statements that verified many withdrawals and, surprisingly, several computer-printed deposit slips. I placed those in the stack. "Yeah. Went oh-for-three but hit the ball hard twice. Their centerfielder made a heck of a play."

"What about Tomlinson?"

There were two glossy photographs. The first was of Gail Richardson Calloway and ex-husband, Frank. She hadn't changed that much since the photos I had seen years ago in Cambodia. Dark hair that swept across her forehead and curved to her shoulders. Cheeks and chin and eyes, those eyes. I could picture her in an aerobics class, dark leotard, a mature woman working hard to stay fit . . . or in a 1940s movie, black and white, with a lot of night scenes, streetlights and bus stops, the kind of film where women with faces as haunting as hers paused on street corners to light cigarettes. Frank looked articulate, moneyed, smart. I said, "Tomlinson has had better games."

"Yeah? What, he make a few errors?"

I put the photo of Gail aside. "It wasn't so much that as he just kind of . . . well, he wasn't there."

"You mean he didn't show up?"

"No, we rode in together, like always. But bottom of the first inning, he hit this shot into the gap, and he just kept running. From second base, he veered off into the bullpen, then ran out of the stadium. Never changed stride. We didn't see him again until just after the game."

The other photo was on the table now, and I glanced at it—my first look at Jackie Merlot.

Felix said, "That Tomlinson, he's a weird one. But a good guy."

"Yeah."

"Sometimes he says stuff, I don't have a clue what he's talking about. The other guides, it's the same with them, too. Was he drunk?"

I said, "Huh?" I was looking at this hugely overweight man, spray-hardened hair on a head the size of a pumpkin, his haunch of an arm wrapped around Gail Calloway's waist.

Felix said, "Tomlinson. Why would he do something like that? Get to second, then run off the field. Was he drunk?"

I looked up from the photo, but my eyes drifted back. There was something compelling about a combination so . . . grotesque? Yes, grotesque. No other word fit. Bobby Richardson's widow, healthy, fit and breasty in designer jeans and dark sweater, dwarfed by a man who had to weigh three-eighty, close to four hundred pounds. He might have been a sumo wrestler or an NFL offensive lineman but for his face. Amanda had described it accurately. It was the face of a prepubescent boy; a strangely feminine face, hairless, very pale, with tiny, tiny dark eyes.

Something about his expression made me uneasy, set me on edge. It was the expression of a man who was working hard to project personality. Big smile, lots of teeth, big dimples above the folds of double chin. Hair combed perfectly and gelled in place . . . or maybe a toupee. Yeah, probably a wig.

But that's not what troubled me. It took a moment; I couldn't figure it out, but then I knew. Part of it, anyway. There is the certain rare child, because of chemical imbalance or neurosis or freak genetics, who is so genuinely manipulative and evil that he or she must necessarily learn to communicate an air of perfect innocence. It's more than an expression, it's an attitude, it's body language . . . and it is a totally contrived act. They perfect that act quickly because their survival depends on it . . . and they feel nothing but contempt for those gullible enough to mistake the act for honesty.

Merlot's expression reminded me of that . . . but there was more, too. There was something in his eyes, those tiny dark eyes. They were not much bigger than black pinholes in the folds of white flesh, but there was an intensity in them that misrepresented their size and that seemed vaguely reptilian.

I had to think hard to remember, and then it came to me: A monitor lizard, that's what I thought about when I looked at his eyes. Komodo dragon: another name.

I'd seen monitors on the islands off Sumatra that were the size of rottweilers; animals that wind-scented carrion with their viper tongues.

Their eyes had that same black, bottomless glare. With the huge face, the massive folds of fat and those obsidian eyes, Jackie Merlot was a strange-looking man indeed.

"Doc? Hey, Doc! You okay?"

Realizing that Felix was all but yelling at me, I jumped slightly. I said, "Huh?"

"I asked if you're all right. You look like somebody just walked over your grave, man."

I said, "Sorry . . . wasn't paying attention. You were asking me something . . . ?"

Felix was giving me a very odd look. "About Tomlinson. Why he ran off like that, left the game."

I forced myself to look away from the photograph of Jackie Merlot, his massive arm locked around the waist of my dead friend's wife. "Why Tomlinson did what? Oh! The baseball game. Yeah, he said the feeling was so good, hitting a ball into the gap like that and running, he just didn't want the feeling to end right away."

"You're kidding."

"Nope. So he kept running. He said he ran clear to the Cape Coral bridge and back. Stretched a double into a ten-K jog."

"Good Lord."

"Because in baseball, he said, the good feelings don't last long enough and the bad feelings, when you screw up, they last way too long. He told me the same with life. So why stop running?"

Felix was quiet for a moment, then he said, "Know what? I used to play baseball back in high school and the man is absolutely right. It's pretty weird what he did, but, when you think about it, yeah, hit one in the gap and just don't stop. You think he's a dope, a real goofball, until you think a little more and then he seems like the smartest guy around. Not normal. No one would say that. But smart."

I said, "Yeah. I know what you mean." I was putting the photos, the bank statements back into the envelope. I looked beyond the docks to where No Más, Tomlinson's old Morgan sailboat—white hull, green canvas—sat bow-tethered on a strand of anchor line two hundred yards off the channel that led to Woodring's Point and the mouth of the bay.

Sailboat out there all by itself, fusiform shape on a blue-green plain, mangroves in the background . . . the water-space where the man had lived for the last nine years.

His new Avon dingy, a bright orange husk, was tied off the stern. The man was home.

I told Felix I had to go.

I needed to speak with Tomlinson.

9

Tomlinson said, "I'm surprised at you, man. Thinking viscerally like this. Gathering information with your instincts, finally letting yourself cut across the meadow instead of taking that long-ass linear road. Yep, I think you're making progress. Becoming an actual human being."

We were face-to-face at the dining booth in the cabin of his boat. I could smell kerosene and wood oil, hemp rope, old books and diesel fuel. There was something else . . . soy sauce maybe, and cold rice. Yeah, and incense, too. Sandalwood, that burned-musk smell. He must have just finished lunch. Or meditating.

I was sitting with my back to the cockpit. Up the varnished steps, through the open hatch, if I turned, I could see the binnacle, the boat's big stainless steering wheel, the folded steering vane, a black plastic bag with black tube hanging from the boom: a solar shower.

On the table to my left was a paper tube unevenly scrolled: a chart of the Dry Tortugas, an anchorage off Garden Key marked in pencil.

Tomlinson was planning a trip. I'd looked. A straight-edge course, Sanibel lighthouse to Tortuga's Channel, with compass headings and the piddly little amount of deviation figured in.

And the man chided me for being obsessive?

I said, "I didn't come here to discuss my heart or my brain. I came to get your advice. So let's try to stick to the topic."

But he wasn't done with it. "Nope. Sorry. No can do. This is what my first sensei, Jasper Freeberg, would have called a minor break-through. You said the guy seemed dangerous from the way he looked in his picture. That was your strong first impression, the way you felt. Don't deny it."

"Freeberg? Jasper Freeberg? You're telling me that you learned Zen Buddhism from a guy named . . . Jesus, I don't want to hear it. I was asking what you thought about the bank statements. Here . . . you haven't even read them yet. The bank statements and the photographs."

He wouldn't relent. "Any other time in your life, you take a look at the photograph of a first rate *maloojink* like . . . like this oddity, this dude Jackie Merlot, you'd say, 'The human eye can't communicate emotion.' You'd say, 'Some of the most prolific killers in history had faces like choir boys.' You'd say, 'I don't judge people by the way they look,' when, in fact, we all do. You've never admitted any interest at all in letting your senses interpret what your eyes see. Until now."

"Mal-what? *Mal-oo-jink?* What the hell does that mean?"

"It's Tahitian. Or maybe from the lost language of the Easter Is-landers. It means evil man. No . . . that's not a precise translation. It means evil *being*. I look at this guy, the first thing I see is something . . . unhealthy in there hiding behind that smile. You felt the same way when you saw his picture, I'd bet on it. The intuitive knowledge, go ahead and 'fess up. This person is . . . different. I'll tell you something else"—Tomlinson's iridescent blue eyes seemed amused—"this person scares you. The first man I could ever say that about. Not that you're some asshole macho kind of guy, Doc, no. It's just that you're always in control, the way you size men up, like in two seconds, because you've met about every kind of man there is. You know what they're like, so what's there to fear? But you've never met a guy like Jackie Merlot, be-cause he's not really a man. He's a being and that scares you. You want to know something else?"

I waited.

"He scares me, too."

I said, "Oh?" wondering if it was true. Was I frightened of the man in the photograph?

Tomlinson said, "He scares me because he's empty. Like a pit. That kind of emptiness."

When Tomlinson takes off on a tangent, the best course is to play along. In the long run, it saves time. I said, "You can tell all that just from looking at his picture?"

"Can't you?"

"No. You're taking the few facts we have and dramatizing the guy's negatives. His powers, too. What I think is—and I'm not judging him by his appearance, understand—but what I think is, he's a user. A small-time con man, that's my guess. Nothing more."

"So you don't think you need to be in a big rush to find your old buddy's wife?"

He had me there. Since seeing the photograph I had, for the first time, felt a pressing urgency. Gail Richardson Calloway was in trouble. How I knew, I wasn't sure, but I was now convinced that it was true. "Seeing the guy's picture has had an effect on me," I said. "I'm willing to admit that."

"I thought so. All things in nature are repetition on a theme, man."

"So you've said many times," I replied dryly.

"Make fun of me if you want, but you've heard of what the astronomers called 'dark anomalies'? They are these extraordinarily dense . . . I forget the name for them . . . uhh-h-h, these *things* in space. Not planets, not suns, nothing that's orderly and normal. They are energized globs created by negative energy. Anti-matter. Black holes. You've heard of them, haven't you?"

I sat there listening.

"Mark my word, amigo, certain people have that same kind of anti-matter energy. Strictly negative. You've met women like that. Destructive bitches unrelated to their sex. Same with men. A very, very heavy counterproductive gig that gauges success by the amount of chaos and pain they can cause. You don't believe me, take another look at this photograph. Not just at his face, but what the dude is doing."

Tomlinson slid the photo of Merlot across the table. Looked once more at Gail's mild, expectant smile; saw the shape and richness and warmth of her, plus something else. Uncertainty? Maybe. She appeared uncertain and there was a curious glaze to her eyes, an expression that I associate with people in shock. Then I turned my attention to Merlot. Studied him for a while before I said, "The way he's got his arm around her, it's a possessive gesture. Is that what you're talking about? Merlot's hand is on her ribs, but his thumb has been elevated just high enough so that it touches the underside of her left breast. He's making a statement. Familiarity. Intimacy. Ownership. He could be saying any of the three."

Tomlinson was leaning across the table, head tilted to see, twisting a strand of his shoulder-length hair, a familiar gesture. "Right, right, that's exactly what he's doing. But he's claiming more than intimacy. You're trying too hard, man . . . which is so typical of you. Relax, soften your senses, look at the picture and just let it happen." Tomlinson waited impatiently for a few seconds before he added, "Don't you see what he's doing with his fingers, man?"

Once he said it, I wondered how I'd missed it before. The middle finger of the hand Merlot had placed around the woman's waist was extended ever so slightly, as was the middle finger of his right hand, the hand he had folded on his bloated marshmallow stomach.

Tomlinson said, "He's looking at the camera, flipping everyone the bird. Merlot picked out this photo. I'd bet anything on it. The daughter said she found it framed on her mother's mantelpiece? Guaranteed, Merlot's the one who had it framed and maybe even placed it over the fireplace where it was easy to find. See how the lens caught the woman's eyes? A flash was used and it created a glare. She wouldn't've had a picture like this framed, because she doesn't look her best. That's how I know Merlot did it. He had it framed because he's telling the ex-husband, his old business partner, fuck you. Using finger-a-grams to do it. Probably got a big kick out of imagining this rich guy, the guy who helped put him in jail. Calloway? What's his name, imagining Frank Calloway walk into the room, finding the picture and going ballistic. Saying to him, *I'm screwing your wife, asshole!* Like that. You see it now?"

Yeah, I could see it.

"The guy is evil, Doc. Slimy. One look and I knew. Your instincts are right, so why bother to be so intellectual about it? He's sneaky evil but a force, so it's no wonder he scares you."

No . . . that wasn't true, I decided. I wasn't frightened of Merlot; not just from looking at his photo, anyway. That he used his middle fingers to send a message seemed idiotically adolescent, not evil. What else? I didn't like him . . . okay, that much I was willing to concede. And partly because of the way he looked. I could understand now why Calloway had reacted the way he did when he learned that Merlot was sleeping with his ex-wife.

Revulsion, yes. There was something about Merlot's expression, his appearance, that triggered the gag reflex. Another admission: The fact that Merlot was apparently manipulating Gail infuriated me on a visceral level. The worth of a man or a woman is established wholly by the worthiness of the people who are devoted to him or her. Gail had been the lifetime love of a good, good man, Bobby Richardson. That a person like Jackie Merlot could defile that bond seemed to illustrate the tragic potential of all life.

What I knew of Merlot didn't frighten me, though. Indeed, what I knew gave me confidence. Yeah, the guy was gigantic, but he was prissy huge, all fat. Something else: Demonstrations of ego—like pyromania—were strictly for amateurs. Clearly, the guy was an amateur.

No, I was not frightened of Jackie Merlot.

When I explained that to Tomlinson, he shook his head, refusing to believe me. "You fight your own instincts, man. You always have. Already you're intellectualizing, telling yourself there's no good reason to feel what you really feel."

"I'm afraid of a lot of stuff, Tomlinson. More things than you realize. But not of photographs. And I've got no fear of a tub like that."

Tomlinson's expression said, *You should, man. You should.*

He put the photograph away—end of subject—and began to inspect Gail's withdrawal and deposit slips. Abruptly, then, he stood, removed the wooden hatch to the ice locker and began to paw around, searching for something.

"Good God," I said. He'd been sitting shirtless across from me. I'd assumed he was wearing shorts. Or maybe the sarong he favored. But I was mistaken on both counts.

I said, "You mind putting some pants on, Tomlinson?"

He was now holding a bottle of Hatuey, that fine Cuban beer, in hand, blinking at me, bare-ass naked. Seemed surprised that I'd noticed or that he'd forgotten, one or the other. Said, "Whoops. Sorry. Gets to be a habit living out here all alone. I was up on the bow taking an air bath. You know, letting oxygen molecules cleanse my pores. Refurbish all the little shadowy places that don't get much sun." He looked down and spoke in the direction of his waist. "Isn't that right, boys?"

I stood to leave. "I'm going. Take a look at the bank slips when you get a chance. You want, we can have dinner tonight and talk about it. I'll call for reservations at the Timbers or maybe drive to the mainland and try the University Grill. I hear it's pretty good."

Tomlinson's chin was still on his chest. "Know something, Doc? Every problem I've ever had in my life started with this little bastard. Hey-y-y-y . . . I'm talking to you. Hello, hello!" Tomlinson chuckled, as if not the least bit surprised. "See that? The little son-of-a-bitch is listening to every word. And things haven't much changed 'cause he's still causing problems."

I was standing on the top step of the ladder. "The Timbers would be good if it's not too crowded. We can walk there and have a few beers, don't have to worry about driving. I'd like to get this thing with Amanda's mother in better focus. That's why I want you to look at those bank slips, give me an opinion. Some behavior-and-cause scenarios."

"You want me to just look at the withdrawal slips? Or do you want me to get down and dirty, really try to figure out what the hell's going on? We've got like five or six hours till dinner time. I can do some serious kick-ass research on the subject by then."

"Then do it. It's just possible I may have to fly down to Colombia and shake her loose from the guy. You could be right: She really could be in trouble."

But Tomlinson was once again lost in his own thoughts, alternately speaking to me and his own male member. He said, "You're the only one I've confided in, the only one who knows I've been trying to get back together with Musashi."

"Me, you mean?"

"Of course. Who you think I'm talking to? I invited her down from Boston to go on a cruise this week. The Dry Tortugas in spring, catch some dolphin, maybe see some sooty terns. Told myself it was to spend time with the mother of my sweet little daughter, but I'm afraid the truth is that Mr. Zamboni and the Hat Trick Twins are up to their old tricks."

"Mr. Who?"

"Yes, they're aching to win that little Japanese vixen back again. Musashi I mean. Set her free from the asshole politician she's been sleeping with. And don't mistake that for some kind of racial slur."

"Right, of course not. Not from an enlightened person like you."

"Little Japanese scum."

I was still lost. "Mr. Zamboni and the Hat Trick Twins? Who the hell are . . . oh. Okay, okay, a reference to your hockey days at Harvard. Now I know what you're talking about. Yep . . . I've really got to run."

"Thought maybe the air baths would help, that's what I was hoping. So . . . what you think, boys? Feeling any better after all that fresh air?"

He looked up at me for the first time since starting his strange dialogue. "Let them breathe free, that's my motto. I do my best, but you think it makes a damn bit of difference? Nope. Oxygen and assholes—the two most common elements on earth."

I shrugged.

"They're still obsessed with Musashi, and I can't do a damn thing about it. Something about her body, those Japanese knobs of hers. And her voice. Zamboni is crazy about her voice. I'll tell you something, Doc: Just 'cause I can aim this bastard doesn't mean I'm in command." Then, to himself: "So I'll tell you what, my stubborn little friend. How does a pair of bikini underwear sound to you? The tight kind without that little fucking escape hatch! No more midnight maneuvers. Think about it!"

I was stepping out onto the cockpit, looking astern where my flats skiff was cleated. I said, "Call me on the VHF, Tomlinson. About dinner, I mean. Nels just sold them some fresh pompano. I know that for a fact, so even if it's not on the menu, Matt will make sure we can have it if we want."

Speaking a little too loudly, as if he wanted to be overheard, Tomlinson answered, "Oh, I'll be ready. You can count on it. And if I'm walking a little *funny*, we'll *all* know why."

❋

In April, Sanibel and Captiva Islands are as crowded and animated as any Carnival cruise ship, but with a basic difference: People who come to the islands tend to be like-minded, outdoors oriented and energized by a longing for quiet beaches and immersion in the subtropics: wading birds, gators, crocs, manatees, littoral fish, coconut palms, ospreys, you name it. Look at the people who come year after year, who make the islands part of their lives, and you will think of L. L. Bean catalogues. You'll think of *Audubon* magazine. Or maybe *Outside*. The fact that the islands maintain more wild space than hotel space is precisely why they continue to be so widely treasured.

Which is the reason I don't mind getting out in the tourist rush occasionally, eating dinner at a favorite restaurant. The people you meet are usually pretty nice. Interesting, too.

Tomlinson came tapping at my door at twilight, looking dapper in blue jeans and silk Hawaiian shirt, pink flamingos and golden tiki huts thereon, his bony hands offering two cold bottles of beer.

"Its very important to rehydrate in this hellish spring heat," he explained. "But if you want to wait for dinner, I'll drink both bottles. Waste is a terrible thing. As we speak, there are Christian alcoholics absolutely Jonesing for a drink in places like Iraq and Libya. Parts of . . . somewhere else, too. Arkansas? Yeah, probably Arkansas. I'm telling you just in case you feel like refusing this beverage."

I took one of the beers from him. "Nope, I'm thirsty."

"Just checking."

"Did you go over Gail's bank slips?"

"I did indeed. Three, nearly four solid hours of pure cerebral exercise. I made a few phone calls, too. So . . . I have some ideas on what's going on. Some very strong opinions, you might say."

"I thought you might. Frank Calloway left a message for me at the marina. He wants to get together in Boca Grande on Thursday. Which means I can work all day tomorrow. I hope. I've got to call him back."

"I don't know why the hell you just don't get an answering machine like everyone else. This fucking decade has cut the nuts off every male between here and Fumbuck, Egypt, but it hasn't even scratched your paint. I think it's because you haven't been paying proper attention. Seriously, Doc, you haven't been playing fair. The damn decade'll be gone before you even realize it was here."

"Spare me, Tomlinson. But . . . yeah. I may get a recorder. I keep thinking maybe someone important has tried to call and I wasn't home. That feeling, like I've missed something . . . I don't deal with it as well as I used to."

"I know whose call you're afraid of missing. Pilar calling from Central America."

"Nope. I don't even think of her much anymore."

"*Right.* Just like you seldom think of Hannah Smith anymore. I'm going to tell you something you may not like: I still miss Hannah. She was the most sensual woman I've ever met in my life."

"If you know I don't want to hear it, why say it?"

"No disrespect intended."

"None assumed. So let's not discuss her anymore."

"The island bookstores, they all say they've sold a bunch of her books."

"That ought to make you pretty happy. You wrote it."

"Hannah wrote it. Orally, at least. I just typed it up."

I increased my pace. "Is there a reason why we're still talking about her?"

※

We'd crossed the boardwalk, through mangroves, onto the island. Now we were walking the shell drive from the marina that became Tarpon Bay Road. It was an hour after sunset. Dark. I could hear chuckwills-widows making their whippoorwill sounds. I could hear screech owls and car traffic and Ralph Woodring running his bait shrimper on the grass flat outside the mouth of the bay. When he cranked the nets up or down, the rusty booms screamed like something that should be chained behind bars.

Through tree limbs overhead I could see the demarcation between night horizon and stars. That line of trees, the muted colors, were as distinctive as a Navaho sand painting. It was a warm night with lots of island smells: jasmine and sulfur and windy beach. It was nice seeing the stars through the trees.

We crossed Palm Ridge past the gas-pump fluorescence of the Pick Kwik and stayed on Tarpon Bay Road. The Timbers was just off to the left, across from the fire station, a restaurant decorated as if by beach-combers: life rings and mounted fish, bamboo umbrellas, driftwood and shadows.

After Matt showed us to our corner table and after Lin brought us each another beer, Tomlinson folded the napkin across his lap saying, "The withdrawal slips and the deposit slips. I went over and over them. I even called a banker friend of mine to see what he thought. Well . . . actually, he's not a friend, he's an acquaintance. Bankers, the re-spectable types, tend to . . . let's just say they tend to be very uncom-fortable around me. As if I'm widely known as the islander voted most likely to climb the fucking bell tower. With a firearm, I'm talking about, which frankly, Doc, really pisses me off because I've never even fired a damn cap pistol . . . at least, not since that ugly incident in Chicago—"

"Tomlinson . . . Tomlinson. You've drifted way off the subject."

He appeared surprised that I'd interrupted. "What?" Then: "Oh. *Right*. Okay, what the banker said was, with all that activity, the woman was either investing in something or gradually changing banks. Maybe transferring the money to accounts outside the country. Which can be illegal if you don't go about it the right way." He paused. "So that's one possible explanation we've got to consider."

"Not just possible," I said, "but probable. In any circumstance like this, the simplest solution is almost always the correct solution. So that's your best guess? That she was moving her money?"

He said, "No. As much as you hate to admit it, Doc, we think so much alike about stuff like this, the serious stuff, I bet you already know what my best guess is."

"Tomlinson, we so seldom think alike that I can count the times on one hand. Five times, max."

"Oh, is that right?"

"That's right."

"Well, it's six times now. Or maybe six dozen."

"We'll see. Tell me why Gail Calloway withdrew so much money before she left the country with Jackie Merlot."

He smiled. "You've gone over those withdrawal and deposit slips as many times as I have. Why do YOU think she was moving around all that money?" Before I could answer, he chimed in, "Blackmail, that's my guess. Judging from the deposit slips, it's blackmail. Same with you, huh? Tell the truth now."

I said, "I've got blackmail down as one of three possibilities."

Tomlinson's expression said that he wasn't surprised. "Damn right, blackmail." He smiled. "You want me to tell you the other two most probable scenarios?"

"No. I'd rather hear about the deposit slips."

I told him that the deposit slips were the only things I couldn't make fit neatly into a plausible chain of action. I meant it.

"Don't feel like the Lone Ranger," he said. "It took me a solid hour of very intense brainwork to figure out why they're important. You got any ideas at all about them?"

I shook my head.

"But blackmail, you figured blackmail as a possibility. How the feds could miss this one is beyond me. See? We do think alike."

"Two peas in a pod, you and I."

"Exactly. I meant it when I said you're starting to come along. That's great news for the people who think your heart's about half the size of your brain. No offense, Doc, but you're working your way up to becoming a real human being."

✳

Tomlinson surprised me by ordering the pompano cooked in parchment paper. He's been an uncompromising vegetarian since the day I met him but, in the last few months, he'd broken form often enough for me to know that he was going through some changes in his life . . . as we all do.

"I've decided that eating animal flesh is a way of ingesting cellular communion," he explained when the waitress had finished taking our orders. "And let's face it, if I dropped dead in a field tomorrow, every goddamn animal for miles would be scrambling to bite a piece out of me. A chunk of biceps, a chunk of my beezer. They wouldn't give a damn. Protein is protein, when the shit really hits the fan. For those omnivore bastards, it's any port in a storm."

I said, "I never looked at it from an animal's point of view before."

"You're damn right. The realization about how the food cycle really works flashed into my brain one night. The vegetarians of the world? If animals were in charge, every two legged tofu humper would be gutted, jointed and deep-fried in about the time it takes to watch a couple of episodes of *Wild Kingdom*."

"Wholesale slaughter," I suggested.

"Jesus, you know it. Culinary anarchy. And there's nothing a vegetarian hates more than looking stupid. The way it came to me was, I imagined myself out sailing and what would happen if I fell overboard and couldn't get back to the boat. The damn fish would think they'd died and gone to heaven, man. We're talking feeding frenzy. And then I pictured myself visiting a farm, nobody around but me and Mr. Zamboni and the two of us have a heart attack near the hog pen. Jesus Christ, what an ugly scene! The cloven-hoofed scum were on me like red sauce on frijoles."

He was shaking his head . . . yes, he'd given the subject a lot of thought. "Fair's fair, man, that's what I say. They'd swallow me down like beer nuts, so what makes me better than them? Not that I plan to eat meat regularly. No. Only when, say, there's fresh pompano available or a really outstanding piece of beef."

"Selective vegetarianism. That actually makes a little bit of sense."

"A way of paying tribute to all life forms."

"Sure. Why avoid something just because it tastes great?"

His smile illustrated tolerance. "That's my point. And by the way, I was kidding about the beef. I draw the line at anything they didn't gather and eat on *Gilligan's Island*. Unknowingly, those seven stranded castaways pioneered the recipe for a healthy, happy life."

Tomlinson went on to explain that the professor wasn't the only one who was ahead of his time. I listened and nodded along, saying, "Uh-huh, Uh-huh. Yeah, sure. Ginger and Mary Ann, you bet." I almost asked, "So what was wrong with the skipper?" but decided screw it, never ask what you don't really care about knowing.

When Tomlinson gets on a subject like that, something that's strange and far off the charted byways, even I sometimes wonder if the man has all his faculties. But then he'll say something so rock-solid reasonable or so insightful that I'm actually a little ashamed that his oddities continue to give me pause.

❊

I'd ordered stone crab claws with lime wedges and a brick of garlic toast. As an appetizer I had the waitress bring grilled shrimp and slices of fresh mango. Tomlinson, who knows something about wine, ordered a bottle of cold Riesling from the snow country of southern Australia. He insisted that I try a glass with the shrimp. Not bad. We both peeled shrimp and sipped wine and talked about Gail Calloway while we waited for dinner.

I told him that, in my mind, three consecutive withdrawals of $40,000 suggested payments. And it was unlikely that any of those payments had been anticipated by Gail. The fact that the withdrawals were made only a couple of weeks apart indicated unconventional circumstances or an unconventional billing source. "If she was going to buy something for $120,000 and had the money, why not write a check for the whole sum?"

"Plus a big chunk of the money was transferred to other accounts," he pointed out.

"Exactly."

"That's one reason I think it's blackmail. I can just see some asshole deciding, okay, we sent one note or made one call and she sends us forty thousand. Nothing to it. So let's keep writing notes or making calls until she stops sending money. Which is where the deposit slips come in."

That's what I wanted to hear about.

"Did you take a close look at all the information on those slips?" he asked. "I described them to my banker friend. What they actually are are receipts from wire transfers. There are ten slips total and the deposits are divided evenly among twelve numbered accounts."

"You're kidding me. I didn't notice that."

He was nodding. "Twelve different accounts for a total transfer of slightly less than one hundred and ninety-eight thousand dollars. The reason you didn't realize there were so many accounts involved is because there are no individual names listed on the slips. I missed it, too. Just numbers."

"I don't know much about numbered accounts, and I've *got* one. An account in the Caymans. But there's always a name associated, right?"

"Nope, I don't think there has to be. It's weird to us because American institutions, they've got a thing called the Banking Security Act. For someone to open an account, they have to provide creditable identification. In other words, there has to be a name attached to the account. It's to put a crimp into money-laundering, among other things."

"So you're saying Gail's money had to have been wired to a foreign bank."

"Foreign banks, plural. I know where the money went because each of the wire receipts has a numerical code that corresponds to the bank where the money was sent. It doesn't mean that the money has to leave the country. Miami's got plenty of foreign-based banks. Among them are the Banco de Colombia and the National Bank of Panama." Tomlinson used his fingers to pick up a slice of mango. "That's where Gail Calloway's money was wired."

"Jackie Merlot spends most of his time outside the country," I said, "Frank Calloway told me that."

"Uh-huh, uh-huh, but wait till you hear the rest of it. After my banker friend translated the numerical codes, the first thing I asked him was why would anyone go to so much trouble? Why divide the money among twelve different accounts? The banker says the obvious: There must be twelve different people or businesses involved. But I don't think so. You know what I think's going on?"

"You're still operating on the premise that Gail's being blackmailed."

"It's making sense so far, right? See . . . the problem with blackmail is how to collect the money. Blackmailers and con men always get nailed when they pick up the ransom. Drop the money at X-spot, throw it out of a moving car, follow directions from phone booth to phone booth, it doesn't matter. I don't think anyone's ever come up with a safe way to make an exchange like that."

I said, "So?"

"So, I think the person who got Gail's money is smart as hell, because I think they finally did it. Found a safe, untraceable way to get ransom money. What I think they did was set up these foreign accounts, probably used fake names to do it, but it doesn't much matter because everything goes by a PIN number and they have no reason to return to those banks ever again.

"They have Gail wire her payments to the account number they've provided her with. Once the money's been transferred, they can visit any ATM machine in the world and drain the accounts dry. They can tell her they're in Lauderdale, just around the corner from her house when they're actually on the other side of the earth. No way she can find out. Same with the feds—not if the blackmailer stays on the move. Pop the card in, punch in the PIN number and the cash comes shooting out in guaranteed unmarked bills. A week, two weeks later, the feds get a black-and-white picture from the ATM camera. Some dude or chick in a floppy hat and glasses and a scarf. What's that gonna tell them?"

I said, "You figured all this out from the deposit slips."

"No, from the fact that there were twelve numbered accounts on each slip. You're the logical one. It was unlikely that twelve kidnappers were involved, so why have so many accounts? Answer: Keep the balances low enough so they can wipe out each account fast."

"But even with the money in that many fake accounts," I said, "it would still take awhile to drain it from ATMs."

"Not really. Twenty-some days, that's all. But what do the blackmailers care? There's no rush, no way the feds can anticipate where they'll be. Like I said, as long as they stay on the move. The way I fig-

The Mangrove Coast
139

ure it, it was so clean and easy, they probably got greedy, which is why Gail's final transfer was for seventy-five thousand.

"Maybe their last ransom note or call demanded a hundred grand, but she tells them she only has seventy-five left, an uneven number. Why? She's trying to be smart for once, make it believable. She's tired of the whole gig. She doesn't want to do it anymore. She's willing to try anything, so she lies and says that's all I've got left, screw you."

I said, "It's plausible. It really is. But think about this finesse: Merlot's right there with her the whole time she's being blackmailed. He's offering her advice, pretending to be her friend when, from the very beginning, he's the one behind it. It's his idea, he's coordinating the whole thing."

"That picture of him, man, that picture really got to you, didn't it? Admit it."

"I'll admit I think the guy's a user. I already said that. I think it's possible that he had something to do with Gail's withdrawing so much money."

"Sure . . . I can see something like that happening. But if he's behind it all, why didn't he clean her out completely? He hates the ex-husband, so why not go for the kill?" Tomlinson came up with the answer before I could reply. "Okay, okay, he lets her keep a little money so he's entirely above suspicion. He not only doesn't want the cops to catch on, he doesn't want the woman to doubt him even for a second."

I was nodding. "Right, I thought of that. It's one of the things that really bothers me. If he's doing this crap for revenge, he'll ultimately want her and Frank to know that he's the one who conned them. It's his final move, the way he wins. As in checkmate. The act isn't over till he sees the hurt in Gail's face and he hears the anger in Frank's voice. So, if he's taken precautions against Gail finding out, it means he's not done with her yet. He has other ways he can use her."

Tomlinson's expression was grim. "The word *checkmate* in chess," he said, "I hope it's not appropriate."

"What?"

"*Checkmate*, the word: It comes from the Persian phrase *Shah mat*, which means 'The king is dead.' Jesus. That's just so sick. He takes her money and he still wants to take more."

Where did Tomlinson come up with this stuff?

I said, "Yeah, it's a bad deal . . . if we're right about the blackmail angle. But neither one of us knows for sure if we're right."

I told him there were other possibilities. We talked about them, batting them back and forth. I described two different cons that weren't much better than blackmail. One, Merlot weasels his way into her confidence. She's emotionally damaged, very vulnerable. Sleeping with her's not enough. To get back at the ex-husband, he wants the woman's money, too. That old saying that you can't cheat an honest man is baloney. Honest, caring people are the easiest marks in the world and, according to Amanda, her mother was sensitive and caring to a fault.

"The guy knows she has money," Tomlinson added. "All he's got to do is find the right approach."

Exactly. I kept going, thinking out loud, trying to put myself in Merlot's place. With a woman like Gail, my guess was he either played on her sympathy or he leveraged the trust he'd very carefully built in her. One possibility? He goes to her and says he's sick. Or a friend of his is sick. Or there's a sick child and the only surgeon who can help has to be paid up front because it's South America and insurance doesn't cover it. Merlot's not sure how much it's going to cost, but she can start by sending forty grand.

Tomlinson was following along. "Yeah, I can see how that would get to her. One of the scenarios I came up with had her making these huge payments to keep some Colombian orphanage from being repossessed. Or an old persons' home. A hospital maybe, it's the same angle. Any variation would work. The big lie, man, the big lie. Honest people always fall for the big lie."

I said, "I know. It's infuriating, because it speaks so badly about how we've progressed as a species. Except for the predators among us. They've gotten better. They've gotten smoother. The predatory types, they've got an instinct. Frank Calloway said that about Merlot. They realize that emotionally troubled people are very pure in their motives. People who've been hurt want the hurting to stop. It's as simple as that. People who are damaged want to be whole again. They tend to be very kind and without device and ready to give anything they have if it will help take the pain away. That's what's so damn sad about someone like Gail being nailed by a jerk like Merlot."

Tomlinson looked at me for a moment. "You don't even know the guy. Isn't that what you told me earlier?"

"Okay, I hate the way he looks. His picture gives me the creeps. You satisfied?"

"Now you're showing an empathetic side, too, man."

"I'm just parroting you," I said.

"Bullshit. You're growing as a person, but you're too damn stubborn to admit it. Hey . . . you know what we really need to do? To get a handle on this whole thing?"

Tomlinson said what we needed to do was read Gail Richardson Calloway's E-mail. If I'd been right when I told him that their affair started through E-mail, then we needed to read the letters, get a feel for how he played her.

He said, "I guarantee you, if they wrote much, every trick he pulled is right there in black and white. I've been involved with E-mail for mucho years, man. People will say shit in E-mail that you seriously would not believe."

I told him that Amanda had promised to go to her mom's house tonight and track down the correspondence if she could. "We can call her cell phone number when we get back to my place, see how it went."

The waitress was bringing the food on heavy platters. It looked good. The aroma of baked pompano is meant to mingle with beach air.

Tomlinson said, "I'm surprised she has her mom's password, man. People don't give out their passwords."

I had the first stone crab claw off the plate and was tapping it with a spoon, creating fault lines in the heavy shell. The claw was shaped like a boxing glove, orange and white.

When I'd explained to him about Gail's password, he told me "Yeah, well . . . if Merlot had the kind of control over her that we both think, he didn't let her leave Florida without covering his tracks. You know that as well as I do. He would've made her change the password. Or dump the whole account."

He had a point. "If the password's been changed, does that mean we've lost all that information?"

"Nope. Just access. There've been whole civilizations lost out there in cyberspace, so the words of two little people don't amount to a hill of beans. Poof! All gone."

What the hell did that mean?

I looked across the table at Tomlinson. He'd brought his own chopsticks and was using them to pinch off the tentative first chunks of steaming pompano. I said, "You're the only computer expert I know. If Amanda can't get into her mom's files, do you think you could do it?"

"Try to figure out some random password? I wouldn't get your hopes up on that one. We've got a better chance of finding pearls in those claws you're eating." He continued using his chopsticks, but his eyes never wavered from mine. After a time, he said, "But there ARE people who've got access to software that can find passwords, track activity, recover just about any file that hasn't been drowned or gobbled by some badass virus. Get on the horn to one of your old CIA buddies and they'll know just what we need. They can send the program to my computer or Gail Calloway's computer as an E-mail attachment; won't even have to put it on a disk."

I poured myself another glass of the Riesling. Why was I drinking wine when I wanted a beer? I connected with his eyes as I sipped the wine. "Some things you just won't let drop. I'll tell you again: I never worked for the CIA."

His smile was not entirely sympathetic. "Well, if Amanda calls tonight and tells you she can't access her mom's account, my advice is get on the phone and contact whatever hot-shit-right-wing-deep-spook agency you DID work for and tell them what you need. If the bastards aren't too busy fucking around, destroying some small country, I mean. Personally, I'd rather spend my day watching the weather channel and whacking off in a hanky than trying to guess someone's password."

Gail Calloway's password hadn't been changed, though. That's what Amanda told me over the phone when we got back to my stilthouse.

"But there's nothing in her letter files," she added. "Not a word. So I guess it's like one of those good news, bad news things."

When I told Tomlinson, he said, "Same difference. If you're serious about getting all the information you can about this weird love affair, you better seek help from one of your warmonger compatriots. Also, I think we better drive to Lauderdale tomorrow or Thursday. Better use me while you can, man. Musashi arrives Friday. After that, we're aboard *No Más* and out of here."

I told him fine, then he needed to give me some privacy.

I had a couple of calls to make.

※

When I heard the outboard on Tomlinson's little inflatable clatter to life, I picked up the phone and dialed a two-one-two area code, plus a number which, as fewer than a hundred Americans and well-placed Israelis knew, actually rang at a secluded, nondescript but beautifully tended farm on the border of Virginia and West Virginia.

When a woman's voice answered, "Malabar Grain and Silo," I spoke a four-digit identification number and was immediately transferred to a computerized security system which, I knew, was searching its own memory banks, attempting to match a graph of my recently-recorded voice with the vocal prints of men and women who had sufficient security clearance to speak with an actual human being.

I did not have to wait long. From this fastidious place, this picture-perfect farm with its forest of grain silos (and a forest of complex trans-global listening systems, passive and invasive, housed therein) came a voice on a screechy, scratchy answering machine that told me, "Sorry, neighbor, you've reached Malabar Grain and Silo and we're probably uptown shopping. If you think you got the right place, leave your name and number and we'll catch you on the comeback!"

Which meant that the computer had recognized me as a person who had once had full security clearance but who was no longer operative, was no longer considered an asset, was, most likely, a potential liability but who might, just might, have a useful tidbit of information to offer.

Without hesitating, I spoke a second four-digit identification code and then, after a series of beeps, I said, "Ford, Marion D. Secondary listing: North, Marion D. I'm calling for Bernard Objartel Yager. My telephone number is—" and I gave it.

Four beeps later, the jolly farmer's voice told me, "Sorry, neighbor. You mustuh got the wrong number. Nobody here by that name. Have yourself a great day!"

I hung up the phone and began to futz around the lab, neatening this, straightening that. As always, I was annoyed by the high-tech game-playing and the Hollywood-style trappings that, to me, seemed an adolescent adjunct to a business I had once found as complex as it was dangerous.

Why couldn't they have a secretary like everyone else? Someone trained to screen calls? What was so compromising about a real, live human being who could decide to accept or refuse a telephone call?

But no . . . they reveled in theatrics and their own little venues of power . . . and every year it seemed to get sillier. More tricks, more complicated electronic gags that suggested to me that the intelligence-gathering community was becoming a parody of its own excesses, and so probably was neither as powerful nor effective as it had once been.

I kept reminding myself: *Ford, aren't you glad to be out of this business?*

I continued working in the lab, going over how I was going to ask Bernard Yager, a computer and electronics genius by all accounts, for his help in breaching the security of a housewife's desktop computer. To even make such a request was embarrassing.

It was Yager who had single-handedly unscrambled the Soviet/ Soviet nuclear sub code progression. It was Yager who had invaded and compromised computer communications between Managua and Havana during the Sandinista wars in Nicaragua.

His was not a name seen in the newspapers, nor would it ever be seen. Yet the man had been a legend in the business for more than a decade. By now, I suspected that his underlings looked upon him as some kind of wizened old electronics guru.

About fifteen minutes later, when my phone rang, I answered to hear, "Hey Doc, you old so-and-so! It's Bernie!"

I began by saying, "Bernie, is it safe to talk?"

"On my line? You're making a joke, right? Such a funny man with the jokes. The president, he should be so confident in his phone security. What? You think I'm such a *nebbish* that I've gotten old and rusty like a certain Viking-sized field hand? Why do you waste our time with such questions?"

"So I take it my side of the line is also fine."

"Marion, Marion, you are trying an old man's patience. Is my line okay? he asks. Is your line okay? he asks. We're having this conversation, you hear words coming from my lips, so of course the lines are okay. What else do you need to know already? Why don't you just come out and ask me, 'Bernie, my old friend, have you become old and senile and stupid?' Because that's what your questions say to me."

"Hey, that's not what I'm saying, Bernie."

"To me, that's exactly what you're saying. You're saying that you no longer have confidence in my expertise. This from the man whose ass I personally saved after he'd slept with a certain president's wife in Masagua. Name another person in the business who could have electronically lifted information from the poor husband's office and still had the good sense to telephone you in the bedroom of His Excellency's beautiful wife? So what did you have to spare? Five minutes? Ten minutes, tops. The man's elite guard hunting you like dogs, but you were warned in time. All thanks to the person you keep asking these offensive questions."

I was laughing. Everything he said was true. I said, "Well, I've got to risk offending you again."

When I told him what I needed, he feigned indignation. "Any teenage hack can do what you're asking me to do. Such a waste of time and talent!"

"It's what I need, Bernie. I don't think you ever met Bobby Richardson, but his wife is the lady in question."

"I've heard of Commander Richardson, so I don't need to meet him. He's a friend of yours, so he's a friend of mine. The man was part of the old guard. One of the rare good men. So what else do I need to know?"

"What you need to know is that Bobby and I went through some very heavy business together. You know the kind of stuff I'm talking about. I owe the man. He's been dead a long time, but I still owe the man. His girl is in trouble and so is his daughter. I'm going to do whatever I can to help out."

"Okay, okay, so maybe I owe you a favor or two myself. You ask, it'll be done. What you need to do is tell the daughter to switch on her mother's machine and modem. It's a PC or a Mac? Of course, someone like you wouldn't know. Doesn't matter. I'll have my equipment invade the poor little thing and install the software you'll need in a program called . . . I think I'll label the folder *Pilar*." He had a curiously high-pitched giggle. "Will you be able to remember that? If remembering is such a problem, I'll have everything on her screen changed to red, but the folder—the folder, I'll make green. Or maybe interesting colors. Just so you can find it."

"You're a bastard, Bernie Yager."

"A bastard I am not. And neither do I ever forget. When my poor sister, rest her soul, got herself in trouble in Boulder, you were the one, the only one, who went there and spoke with her and helped bring her home. Eve liked you, Doc, she really did. And she trusted you. You may have been the only person in her life that she truly trusted. I don't know why she went back to the streets, but she did. God rest her soul and the souls of all who loved her. Her going back, that I will never make sense of."

I said, "She was a good woman, Bernie. And thanks a lot for your help."

"There isn't something else you want to tell me, Doc?"

I said, "No . . . I don't think so."

Bernie Yager, the tough electronics guru, said, "The number, I need her mother's phone number. And her E-mail address. I need to be able to access the machine if I'm going to upload software. What, I've got to take your hand and lead you through this?"

10

The Calloway family home was in the Lauderdale suburb of Coral Ridge south of Oakland Park and north of Plantation. Probably one of the original gated communities on the Intracoastal Waterway, built back in the fifties when dolphin-finned Cadillacs and pink stucco defined the sunrise coast.

There were banyan vines and shadows on streets that never took the full heat of summer because of moss and filtered light. The brick gatehouse was unattended, but the neighborhood still had the solid look of corporate money, good benefits and upwardly mobile executives. Not old-time wealth, but high-salaried position players with plenty left over for pension plans and toys.

Tomlinson was taking it all in. "The people who first lived in these houses, I bet they voted for Eisenhower and bitched about Elvis back when they were built. Caddys, yeah. Can't you picture great big land yachts sitting in the driveways?"

We were in my Chevy pickup, windows down, driving through the shade of ficus trees. We'd crossed the saw-grass flats of Alligator Alley to I-595, then north on U.S. 1 past Freddy's Anchor Inn, tattoo parlors and Comfort Suites, then through the Kinney Tunnel into a gray corridor of furniture stores, Burger Kings, Porsche and Ferrari dealerships, Chinese restaurants.

Now we were looking at houses that were set back behind thick brick fences, the yards hedged with sea grape. Dominant colors were conch pink and Bermuda white. Not many Cadillacs in the driveways, though. Mostly sport utility vehicles in earth colors, but a few BMWs and Lexuses hitched up close to large ranch houses with red tile roofs showing through the trees.

"Can you smell it?" Tomlinson said. "The Atlantic Coast, man. It . . . smells different. Big ocean, big seas, lots of wind out there beyond the condos, even if you can't feel it."

I was cruising at maybe ten miles per hour and the truck cab was filtering odors.

I said, "Yeah, nice air. Not as dense." Meaning not as heavy as the air on Sanibel Island.

No matter where I've been in my life, I can get within ten miles of an ocean and feel it. Can sense the implied weight of the sea even if the horizon is blocked, fogged in, you name it. Thatch-roofed huts or trees or mountains or high rises, it didn't matter what stood between us. The convexity of sky is always different. Brighter? No, but there is a distinctive sheen to it, as if rarefied by lightning or chemical reaction: saltwater, oxygen, wind, isolation. I always, always know if the sea is near.

The Calloway house was several blocks from U.S. 1, just off Bayview at the corner of 8th Street and Middle River Drive, not far from Bayview Elementary and the Coral Ridge Yacht Club. Very solid-looking brick one-story painted key lime yellow with vines that trailed up the walls and framed the bay windows. Pie-shaped quarter-acre corner lot, old tropical vegetation, the weathervaned masts of sailboats showing above the roofs of neighboring homes.

A yachting community. Each house with its own dock out back.

I noticed a frayed rope hanging from an oak tree in the side lawn. Presumably it had once held a swing. I noticed the plywood remnants of a tree house in said oak and thought about Amanda with her tomboy attitude. Sometimes you can look at a house and read what's gone on there. This had once been a child's place; a family place. A little girl had once lived here with her mother and stepfather. Not now, though. The property had the sterile look of weekly yard maintenance and vacant bedrooms.

You take one look at such a place and you guess that someone's dream came unraveled here.

The front door of the house was cracked open, though, as if to let stale air escape.

Amanda's little car was in the drive.

※

"Jesus Christ, what happened to my mom's computer?" Amanda, wearing gold wire-rimmed glasses, sat at a desk in a study just off the master bedroom, her face illuminated by the monitor screen.

No T-shirt for her now. She was wearing pantyhose, a pale gray pleated cotton skirt, white blouse with pearl buttons and a navy blue blazer. The way she dressed, it not only changed the way she looked, it changed the way she handled herself. An athletic-looking redhead with some lanky size, maybe handsome but not pretty. Interesting face, with her mom's great cheekbones but her dad's tough-guy nose. Not a person to take lightly. She moved and spoke without hesitation, the modern businesswoman.

The backseat of her car, I'd noticed, was crammed with boxes and folders and pieces of some kind of plastic shelving, maybe something that had to do with dispensing medications. Just a guess. It looked as if she'd been making the rounds, calling on her clients, and had interrupted a busy day to meet us at her old house.

"What kind of friends do you have, Doc? A person who can do something like this to a stranger's computer . . . my God! He changed all this through the telephone modem?"

It was hard to tell if she was impressed or spooked. Bernie had re-colored each and every screen icon in rainbow shades. They appeared to drift randomly, not unlike pinballs, on a fluorescent wallpaper backdrop of pink flamingos in flight.

The exception was a folder labeled PILAR.

It sat in the center of the screen, many times larger than any other icon, and it flashed as methodically as a small-town caution light. One of his little jokes.

"What's *pilar* mean?"

"It's Spanish. It means, well . . . like a support or a column. Something that will hold up a building."

"But here he means like support for my computer program, right?"

"For the computer . . . sure. That kind of support. What else could he mean?"

"Is he some kind of drug freak or something? These colors, all the activity, just looking at the screen is giving me a headache."

"A drug user, you bet," Tomlinson said, nodding. He was looking over Amanda's shoulder, riveted. "This kind of genius, there almost has to be synthetics involved. Yes . . . yes, I'm sure of it. It's a professional guess, but still a guess . . . yeah, I believe this whole scene demonstrates certain signature effects that I associate with what may have been the bitchingest acid ever produced. The Hitchcock Estate, Dutchess County, New York, nineteen sixty-seven. Dr. Leary had a hand in that one, God bless him." He turned to me. "If this buddy of yours has a tab or two to spare, I'll pay top dollar. I know you don't approve, but I just got a nostalgia rush you wouldn't believe. All I want is enough so I can go back and revisit some old friends. Maybe talk to the dead, visit my own karma in the afterlife. Nothing fancy. You don't mind, why don't we take a second and jot his number down—"

Amanda said, "Hey, be quiet a minute."

Tomlinson said, "Huh?"

"Look at this. There's something wrong here."

I watched Tomlinson's face as he looked at the screen. Maybe from his reaction I'd be able to read what was going on.

She said, "I just tried to sign on to my mom's account, but I get this damn thing."

There was a message corralled by a blue border: "Invalid Password. Please try again."

"I thought you said that her password still worked. That you'd tried it."

"It worked fine last night when I came over to turn on the computer."

"Maybe her bill hasn't been paid and they've terminated her service."

"Nope, it's a credit card thing and the money's taken out of her account just like everything else. She's got plenty of money left for stuff like this."

"Try signing on again."

She did.

The response was the same: *Invalid password.*

"Someone's changed it," she said. "That's the only explanation. Someone had to. Which means it had to be my mom." Her voice gathered a little energy. "So that's good, right? It means that she's near a computer and she's still . . . that she's still okay."

Tomlinson was patting her shoulder, comforting her but also asking her to move. "Tell you what, let me dig into the folder that Doc's hipster friend sent. Maybe it's got the juice to find the password, recover the old files, the whole works." He glanced at me. "Your buddy said everything would be self-explanatory, right?"

I had my arms crossed; stood there trying to picture someone with a computer on a sailboat in Colombia. But yeah, why not? There were phone lines and notebook computers everywhere. I said, "I told him you'd done some of your own programming, that you knew all the basics. He said no problem then."

To kill time while Tomlinson worked, Amanda walked me through the house. The furniture was draped with white sheets. Her old bedroom was pink with flowers, neat as a museum. There were trophies on the shelves: tennis and softball. An athlete. One big window looked out onto the screened pool and the canal beyond.

"See all those Australian pines across the Intracoastal? That's Birch State Park. At night, when I was, like, a sophomore or something, I used to sneak out and paddle our canoe across. I'd have the beach all to myself. Not too far from here, you look across and you can't see anything but condos. Bahia Mar, where Frank and his little soulmate moved. Places like that, there's no skyline, just buildings. The people there, you got these old men the color of bagels, plus all the yachties and the beach bunnies."

Playing tour guide while Tomlinson worked.

I noticed that the closet door was wide and the boxes therein were open, scattered, as if someone had recently ransacked them. She replied to my quizzical expression: "I was looking for more photographs. While I was waiting for you guys to get here."

"Why? You already sent the ones of your mom and Merlot. That's all I wanted."

"I know, but I started wondering after you asked me. The pictures of me when I was a little girl? I thought I'd piled them all in the same box. Now I can't find the box. My mom must have put them somewhere, someplace she thought was safe."

"You can't find them."

"No, but it's okay. Mom probably hid them. She knows how sensitive I am about how . . . about, you know. How my eyes looked."

Like she was kidding, Amanda said, "Mom was probably worried I might burn the whole bunch."

✳

It took Tomlinson slightly less than three hours to nail the password and recover the lost correspondence between Gail and her E-mail friends. Three intense nonstop hours, during which he shouted orders and updates to us from the study:

"Beer! Bring me beer! My fluids have been sapped. I need to rehydrate!"

"This fucking computer can kiss my ass on the county fucking square! Killing's too good for it! Burning this noxious bitch would be a kindness. Where'd your mom GET this piece of junk?"

"Amanda, dear? *Ahum-m-m.* Oh-h-h-h-h Aman-N-N-N-da? Would you mind very much if I, uh, have a smoke in your mom's study? Now . . . before you even answer, I know what you're thinking but you're wrong: It's not tobacco, so you'll hardly even notice the smell."

She said yeah, sure, he could smoke a joint.

That surprised me.

Dressed in her power clothes, she was still coming across as a much different person than she'd been at Dinkin's Bay Marina. We were the guests here and she was comfortable with being in charge. Wasn't self-conscious, not at all reluctant to show little bits and pieces of herself.

Every now and then, she'd flip open her cell phone like it was some kind of Star Trek communicator. I'd listened to her say, "Larry . . . Larry, I *realize* the woman's a pain in the ass and I *realize* what she's asking is unfair. But it's her hospital and it's a major account and I want you to do whatever it takes to make her happy. . . ." I listened to her say, "Kath? Amanda. Look, girlfriend, about dinner tonight . . . I'm up to my ass in work and I don't think I'm going to be able to get away." She gave me a sly glance before she added, "Yeah, I've got company, but they're a couple of gorgeous hunks, so it's okay."

Once her cell phone rang and I listened to her say, "Steve, I'm going to make this short and sweet. I don't want you calling anymore. I don't want you leaving any more messages. I'm sorry, but I don't feel that way about you and there's nothing you can do about it. No . . . no more of your idiotic lines from *Casablanca*. We never crossed the Broward County line, so don't even fucking talk to me about Paris."

After that, she stomped off toward the study and came out a few minutes later, exhaling smoke.

Behind her, I heard Tomlinson say, "Pretty good shit, huh?"

I said, "Dope fiends, I'm surrounded by dope fiends. Jesus." And I watched her smile at me.

She had removed her blazer. Through the white blouse I could see that she wore a gauzy-half bra. It showed her washboard body like a relief map. I pretended that I didn't notice. It was an old buddy's daughter, for Christ sake. Which was probably why she was going out of her way to show me that she was now an adult woman making adult decisions.

Mostly we sat around and waited.

I used her cell phone to make a couple of calls. She gave me the number and the name and I reached Deputy Melissa Grendle at the general investigations desk, Broward County Sheriff's Department. Amanda had already told Grendle about the money that had been withdrawn from her mother's accounts, but I decided to give it a try myself. Grendle was still uninterested, unimpressed. Polite indifference is a common buffer mechanism and she used it.

I hung up disappointed, but not surprised. Law enforcement may be the most demanding yet thankless job in America. Cops are underpaid, overworked and held up to public inspection and public ridicule to a degree that no other profession would tolerate. Which may be why the demarcation between outstanding cop and incompetent cop is becoming increasingly wide. The good ones, the really good ones, do it because they love it and they are intelligent enough to accept the job's drawbacks philosophically. The bad ones do it because it answers some tough-guy film fiction they have chosen to portray, and they are too stupid or lazy to actually do it well.

Officer Grendle was one of the lazy ones. Perhaps one of the stupid ones, too, although I didn't speak with her long enough to pass judgment.

When I clicked off, Amanda gave me a look like: See? I told you.

FBI agent Mitchell Wilson, however, was neither stupid nor lazy. "It's like I told the daughter, Mr. Ford, we've got a copy of a written report, the local sheriff's department, saying the woman stated that she planned to leave the country willingly. That's not kidnapping, no matter what the daughter thinks. Now, okay, this other business, the money, all those withdrawals, yeah, I agree, it has an odor to it. Maybe it stinks. I want you to keep me informed about it because you sound like a reasonable guy and, like I said, what's going on has an odor. A little bit of a smell; something may not be right. But we don't know enough yet to warrant an investigation. Understand what I'm saying?"

I understood.

The last call I made was to Frank Calloway's Lauderdale office where the hardworking Betty Marsh confirmed that Mr. Calloway hoped to meet with me tomorrow afternoon in Boca Grande, but that, yes, he would call me personally to confirm.

"Thursday," she said, as if double-checking an appointment book. "In the late afternoon. He said something about you coming by boat?"

I said, "Yep. But have him call me early, just in case the weather's bad and I decide to drive."

I gave her Amanda's cell phone number as well as my home number.

A couple of minutes later, I heard an electronic voice say: "*Welcome. You've got mail!*" And then Tomlinson was calling us: "Hey! Looky, looky, looky at all the letters this lady got. Your mother, I'm talking about. Lots of letters. They were all deleted, but I got 'em back."

Shouting because he'd cracked the code.

✳

There were a couple of hundred letters, counting the junk mail ads for porno shows and moneymaking schemes. Maybe three hundred letters. A bunch.

I said to Tomlinson, "So this is the great educational network you've been telling me about. Finally, I get to see what I've been missing."

The cursor was highlighting one of the letters. It was titled *Betty Bell and Her Twin Liberty Bells. Free Sex Show!*

"You see, Amanda?" Tomlinson said. "You see how cynical he can be? At least admit that this one's patriotic. Man . . . we've got a lot of reading to do, huh? Your mom had plenty of spare time on her hands."

A middle-aged divorced woman, yeah, with enough money. Nothing to do but sit at the computer.

We started going through the letters at random, concentrating on the ones written by people whose screen names reappeared over and over. *Merl* was one of the two most common screen names. The other was *Darkrume*. There were dozens of letters from each and dozens of replies.

"Merl," Tomlinson reasoned. "Pretty safe bet that's Jackie Merlot. One of those friendly sounding screen names. Harmless. Trying hard to sound harmless anyway. The other one . . . what? Someone who likes fantasy novels? *Darkrume* . . ."

Yeah, *Merl* was Jackie Merlot. According to the status bar, the first E-mail that Gail received from him was dated just less than a year before. The three of us scanned the first couple of letters. He wrote long, windy sentences. They seemed stuffy-formal. Had a pseudo-intellectual tone that masked a false sincerity impossible to miss.

Well, not impossible. The lady had apparently been fooled. . . .

"Dear Gail, It has been a long time since we talked. I heard it thru the executive grapevine that you and that salesman you married, Frank something, are divorced. So here I am to say that he has to be a very un-

stable person to let go of someone as beautiful as you. You may remember from the past that I loved doing volunteer social work. I love
helping people. I want you to know that I am volunteering to help you
any way that I can. My business is so big now and demands so much
time but I don't care. It is an international company and I am C-E-O and
C-F-O. I cannot live in the United States because it would be an unwise
move due to tax obligations. It does not matter. Fifteen years ago I was
there for you and I am still your loyal servant if you require assistance."

"My God," Amanda said. "I can't believe she even bothered writing the guy back. What a jerk. I've got all kinds of E-mail friends but
none that illiterate. This noble-knight-on-a-steed stuff tells you how
lonely she really was. The fact that she would write him back, I mean."

The next letter was dated two days later. Yeah, Gail had replied, so
Merlot repeated his offer to help. He wrote: "I would love to be the
shoulder you need to rest your head on. I am a man of honour. You
never judged me by the way I looked but how I looked in my heart.
These small people who are losers and quick to judge make me sick.
That is because you are smart enough to see me for the real person I am.
Anytime you need my shoulder, write me. I'm thinking about renting a
place in Lauderdale for a few months to take care of some business. . . ."

She said, "It was like he could sniff the wind and smell how lonely
she was. Thinking about renting a place in Lauderdale, my ass. He was
tracking her."

"It does indeed seem that way."

"He sounds like he dropped out of school in the tenth grade."

"Let's skip ahead twenty-five or thirty letters just to see where it
takes us."

I was in the chair now and I used the mouse to scan down. Most of
the letters from *Merl* were labeled NO SUBJECT. But there was one from
Darkrume that was labeled HOW YOU MAKE ME FEEL, and that's the file
I opened.

Amanda was apparently a faster reader than I. I was only a couple
of sentences into the letter when she grasped my shoulder and said,
"Oh . . . God. I'm not up for this."

She had a strong grip; I could feel her nails digging in.

The Mangrove Coast
157

She said, "This is just . . . just sick. I can't read this crap. Anybody who'd write that kind of trash to my mom is . . . and I thought Jackie Merlot was an asshole." Then she turned quickly and left the room.

I returned my attention to the letter as Tomlinson said, "Know what? I don't blame her."

The letter wasn't just sexual, it was detailed, graphic, aggressive. It combined the language that I assume is in porno novels with terms of endearment that I associate with people who feel genuine affection for one another. Gail was "My dearest darling." She was "My soul mate, the kindest, funniest, sexiest woman of all time." She was the woman who "writes like an angel and thinks like a whore."

The first several paragraphs of *Darkrume*'s letter described in detail what he wanted to do to her, what he wanted to use on her body and inside her body to help bring her to the brink of "ecstasy." The second part of the letter described what *Darkrume* wanted Gail to do to him.

At least, I assumed that *Darkrume* was a him. From the way he described himself, there was nothing left to the imagination and little doubt. The letter was picturesque, playful, and left me with the impression that this was a game that he and Gail enjoyed playing and it wasn't the first time.

I was struck by a line in the letter: "When we finally do meet, I want to photograph you. Maybe find a secluded beach near a harbour I know. On the Pacific, of course. A woman as beautiful as you deserves to be photographed by an artist. I am an artist. . . ."

Tomlinson was apparently reading the same passage, because he said, "Ah-h-h, a photographer."

The screen name, yeah. Darkroom. That explained it.

Another line from the letter that caught my eye: "I love the videos you have sent. I watch them alone almost every night. But I can't get past the dream of touching you in person. My God, you are truly gorgeous!"

I thought about it for a moment before I said, "Is he making this up? Or did she really send him videos?"

"I . . . I think she really did send this dude videos. A very heavy gig going on here, man. And she hadn't even met the guy. Unusual."

"But why? This is a nice woman. An intelligent woman."

Tomlinson echoed what I was already thinking: "Her husband tells her she's fat, rotten in bed and then he shacks up with a much younger woman. Isn't that the way Amanda explained it? So she needs reassurance and she needs it quick 'cause she's at about rock bottom. Maybe headed for a nervous breakdown. Yeah, she is a nice lady and she's smart. Smart enough to know that it's dangerous these days to get out there on the dating scene. Plus, she doesn't know any men. So she lets herself get involved in a hot cyberscrew. You know, an on-line affair. No muss, no fuss. No blood tests required, no need to hose down the decks afterward. Oral sex. *Real* oral sex, because it's nothing but words. A mind-fuck pure and simple. That much makes sense."

"Does it?" I said. The tone I used told Tomlinson that I thought it was idiotic.

He was unruffled as always. "It's like weed, man. Don't knock it unless you've tried it. Right now, I've got three cyber affairs going. All with happily married ladies. Or so they say. Honestly? I think one of them's a guy. You never know on-line. Hell, you can say you're anything, how you gonna check? Him I only write out of a sense of fair play. Nothing against the flute-tooters—they've got to be born that way, right?—but I just don't see the charm."

"But why? Why would you do something like that?"

"Because they're lonely, man. And I understand what it's like to be lonely. You know me, I'll do anything to help another human being to get over the hump. It can be one painful bitch of a life, so why not co-operate when someone asks. Hey, don't look at me like that"—he was smiling—"I can't whack off and type at the same time. I've tried it, it just doesn't work. So it's more like a . . . a public health service I'm of-fering. If the ladies want to type sexy notes back and forth with a man they've never met, who's it hurt? These two women, my cyber mis-tresses, they got kids and professions and happy husbands. But we screw like crazy through E-mail and instant messages."

"You don't even have a telephone on your boat."

"I plug the modem into the connecting block outside the gift shop. You didn't wonder why I was spending so much time at the marina? A couple of nights ago, I had sex with one of my cyber girls while we were hidden by a curtain in a crowded restaurant. No panties and she pulled her dress right up over her head. Her idea, man, not mine, although I loved it. She says that the things we do, I've saved her marriage."

I couldn't believe what I was hearing. "And it's all imaginary. You've never really met her."

"Don't even know her name. Not for sure, anyway. She calls herself *Phaedra*. And yeah, she definitely has a couple of kids and her husband's a big successful honcho. That much I'd bet on. We met in a chat room and we've been having sex for two, maybe three months. An online affair, it always starts with little hints about horniness, then escalates pretty fast. The first few letters, I'm talking about. We follow *Darkrume*'s letters back, I'd bet that's what we'd find. Little hints about this and that, just joking around, but mostly writing about what nice, thoughtful, honorable people they are, before one night they decide to let it happen. Sending videos, though, that's above and beyond the call of loneliness."

I was looking at *Darkrume*'s words on the screen—something else troubled me about the letter. It wasn't the content. It was a word or a term or phrase . . . something that was out of place. What?

Tomlinson said, "I know why you're shaking your head. It's because none of this makes sense to you. The first time we met, Doc, I took one look at your face and I thought: This man is living a chronological nightmare. That face of yours, I've seen it in photos by Matthew Brady. John Ford's films, same lost expression. It's like the karmic mailman stuck you in the wrong slot."

I said, "What?"

Tomlinson said, "You, Doctor Ford, were not made for these times. That's all I'm saying. Know who's got exactly the same problem? Your uncle. Yeah, Tucker Gatrell. Both you guys got sent to Earth a couple of generations too late."

Tomlinson and Tuck: Each assumed he was an expert on the other.

He said, "This whole Internet business has got to be like fingernails on a blackboard to you. Or like teenagers arguing."

After two joints and three hours looking at a computer screen, this is what I had a right to expect from Tomlinson.

Time to change the subject.

I said, "What I want to do is read all these letters in order. All of

Darkrume's first. He and Gail had this weird relationship going and I don't like the business about her sending him videos. We need to check around the house, see if she really does own a camera."

"She does. I was snooping in one of the closets while I was waiting for you to get out of the head. She's got a video camera on a tripod. Perfect for taking self-portraits. No cassette in it, though. I checked that, too."

"Then I don't like it. Some guy wins her trust, she sends him self-made videos and he uses them to blackmail her. I can see that happening. How long were they E-mailing each other?"

Tomlinson reached over my shoulder and took the mouse. He clicked it, clicked again. "*Darkrume* started writing her about two weeks before Merlot did. The letter we just read was sent in late August, so they'd had a couple of months together. Plenty of time to get a hot and heavy cybersex deal going. It's scary how easy and fast you can win someone's trust if you're writing every day."

I started to tell Tomlinson that something about the letters still troubled me. Was it a word? Yeah, maybe . . . maybe a word. So what I wanted to do was spend the next few hours and read each and every letter. Use the laser printer beside the computer to get them all on paper. That way, maybe put everything in perspective and figure out the detail, the nagging little detail, that continued to bother me. One by one, read *Darkrume*'s letter, read Gail's reply. Read Merlot's letter, read Gail's reply. Go back and forth. Keep it orderly.

I said, "We've both seen her photograph. A woman this classy, it's tough to imagine her writing graphic sex scenes to some stranger."

"Not a stranger, he was her E-mail lover. There's a big difference. This is America, man. For the last forty years, we've learned that our dreams can come true on a television screen. A TV screen is exactly what we're looking at now. We trust this screen, man, it's part of our family. What better place to find romance? You don't believe she'd do it? Let's check the lady's letters and see."

We checked and, yes, she'd replied to *Darkrume*. Replied with enthusiasm, too. *Ooohhh*, it was okay to do that and that and that to her, but what she really wanted was for him to do this and this and this. . . .

The description went on for many paragraphs.

After reading the letter, Tomlinson said, "Far out! Now I can understand why your buddy was in love with this lady. Match the photo I saw with these words, and this is one of the great bedroom women I've ever had the honor to be associated with."

Feeling an irrational animus, I flipped his hand away from the mouse and closed the file. He gave me a look like, Whoa, buddy, lighten up!

But enough. I'd read enough.

I said, "Just for the hell of it, let's see what Merlot was writing at the same time. These letters are listed chronologically, right?"

I opened another file and surprise, surprise. Merlot was also concerned about Gail's involvement with her Internet lover. A couple of lines written during the same week in August: "My beautiful friend. When I left your house tonight I was so worried about you I drove straightaway to the beach. Even with all my investors hounding me for details, all I could think about was you and the mistake you might be making in trusting *Darkrume* too much. . . ."

And: ". . . you don't know this person. If he cares so much for you, why does he refuse to write to me, your closest friend?"

And: ". . . I promise you this. If he ever hurts you, I will be the friend there to help you. Why? Because you see me the way I am. Not the way I look. I will always be your servant because of that."

I removed my glasses and cleaned them on the sleeve of my blue chambray shirt. I was about to comment on the obvious way that Merlot had manipulated her. By telling her over and over why he admired her, he was giving her subliminal instructions about how she should behave toward him. No, he wasn't physically attractive, but that wasn't important. It didn't matter to her. She thought he was beautiful. Right? Right? *Right?*

Told repeatedly, the time would come when Gail would feel obligated to behave accordingly. And maybe she was actually suggestible enough to believe it. It was a concept that Tomlinson would quickly grasp. But as I turned to speak, I was interrupted by a fairy-dust sound coming from the computer, a riff of bells.

Tomlinson whistled and said, "An instant message for the lady in question, man. How weird!"

I said, "What?'

"An instant message. Gail just received an instant message."

A bordered rectangle within a bordered rectangle, typed words inside, had appeared on the screen.

"We're in direct contact, man. Just him and us. See the screen? It's from *Darkrume*."

Tomlinson's voice dropped a little, as if he didn't want anyone to hear. "He's out there, man. His computer, he must have it locked onto Gail's screen name. He knows we're here. He knows where we are."

The message read: *Is it you?*

After a few more seconds, the screen read: *I'm waiting.*

11

I called Amanda back into the room. She needed to be part of this.

She was staring at the screen, looking at the name—*Darkrume*—when I asked, "What do you think we ought to do?"

"Tell him to kiss off. Never write again or we'll notify the AOL people. The jerk."

I told her, "You don't see this as an opportunity? I think you ought to write the guy, find out whatever you can about your mom. Maybe he knows where she is. Maybe he knows what happened to the money. Any information you can get, we'll take it."

I was standing, trying to make Amanda sit in the chair so she could use the keyboard. She wasn't eager. She had her hands up, palms out—a "screw this" pose—as she said, "You think I'm going to be nice to this guy after the trash he wrote my mom? All that really sick stuff. No thanks. No way. Not me."

The way she said it, there was a frustrating, petulant quality in her voice that I found irritating. The last time I'd heard that same infuriating tone was years ago in the jungles of Cambodia. No doubt that she was her father's daughter.

"Just throw away a chance to get information? You don't have to be nice. Get a conversation going and let's see how we can use him.

Pump him for whatever he might know. You think he wrote some sick, ugly stuff? Fine. Get even by tricking him. He thinks he's writing to your mom. That's what we want him to think."

"If it's so important, why don't you do it?"

"Because you're her daughter. And you're a woman. The way you write is way more likely to resemble your mom's sentence patterns. These two exchanged letters for months. Thousands of words. Even if they never met, they know each other intimately. He's not going to be easy to fool."

She turned away from me, arms folded. I felt myself coloring, getting angry. "Goddamn it! Your mother was a sexual person—what a hell of a shock that must be to someone as high minded as you. Gee, she had men friends. They talked dirty to each other. She probably looked forward to it. She probably thought it was fun. Maybe she even had orgasms. Isn't that just awful!"

"Knock it off, Doc! That's not fair."

"Yes, it is fair. It's not only fair, it's the truth. You want me to help find her? Then you'd better sit your butt down in that chair and cooperate."

She glared at me. She turned to look at Tomlinson, as if he might offer her refuge. To his credit, he slowly shook his head. Nope. He couldn't help. It was only then that she put her hands on her hips, made a fluttering noise of contempt through her lips, plopped down in front of the screen and placed her long fingers on the keyboard.

Gail73679: How've you been?
Darkrume: Great as always. :~} But I don't think this is Gail. This really the whore queen?

Amanda repositioned herself in the chair as she whispered, "Asshole. What a creep."

I patted her shoulder as I watched the screen. Beneath my hand, I felt her take a deep breath.

Gail73679: It's me all right. And I'm so horny you wouldn't believe.

There was a pause. A very long pause. Was he thinking about something? Maybe.

Darkrume: Is it really you? I missed you. Missed you a lot. Where you been? : ~ ?

Gail73679: Been really busy.

Darkrume: Sure but where you been busy?

I touched my hand to her wrist. Made her take a few seconds before replying. "What do those little symbols mean? The little things he adds after sentences?"

"Cyber faces. Look at them kind of sideways, you'll see facial expressions. It's what people use on-line to show emotion. You know, happy, sad, joking. Like that."

My recurring question: *Adults do this?* I said to her, "Keep playing him along. If he and your mom are still close, he knows where she went. No matter what he says. Find out."

Gail73679: I thought I told you about the trip I was taking. Come on, my love. You forget already?

Darkrume: You told me where you were going?

Gail73679: Of course I told you where I was going. If you cared about me, you'd remember. God, all I can think about is getting dirty together.

Darkrume: <--------- Remembering now. You went on a sailboat trip someplace. With Merl who wrote me those times. Merl who told you to stay away from me. What a jerk. : = (Was it Colombia?

Gail73679: You know it was Colombia. Or maybe you don't. Maybe you don't care enough to remember. I told you the city and where I was going to be staying. Remember the name of the marina?

Darkrume: Maybe. Did you screw Merl?

Gail73679: No way. Are you kidding? He would've crushed me. You're the only man I'm thinking about now.

Darkrume: Crushed you? The E-mail Merl who hated me because he was jealous, your neighbor in Florida. He fat?

Gail73679: Yes, crushed me because he's so fat. Fat and disgusting.

Darkrume: <-------- Laughing. Never liked him. He wrote me those idiotic E-mails, stay away from Gail. Jealous fat man.

Gail73679: Yes, he's terrible. Huge.

Darkrume: Know what's on my mind all the time? Looking down and seeing your eyes. You on your knees looking up at me. >:~{o} The way your lips felt on me when we finally met. God, you are even prettier than I thought you would be.

Beneath my hand, the pace of her breathing had increased. She said, "I can't do this, Doc. I really can't do this."

"Those little arrows at the beginning of a sentence. What do they mean?"

"It's like a present tense thing. The arrow means he's doing it at the time. Laughing, remembering, whatever. With this guy, you can probably add whacking off."

"I'm becoming a little uncomfortable with his approach."

"He's awful. And those little cyber faces. He's disgusting."

"Oh yeah, he's that." I was still patting her back. "Know what Amanda? You're right. I was a dope to get you involved in this, way off base. Hell with it. Sign off. Or . . . whatever it is you do. This guy really is sickening."

"I'm sorry, but . . . this is just too much. Pretending I'm my mom and him writing that stuff."

"I agree. It's awful. We're all better than this. I had no idea."

"But I didn't get any information for you."

"That's okay. Yeah, maybe he knows something. But the key is Merlot. We'll deal with it. You don't need to put up with this kind of garbage. Forget it."

She was still breathing heavily, but also thinking about it. "Look . . . I'm okay now. Let me just try one more thing."

"Nope. Drop the whole act. I feel bad enough as it is."

"What you're forgetting is I can make my own decision. I don't need you to tell me what to do. I'm an adult. I may not act like it sometimes, but I really am a pretty solid person."

Her fingers began to move again on the keyboard.

Gail73679: I wish I was looking up at you right now. From my knees. Can just imagine the way you'd be. Call me on the telephone, sweetheart. Call me right now. I want to finish up hearing your voice. We'll both have a wonderful time.

I patted her shoulder. It was a nice finesse. No one but Gail would risk asking him to call. Very convincing and completely safe.

Darkrume: What you mean, call? Just tried to call you. Thought I'd give you a little surprise. Recording said the line was disconnected. :=(
Gail73679: Damn! I guess the phone company only connected one of my lines. Because of the trip I was on. The dopes. Then let me call you, love. Give me your number so I don't have to look it up.

As she typed she said, "We get his number, we'll find out who he is." There was that fairy dust noise again.

Darkrume: Maybe I'll call later. Know what I'm thinking about right now? Remember the way we both got off the best?
Gail73679: You always got me off. I hope I always got you off.
Darkrume: No, this way was special. We were all naked. We were in a hot tub. We were drinking good wine and all three of us had a bottle of baby oil. Rubbing it on each other. I watched you rub the oil all over her body. It was you and me and what's her name?
Gail73679: Umm-m-m. Sounds wonderful. Tell me her name. I remember her name, but do you? I think I'm in love.
Darkrume: Yes. I remember her name. It was the three of us. You and me and . . . If you remember, say the name. >:+{o}
Gail73679: You say the name. I'm too hot to think.
Darkrume: Okay. Okay. It was you and me and . . . she had these weird eyes you told me. Not like yours. Different. Crossed eyes. Her name was Amanda. You and me plus your ugly daughter.

The chair went tumbling backward when Amanda jumped to her feet. "The son-of-a-bitch. He set me up!"

My hands were shaking, but I had my arms out and around her now.

Behind me, I could hear Tomlinson making a strange whoofing noise. Was he groaning or fighting back nausea?

"Let it go," I told her. "Let it go."

"My mom wouldn't have done that! My mom would never have done that! I don't care what he says! You bastard!" She was yelling and now she smacked the screen with her open hand. "You filthy-minded creep!"

I pressed Amanda into Tomlinson's arms as I took her spot in front of the computer and began to type a reply.

Gail73679: The trick's on you. This isn't Gail.

I could hear Amanda crying, still furious, as I waited for the fairy dust sound.

Darkrume: I know that!) : =)
Gail73679: Why so sure?
Darkrume: Wouldn't you like to know. You're Amanda. The daughter.
Gail73679: Amanda's not here.
Darkrume: You're lying. Either Amanda or some computer nerd friends. Someone to figure Momma's password. Not smart enough to do it alone.
Gail73679: You changed her password?
Darkrume: Just in case. Someone has to protect our privacy.
Gail73679: Pretending to know Gail, pretending to know Amanda, too. You've never met either of them.
Darkrume: <- - - - - - - - - Smile smile smile! Right. Never met you. The ugly daughter.

I was fighting it, trying hard not to get mad.

Gail73679: Why so mean?
Darkrume: Not mean. I'm happy. HAPPY! Want to do to you what I did to your mom.

What then followed was a graphic litany of his sexual triumphs with Gail. Real or imagined, it was impossible to judge. But very specific. Each outrage was listed as a conquest.

I waited patiently. Then:

The Mangrove Coast
169

Darkrume: You want the same things done to you?

Gail73679: Love it. Let's arrange a meeting. Tell me who you are.

Darkrume: Figure it out.

Gail73679: Okay.

Darkrume: I'm serious. Try.

Gail73679: We'll go through your letters, they'll tell us. Lots to choose from. Pick the best ones and take them to the police.

Darkrume: Be my guest. Better hurry!

From behind me, Tomlinson said, "What the hell does that mean?" He still had his arm around Amanda, reading along with me.

Gail73679: Why so evasive? You're a friend of Gail, we're friends of Gail. So what's the problem. What are you scared of?

Tomlinson said, "That's the wrong approach, man. This guy wants to be in charge, let him be in charge. Don't push him."

Darkrume: Why should I care about Gail? Already done everything I wanted to do to Gail. But I wouldn't mind meeting you. Got any videos?

"This is a sick, sick person."

"Yeah, man. He is truly and honestly twisted."

Gail73679: Got a great video. You'll love it. Tell me where to send it.

Darkrume: Find me, asshole.

"He's not going to cooperate."

"Nope, not a chance."

"Then I'm done playing his game."

"Don't blame you. Fire away."

Gail73679: Find you. Exactly what I plan to do.

Darkrume: Oh. You sound so dangerous.

Gail73679: I'm not.

Darkrume: Didn't think so!

Gail73679: No. Amateurs are dangerous.

Darkrume: <- - - - - - - - - - - - - Shivering with goose bumps. That means nothing. You expect me to be scared?

Gail73679: No, I expect you to be inept.

Darkrume: You jerk. I don't waste my time worrying about people like you.

Gail73679: I'm counting on that, too.

Darkrume: On what?

Gail73679: Your stupidity.

Darkrume: Fuck you!

Darkrume: Fuck you!

Gail73679: You illustrate my point.

Darkrume: FUCK YOU!

Tomlinson said, "You're getting to him."

"Apparently. Let's hope he'll hang on until he lets some information slip."

Darkrume: You don't have a goddamn clue who you're talking to.

Gail73679: Wrong. I know the type of person you are. So did Gail. That's why she stopped writing.

Darkrume: She never stopped, you idiot.

Gail73679: But she refused to meet with you and she told me why.

Darkrume: I'm the one refused to meet her, scum. That slut would have met me anytime anyplace.

"There," Tomlinson said, "we just learned something."

Gail73679: Because of the problem you have, she said she felt bad for you. I'm your friend, too. That's why I'm telling you this.

Darkrume: You got the problem, not me.

Gail73679: No, but I'm sympathetic. Impotence or homosexuality, nothing to be ashamed of.

In the long pause that followed, I suspect that he typed and erased a number of replies. I wish that I could have read them. Finally:

Darkrume: You think I'm stupid. You must really think I'm stupid.

Gail73679: Already told you: inept. Is your memory really that bad?

Darkrume: Time to show you how smart I am. How much smarter than a cross-eyed hag like you ever thought of being. You say I don't know you. You're so wrong about that it makes me laugh. <-------- laughing right now. Remember the letters you planned on reading? Read them now. Bitch!

The Instant Message screen was suddenly filled with a series of strange figures.

Behind me I heard Tomlinson say, "What the hell . . . Hey . . . HEY!" He lunged over my shoulder, began to click the mouse frantically, but our cursor was now frozen.

"He's pumping in some kind of . . . he's uploading a file into our system. Look at that crap . . . it's like taken complete control, shooting its way right in here. . . ." Tomlinson slapped the desk with his hand. "Shit! Now he's taken over the whole computer."

The screen continued to pulse with line after line of figures:

```
DARKRUME:  |\`````¯\/¯¯¯/|¯¯¯¯¯¯¯¯¯¯¯¯¯¯¯¯¯¯¯¯¯¯¯¯¯¯¯¯¯¯¯1
DARKRUME:  | |::·.. ·.|\___| |_____·_____|
DARKRUME:  \|::·.· ¯¯1 ʹ|/ /¯¯¯/| |::·.·
DARKRUME:  | ·.·. |¯¯1_,|/____/|¯¯¯1 ·.·|::·.
DARKRUME:  |\_____\-Po0|\___\|___|___|\___\|____|
DARKRUME:  | |     |    | |     |      | |
DARKRUME:  \|_____| ʹ\|____,____|___|\|_____,|
DARKRUME:  «-•¤[ Fate X3 By MaGuS & pyre ]¤•-»2

DARKRUME:  |\`````¯\/¯¯¯/|¯¯¯¯¯¯¯¯¯¯¯¯¯¯¯¯¯¯¯¯¯¯¯¯¯¯¯¯¯¯¯1
DARKRUME:  | |::·.. ·.|\___| |_____·_____|
DARKRUME:  \|::·.· ¯¯1 ʹ|/ /¯¯¯/|  |::·.·
DARKRUME:  | ·.·. |¯1_,|/____/|¯¯1 ·.·|::·. ʹ
DARKRUME:  |::·.· |__| ʹ/¯¯¯/|::·.· |::·.· |::·.· ʹ|
DARKRUME:  | |     |    | |      |      | |
DARKRUME:  \|_____| ʹ\|____,____|___|\|_____,|
```

Randy Wayne White

172

Just before the screen froze, the last instant message from *Dark-rume* read:

You lose! <: +))

✳

"I appreciate the fact, man, that you're trying to concentrate. Trying to pull off one of those total-recall deals. But do you really have to drive so slow?"

We were midway across Alligator Alley, the Everglades holding the horizon in all directions. Saw grass, globes of cypress shadow, gators baking mud gray on canal banks, black vultures cauldroning.

I'd asked Tomlinson to give me some silent time. Let me think about the few letters we'd had time to read.

"I suppose that means no radio, too."

He'd been switching back and forth between WAXY 106 and ZADA 94. Miami and Lauderdale, all the old hard-rock classics.

"The radio's fine. The radio I don't have to think about."

"Yeah, well . . . the radio doesn't make you think 'cause you weren't the one who dated Janis Joplin. But don't get me started on THAT weird episode." He was tinkering with the dials. "Hey . . . you know, it wouldn't kill you to have a tape player installed in this truck. Maybe a set of earphones for your noise-loving buddies."

I just nodded.

What was it about the few letters I'd read and my exchange with *Darkrume* that I found so troubling?

Something. Couldn't manage to nail it down. Perhaps it was tone or implication; a word or a phrase that nagged at me. But if it was important, really important, why couldn't I dredge it up out of the narrowest processing conduits of my brain?

I kept fumbling with it, going over and over what details I could remember. Not that there was any alternative. Whatever data *Darkrume* had uploaded into Gail's computer had destroyed or garbled the entire program system.

A call into Bernie Yager had confirmed it. "So you sit there, don't switch off the machine, and let someone invade you? Doc, the memory bits that were destroyed were in HER computer, you didn't even have to be on-line at that point. Now you expect me to help? Believe me, if there was anything left to save, I'd do it. But the virus you just described, what's left after something like that?"

Nothing, apparently.

"The piranha programs, I've heard you can buy them from the heavy-duty hackers," Tomlinson told me. "I've come across cyber punks who pretended to have them. Same kind of weird crap shoots across your screen. But this was the first time I ever saw anyone actually do it."

Darkrume had indeed done it. All trace of Gail's correspondence was now gone.

So I'd spent my driving time trying to visualize the letters I'd read. Not easy because my brain kept slipping into a replay of the exchange with *Darkrume—It was your ugly daughter!*—and I became furious all over again.

Now Tomlinson said, "Maybe if you speed up to like seventy, it'll bounce something loose in your noggin. Can't hurt and might help."

"Know what, Tomlinson? That was one of the cruelest things I've ever witnessed. What that guy did to Amanda. Gail Richardson must have extraordinarily bad judgment to get hooked up with someone like that. And to send him videos?"

"We've been through all this. Why keep going over it? Women in that situation, especially the nice ones, they're just too damn vulnerable. Hey—you want me to drive? We can pull over, take a whiz and let me get behind the wheel."

Tomlinson was a tailgaiter, a lane-weaver, a terrible driver.

"Nope."

"I wouldn't mind getting to Dinkin's Bay before sunset, man. Brewskies on the dock with the guides. Maybe order in some appetizers. Chicken wings, they're sounding tasty."

"I'll go faster."

"Man, I wish I had a bottle of beer for every car that's passed us this trip. Sixty-five, man, that's Winnebago speed. Zoom zoom zoom the cars just crackin' past and us tooling along like two catheter cadets in a Caddy."

He chuckled. The alliteration was unintentional and pleased him.

I started to remind Tomlinson that he'd promised me at least twenty minutes of silence, but I stopped in mid-sentence.

I said softly, "Straightaways."

"Yeah, man, you go slow, no matter what. Dozens passed us."

I changed the inflection. "Straight away. Straight *away*."

"Uh-huh, which is embarrassing 'cause a couple of those cars were from Ohio, Indiana, the neck-bender places. No offense."

"In Merlot's letter to Gail, what did he write? 'I was so upset that when I left your house, I drove straight away to the beach.' Something like that. You remember that?"

"Yeah, of course."

"That's more British than American. 'Straight away,' used like that. Or a phrase you might hear in the British colonies. Hong Kong, maybe Kuala Lumpur."

"Sure, it jumped right out at me, man. But then I'm a scholar. Colonial English—Merlot's sentences had that kind of weird syntax. And honor, the way he spelled things. He spelled it H-O-N-O-U-R like the Brits do."

Was it true? I couldn't remember.

I said, "He used British spelling as well? You're sure?"

"Positive. There was this line where he said that the first thing he wanted to do was take her to the beach, some secluded harbour—he spelled it O-U-R—" Tomlinson stopped talking and looked at me, a new awareness in his expression.

I finished his sentence for him: "He spelled harbor H-A-R-B-O-U-R. But Merlot didn't write that."

"He . . . shit! You're right. It was *Darkrume,* that's what he wrote to her."

"Exactly. *Darkrume.* The same British usage, the same spelling."

"You're saying . . . I'll be damned. Okay, okay, this is really fucking with my composure, man. You're telling me that *Darkrume* and Merlot, they're the same person."

I was waving my hand at him, telling him to be quiet. "Give me some time, let me think about this a little bit." After a couple of minutes I said, "Yeah. Two different screen names, but the same person. Can you have two different names on the Internet?"

"Absolutely. And the dude could have been anywhere, Colombia, Fumback, Egypt, you name it, and sign on with either name."

"What do you think the chances are of two people in different parts of the country, two American men who don't even know each other, affecting the same limey style?"

"Zero. Almost zero anyway."

"Then that's what happened. *Darkrume* said he's the one who refused to meet her. That's what kept nagging at me. He was furious by the time he said it, which is why it had the ring of truth. But why would an on-line hustler refuse to meet with the woman he's hustling? He's seen her videos, he knows she's beautiful. You're more familiar with this business than I am, but my impression of this on-line romance stuff is that it attracts the lonely, the desperate and the predatory. Does that seem accurate?"

"Hey now, man, don't forget I've got a couple of cyber mistresses myself."

As much as I would have liked to, Tomlinson's oddities were not easy to forget.

I said, "But generally speaking. Give me one other reason why *Darkrume* would have refused to meet with Gail. She expected to have sex, right? That's a hustler's whole objective, yet he chose not to. Why? Because if they met, Gail would know he wasn't some handsome photographer from California. He was her fat friend, just down the street."

He was nodding. "Somehow I felt it all along but didn't know why. Merlot invented *Darkrume*. He orchestrated the whole thing, which is some serious sick shit, man. Very serious."

I said, "He plays good cop, bad cop. He sets her up, has her send the videos to some mail-forwarding service with a P.O. box. Maybe in Florida but probably another state. Maybe sends her pictures of some good-looking guy through the same service and says it's him, *Darkrume*, this sexy professional photographer. Then he springs the trap, blackmail, and Merlot is right there saying I told you not to trust *Darkrume*. Let me help you get out of the mess you're in. He tells her, yeah, the smart thing to do is just pay the guy off. And the whole time, she's becoming increasingly dependent on Merlot 'cause only he knows her terrible secret."

I mulled it over for a minute. "If he sent a blackmail demand by instant message, there're no handwriting samples to worry about. And no record of it either, right?"

Tomlinson said, "Unless Gail copied it and saved it to a whole separate file, no."

"Then that's probably the way he played it."

"Or maybe he's got a partner. Some guy and he had him call Gail and play the roll of *Darkrume*. A guy with a nice voice. Convincing."

We talked about that. There were several ways to make it work.

I said, "I'm supposed to meet with Frank Calloway tomorrow. He hired an investigator to dig up dirt on Merlot, and he's going to let me see the file. But I think I'm going to call tonight and make reservations to fly down to Cartagena. You're right, it seems serious. Leave Friday or Saturday if I can get a flight."

"The sooner the better."

"I agree. What I should have done is head down there right away. Now I'm worried. This guy really is a freak."

When Tomlinson is very serious or concerned, he speaks more softly and becomes more articulate. "I think you need to find this lady, Doc. I really, truly do. Find her and make her believe the truth. Or scare the fat man away. Whatever it takes. He's making a fool out of that nice woman. He may try to do worse."

Yes, maybe a lot worse.

※

I drove in silence for a while, looking at the saw grass and the sky: gold on blue. The saw grass, the way it showed currents of wind, reminded me of elephant grass, the twelve-foot-high grass of the Mekong River and around marshy Tonle Sap Lake, Cambodia.

Once Bobby and I hiked into a bamboo village, drawn by the amplified buzzing of what we thought might be hiving bees.

But no . . .

It was the sound of flies, fat iridescent green flies. Thousands of flies, millions of flies, a gray haze. All drawn to what had been hung on hooks to die at the center of that village . . .

Thinking about it, seeing it again but not wanting to see it, I said to Tomlinson, "If Bobby were alive today, and someone like Merlot hurt his wife or child, I think he would probably—" I stopped. Was there any way to exaggerate what Bobby was capable of doing?

No. Just as there was no way to communicate some of the atrocities we'd witnessed in the jungles of Southeast Asia. So why discuss it?

I, on the other hand, was far removed from that place and time, so I would handle it differently.

Right?

I would have to handle it differently.

I listened to Tomlinson say, "I wish I could go with you to Colombia, man. But tomorrow, Musashi gets here with my little girl. I've been looking forward to it for months."

I told Tomlinson not to worry about it. If Merlot and Gail weren't out cruising, it probably wouldn't take me more than a couple of days to locate them. I had photographs. There weren't that many marinas. And very, very few hugely fat gringos visited the land of cocaine, cartels and kidnappers. So I'd track down the boat, play it by ear. And tomorrow what I might do is ask Frank Calloway to go along with me.

Tomlinson said, "You serious?"

Yeah, I told him, but first I had to meet the man, get a feel for how he'd handle himself on the road. A place like Colombia, you didn't want a whiner tagging along, but I needed someone to vouch that I was on Gail's side. Not Amanda, though. Not if I could talk her out of it. I'd had bad luck traveling with women in the past.

But Calloway, that was a different story. He should have a personal interest. Jackie Merlot had taken a lot of the man's money.

※

I made plane reservations that night from the phone in my little stilt-house cabin. I also spent nearly an hour calling old friends and former contacts around the U.S. as well as Nicaragua and Panama, trying to get a line on any mutual friends we might have in Colombia.

I knew there was a naval amphibious base on Cartagena Bay because I had billeted there years ago. But the people I had dealt with were long gone. So I called old friends and contacts and played the game of Hey, is what's-his-name still doing this-or-that? And, When was the last time you saw . . . ?

The more connections these prospective mutual friends had in Cartagena, the better.

I didn't come up with a name, but I did come up with a description: an Australian expat who ran a little marina on the island suburb of Manga, which is just across the bridge from the old walled city of Cartagena. The Aussie was the friend of a friend, maybe a former SAS guy, maybe not, the woman I was speaking with didn't know for sure.

The name of the marina was Club Nautico, and the Aussie, she said, might be a good source of information.

"Down there, everyone knows everyone else," she reminded me.

She was speaking of the broader community of English-speaking expatriates in Central and South America. She was exaggerating—but not by much.

Club Nautico: It was a place to start, anyway.

Something else I did was risk a phone call to my Tampa workout friend, Maggie. Always, always, she'd called me to arrange our meetings. What would I do if her husband answered? I felt ridiculously illicit as I dialed the number. We were just friends; I wasn't doing anything wrong, so what did I have to feel guilty about?

Maggie answered. She sounded delighted to hear from me. Her husband was out playing softball, so she could talk as long as I wanted.

We didn't talk long. I told her I was going away for a few days. Told her that we'd probably be able meet in Pass-a-Grille next week.

"Dinner at the Mermaid," I told her. "Run five or six, swim maybe for half an hour, then ruin it all with food and lots of beer."

She laughed. Maggie had a nice laugh.

Before we hung up, she told me something that was not a surprise: "Doc? I'm thinking about leaving him."

✳

While I was on the phone making reservations, I could look through the window at the porthole lights of Tomlinson's sailboat throwing yellow tracks across the water.

Tomlinson over there getting everything shipshape, nice and neat and orderly. His daughter was coming to visit. His young daughter and the mother whom Tomlinson was determined to win back.

The last time Musashi had visited him (this had been months ago), I had had the misfortune of overhearing one of her attacks on him. Not that I had a choice. Sound carries across water, and Tomlinson's sailboat is not anchored far from my house. I don't know what shocked me most: the gutter quality of the woman's profanity or her venomous assault on Tomlinson. He was a good-for-nothing impiety impiety who clung to an adolescent past, had wasted his life, was a terrible example as a father and who didn't make enough money to provide his daughter with the eloquent life, the clothes and the private schooling that she deserved.

It was a painful, disturbing attack to hear.

Dinkin's Bay is a quiet place, even serene in a goofy, bawdy, fraternity house way. Yes, there is the occasional fistfight on the dock and more than the occasional drunken beer bash, but the marina community is peaceful, very peaceful, perhaps because individual members are allowed to embrace the private lives of our own choosing. Respect is implicit in such acceptance.

Musashi's attack on Tomlinson, however, seemed designed to destroy the delicate scaffolding of his personal dignity.

The next day, when Tomlinson boated into the marina, I could see him searching the faces of the other liveaboards: Had they heard? Were they embarrassed for him? In our long friendship, it was the only time I'd ever seen him unnerved by that old and eternal debate: Should I be ashamed of what I am? Of who I am?

This was the woman he had invited back to his boat. This was the woman he had asked to go cruising with him to the Tortugas.

There is no explaining or understanding the intricacies of the human male-female relationship and, in such a circumstance of obvious abuse, all a friend can do is stand back and pretend not to see or hear.

I could, however, agree with Rhonda Lister, who told me, "Jesus Christ, what a poisonous bitch that Oriental twat is. Every woman on the islands over the age of twenty-one is wild about Tomlinson, but he's wasting his time getting beat up by her."

It was a mystery.

I booked one of the Avianca flights out of Miami, a direct to Cartagena. The Friday-morning lunch flight and the food on that fine Colombian airline is almost always good. I asked the lady in reservations, tell me honest now, were there plenty of seats available? Told her I needed to know, because I was thinking about taking a friend, but wasn't sure the friend could make it. I didn't mind risking the money, but why bother if there would be seats available?

The nice lady chuckled and, in Spanish, told me, on Fridays the flight from Miami to Cartagena had plenty of open seats but the flight back would be full. The Sunday-night flight was just the opposite. Full going to Cartagena, plenty of seats coming back.

"On weekends," she explained, "the Marimba people like to come to the States and party."

By the Marimba people, she meant the happy people; people who'd made enough money in the drug trade to do whatever they wanted.

So I booked only one seat. A bulkhead seat, aisle.

The next day, among the strangest of the strange thoughts that went flittering through my brain was: *Glad I didn't book a second seat.*

This was upon discovering Frank Calloway, my potential traveling companion, lying dead on cold Mexican tiles in his home on Gasparilla Island, village of Boca Grande, on a sun-dappled afternoon in April, a Thursday.

Calloway had been expecting me, right?

Right.

So why couldn't I find the file on Jackie Merlot?

I went through the whole house room by room, no luck. The more carefully I searched, the more frustrated I became.

The file had to be there. The reason I'd boated from Dinkin's Bay to Boca Grande was not just to meet and speak with Calloway, but because he'd said the information he had on Merlot was too delicate to risk allowing it to circulate outside his personal control.

Well . . . he hadn't said too delicate, but that was the implication.

Read between the lines: Long ago, Calloway had been Jackie Merlot's psychologist. Merlot wasn't being treated for some simple emotional difficulty, there had been pathology involved. Why else would Calloway have observed aloud to Amanda that he was surprised Merlot hadn't yet been institutionalized? Ethically, Calloway could not go to his ex-wife and tell her about Merlot's psychological problems. But he could and apparently did tell a private investigator where to find the information he wanted to share with Gail. Probably directed him to specific places: schools or military offices or police records. And maybe, just maybe, Calloway had told the investigator where his old files were stored and maybe just maybe there'd been a recent break-in.

It depended on how far Calloway was willing to go to circumvent the ethical demands of his former profession and how badly he wanted to get specific information to his ex-wife.

So the file should have been handy, right? Maybe not out in the open, but at least in an accessible place. Didn't matter that Calloway had decided to take a swim before our meeting, the file had to be nearby.

Right? *Right.*

So why couldn't I find the thing?

※

Calloway's study: Heavy wood and leather, chromium steel and thick champagne-colored carpeting. Plaques, diplomas and framed photographs beneath a white ceiling fan.

Frank's face dominated most of the photographs. Dark eyes, fixed smile. The man owned suits. Lots of suits.

There was a shot of him with his arm around Amanda's shoulder. She wore a green cap and gown. They both looked very happy, particularly Amanda. Proud daughter with proud daddy. Maybe she and her stepfather had been better friends than she'd let on. Maybe she was reluctant to admit that she, too, felt betrayed by the man's behavior.

In the corner was a well-organized computer station. Lots of shelves rising above the computer screen in tiers. Through the bay window, the Gulf of Mexico and western horizon were a panel of pastel blue on a ribbon of rust and turquoise.

It was getting late. How much longer did I have before Frank's wife returned?

I was still carrying the dish towel, wiping off my prints as I went. Sound is amplified and sharpened when one is inside the empty home of a stranger. It jabs like a needle. Each time a car slowed outside, I froze. I went through the roll-out drawers. Checked for little hidey-holes behind the desk, beneath the heavy plaques. Got down on my knees and looked under the desk. Had he taped the file underneath?

Nope.

Kept pausing to listen.

Couldn't find the file.

In the massive bedroom, with its bathroom sauna and pool-sized tub, there were all kinds of interesting discoveries to be made in the dresser drawers and beneath the bed.

Frank and the new Mrs. Calloway apparently enjoyed sexual aids and pornography. Lots of plastic toys and interesting photographs and unmarked videocassettes.

If such sexual play had been a part of Gail's life before the divorce, perhaps Merlot had had an easier time talking her into it after the divorce.

But still no file.

I was very happy to leave that bedroom. Snooping through the personal belongings of married couples does not mesh with the self-image upon which I rely to govern my daily activities. I felt like a sneak. I felt like some low-life voyeur.

I'd already searched the downstairs thoroughly. Decided to give it one last quick sweep. I was in the den, looking under magazines, looking under sofa cushions. If I turned my head one way, I could see into the kitchen: Frank's torso and bare feet were visible through the doorway. Turn my head the other way, I could look through translucent curtains to the driveway and street outside.

Good thing, too. I was shuffling through a stack of books when I saw a car swing fast into the drive. A new 'Vette convertible, black on black, top down. I stood there just long enough to see an attractive blond woman slide out. Hair spray and a body that bounced and flexed within an expensive white tennis outfit.

The quickness of her movements suggested that she might be irritable, maybe angry. That was my impression.

I recognized her face from photos all around the house. It was Frank's trophy wife, Skipper. I didn't linger to assess or admire. She appeared to be not just irritable but also in a hurry. In a few long strides, I was through the kitchen and out the busted glass door into the pool area.

It was there that something odd and unexpected caught my attention. Something lying on the deck: A checked scarf lying near the screen door. Bright checks on a white field. The little squares were raspberry red.

What was a scarf doing there? It seemed out of place, accidental. I'm not sure why I did it, but I did: I leaned and swept the scarf up in my right hand like a rider on a horse, then closed the pool door very, very quietly behind me.

A few moments later, I was on the beach strolling along, the scarf bunched up in my big hand. I had a role to play. It was not a difficult role: big wind-burned tourist in khaki fishing shorts and gray polo shirt enjoying the sunshine through his wire rimmed glasses. I did not allow myself to meet the eyes of fellow strollers who now paused to exchange glances that, at first were puzzled, then concerned.

There was a noise. . . .

What was that noise?

Even above the sound of rolling waves, everyone on the beach could hear it: a shrill staccato howl that seemed to grow progressively louder. It originated from the shadows beyond the sea grapes.

A lady in a gigantic sun hat waddled toward me as if seeking shade or protection. She wore a blue polka-dot swim dress and was carrying a basket of shells. Zinc oxide was smeared across her pink face. The rapidness of her breathing illustrated a neuron fear. The next level is panic.

To me, a stranger, she said, "Sir? Is . . . is that the sound of a woman screaming?"

I continued walking, as I answered, "Yes, ma'am, a woman screaming. I believe that it is."

✻

The Temptation Restaurant, a fixture of Boca Grande's tiny cross-roads downtown, is only a few blocks from the beach and so was a short walk from the late Frank Calloway's home. It's in an old stucco building next door to an art gallery, across a sleepy street from Island Bike & Beach, not far from Italiano Insurance and the *Boca Beacon* newspaper offices.

If I'd hustled to Whidden's Marina, hopped in my skiff and really pushed it, it was possible, just possible, I could have been making the turn past Woodring Point and into Dinkin's Bay during the last, last pearly glow of dusk. Truthfully, that's what I would have preferred to do. Get home, speak confidentially with Tomlinson, let him help me decide the best way to break the news to Amanda that Frank was dead.

How do you tell someone that she is now twice a paternal orphan?

But racing away from Boca Grande was not the smart thing to do. Nope.

I needed to be seen around town. I needed to do some talking and be remembered. If asked, the efficient Ms. Betty Marsh would quite accurately inform the police that, yes, the late Mr. Calloway did have an appointment on Thursday afternoon. It was with a man named Ford, a Dr. Marion Ford.

The police might say to me, You want to hear something really strange? After Calloway died, somebody went through his stuff and wiped all the prints clean. They might say, Someone was there, someone was in the house. So why didn't you call us and tell us the man was dead?

If the police had questions, any questions, I wanted my answers to be easily corroborated. The Temptation was where I chose to be seen and be remembered.

Annie was behind the bar when I walked in. She's a large chestnut-haired woman with a good smile. When I straddled a stool, she raised her eyebrows and said with mock anger, "So? You don't have time for your old friends anymore? You too busy to jump in that skiff of yours and fly north more than once or twice a year?"

For all the tourism, for all the transient comings and goings rightfully associated with the ratty, tacky character that is Florida, the community of waterfolk remains tight and dependable and it doesn't change much from generation to generation. Annie had been born and raised on the islands. She knew everyone that I knew and more.

"During tarpon season," I said, "you're always so busy. I hate to come up here and get in the way."

"We look that busy?"

There were a couple of men locked in private conversation at the end of the bar. In the dining room, they'd pushed three tables together and a dozen or so cheerful-looking women were drinking iced tea and eating salads.

"Everybody's out fishing the hill tide," Annie said. "Tarpon'll be on a sure 'nuff feed. So if it wasn't for you and the Sarasota Ladies' Something-or-Another Book Club in there, this place'd be like a tomb. Jim and Karen done left. Hey—how about I read your fortune?"

Annie liked playing with tarot cards. It was her little hobby. I ordered a Bud Light and a bag of chips while I waited on one of Smitty's grouper sandwiches. I proceeded to tell Annie my sad story as she laid out the tarot cards.

"I make an appointment to talk to this guy, I run my boat all the way up here, and the man's not home."

Annie was slapping the cards down on the bar, looking at them. "Geez, what a jerk," she said. Her mind was on the cards. "You're goin' on a trip real soon. Pretty long trip, too. Where you goin'?"

"Colombia. I've got a morning flight out of Miami tomorrow on Avianca, so—" I stopped chewing for a moment. "How'd you know I was going somewhere?"

"You got the Three of Swords up next to the Ten of Swords. The last time I saw that, one of the Hamilton boys met a girl at the Pink Elephant and the two of them drove her mini-van all the way up north someplace. Dee-troit? Maybe Cleveland or a place like that. Those cards, they almost always mean some kinda trip." As she spoke, she was looking at the checkered scarf I had placed on the bar. "Where'd you get that? I don't think I've ever seen one like that before."

I patted it. "Pretty, isn't it?"

"Looks handmade. The checks, that berry color, looks like they mighta used natural dye." Fingers at the top corners, she held it out for a more complete inspection. "Whew! Kinda smells funny, though, don't it. What is that? Like a fish smell."

I sniffed my fingers. Yep, sour and fishy.

She said, "Smells just like some of the tarpon fishermen come in here after a hard day. 'Course then, Doc, maybe that's the way biologists smell, too. 'Scuse me if I don't check." She placed the scarf back on the bar. I balled it up and stuck it in my pocket.

I said, "Did you hear what I was telling you? This guy I had the appointment with, Frank Calloway, that's his name. I was supposed to meet him at his house at six-thirty sharp. But like I told you, nobody home. Stood there like an idiot knocking on the door."

"Knocking on the door?"

"Yeah."

"What, he didn't have a bell?"

The woman didn't miss much.

I told her I'd tried the bell first, but figured it was broken because no one answered the door.

"I don't know any Frank Calloway. Never even heard the name. Where's he live?"

Gilchrist Avenue, I told her.

"Oh, one of the Beach-Fronters. But pretty new to the area, right? The old-timey Beach-Fronters, I know all them."

"Yeah, I think the Calloways have only lived here a few months. Pretty rude, if you think about it. Have me run my boat all the way up here, then stand me up."

"Doggone rude. But maybe he's got a good reason for it. Maybe he had an emergency or something." She was moving the cards around concentrating. "Say, Doc, tell me somethin'."

"Sure."

"You know anybody that just died recently?"

I stopped chewing again. "Why do you ask that?"

"'Cause you got the Tower card faceup. The last time I saw the Tower card faceup the way she is now, it was for this tourist lady, and a friend of a friend of hers got dead somehow. Maybe zapped by a truck or something, but he sure 'nuff passed away. "

"Is that right."

"Yep. The Tower card, positioned the way she is now, it almost always means somebody's ready to cash in their chips."

I looked at the card. It was a gothic drawing of a medieval tower. The tower had been set afire . . . or caught in an explosion, perhaps. Stones were flying skyward in a starburst of orange flames

"I don't believe in this stuff, Annie. You know that."

"Who says I believe it? Readin' the cards, it's just something to do for fun. How else am I gonna pass the time?"

She moved that card, placed a couple of more cards on the bar and stared at them while I sipped my beer.

From the dining room, I could hear the Sarasota ladies laughing about something. Playing some kind of game, it seemed. Friends and mothers, probably, who had the self-amused glow of contented, attentive wives. Good women getting together, having fun.

It was my guess that Skipper would not have been readily accepted by this nice group.

I looked up from the bar. Annie was backdropped by rows of liquor bottles. On the wall were old framed caricatures of local baseball players. The cartoons had been done years ago by Sam the three-fingered artist. Sam had lived down on the Keys, then one day just disappeared. Or so the story went.

I said, "Say, Annie, I was wondering about something: Have you seen a man roaming around town, a really huge guy. Like I'm talking maybe three hundred pounds, probably more, and a head the size of a football. With perfect hair, the kind that looks painted smooth. You would've noticed him."

It was a reasonable question to ask. Not that it seemed likely that Calloway had been murdered. Wet tile, bare feet, blood on the marble countertop and hard kitchen floor. But it was a possibility and it didn't hurt to check with one of the most observant women around if someone matching Merlot's description was in town. Maybe the trip to Colombia, the entire postcard business, was a ruse just like *Darkrume*, Merlot's alter ego.

Annie said, "A really fat guy, huh? Is that the man you come here to see? This Calloway fellow?"

"No. Another guy I thought I might run into up here."

"The carnival people, the ones who winter up in Gibsonton? They drive down to the beach sometimes. The ones they call freak show people, but you couldn't meet nicer folks. The Giant used to visit with the Monkey-Faced Lady. They'd stop in for lunch. Sometimes they'd bring a couple of the midgets along. And the one I think they call

Crab Man, I just seen him. Maybe they got a Fat Man travelin' with 'em."

"No, this isn't a circus person."

Her attention was back on the cards. "You sure no one you know died recently? A woman. I'd think it'd be a woman."

That almost made me smile. Calloway lying stone-cold dead only a few blocks away and the cards were telling her it was a woman. "Yep," I said, "I'm pretty sure I haven't had any lady friends die recently." Smitty had brought out my sandwich. I took my time, napkin on knee, getting ready to eat.

Annie's a nice person. I could see the concern in her face. "Then I sure wish you wouldn't take that trip. Colombia, you say? Some of the local boys have been down there a time or two. They say she can be a pretty dangerous place, Colombia."

"Annie, you're worrying for no reason. I already told you I don't believe in fortune-telling. Tarot cards, palm-reading, none of it."

"I don't either, Doc. I don't either!" Now she was scooping up the cards. Seemed eager to get them back in their box. "I just read them for fun. They don't mean nothin'. Not a blessed thing. Just fun."

I was smiling at her. "Then why do you look so concerned?"

"'Cause sometimes readin' the cards is more fun than others. Now eat your grouper and let's talk 'bout something else."

On the phone, Amanda Richardson said to me, "You're talking about Frank? Why're you being so nice, trying to get me to say that I still feel an emotional attachment to Frank?"

Smart woman . . . and exactly what I was trying to do. The reason was, she'd spoken badly of the man earlier and I didn't want her saddled with additional guilt when I told her that Calloway was dead. Wanted to nudge her into saying some nice things before I gave her the news. Something else: I wanted to get a sense of how she felt for him deep down. She'd already told me her roommate wasn't home, and I needed to decide whether I should contact one of her close friends first. Make sure the friend was nearby when I told her. Or maybe drive over there. It was only two hours to Lauderdale, and I was flying out of Miami International tomorrow anyway.

Would that work? No . . . because by the time I got there, someone else would've already contacted her. The county cops, probably. So I needed to tell her now or find a way to get her out of her apartment; give her something to do until I had time to get to her.

She said, "A question like that, it seems just a tad touchy-feely for a guy's guy like you. Or wait . . . tell me if I'm right: you and Tomlinson went and got drunk and you've got a bet going or something.

About how Amanda *really* feels about Frank-the-jerk. One of those heavy conversations drunk men have."

It was nearly 8:00 P.M. and I was back in Dinkin's Bay, back on Sanibel Island. My skiff was tied bow and stern to the counterweight and pulley system I use when the weather's foul or I might be away for a while. There seemed to be a little preweekend party going on aboard the soggy old Chris-Craft, *Tiger Lily*. Chinese lanterns had been strung around the flybridge and I could hear music drifting across the water: "Rum & Coca Cola," the big band version. Lately, JoAnn and Rhonda had been listening to 1940s music. They had also taken to wearing glossy scarlet lipstick, equally bright hibiscus blossoms in their hair, and flowered sarongs. The Dorothy Lamour look, as if waiting for the GIs to return from overseas.

Fashion is nothing more than gossip in fabric form, energized by hope and dispersed by osmosis. Which is probably why I'd been noticing that men around the dock were beginning to favor pleats and anything olive drab. And probably why, lately, female waitresses and bartenders around the islands were parroting the Dinkin's Bay look: sandals, Lennon Sisters hairstyles and sarongs.

Funniest thing of all, though, it was Tomlinson who had rediscovered and popularized that Stage Door Canteen combination.

The sandals and sarong, anyway. His hair, Tomlinson always wore that down. Even when he played baseball.

With the phone wedged between my shoulder and ear, I told Amanda, "This has nothing to do with a bet. I'm asking for a reason. That question, Do you understand why you're mad at Frank? it's something you need to consider. What I'm saying is, I know you care about the man. No matter what you said about him earlier, I know he helped raise you and you care about him, and . . . that's all a given."

"Christ-o-mighty, you can be so weird sometimes, Ford. Talk about a strange phone day! I get home, there's this hysterical message from Skipper the Bimbo Queen on the recorder, call her immediately. The two born-again dolphins must have had their first fight. Now you're behaving like Father O'Malley. Hey, can you hang on a minute? I've got your uncle on the other line."

So the newly widowed Skipper had been trying to get in touch.

Amanda probably hadn't called her back because she'd been talking to Tuck. The man's timing was extraordinary. This was a rare exception because his timing was almost always, always bad.

I waited . . . and waited. Then: "Your uncle, he really could get to be one of my favorite people in the world. He's so darn . . . I don't know, sincere or something. And so easy to talk to. He makes me laugh. Really laugh."

I was in no mood to hear this. "Do you want me to call later? After you're done listening to Tuck?"

"Come on, now. Don't be snotty. No . . . what I told Mr. Gatrell was I'd call him back when we were done. Know what he said?" Her chuckle told me that she found the man amusing. This twenty-some-year-old woman sitting in a Lauderdale condo linked by fiber-optic thread to an Everglades gangster who'd driven cattle on horseback and poached gators for a living. "What your uncle said was, 'Well, lil' lady, then you'll be calling me back real soon, 'cause Duke, he's not a man to use two sentences when one word'll do.'"

Her impersonation was pretty good, but I didn't want to encourage her.

I said, "Really."

"Yeah. You two guys . . . do you want me to tell you why it is I think you don't get along? It's like when my mom and I get into these spats, it's not 'cause we're so different, it's 'cause we're so much alike."

"Take my word on this one, Amanda. Tucker Gatrell and I are nothing alike. Nothing."

"Jesus, you don't have to bite my head off. It should be something we could at least sit down and talk about."

"I don't have a lot of time. I'm leaving for Colombia tomorrow. I'm taking the morning Avianca flight, and I've got a checklist of things to take care of before I leave."

She was very quiet for a moment before she said, "If you're going to Colombia looking for my mom, I'm going. But you coulda at least given me a little warning. Your uncle, he wants to go, too."

"Tuck's not going and you're not going, either. There's something I need to tell you—"

"Hold it!"

I raised my voice to make her listen. "Amanda, I have something very important—"

But her voice was louder: "What you have to say can just wait, 'cause I have something I need to tell you, too!" She practically shouted the last of it. Yep, she could be forceful and had chosen this moment to show it.

In a normal tone, I said, "Okay, okay. We'll do it your way."

"Damn right we will. What I need to tell you, buster, is you're not the boss. I asked you to help, yeah. But if I want to go to Colombia, I'll go. And if Tucker Gatrell wants to go to Colombia, he's my friend and we'll both by God go."

Her voice had more chill than fire. I was smiling a little, her tone was that familiar to me. The same pissed-off intonations that had been in Bobby's voice when he was mad.

First Bobby, now Frank Calloway.

This woman had lost them both and didn't even know it yet.

Speaking of the death of her dad, Amanda had once told me, "You don't know what it's like."

Didn't I?

Standing there with the phone to my ear, alone in my house, I decided to tell her something I'd never told anyone, not even Tomlinson. The circumstances made what I had to say relevant, but it was more than that. There was something about this girl that I liked and trusted.

I said, "I want you to calm down. And I want you to sit down."

"If you think you're going to talk me out of going—"

This time, instead of raising my voice, I spoke more softly. "I'm not going to talk you out of anything, Amanda. If you want to go to Colombia with me, that's fine. Or meet me there later. Whatever. But we need to have a talk first."

She was listening now.

"I'm going to ask you a favor. It may seem like a strange favor, but if I'm willing to help you, then you need to be willing to help me. I'm going to tell you why I don't want Tucker Gatrell around me. Or even near me. Let alone with me in Colombia. It's something I've never told anyone, but I've decided to tell you, because . . . well, you'll understand when I'm done."

She must have read something in my tone; hadn't heard me this serious before. She said, "This isn't about my mom, is it? My mother, she's okay, isn't she? If that man's hurt my mom—"

Her voice had a little-girl quality when she was frightened.

"No, it's not about your mom. But look . . . this favor I'm going to ask is important to me. What I'd like you to do right now, the moment we hang up, is get in your car and drive to . . ." Where? I'd thought about asking her to pick a hotel on Lauderdale Beach. Take her for a walk, give her the news that way, very gently. But no . . . it'd take me two hours to get there, which meant that she'd probably spend the next hour or so in her own apartment waiting. By then Skipper or the Sheriff's Department would have been in touch.

I said, "What I'd like you to do the moment we hang up is get in your car and drive to . . . to Everglades City. You ever been there?"

"Well . . . sure. But that's more than an hour from my place. I take Alligator Alley west, then south on highway twenty-nine. It's a really narrow road; lots of swamp. So more like an hour and a half—"

"It's about the same distance from Sanibel. If we both leave now"— I was looking at my watch— "we can meet there by ten. Earlier, if we push it. You know where the Rod & Gun Club is? The old hotel right on the river?"

"Sure, the Rod & Gun. The mansion-looking place with the alligator skins on the walls and the big fireplace. Yeah, I've had lunch there with clients. In fact, I was planning on driving over that way early next week to call on my accounts in Marco and Naples. So . . . I guess I could change things around, see them tomorrow, if it's really that important to you."

I said, "Whoever gets to Everglades first, go ahead and get a couple of rooms and order dinner. Better yet, I'll call ahead and make reservations. It's a nice night, so tell the woman there—her name's Hortensia— tell her who you're waiting on and that we'll eat out on the porch by the water. All on me. My treat. She's from Costa Rica, a friend of mine."

"You're serious."

I said, "Very much so."

"The reason you want me to leave my apartment, it's not because I'm in some kind of danger or something is it?"

"Nope."

"You scared me there for a minute. I thought there was something wrong with my mom."

I said, "The Rod & Gun. I'll meet you at the bar for drinks."

❇

I told Amanda, "The reason I don't trust Tucker Gatrell, the reason I don't like being around the man is because he managed to get both of my parents killed. I hadn't quite reached my teens when it happened."

She whispered, "Dear God."

I told her as we were walking deserted streets along the Baron River. It was an hour before midnight on a moonless night with stars. Everglades City is a mangrove town built at the nexus of saw grass and brackish backwater that is the Ten Thousand Islands. It has had the same streetlights since the 1930s, milky glass bowls on elegant iron stems. The globes created incremental pools of light along the river. In each pool was a precise island of asphalt and lawn, of wooden dock and flowing black water. In some places, the streetlights found a framework of ficus limbs, vines and leaves.

When I said it—"He managed to get both my parents killed"— Amanda took a few more steps and then stopped as if frozen. Maybe it had taken a few seconds for her to realize what I was telling her. That's when she whispered, "Dear God."

Then: "Oh, Doc, I . . . I'm so sorry. I had no idea." She put her hand on my elbow, then found my hand, meshing her fingers tightly into mine.

I found myself oddly uncomfortable with her reaction. The fact that she felt I would welcome an emotional demonstration so obvious and familiar surprised me a little.

I said, "I'm not telling you this because I need sympathy. It happened so long ago I don't even think about it anymore. I'm telling you for a reason."

"I know, I know . . . because it hurts. I know how much it hurts."

I remained patient, evenhanded. "No, that's not the reason."

"But . . . how did your parents die? You're uncle's such a nice man. Why?"

"I don't know why. Is there ever a reason good people die? But how it happened, that's another story. It was an accident, but an accident that was completely unnecessary. The whole thing was pointless. But it did happen and all because of Tucker's idiotic . . . his idiotic selfishness and his sloppy approach to life. That's exactly how I define Tucker Gatrell as a person: selfish and sloppy. And what Tucker is as a person killed my mother and father. He's careless. He has a random approach to everything. Tucker is the center of his own universe . . . his own *chaotic* universe, and that is the height of indifference."

Now she locked her arm into the crook of my arm. "You've never told anyone this before?"

"No."

"Will you tell me?"

We continued walking.

I didn't embellish. Didn't dramatize how it happened or romanticize the notion that I had suffered because of it. I gave Amanda the facts as coolly and unemotionally as I could.

She listened. She made empathetic sounds. Once I think she started crying, but didn't want me to hear.

I told her that, while I never knew either of my parents well, I suspected I would have come to like them. My father had played a couple of years of pro football for Chicago and the old Atlanta organization before he took up running lobster traps down on the Keys. That and pompano fishing.

My mother by all accounts had been a gifted amateur naturalist and one of the earliest advocates for a save-the-Everglades movement. She spent a lot of time giving talks in the moneyed tourist cities or lobbying hard up in Tallahassee. There is a little brass plaque almost hidden by mangroves in Flamingo, once an isolated fish camp, now headquarters for Everglades National Park. My mother's name is on the plaque, second column, about midway down.

I saw it once. I happened to be in Flamingo with nothing to do. I found the plaque and cleared some of the brush away. Had to get down on my knees to do it.

I told Amanda that a friend of my parents had once (not unkindly) described them as separate planets in the same orbit. Not that it mattered much to me. Early on, I discovered the more predictable and articulate world of biology and the natural sciences.

At one point, Amanda interrupted me to say, "The way you're talking right now, the way you tell it all so coldly, so . . . like you don't really care. Hardly an emotion at all. It doesn't bother you talking about it?"

I asked her how something that happened so long ago could bother anyone. I was simply trying to tell her why I would never trust Gatrell.

"The one thing that my parents had in common," I said, "was they loved poking around the Everglades and the Ten Thousand Islands. They did a lot of boating. My father had a thirty-six-foot Daniels designed in Boca Grande and finished by a man named Preacher Brown in Chokoloskee. It was a fine boat. Beautifully done, solid as stone.

"I know how well it was built because, after it blew up and killed my parents, I spent the next two years putting what pieces I could find back together. About every spare minute I had, that's what I did. You know how the FAA reconstructs wreckage after a plane goes down? I used the same method, but by pure coincidence. It seemed like the most reasonable way to do it, so that's what I did.

I said, "What I want you to understand is, I wasn't motivated by pain or a sense of loss. I was trying to determine what the authorities who investigated had tried but failed to figure out. I was trying to determine why the boat exploded. To me, it seemed so . . . haphazard to allow such an important question to remain unanswered."

Amanda said softly, "You were only, what? Twelve or thirteen years old?"

"*Um-m-m-m* . . . something like that. But what matters is, I discovered why the boat exploded. I figured out *exactly* why the boat exploded. Tuck has always fancied himself an inventor. An inventor and a songwriter—ask him and he'll tell you. Not that he ever stuck with anything long enough to be good at it. No. He just dabbles and leaves the real work up to others.

"What I discovered was that someone had removed the boat's brass fuel shutoff. It's a little butterfly valve usually found astern on the transom. Or sometimes closer to the engine itself. This person replaced it with a type of pressure valve made out of PVC pipe. It was an ingenious idea, really, but for one thing. To fix the valve in place, the person used Superglue. That or some kind of similar bonding agent. Switched the valves and didn't tell a soul.

"Unfortunately, the person who did it didn't take the time to test the valve under real conditions. If he had, he'd have realized that gasoline dissolves Superglue."

Amanda said, "Your uncle, it was his invention."

"Of course. He never had the courage to admit it, but, yeah. It was him. One Saturday morning, my parents headed out across Chokoloskee Bay for a romantic weekend. Fuel leaked into the bilge and the boat blew up. Quite an explosion. We lived in Mango, just a few miles from here. I was in my bedroom at the time, alphabetizing my beetle collection. The percussion blew out my windows."

She was crying again. "I'm so . . . Doc, I'm so sorry. I like your uncle. I still like him. But I understand. And I understand now why you're telling me this. Thank you for choosing me. . . ."

No . . . she didn't understand.

I turned, faced her, put my hands on her shoulders. We were at a place where the deserted road curved away from the docks; stood near the water at the outer periphery of streetlight. There was the sound of our own breathing, the vectoring resonance of mosquitoes. Across the river in the Everglades darkness, mangroves created a surreal skyline of charcoal figures—"the Sentries of Isolation," as Tomlinson had once described the night fringe of our own mangrove refuge, Dinkin's Bay. The tops of the trees were individualized and set apart by a haze of stars. They were bonsai shapes, ancient and gothic, against the brighter sky.

I told Amanda about Frank. Told her that Frank Calloway, her stepfather, was dead. Told her about finding him and that his death was probably accidental, but that I wasn't certain.

"I'll be in Colombia," I told her. "If the police have any reason at all to suspect murder, I need to know. I need to know just as soon as I possibly can. If Merlot was behind it, there's a big difference between tracking down a con man and tracking down a killer. You need to keep tabs for me. You need to find out what you can."

I watched her face. She was puzzled. Frank is . . . dead? Then there was the numb, confused look of shock. He's *dead?*

I said, "There's something else." I took out the scarf I'd found. "Did this belong to Frank or his wife?"

She took it. I noticed that her hands were trembling. She moved closer to the nearest streetlight and inspected it carefully. She sniffed it, then looked at it again. "You know . . . it seems familiar, but I'm not sure why. Frank's? No, it isn't Frank's. God . . . I mean it *wasn't* Frank's. And not my mom's, either."

"Then how could it be familiar?"

"I don't know. Just an impression, that's all. Maybe I saw a scarf like it someplace. Where'd you get it?"

I told her.

"Shouldn't you have left it for the police? Frank wouldn't have owned anything like that, and it's too . . . cheap and common for a woman like Skipper."

I stuffed the scarf back into my pocket. "I don't know why I took it. But I did."

Amanda seemed determined to remain aloof, untouchable. For an hour, maybe more, she didn't allow the news to bother her and she refused to demonstrate to me that she took anything more than an objective view of her stepfather's death.

Well, his dying so young, it was a shame, because Frank was starting out on a new life and while they were no longer close, she certainly never wished him ill. Yes, she would contact the private investigator Frank had hired—Castillo was his name?—and try to finagle a copy of the report on Merlot. But if she did that for me, I had to promise to call her when I found her mother.

"When you find her, I'll fly down. I can't wait to see my mom. I miss her so much!"

Amanda told me that she was so eager to hear about what I found in Colombia that maybe she'd get another phone line installed in her apartment. That way, she could still mess around with the computer, stay in touch with her E-mail pals but not risk missing the call from me.

I said, "You really spend that much time on the computer?"

Her reply seemed a metaphor for an entire generation: "You kidding? The Internet's the future. And what else do I have to do?"

The way she behaved—very rational, completely in control—she seemed to be saying to me, "See? Doesn't bother me a bit. I don't need him or any other man in my life."

About 3:00 A.M., though, lying sleepless in my little cabana room near the Rod & Gun Club's main building, her tough-guy façade cracked and then crumbled.

I heard a tentative tapping at the screen, then louder.

When I opened the door, she whispered, "That poor . . . poor man," and then she fell into my arms crying, crying, trembling like a small wounded creature. She moaned: "He used to hold me. When I was a little girl and frightened, Frank used to hold me."

Which is exactly what I did for her then.

Held her. Let her bury her face in my chest, sobbing. Allowed her to walk me backwards until we were both on the bed, wrapped as tightly as we could wrap ourselves together, not alone anymore or isolated or set apart, either of us. I could feel her skinny little washboard body spasming beneath my hands, bare-legged and wearing nothing beneath her T-shirt, her face wet against my neck, then . . . and then . . . my face wet and buried in her hair . . . both of us unprepared for the degree of emotion that we felt and the depth of that which neither of us had probably ever admitted: our pain.

More than once during the night, I asked myself: *Is this wrong?*

More than once, she answered for me: *No.*

But it wasn't right; something about it just didn't work. There was an undefined tension; a sad, sad unwillingness that seemed to go to her very marrow. I realized it and then she admitted it. Not verbally, but by accepting what it was and the way we were and by not posing or pretending. It was okay. We were just fine.

We held each other.

We held each other.

The next morning, in the first water-colored light of morning, I saw her T-shirt on the floor: *Thirty-Second Rule Strictly Enforced.*

She was still asleep, hair mussed on the pillow in a rusty halo around her tomboy face, as I closed the door quietly behind me.

In that soft light, she looked very pretty. Amanda looked at peace.

14

On the air approach to Cartagena, the parrot-blue of the Caribbean Sea is gradually murked by a long cusp of beach that flattens into a hardpan of mud and mangroves and plum-colored slums. Beyond is a fortress city that looks like something dreamed up by Hollywood, its bastion walls built by the Spaniards in the 1500s to intimidate pirates, its narrow streets clogged with motor scooters and smoking cars and wooden donkey carts.

Fortresses and pirates are still an intricate part of Cartagena today.

I stepped off the plane into the rain forest heat, Loomis travel bag in hand. At immigration, a little man in a blue uniform checked my passport, eyed me carefully, then rewarded me with a huge smile. "Welcome to Colombia!" He seemed surprised that I was there.

No wonder.

U.S. citizens do not visit Colombia much anymore. The lone exception is Bogota which, of late, has been doing a brisk business in the mail-order-bride business.

To be accurate: computer-ordered brides.

I've never heard anyone argue the point: Colombia produces the most beautiful women in the Americas. Single U.S. men, perhaps tired of being treated as social villains, have been flying here in ever-growing numbers to find kind and gentle mates to marry.

There is a second, darker attraction: Because of its beautiful women . . . and its hungry and desperate children . . . Colombia is also a favorite destination of sexual predators. Unknown to most, impoverished Third World countries have little choice but to turn a blind eye on their own booming sex trade. They need the money. They have come to rely on it. Behavior that is considered felonious back in the U.S. is, in poor countries such as Colombia, not only tolerated, it is accepted.

That is a tragedy. . . .

Contributing to that tragedy is the United States Congress, which has done absolutely nothing to discourage our sexual deviants from crossing the border and preying on poor and desperate children.

But, aside from men seeking women, U.S. tourists seldom visit Colombia anymore. Not even the cruise ships bother to make landfall. Too much bad press. Maybe the little man at immigration took my arrival as a good omen. A North American tourist? Perhaps the world's attitude toward his country was changing!

My smile told him: Maybe soon but not yet.

Which is unfortunate. Colombia is one of the most beautiful countries in the Americas and its people are among the most gifted, the friendliest and attractive people in the world.

But Colombia is also the world's chief exporter of cocaine. Each and every drug cartel has its own meagerly equipped small army. When a cartel goes under, its army tends to stay together because there's so little work available. How do these guerrilla bands survive? Their members have embraced the very profitable vocation of kidnapping and extortion to keep food on the table.

It is estimated that between a hundred and two hundred people are kidnapped and ransomed each month in Colombia. If relatives of the victims do not pay the ransom quickly and in full measure, the victims are executed in cold blood. There is a spoken procedure: *Get down on your knees and I will then press the muzzle of this pistol to the back of your head.* . . .

The second casualty of poverty is conscience. The first is the local environment, so it is business, nothing more. Kill a hostage promptly and efficiently and you may be sure that relatives of the next victim will be more highly motivated to cooperate.

The irony is that Colombia, in terms of overall violent crime and theft, is no more dangerous than Miami or L.A. Tourists don't hesitate to visit those places. But mention the name "Colombia" to an unseasoned traveler, and the reaction is predictable: Colombia? Too risky!

Not really. Besides, such statistics mean very little to me when it comes to travel. I love Colombia, have always loved Colombia, so facts and figures about crime carry little weight. Not when the beauty of the country, the kindness and humor of its people, are weighed in the balance.

Which is why I was both chagrined and irritated at myself when I realized how long it had been since I'd treated myself to a return visit. Had I unknowingly become so tangled in the cheerful social web of Sanibel that I was now what I had always dreaded: dependent, addicted to routine, immobile?

When I got home, I'd force myself to take a hard look at my life. Do some reassessing, maybe make some changes.

For now, though, I felt the thoracic glow of being alone again, focused and under way far outside the boundaries, on the road once more.

※

I worked my way through Cartagena's small terminal to the street outside, where four or five taxi drivers stood braced against their little cars, dozy in the heat. By old habit, I chose the third cab in line (never take the first or second car in a country where an attacker might anticipate your arrival). It was a punch-drunk Toyota with a parade of dashboard saints. The car might have once been red but was now sun-bleached pink.

Before opening the door, I paused to ask the driver how many marinas there were near the old walled city.

He said two.

I asked him which of those two marinas would be most comfortable for a gringo couple on a sailboat.

That was easy, he said. There was only one marina preferred or used by foreign yachters (sea travelers, he called them). That was the little marina in Manga.

Good news. Very good news.

I explained to the driver that I might need a hotel, but first I wanted him to drive me to this place, the marina called Club Nautico. I told him that I planned to spend an hour or so at the marina, get something to eat and hopefully make contact with the Aussie who owned the place. If he was a good driver, if he didn't put my life at risk or try to maneuver me to a friend's shop or a store or a restaurant in hopes of a kickback, I'd hire him for the day.

I hadn't quite finished explaining what I wanted when a familiar voice interrupted me from behind: "God dang, Duke, I was beginnin' to think you wasn't gonna show up a'tall."

I felt a sickening feeling. How could this have happened?

I was tempted to slide into the cab, shut the door and never look back. In hindsight, that's precisely what I should have done.

But I didn't.

Instead, I turned to see Tucker Gatrell.

He wore a stained gray Justin cattleman's hat tilted jauntily on his head, skinny-hipped Levi's, a black western shirt with plastic pearl buttons and a white sports coat that a piano-bar hustler might have chosen. On the macadam, braced against his boots, was a large cardboard suitcase. The thing had to be forty years old.

Tucker Gatrell in travel uniform. I was not amused and I wasn't sympathetic.

"What the hell are you doing here?"

"Come to lend a hand. What you think?"

"What I think is, you weren't invited, so my advice is don't expect a hell of a lot of consideration."

"Wasn't asked, my ass. That pretty little girl asked me. Called me on the phone last night. Said you was headed for Colombia and you might need some help."

"Amanda? You're telling me she called you after she spoke to me. And told you I'd need help?"

"That's right, after. She called me back and told me, 'You make sure you look after Duke.' That li'l girl likes you. She truly does."

"Amanda referred to me as Duke."

"Well . . . no, she called you by the other name, Doc. But it means the same."

I looked into his face. Was he lying? The man had the craziest, brightest blue eyes I'd ever seen in my life. It was as if each iris were independently wired and energized with chromium filament. There was madness in there. And a terribly driven . . . something. But was he lying?

Couldn't tell. It was always nearly impossible for me to tell if he was lying. Although with Tuck, it was usually safe to assume that he was.

"I'm going to be real honest with you, Tucker. I don't want your help. I don't want you near me. And I don't have time to waste keeping you out of trouble. So do me a favor: Turn around and take the next flight back to Miami. Or anyplace else you want to go."

He was already loading his suitcase into the trunk of the taxi. "Miami? You drunk, Duke? Hell, boy, I just flew in from Miami. When Amanda—ain't she the nicest girl?—when that Amanda told me you was takin' the mornin' flight, I figured that meant like close to first light, knowin' you. So I got me a seat on LACSA's first and best. Been here waitin' for more than two hours, but I'm still burpin' red peppers from that breakfast they served." He was grinning, showing me what a good-natured and all-around cheerful old guy he was. "Goddamn, boy, airplane food, I figure it's just about the best stuff in the world."

I used studied, articulate patience to show him just how impatient I was. "I'm not taking you with me. You might as well gather your gear and go home."

I watched the grin fade from his face. One thing I've never doubted about Tuck is his capacity for anger and violence. "You don't want me?"

"That's right, I don't want you."

"You think I'll get in the way. Maybe slow you down."

For some reason, now that we were away from Florida, I felt free to tell him exactly what was on my mind. "That's right, I think you'll get in the way. Not only that, I think you'd find a way to embarrass me if you stayed. Or get me killed. You've got some experience at that, right?" I waited, looking at him. No reaction at all before I continued,

"So do us both a favor and take the next flight to Miami. I'll pay for it. Whatever. Just get the hell out of here because I've got work to do."

He looked at me with those sled-dog eyes and, for a moment, a crazed moment, I think he came close to punching me. In barely a whisper, he said, "Let me tell you somethin', boy. Don't fuck with a falcon unless you can fly."

That was supposed to make sense? I said, "O-o-o-kay."

"There's never been a day in my life I couldn't carry my own weight. And I was kickin' ass in these shithole taco towns back when the big news was that you'd taken a dump that wasn't in your diapers."

"Um-huh."

"I've put in the miles. There are worse men to do the river with."

"If you're saying you're not a young man anymore, Tucker, I agree."

"You ain't listenin', 'cause that ain't what I'm sayin.'"

"But it's what I'm saying. So get on a plane and go home. I'm starting to lose my patience."

I watched him visibly compose himself, but then he was mad again within seconds. "You don't think I know the story as well as you? Amanda's mama's gone off with some lard-assed Yankee that's diddlin' her and takin' her money at the same time. You come down here to fetch her home, but you're too damn stubborn to admit you might need some help if lard-ass won't let her go. Goddamn it . . . quit bein' so goddamn stubborn!" His face, which was as wrinkled as parchment, had turned a Navaho red. For the first time, I realized something: This really was an old man. What if I kept at it, made him so furious that he had a heart attack right here at the airport? That's all I needed, dealing with Tuck and mounds of idiotic paperwork at some Colombian hospital.

I said, "Okay, okay, calm down, Tucker. There's no need to get so upset. People are looking."

"I don't give a hoot in hell who's looking. They can kiss my ass on the county fucking square for all I care! And you, too, Mister-been-all-over-the-world-know-it-all! 'Cause here's something you don't know: When things go bad in a place like Cartagena, the shit comes down so fast, you'd better have wings to stay above it or a shovel to dig your way out. And you'd better by God have someone you can trust watching your back."

I nearly said, yeah, like I'm supposed to trust you? Would've but veins were sticking out in his neck and he'd gotten redder.

"Take a deep breath, just relax." I was shushing him with my hands. "Get in the cab and we'll talk about it. No need to get upset."

"I ain't exactly inexperienced at this business, you know! I've been in plenty of tough spots. Shit"— his voice softened—"I hate to admit it, but I've done the worst thing a Christian white man can do. Yes sir, I done killed me a human being. A Mexican. Great big fat one, but he was quick and them bastards ain't exactly easy targets." He paused for a moment; let his eyes blur at the horizon. "Duke, that greasy beaner haunts me to this day."

The man was insane. He hadn't killed anyone—Tuck's old partner, Joseph Egret, had told me the truth. One more example that Tucker was the creator of his own sloppy reality.

I opened the door of the cab and slid inside as the old man said, "I won't get in the way. I promise. And I might help."

I was shaking my head. Why had Amanda told him my travel plans?

Now he was in the car beside me, hat on his lap because the car was so small. "I hate to admit this, Duke, but I been kinda lowly lately. This ain't been the best month for me."

Trying to keep peace, hoping he would calm down, I said, "Amanda told me about Roscoe. I'm sorry. You two had been together a long time." Tuck and his big appaloosa gelding.

The expression on Tucker's face demonstrated surprise, then indifference. "Huh? I ain't talking about my damn horse dying. That worthless bastard? Roscoe, I ain't . . . hell, he'd been so damn contrary lately I was half tempted to put a bullet in him myself. Good riddance, that's what I say. No, what I was talkin' about, Duke, is my health."

The man was maddening. I refused to ask.

Didn't have to.

As the cab sped us west along a rolling seacoast, I listened to him say, "The last four or five weeks, something's gone wrong with this old body of mine. Hard to believe for as good as I look. I won't argue that.

But the problem is . . . well, shit, I'll just come out and say it. For more than a month, I've had me a permanent case of Whiskey Dick. It's about to worry me sick. Understand that what I'm saying is just between you, me and the fence post. If Joe ever got wind of it, he wouldn't let me forget—"

Tucker stopped abruptly. He'd apparently forgotten that his old roundup and poaching partner was dead.

He began again. "What I mean is, if anybody as black-hearted as Joe found out, I'd never hear the end of it. It wouldn't do me no good with the tourist ladies around Marco and Naples, neither. So I'm hopin' this little trip to the tropics works me some good. The señoritas, they've always liked me just fine, Duke. Just fine."

I was rubbing my forehead with my fingers. I said, "I'm not going to tell you again, Tucker: Don't call me Duke."

❋

Club Nautico was located on Cartagena Bay just a few hundred yards from the Spanish stone garrison that was now an upscale restaurant called Club Pesca . . . one of the nicer sections of Cartagena.

I recognized the fort from previous trips as well as the postcard that Amanda had received from her mother. One being so close to the other, I interpreted as a good sign. Maybe someone would know something about a fat American on a sailboat.

The little marina took its security seriously. A bright pink stone wall screened and protected it from the street. At the wrought-iron gate, a man in a blue guayabera shirt stood guard. He did a quick assessment as I paid off the taxi, then nodded a greeting as he swung the gate open. Gringos with money are welcome almost anywhere, anytime.

Club Nautico could have served as the prototype for every expatriate waterfront bar from Hong Kong to Bombay: palm-thatched roof strung with fishnet and seashells, ceiling fans, bamboo framing and supports, red tile floor, L-shaped mahogany bar near a pool table and laundry room, an elevated dining area with white tablecloths, everything outdoors and open to the water except for the wall that sealed off the street.

This was the tropics, right? All you need is shelter from the sun, protection from thunderstorms, plus some ice, rum and a place to sit.

The rafters above the bar were draped with international flags. An atlas of sailors who had made landfall here from far-flung places—Britain, Japan, Cuba, Vietnam, New Zealand, plus a huge green burgee that read "Nostromos." Tacked to the raw wood pole supports were yacht club pennants from around the world. The rest I knew without having to look: There would be showers and good food and the bulletin board would be layered with uncollected airmail and For Sale notices posted by wanderers trying to scrape together enough money to get home and handwritten notes offering deckhand service for passage to the next port of call by those stranded and desperate for transportation.

Club Nautico was neat, well maintained and protected. Whoever had set up the place knew what he was doing. It was like most small marinas run by expats: it was an adjunct to the country that housed it; a tiny and precise international crossroads that had many of the characteristics and advantages of a foreign embassy, but none of the stuffy drawbacks.

As Tuck and I straddled stools at the bar, I could look through the fronds of palm trees growing up through the decking and see a couple of dozen ocean-going sailboats moored stern-first to the marina's high wooden docks. They were probably owned by voyagers who'd settled in Cartagena for an extended stay. Beyond the docks in a broad mooring area were a dozen or so more sailboats anchored randomly. Their hull colors—mostly fiberglass white but a few painted red or blue—looked brighter for the marl-blue water. The marina seemed to have a pretty good business going.

Across the bay was a Colombian Navy Amphibian base where I had once billeted for three interesting weeks. I could picture the way it would be beyond the sentry gates: massive grounds, trimmed golf-course, neat barracks and buildings and Quonset huts freshly white-washed, a military park with ships tied along the cement quay.

"You like a drink, *señor?* Cold beer perhaps? Perhaps menus?" The bartender was a tall man, very black, with a heavy Spanish accent. A putty-colored scar, razor-thin, ran from his ear to his neck. First look at the man's face, I thought: *Maybe knife fight.* Second look: *Undoubtedly a knife fight.*

Improbable adventure movies aside, it is hard to imagine two men drunk enough or crazed enough to fight with knives.

I told the bartender in Spanish that we would, indeed, like menus plus a couple of bottles of Polar or Aquila. We would try both. Plus glasses with ice, for that is the way beer is sometimes drunk in the tropics. And, by the way, was the owner around? The Australian man. What was his name?

"Garret," the bartender said, choosing to continue in broken English. "Are you a friend of his?"

"I think we have mutual friends, but I'm not certain."

"He go to the Magali Paris for the kitchen."

After we'd ordered, Tucker tapped the bar and made a noise of frustration. "I'll be damn, that's too bad. The man you wanted to see, he's off in damn France."

I said, "France?"

"Didn't you hear the bartender? Gone to Paris. Even back in World War Two, I hated those bastards. The French, I'm talkin' about. Stinkin' wine-drinking sons-a-bitches. Down there in the South Pacific when we was fightin' the Japs so they could have their damn country back. Run around pissin' in the streets, what'a they care?"

The Magali Paris is a supermarket chain popular throughout South America. I shook my head slowly; said nothing.

※

We were drinking our beers from the tall glasses filled with ice. Tuck gulped his half down, wiped his mouth on the back of his sleeve. "You know what we got in common, Duke? The both of us, we're nothin' but tramp steamers on two legs. Tropical junkies. In my heart, I feel like I'm about half-beaner. I really do. Can't count the times I've come *this* close to growing me one of them skinny Ricky Ricardo mustaches. Know what I mean?"

Get some drinks in him, Tucker loved to talk. When he asked a question, though, it wasn't because he wanted an answer. He asked questions because they required pauses that added pace and timing to the stories he told. I said, "Yeah, that would fit your whole act. Perfect, pencil-thin mustache."

"Exactly the way I see it! 'Cause that's the way I feel in my heart, understand? It's like this craving I get. It's like a craving for the sea, but, at the same time, it's for the jungle." Gave a little shrug: *Can't explain it.* "I want them both close enough to step outside and know they're there when I take a breath. You're the same, that's my guess. I bet we ever set down and talked, really talked, we'd have a shit pot full of stuff in common, you and me."

I was drinking a Polar. Ten-ouncer in a lime green bottle. Good beer. "Yep, I'm just a chip off the old block."

"Now . . . there's somethin' I never told you about my life, 'cause I didn't want you to think bad of me. Thing is . . . as you know, I spent a lot of my time down here in these little banana republics. Me and Joe Egret, we went about everywhere a man can go without needin' an airboat or a ladder. Know what we was doin'? Pot haulin'. Yep, run a seventy-, eighty-foot crab boat over here, have the colored boys fill'er up with bales of pot, haul 'er back."

When I didn't react to that, Tuck added, "It's illegal, you know. Pot-haulin'."

I said, "Uh-huh, I think I read somewhere that bringing tons of marijuana into the United States is something that, yeah, they can arrest you for."

"But we never got caught. Nope. Trouble was figuring out what to do with all that money we made. Joe and me? What we was scared of was the IRS net-worthing us. A man can't outrun the multiplication table no matter what kinda horse he's riding. A calculator can stick your ass in Raiford just as fast as a .38. At one time we had close to three million in cash between us."

Didn't want to react, but I couldn't help myself. Three million cash? Or . . . maybe it was just another one of his lies.

Tuck said, "Hell, countin' all that money, we'd get pissed off if we came to a bill smaller than a twenty. I once used a stack of tens to wipe my business after takin' a good 'un. Just too much damn trouble to bother with, know what I mean?" Tucker glanced at me for a moment, returned his attention to his beer. "Now . . . a great big chunk of that money I got hidden away. Not in the U.S., that's all I'm gonna say. When the time's right and the coast is clear, I'll go get her. Maybe ask you to go along, ride shotgun. But know what Joe and me did with the rest of it?"

"Nope. Don't have a clue."

"Invested it like smart businessmen. Sure did. We opened us a string of seven tanning parlors. This was back before tanning parlors got to be real popular. Like we was pioneering that particular business."

"Where?"

"Panama City."

"Panama City, Florida?"

"Nope. Panama the country. All right downtown, too. Good locations. Couldn't risk bringin' the money into the states."

I wondered if I should even bother. Yeah, I had to. Couldn't pass it up. I cleared my throat. "You know, Tucker, Panama's only, what? a couple of hundred miles off the equator? And Panamanians, a lot of them are pretty dark to begin with. I wouldn't think tanning parlors would be such a good investment."

Tucker was nodding, way ahead of me. "Gawldamn it, when you're right,, you're right! I wish I'da talked to you first, 'cause every one of them bastards went bust. Joe and me, we lost us close to a million dollars cash. But you know me, I always try to look on the bright side. You want to talk about a good tan? I had me the best tan you ever seen in your life. No shirt marks or nothin'."

Tucker was wagging his fingers at the tall bartender. "Hey there, *amigo!* We'll sail again here." He clumped his glass down on the bar. "Bring me a shot'a that white rum on the side, too."

※

Tucker said, "Since the owner's not here, what you bet I can get that bartender to talk?"

He had finished the rum, was still working on his second beer.

I said, "Talk? Talk about what?"

"About that guy Amanda hates. Merlot. If Merlot was here with his sailboat, I guarantee you I can get the bartender to tell me. You got those pictures?"

"Yeah, I have the pictures. But I'll do the talking. You just sit there and drink your beer."

"I don't think the man'll talk to you. That scar, a man with a scar like that, you got to figure he knows the price of admission. He's not gonna go runnin' off at the mouth just 'cause you ask."

I said, "But he'll talk to you?"

"That's what I'm bettin'."

"I guess we'll just find out, won't we?"

I placed the photograph of Merlot and Gail on the bar. Looking at the glossy print—the way the man's fat thumb strained to touch her breast—irritated me, so I took pains not to allow my eyes to linger. The bartender, however, stared at the picture intently. As he did, I watched his eyes. They focused, then they appeared to refocus from the general to the particular. His expression struggled to remain relaxed, unreadable.

Yeah, he knew who he was looking at. . . . I was convinced that the bartender had seen Gail and Merlot before.

He said, "This woman, she is beautiful, very beautiful, no?" Still speaking English . . . probably because he didn't want the rest of the staff to know what we said.

"Beautiful, yeah, I guess so. I've never seen her in person before."

"That is *verdad?* Then why do you carry her photograph?"

You have to play these things by instinct. The bartender, whose name was Fernando, was smart, savvy and necessarily tricky. Serving drinks to foreigners in a wide-open town like Cartagena required the rare combination of diplomacy and cold-blooded indifference. In any circumstance, the most convincing approach is the one that sticks closest to the truth, particularly with someone used to listening to drunken lies. So that's the approach I tried. The truth. "I'm carrying her picture because I'm looking for her." When Fernando glanced at Tuck—now done with his second beer—I added, "*We're* looking for her. My uncle and I. We flew down this morning from Miami to find this woman, because her ex-husband just died and we have to tell her."

Tucker's head swiveled toward me. "You're shittin' me! Her husband, that asshole Frank what's-his-name, he really is dead?"

I felt like knocking the old bastard right off his stool.

I was chuckling. Letting the bartender know it was a big joke. "My uncle knows the man's dead. My uncle's a drunk. A troublemaker. He doesn't know what he's saying half the time."

Fernando had been following along, accepting my story until Tuck interrupted, but now his thin smile told me he didn't believe a word I was saying. "I wish I could help you," he said with a shrug. "But I'm afraid I don't know these people."

I had a $20 bill folded in my hand—a week's salary to restaurant help. I slid the bill under the photograph so that just the corner was showing. "It's very important. What I told you's the truth. The woman's ex-husband is dead. There will be legal complications. We need to find her and take her home."

Fernando, I could tell, wasn't going to budge. "At the Club Nautico, *señor*, a man's business is his own. We do our jobs. We give the good service, the good food, and that is all. If you have other questions, you maybe ask Mr. Garret. But I warn you as a humble person"—he eyed the $20—"I would not use your money in such a way with Mr. Garret. He is the owner of this place and not a man to insult."

Fernando wheeled away, reappearing a few moments later with our food: platters of fried snapper and black beans with wedges of lime.

"Damn almighty, Fernando! That smells even better than the grub I had on the plane and, by God, that's sayin' something!" As an aside to me, Tuck added softly, "That son-of-a-bitch really is dead?"

"Yeah, and thanks for handling it so well."

He missed the sarcasm. "How?"

"I don't know. I'll call Amanda tonight and maybe find out something. As it is, you just screwed up any chance I have of getting information out of the bartender."

"I already told you, he'll talk to me."

I took a bite of the fish. Why even answer?

"Talk about touchy! You want me to get the information out of him now, or you mind if I eat first?" Throwing it up in the air like he didn't much care one way or the other, letting me decide.

I said, "We'll wait for the owner. Just drop it."

"So you don't think he'll talk to me?"

"No."

Tucker pushed half a fillet of snapper into his mouth, a chunk of bread and said something—no way of knowing, his mouth was so full. He may have said: "Watch me."

Which is what I did.

I watched Tucker corner Fernando by the entrance to the kitchen, near the telephone and a sign on the wall that said in Spanish and English: *Log all calls.*

I watched Fernando's scarred face glaze into a mask of indifference . . . then surprise . . . then enthusiasm and pleasure. I watched the two men shake hands and—this was unbelievable—I watched them hug slightly and whisper something into each other's ear . . . or so it appeared.

I wasn't eating. I couldn't eat. I felt as if I were witnessing some bizarre theater. Tucker Gatrell, an Everglades gangster and unrepentant racist, was suddenly bosom buddies with Fernando, the onyx black Latino who had experience with knives but was too ethical to accept bribes.

I watched them talk. I watched them laugh. Translation seemed to be a problem. When Fernando didn't understand Tuck's English, Tuck simply—and idiotically—spoke louder not slower. He used hand language, too, like some bad actor conversing with Indians in an old Western film.

Finally, they shook hands again, hugged again, and Tuck returned to the bar, walking his gunfighter walk. He straddled the stool and began to eat. Didn't say a word.

I waited. . . .

I waited. . . .

Jesus, he was going to make me ask. Finally, I did:

"Okay, okay, you and Fernando are suddenly best friends. I apologize. He told you something, what?"

Tuck had a mouth full of beans. "Told me everything. Just like I knew he would."

"I don't get it. I didn't lie to him, didn't try to trick him, I even offered him money. You knew he'd talk to you—how?"

"'Cause he's a Freemason. We're both Freemasons."

"Freemasons? I don't understand . . . like a club? You're both Freemasons, so that means—"

"I'm a thirty-second degree Master Mason, Scottish Rite *and* Knight Templar. Not a club, it's a what-you-call-it, an exalted brother-hood. Tropical Lodge Fifty-six, which is one of the oldest in Florida. Fernando there, he's just out of Blue Lodge, only a third degree Master and he wants to be a Shriner. If we get some time, I told him we'd sneak off alone and work on it. I'd help him along."

I tried to picture Fernando, with his murderer's scar, wearing a bur-gundy fez, driving one of those little clown cars at parades. "A Shriner? He gives you information for free just because you belong to, what is it, the same lodge or something? You're fraternity brothers, that's what you're telling me."

This was lunacy.

"Shows how much you know. Freemasonry is a . . . hell, you won't understand. Nobody's not a Mason can understand. What Freema-sonry is is an ancient and honorable union that dates back to the time of the pyramids. The vows a man takes when he gets married? They ain't close to bein' as sacred as the vows a Mason takes. You doubt how serious bein' a Mason is, check the back of a Yankee dollar. The Eye of God on the pyramid, that's a Masonic symbol put right there by my fel-low Freemasons who started the U-S-of-A."

He was serious about it, maybe telling the truth for a change, too.

"I got brothers all over the world, mister man. Joe Egret? He was a Mason. Dumb as that Injun was, he put the time in and learned what he had to learn. Why . . . Joe actually worked so hard at it, he got to know his stuff better than me. I ate and drank with some brothers down on Cat Island—the Bahamas, I'm talkin' about—who were the head voodoo chiefs . . . only they called it something else. Talk about black? Those brothers down there make Fernando here look like an albino-fucking-Swede. Nothing they wouldn't do for me 'long as they can put their family and their work first. Me same with them. You didn't see Fernando's ring? That's why I knew he'd talk to me. Has to. Masonic Code. 'Cause he can trust me and he knows it. Doesn't matter he's a beaner or not. Once a Mason, always a Mason."

"Did he tell you anything about Gail?"

"Yep. Seen 'em both. The fat man had a boat here till the owner, the Austrian guy, kicked 'em out."

"Australian. The owner's not Austrian, he's Australian."

"The one who took off for France?"

I ignored that. "Where did Fernando say they went?"

Tuck made a slow-down motion with his open palm. "You'll find out. In good time, you'll learn it all. What Fernando suggests we do now is stroll out to the end of the dock—see that great big rusting three-master out there? Big enough to carry a small herd of cattle and old enough to sink like a damn tire iron. He says we need to go out there and ask for a man they call the Turk. But we're going to have to kill some time around here, wait for the man to wake up. He sleeps most the day, stays awake all night. Fernando says we should ask the Turk about real estate, make him think we want to buy something. That way, nobody at the marina will have to tell you where to find the fat man and the lady, 'cause the Turk'll let it slip just discussing real estate."

"We say we want to buy real estate?"

"Isn't that what I said? Merlot, what Amanda told me was, that Merlot was involved in real estate, so it makes sense."

"Fernando wouldn't tell you the rest of it. Where they went?"

Tucker smacked his lips. More fish, more beans. "Didn't say that. Fernando told me exactly where they are. Told me everything he knew. But I'm not allowed to tell you. Part of the Masonic Code."

"That's absurd. If you know, why bother with the charade of—?" I was shaking my head, frustrated, irritated. "What kind of code are we discussing here?"

Tucker finished his beer and signaled a smiling and eager Fernando for another round. He said, "Sorry. Can't tell you that either," before he called, "Brother Fernando? We'll sail again here, *amigo!*"

15

The Turk's name was Jamael Hasakah. Lean man in his mid thirties, six feet tall, black hair, very thick eyebrows, facial features that were delicate, waxen, feminine. The white cotton pullover and drawstring pants he wore made his skin even darker, almost black. He had wide full lips, an Egyptian nose and remarkably long, thin fingers like splints of brown bamboo that he moved constantly, almost experimentally, as he talked. He might have been playing an imaginary accordion.

The Turk was talking now: "You gentlemen are truly interested in our new community? Our very special real estate opportunity? Then, by all means, come aboard. Come aboard my home! I am the only authorized representative in Cartagena. It is true!"

His home was an oceangoing motor-sailer over 150 feet long; had to displace 250 maybe 300 tons. Looked as if it might have been built to ship bananas during the days of United Fruit, back in the thirties. Or maybe dates and casks of olive oil through the Suez. The hull was a rust-streaked enamel-white hulk that was made to appear delicate and geometric by a labyrinth of hawser lines and rigging that angled skyward to towering masts. The deck area was massive, with elaborate skylights, an elevated wheelhouse and an open gallery astern: a big-time, old-time, sailing freighter that had seen better days, much better days.

On its rounded stern, I'd noted the name:

MOON OF KIZ KULESI
ISTANBUL

"Follow me, follow me!" The Turk continued to wave us along, apparently excited to have company. The deck was a maze of crates lashed as if for shipping. There were bicycles, motor scooters, potted plants, exercise equipment, a couple of sea kayaks. There was a whole row of waste-high bushes growing in plastic boxes. The leaves of the bushes were saw-edge, five-leafed.

Cannabis? Yes . . . no doubt about it. Right out there in the open, no big deal.

There were some chilies growing, too. Beefy-looking green chilies. Made me think of Tomlinson. He, Musashi and their toddler daughter were probably under sail right now, headed for the Dry Tortugas. If nothing else, maybe I could get some chili seed stock for him. . . .

"You really must excuse the mess, gentlemen. I've acquired so many things. So many things since we arrived in Cartagena! I hired one of the fruit ladies to clean for me, but she didn't come today."

"Fruit lady?"

"You're unfamiliar with Cartagena? It's an absolutely delightful place. Every morning, the fruit ladies come carrying baskets on their heads while the merchants sweep the streets. Baskets of fruit, understand. These women, they scream like cats. '¡Piñas! ¡Bananas! ¡Aguacates!'" The Turk was attempting to imitate them, shrieking out the words. I realized that he was very drunk or very stoned.

Five in the afternoon. Probably both.

We were still following him—down a ladder that was peeling varnish; ducked through the steel frame of a watertight hatch—as he said, "So I hired one of the fruit ladies to do my cleaning. She brings me breakfast, cleans all the cabins, absolutely anything I want her to do. If I haven't had a woman for a day or two? She takes care of that, too. All for just a few pesos. In your money . . . American money, perhaps two, maybe three dollars." The Turk seemed very pleased with the situation. He was smiling. Had a nervous laugh that was more like a twitch. He also had a very noisy case of the sniffles. "Have you gentlemen noticed? The poorer the city, the more passionately a man can live! I've been in Cartagena a year. I may stay another year!"

The poorer the city, the more passionately a man can live!

Undoubtedly, guessing from the Turk's satisfied expression. Also judging from the vast number of men like the Turk whom I'd met around the world.

Now we were in a large salon area: dining booth, sectional couch and chairs, big-screen television, VCR, teakwood cabinets that held stereo gear, books, plastic controls for video games, a pinball machine in the far corner, a ship's coffee table made from a massive porthole bolted to the deck in plush carpet at the center of the room. On the coffee table was an ornate jade water vase with small hoses dangling out the top. The hoses were tipped with gold. Smoke drifted out of a brass bowl near the bottom of the vase, little tendrils of steam. A Bedouin's hookah.

The salon smelled of marijuana and diesel fuel, rotten fruit, electrical conduit and paint.

The Turk made a welcoming gesture. "Smoke if you like, gentlemen. We grow it ourselves. *Viajera de Cartagena,* we call it. In English, the 'lady traveler of Cartagena.' Because people will travel through time zones and risk much to find it. An absolutely wonderful product. If you're interested, I have some I might be willing to sell you."

Was the Turk really in the drug trade or simply offering to share? I was curious. "How much product do you have available?"

He paused for a second or two to think about it. "At the moment . . . a thousand . . . perhaps two thousand kilos, I believe. But I can get more if you are serious."

Laughter . . . *sniff!* . . . laughter.

Yes, he seemed to be in the business.

"I wouldn't mind having me a quick smoke. Bought a whole roll of Copenhagen for this trip, but damn if I didn't go off and leave her at the ranch. Where the hell's my brain lately?" Tucker had one of the rubberized stems in his fingers, looking at it. "There'uz this bawdy house in Tampico, they had them one of these here kind of pipes. Suck on her, she made bubbles. Coolest smoke I ever had."

I took a step to warn him . . . then thought, hell with it. Let him think it was tobacco. Maybe he'd get high, pass out, go to sleep, leave me alone.

Tuck took a couple of puffs, then a couple more. Finally he smiled, blowing smoke out of this nose. Surprised me, saying, "Yep, same thing like in Mexico. First-rate shit you boys grow down here."

※

The Turk explained that their development was so new they didn't have their brochures printed yet. But what they did have was a superb Web page. They'd just got it up and running. This American, the CEO who put the whole syndicate together, was a real computer wizard. Probably could have done the whole thing himself, but he had the cash, so why not hire the best?

The Turk said the American paid some Taiwanese Internet specialists like twenty thousand U.S. to design the entire Web page. Made the thing interactive with audio and little videos and all kinds of rooms. "But some of those rooms"—his tone was telling us "naughty-naughty"—"some of those rooms, we have to restrict, because U.S. authorities will not allow certain things to be shown. Even to adults."

I was thinking about Gail's money. A project, any real estate project, arrives at a point where it requires fast cash. She'd been right there with lots of it. Gail had almost certainly paid for the high-tech Web page he was describing, X-rated rooms and all. That and probably a lot more.

"They're just plain tightass idiots," Tucker said. He was referring to whoever it was who made them censor whatever it was in their Web page rooms. He visited often enough with Tomlinson to be more familiar with computer jargon than I, but his concern was manufactured. He had to concentrate to speak, enunciating very carefully. He'd been smoking right along, still carrying a beer from the bar. He seemed to know what he was doing with a hookah in his hands, I noticed.

The Turk was nodding, very eager to agree with him. "But here in

Colombia, I can show you anything. Everything. We have freedom here! The entire program. Anything you want to know, it's very simple, just point the arrow and click. But you'll see. Our company is having the Web page, the whole layout, put on CD. This CD, we will send out to perspective buyers. Even the scenes certain people find so offensive." That laugh again . . . *sniff!* Very nervous, slightly crazed, lots and lots of drugs. That's what the laugh told me. He said, "But I don't have the CDs yet, either. So you'll have to look over my shoulder, I'm afraid."

The computer was on a three-tiered desk near the TV. It was small, about the size of a reference book. A Macintosh Powerbook G3-something with a color screen that reminded me of Tomlinson's machine.

Tucker and I stood behind the Turk as he tried to get the thing going. But something was wrong. Couldn't get a dial tone; couldn't get on-line. He checked the beige telephone wire that was plugged into the machine. The wire ran across the floor on top of the carpet and out an open porthole on the marina side of the freighter.

The Turk shook the wire, said something loud, furious in Turkish, then charged across the deck to the porthole where he yelled, "Garret . . . ! Mr. Garret! You have unplugged my telephone line again!"

Didn't wait very long before he screamed the same thing again.

Finally, there was an answer: "Stick it up yer arse, you fuckin' raghead! I'm busy!"

"I need my telephone, Mr. Garret!"

"If you don't like the service, pay your bloody bill and tow that garbage scow out to sea. The *federales,* they'd love that! You wouldn't make it past Bocachica before they had you in cuffs!"

No mistaking the bush brogue of northern Australia. So . . . Garret, owner of Club Nautico, was back from his shopping.

The Turk fixed us with a look—Give me a moment, I'll get this straightened out—before he yelled through the porthole. "Mr. Garret! I have clients here. Americans who may be interested in buying a membership in Mr. Merlot's project."

Tucker and I exchanged looks at the mention of Merlot.

The Aussie yelled back, "They ain't my bloody problem, Turk! You want the phone line hooked up, I'm gonna charge you double this time. Them long-distance access calls for your bloody computer bullshit ain't bloody cheap. Fifteen . . . no, twenty dollars U.S. for the first half-hour and then I cut you off."

The Turk was smiling—okay, things were all arranged now. "Yes, of course. That is acceptable. To show my appreciation, Mr. Garret, I will pay you twenty-five U.S. It is worth it to me! Put it on my bill."

As the Turk sat at the computer again, he said, "It is a game that Mr. Garret and I play. He pretends to expect payment from me and I pretend as if I expect to one day pay."

He was working at the keyboard.

"You stay here for free?"

"I owe Mr. Garret a year's back dockage. Plus utilities. Plus our restaurant bill and tips." He looked up at me briefly, very serious. "I am the grandson of a Sultan, you must understand. I am accustomed to living comfortably; to the better things life has to offer. It is what I deserve, so it is what I demand. In my country, my family is of the highest social station. President Demirel is a second cousin to my mother. Prime Minister Erbakan attended the same British preparatory school as my father. You can understand, then, why I refuse to allow money to dictate my lifestyle. Plus, I entertain many ladies here, many, many ladies. As a part of our new real estate venture, understand." The laughter, that cocaine *sniff!*

"The owner lets you stay here even though you don't pay?"

"Mr. Garret? He would prefer not to be paid because he hopes to take my yacht. Naturally, he would be very disappointed if I paid even a portion of the bill. Already he has filed papers with the Colombian court. So I live here and he keeps charging me and the bill keeps adding up. See? It is now a game that we play! *Ah-h-h-h,* here we are!" The Turk gestured with his hand. "Our Web page!"

※

The Turk said, "You were under the impression our property is in Colombia? No. It is in Panama. Over the water and through the jungle. Not far! Just as Ohio is next to . . . next to an adjoining state in your country. Illinois? Very close, very, very close. And if you like what you see on the computer, we have a plane. We will fly you there. At no charge, of course."

I don't know that I'd ever seen a Web page, but this one certainly seemed professionally done. What Merlot and company were offering was membership and time-share participation in a converted country club in an old Panama Canal Zone village, a tiny place called Gamboa. The locator map showed it to be about midway between the Pacific coast and the Caribbean coast, on a paw of jungle where the Chagres River entered the canal. The Isthmus of Panama, where the canal cuts through, is less than fifty miles ocean to ocean, so Gamboa was close enough to Panama City to make for easy access.

But Merlot was offering more than just property.

The home page headline read:

Gamboa
A Private, Protected Community for Fun-Loving People

Then in smaller letters:

Gamboa
Finally! The Freedom to Live Our Dreams!
Anything you want . . . because you've earned it.

The script was backdropped by a stunning photograph of classic tropical homes overlooking the canal on a hillside of dense rain forest. There were flowers, gigantic luminous leaves, clapboard and wedges of bamboo fence showing through. The houses appeared to be from another time: wooden, perfectly maintained, elevated off the ground like tree houses.

The jungle that dwarfed the houses implied components that jungle always implies: shadows, waterfalls, vines, earth as black and potent as gunpowder, wild parrots.

I'd driven through Gamboa once years ago, but it was at night. Didn't see much, but remembered the smell of the jungle there, and the solid look of the houses that drifted past in our Humvee's headlights. Like most structures in the Zone, the houses had been built back in the

1920s and '30s by American shipwrights. The guy who'd been driving was an old hand from the Jungle Operations Training Base at nearby Fort Sherman, and I remember him telling me how the houses were built: redwood imported from California, hardwood floors, copper plumbing, even roofs layered with copper sheeting, for God's sake, everything pegged and bolted and dovetailed solid as a ship, built for the long haul of colonialism. Only the best if the U.S. government was buying and building it. Also told me something about the work-hard-drink-hard locals . . . yes, he'd told me what they called themselves: *Gambodians*.

Right . . . and I had certainly passed Gamboa while transiting the canal by ship or boat. I had a vague recollection of white houses on a hillside, a little working tugboat and dredge marina. But I had not realized what a truly lovely place it was.

The Turk was clicking through a scrapbook of photos: houses, interiors and exteriors, swimming pool, tennis courts, a refurbished bar and restaurant on a high hill. "The Gamboa Country Club," it was labeled.

"Is it not beautifully done?" The Turk asked.

"The Web page? First-class. Really nice."

Looking at the computer screen, reading the words, I felt a chill . . . the kind of chill that precedes nausea. It is always troubling when innocent words are used to mask a broader meaning: If the buyers Merlot wanted to attract were nothing more than fun-loving people, why did they need to be protected? If they had legitimate dreams, why was it so difficult to find a place where those dreams could be realized?

The Turk wanted to ask us something, I could tell. But he was having difficulty finding the right approach. Finally:

"You are men of the world, I take it."

"I've been around."

"Gawldamn right we have! I'd barely scratched the surface when I told you about that bawdy house in Tampico. Tampico, the best place in the world to buy hand-tooled boots. Also, maybe the toughest city in Mexico to leave without takin' a case of the clap home as a souvenir. Lotta people don't know that, either."

The Turk smiled indulgently. "So you appreciate the more pleasurable . . . the more sensual needs that all men of health and vitality share. Of course! Why else would two successful American men come to a place such as Cartagena."

Yeah, the sex trade. Why else would a Yankee come to Colombia?

I nodded, hoping Tucker would keep his mouth shut for once, just let it happen.

The Turk said, "Gentlemen, what we are offering for sale here are not simply beautiful time-share duplexes and homes in one of the most beautiful rain forests in the world. What we are offering is a private, a very private, members-only club where a man—or, yes, a woman—may come and indulge any . . . any appetite or fantasy they wish. Indeed, the management of Club Gamboa will . . . strive to provide whatever . . . whatever is required to make your fantasies a reality."

I wanted him to come out and say what he meant. "What you're telling us is there'll always be women available. So it's like a whorehouse village. Or are there options?"

The laugh, that *sniff!* "Gentlemen, why am I talking when our Web page is designed to show you? Here . . . please consider what we have to offer. This feature"—he was moving the cursor, closing windows, opening others—"it is called . . . it is a video, a QuickTime video. Watch and you'll learn much of what I'm sure you want to know."

16

First I had to sit through a little bit of history on the Panama Canal. I watched the video patiently, already convinced that Merlot and Gail were at Gamboa, but also knowing that my best approach to Merlot was probably as a potential buyer. I wouldn't receive a very warm welcome if I just walked up and said, "Hey, that lady you've been blackmailing? I've come to take her home."

To convince Merlot that I was a legitimate buyer, I had to first convince the Turk.

Tucker was still smoking . . . Christ, wobbling now and humming country-western songs to himself . . . moving back and forth between the hookah and the computer as I watched helicopter footage fly me over locks and down a straight brown conduit of water, jungle on both sides, as the Powerbook spoke to me as if it were guiding a tour of Disney World:

"The independent nation of Panama is completing its takeover of the Panama Canal and the land that sides it. It is the world's most lucrative shipping route!

The United States opened the canal in 1914 and, over the years, built ten military bases and American-style villages in prime areas of the fifty-mile-long, ten-mile-wide Canal Zone. Those facilities will soon be abandoned by the U.S.!

The Zone is so beautifully maintained that outsiders often compare it to a national park. It consists of 560 square miles of prime land, much of it uncut tropical rain forest . . . and one of the Zone's most beautiful little tropical colonies, Gamboa.

Gamboa's rain forest is the richest on earth. That's no exaggeration. Honest. Biologists have counted 184 varieties of tree per hector there, a world record! Tiny Gamboa also holds the world record for the most birds counted in a contained area—525 species! In and around Gamboa you can also find more than 120 kinds of orchids plus all kinds of wild fruit and flowers. But know what? You'll probably be too busy having fun to spend much time outside."

The Turk interrupted, saying, "What it says next is important. *Very* important. As how you would say . . . background information that will make you feel secure about your investment."

That seemed to be the sole objective of the video: convincing potential members that Panama was a safe investment.

"Want to know why investors like you and me are being offered this extraordinary opportunity? Here's the fascinating story: In 1977, the Carter Administration agreed to gradually turn over the canal and the land to Panama by December 31, 1999. It was also agreed that the so-called Zonies—mostly Americans from families who'd worked in the Zone for several generations—would be phased out. Prior to the Carter treaty, there were nearly twenty thousand Americans, or Zonies, living and working in the Canal Zone. On the afternoon of the transfer, fewer than 800 remaining Zonies will finish their last day at work and leave for good. Why should that be of interest to people looking for a unique new vacation paradise?

"Here's why: The Panamanian government considers the beautiful housing and facilities long provided for the Zonies to be among Panama's most valuable assets. The Authority for the Interoceanic Region is willing to make these facilities available to good people like you and me at bargain prices . . . but only through select companies and individuals that they have chosen to administrate these properties . . ."

Meaning Merlot. But why had the AIR chosen someone like him?

As I started to ask, the Turk pressed an index finger to his lips . . . then went ahead and spoke anyway. "What comes next, it will explain more. Why you will have wonderful security and support in Gamboa."

The person doing the explaining was Club Gamboa's founder and CEO, Jackie Merlot. Big smiling close-up of that hairless face and those BB-sized black eyes. How Merlot happened to be entrusted with control of a defunct golf club in a beautiful Panamanian village was not immediately spelled out. He was just there, a smiling giant, blond hair as if it were glued in place. The little video zapped through a montage of shots to keep it interesting—wildlife, hot springs, jungle rivers—while we were told that, in Panama, Mr. Merlot was a man who got things done. . . .

And then Merlot was on camera. He looked massive in a tent-sized beige guayabera, a style of four-pocket linen shirt that all fat men wear in Latin America. He was walking through the flowered streets of what I assumed was Gamboa, talking to the camera. He had a smoky, curiously high-pitched voice, in which he began by speaking about his connections with "many important" Asian businessmen.

Strange. It seemed an odd choice of topics, but there it was. He had to be working some kind of angle.

I stood and listened to him explain that his "connections" were instrumental in approving an ingenious plan: The virgin rain forest on the Gamboa property would be harvested and a portion of the income would become a financial asset to all members. The timber revenue would finance remodeling and maintenance for the whole project, plus create more room for construction.

That, at least, made sense. Despoil a mountainside, despoil a human being. What was the difference?

Then he said, "Our project will be of particular interest to my many good friends from Chinese Hong Kong and Taiwan. I have personal knowledge of the modern Far East's high standards of service, whether it's business or pleasure. We know quality. That much you can be sure of."

He didn't seem nervous; was perfectly at ease, a man used to being in charge. No doubt about it, he was tailoring his sales pitch for Asians.

Why? And what kind of connections could he have in Asia?

I waited to find out as he told the camera that "Panama's friendship with Asia has always been important. But now it's more important than ever." The reason? Huge smile. "Because there would be no Club Gamboa, that's why. Not if some of the most successful corporations in Hong Kong and Taiwan weren't committed to playing major financial and organizational roles in the future of the New Panama Canal."

One of the Chinese companies involved, he said, was Panama Ports, a subsidiary of a major Hong Kong conglomerate. Panama Ports had been awarded control of Panama's two most valuable properties—the ports on either end of the canal, Colón and Balboa—with a twenty-five-year contract. The company would pay $22.2 million a year, plus would invest many times that in improvements!

Which was a big surprise to me—the Chinese were now in control of both ends of the Panama Canal?

And maybe that's why Merlot was targeting Asian clients . . . but, in a strange way, he also seemed to be using Asia's participation as a bona fide for his own small project.

Another very important addition to Panama, he said, was Evergreen, a Taiwanese shipping company that was beginning construction of a fifty-nine-acre terminal near the Colón Free Trade Zone. The project would cost about $100 million.

A third Chinese company, Tainan Ltd., solely owned and controlled by one of Taiwan's wealthiest families, had also received major concession contracts from the Panamanian government. Among them were several tracts of housing, including Gamboa.

Merlot was grinning into the camera, as he said, "I spent my early years living with my mother in Taiwan, and I have known the fine people at Tainan all my life. They have my eternal respect . . . as do all the companies that are working hard to make the Panama Canal bigger and better than ever. In their free time?" His smile broadened. "I hope the honored workers of these fine companies will join us at Club Gamboa and let their fondest dreams come true. Just as I hope you will do the same. Our club motto is simple: Anything you want . . . because you've earned it."

There it was: Merlot was telling potential buyers that he had the political blessing of a major Taiwanese company. That was all the guarantee anyone needed. He had connections with Tainan, a corporation that was investing millions in Panama. Which was probably why he'd been awarded the Gamboa concession. Choose a reason: maybe he was old school buddies with a member of that powerful family . . . or maybe he had some kind of blackmail leverage . . . or maybe, just maybe, Amanda had been right when she guessed Merlot had a touch of Asiatic blood.

It didn't matter. He had this village and he apparently had the political juice to make it work.

I placed my hand in front of the screen. "Look, you're kind of wasting my time, Turk. I'm not here to listen to history and crap about the Chinese. All I want to know is exactly what Gamboa's offering me and how much is it going to cost? You got something interesting to show me, show me now or I'm going back to the bar."

The Turk looked up at me and shrugged—Okay, tired of this screen? Let's try something else. He was closing windows again, moving the show along as he said to me, "Some Yankees . . . forgive me, Americans, are easily offended. They have a very narrow view of what is improper or immoral when it comes to a man's pleasure. Our chairman, Mr. Merlot, put it very well when he said that Americans are . . . what's the word . . . ?" The Turk was thinking hard, eyes wrinkled shut.

"Prudes?"

"Exactly! Prudes. That's precisely the word. Are you and your old friend like most Americans? Or do you agree that we all have different . . . needs?"

Tucker was now sitting on the couch, staring into the hookah's smoky glass globe. He was still wearing his gray rodeo hat, white sports coat, ankles crossed showing his fancy boots. He stirred, looked around, finally found the Turk with his eyes. Said, "Old? Fuck you."

"A generous offer, but no thanks," smiled the Turk.

"Well . . . who the hell you callin' old, boy? How'd you like to go home and tell your mama that some boy just spanked your . . . your . . . spanked your . . ." Tuck's voice flattened and disappeared. He'd lost the thread . . . but he'd found the hookah again, something easy to look at, not loud, not penetrating.

He sighed; folded his hands in his lap.

I watched his head fall before I said, "I'll look at anything you've got to show me. I'm wide open."

"Open to anything?"

"You think I came to Colombia for the fishing?"

The Turk's laughter said okay, he was convinced. Sounded very enthusiastic as he said, "Then you will love Gamboa. Because in Gamboa, you can have anything you want."

"I know, the motto. Because I deserve it." Like it was bullshit.

"No, when I say anything, that's exactly what I mean. The Chinese, the Japanese, they know how to relax. Gamboa is being created for them . . . and for Mr. Merlot's own personal interests."

On the screen now, new images were appearing. I stepped back a little, watched.

Felt that chill again. A swelling nausea . . .

※

The Web page had a very complete catalogue of pornography, most of it shot at Gamboa, I was told, but a few things from Mr. Merlot's own personal collection.

The stuff from Merlot's collection, I didn't see till the very end. . . .

The way it worked, the Turk told me, was that he recruited "help" to work in Gamboa. In return, Mr. Merlot paid him a small finder's fee, promised him a prime vacation time-share on the canal, plus allowed him to be Gamboa's sole agent in Colombia. He got 10 percent of anything he could prove that he moved.

"If I can sell a few of these time-shares," he said, "I can pay Mr. Garret enough to get the case out of the courts. I can save my yacht in this way."

I said, "So convince me. Make a good case for your project, and I'll buy."

The shrug, the hands, the facial expression, all said no problem. "First thing, Colombia has the most beautiful women in the Americas, perhaps the world," the Turk said. "If you sign the contract, purchase a time-share with us, what you do then is tell Mr. Merlot what you want while you're in Gamboa on vacation. Anything you want, I can find it for you. A beautiful Negro housemaid? A young Latina cook? Or perhaps . . . perhaps a teenage boy." He held his palms up—whoa, he wasn't judging, just giving an example. "You want all three at once . . . or five at once, you can have that, too. If we get your order in advance, I find what you want in Bogota or here, in the slums of Cartagena." The palms again. "Poor, yes, but very clean and beautiful. You pay a small fee for each and they will do anything you wish them to do. Truly, Gamboa is the place to make your fondest dreams come true."

"So what happens if I happen to be visiting Panama, I've got some clients with me, but the time-share I bought is for a different time of the year?"

"As a member of Club Gamboa, you may rent by the night, by the week, whatever you want. True . . . on such short notice, we may not be able to provide precisely what you want. But the club's entire staff will be made up of very beautiful women and very willing boys and they are always at the members' disposal. But here—let me show you the kind of pleasure we have to offer." As the screen changed, he said, "Are you sure you would not like to smoke a bit while you watch?" A minute or so later, he said, "You don't mind if I do?"

I wasn't looking at the screen. Had long since turned my eyes away . . . not out of disgust, but out of . . . sadness? No, but an emotion that was close to it. More like a . . . hollowness.

I did not look at the computer screen for the same reason that I do not go to topless bars or strip shows or watch pornographic films. Sex? Yeah, I love sex. Love the tender anything-to-bring-her-pleasure kind and the sweaty belly-slapping variety and anything, absolutely anything else, that will make me or my like-minded partner happy. But when the debasement of an individual is viewed as entertainment, we are all diminished . . . plus I am always, always perplexed by a very basic question: How does it come to pass that the lives of otherwise-healthy men and women are so tragically compromised?

The Mangrove Coast

235

"Mr. Ford. Do you not find them very beautiful?"

I had signed a one-page form, printed in English and Spanish, acknowledging that Jamael Hasakah had introduced me to the glories of Club Gamboa, thereby confirming his legal right to a finder's fee as well as elevating me to the status of a man who deserves a respectful prefix.

Tucker had dozed off on the couch. Had his cowboy hat tilted down over his eyes, boots up on the coffee table. He'd had six or seven small beers plus the dope. He was out.

I said, "Yes, the women are gorgeous."

"But a trifle old, perhaps?" The Turk's words were saying one thing, but his tone was saying something else. Maybe asking me a delicate question. What?

So I played along. "Sure, maybe a bit too old." I glanced at the screen. The two girls soaping each other beneath a waterfall couldn't have been more than, what? fifteen, sixteen? They were cold, had goosebumps, but were toughing it out for the camera. A third woman, performing oral sex on an Asian man, looked to be about the same age.

"The girls you see here, they all work as housemaids at Gamboa. You will meet them. Very nice. I selected them myself. From Bogota!"

The Turk's professional pride showing.

"But if you're feeling adventurous, let's go to Mr. Merlot's personal room. Is that all right with you?"

"Sure. I want to see it all."

"Then you shall!"

Click.

I looked at the screen, then looked away quickly, as the Turk said, "Mr. Merlot's tastes are not as unusual as many people think. Perhaps you agree? Mr. Merlot enjoys and appreciates children. It was a preference that he says he learned in China when he himself was a child.

"Here . . . in this photograph, you are introduced to a man you will come to know if you become a member. His name is Akibar, but everyone calls him Acky. Not only is Acky"—I noted the meaningful chuckle—"quite a man, as you can see, but he is the reason why Gamboa is guaranteed to be a peaceful place. Acky looks quite terrifying, but that is not a bad thing. There will be no obnoxious drunks or uninvited guests, you may be certain of that. Who needs policemen with Acky around!"

I looked just long enough to commit to memory the face of a man who appeared to be Afro-Asian; half Vietnamese, perhaps, or half Chinese. His face reminded me of the face of an ant but in human form. Big cheekbones like mandibles, skin tight over the bones, black piercing eyes. Big man, probably well over six feet tall, though his height was difficult to gauge.

He was standing before a teenage boy. . . .

But a very powerful man; with the body of a steroid-user, a weightlifter. I remember Amanda telling me about the showdown with Merlot. How Merlot's roommate was there, pissed off at her and Frank, ready to fight.

So say hello to Akibar, the giant ant. That's the way I thought of him. Merlot's enforcer and roommate . . . and who knew what else. . . .

I had to ask: "Merlot and his friends—they don't find it embarrassing being part of a show like this?"

"Not at all. Mr. Merlot feels it's important to set an example. In any healthy culture, my own country, for instance, what you are seeing is perfectly acceptable behavior as long as it is done . . . quietly. I myself occasionally enjoy a child who is utterly pure and without experience. Men loving children. Where is the harm in that? If the adult is kind and thoughtful and not abusive? Something else is, Gamboa Country Club will be a clothing-optional village. The pool, the beach they're building on the canal, the spa."

The smell of the salon, plus the heat, was getting to me. How much longer could I stand to be in the same room with this man? I said, "What do you mean, 'Gamboa will be clothing-optional'? The place isn't open yet?"

"On a very active but limited—only slightly limited—basis. There are still a few Zonians who live in that part of the village—a section called The Ridge. Still a few occupied houses. They run the tugboats until the transfer's complete, but they won't interfere, don't worry. And they'll be gone soon. All of them, all gone. And we'll have the pleasures of Gamboa all to ourselves."

The Turk wasn't done with it. "But the point is, why shouldn't the club's founder appear nude on his own Web page? Besides—" Laughter . . . *sniff!* "I think Mr. Merlot enjoys being what some might consider a porno star. He doesn't exactly fit the mold, does he? Such a big man but not what many would consider to be attractive. Also, I don't know if you've noticed—and I would never mention it to him—but he is always . . . well . . . he's never aroused in all these many photographs. Quite the opposite! So . . . let's just accept this as part of his sexual fantasy. Nothing wrong with that. Not a thing! It's what Gamboa is all about. Truly, it's a dream come true for a certain type of man. The type of man who often has to travel the world to find what he needs. I think Mr. Merlot and his closest friends fit that description. Perhaps you do, too, Mr. Ford!" Laughter . . . *sniff!* "Let's look at his personal collection, and I will show you what I mean—"

My head swiveled automatically; the screen came into quick focus. Just as quickly, I turned away . . . but too late.

It is unfortunate that I was unprepared . . . no . . . make that too damn dull to realize in advance what the subject matter would be. Had I stopped to think even for a moment, the general content would have been obvious . . . which is why I would have been spared the specific vision of something I did not want to see.

But I have a maddening gift for being inept or just plain dumb at precisely the worst possible time.

True to form, I charged ahead without consideration. I looked at the screen. Of course I looked! And what I saw will forever haunt me. . . .

For a photograph that was nearly twenty years old, the resolution was excellent. It contained an Easter egg–bright fluorescence that was painfully, painfully familiar. It possessed the bright colors common to Polaroids of that period . . . the kind of Polaroid that a devoted wife and young mother might have had laminated to send to the man who was the love of her life . . . if the love of her life happened to be stationed somewhere in the monsoon jungles of the Back of Beyond.

But a loving wife and mother would have never taken or sent this picture.

No . . .

Probably couldn't have even imagined such a nightmarish vision. Nor could I.

But I didn't need to imagine it because there it was in front of me.

"Mr. Ford. Mr. Ford? Are you all right?"

The cigarette-butt stench of marijuana, plus the heat and the diesel fumes, now seemed nearly overpowering. I had to take shallow, careful breaths to keep from vomiting.

To the Turk, I said, "I'm fine. Feel great, but I could use a beer. So . . . I'm going to head back to the bar. You can shut down the computer—I don't need to see any more."

"You like? What you've seen pleases you?"

I could feel sweat pressing through the pores of my forehead. Could feel the blood vessels throbbing beneath my skin, as beads of sweat traced their way down my cheek.

"This picture . . . ? It's great." I had to ask: "Who do you think Merlot got to . . . to take a picture like this? Of him and the little girl?"

The Turk considered the screen with professional objectivity. "Such cameras, even the older ones, I think, have those little timer buttons for self portraits. Press the trigger, then hurry to get into the shot. He probably took it himself. That is normally the way with such pictures." He was still considering the photo. "An unusual-looking child, is she not? The eyes are very interesting."

I was forcing myself to read and reread the piece of paper I'd signed; concentrating on it. "Oh yes, lovely. This Gamboa project, the entire presentation . . . I'm very impressed by what Gamboa has to offer. If the housing's nice, I'll buy. You've made yourself a commission. Might as well call the head guy—Merlot's his name?—might as well call him and let him know I'll need a tour. A personal tour, if he doesn't mind. I'll be there tomorrow."

"Tomorrow?"

"He can count on it."

"No . . . I'm afraid I can't arrange to fly you to Gamboa for at least two days. Maybe three. Our company plane is busy—"

"I don't remember asking for your help. I'll find my own transportation."

I paused. Had I spoken too sharply? Tomlinson once told me that the truly insane fear only that their madness is transparent to the world. That's how I felt at that moment. Transparent, out of control. How could the Turk have missed the fury that was cauldroning in me?

I added amiably, "I mean, it's no big deal, I'm happy to book my own flight. I've got nothing better to do"—made myself smile—"and I can't wait to get to Panama."

"Your friend will visit Gamboa with you . . . I say 'friend,' but perhaps he is a relative."

"The old man? He's a pain in the ass is exactly what he is. You don't mind, I think I'll leave him here, let him sleep it off." I was still fighting the nausea. "I don't know if you heard me or not, but you can shut down your computer. I've seen enough."

Finally, he did. But the nightmare image lingered: the grotesque lard-white nudity of a much younger Jackie Merlot, his sausage hands violating the innocence of a pretty, copper-haired child . . . the surprise of what was happening and the pain of it showing on the child's face and in the depths of her wise and lovely eyes; eyes that I liked, had always liked; one of them slightly off center, a wandering brown eye.

The shock of seeing her with the fat man was like a whiff of ether . . . and with that came the realization of another stupidity: Tomlinson had immediately realized what I refused to consider. Amanda's childhood photos hadn't been misplaced, they'd been stolen. By Merlot, on the chance that those boxes contained innocent photos of the two of them together, the cross-eyed child and the deliberate stranger. All photographs almost certainly taken with the same camera.

I wondered what kind of ruse Merlot had used to send the young mother off on an errand while he "baby-sat" her child. Or maybe he had sufficiently charmed Gail so that, for a time, he was little Amanda's regular baby-sitter. A nauseating thought. So get the child alone, use the mother's instant-print camera, hide the prints. What fun!

Merlot had been lucky enough to discover that Amanda's memory of him had scarred shut. The proof was when she'd surprised Merlot at her mom's house. Amanda genuinely believed that she'd never seen the fat man before. Even so, he couldn't risk further association between himself and the daughter . . . or allow a chance encounter with an old photograph to key the memory electrodes. . . .

17

The man behind the bar said, "Hello there, mate, you must be the Yank that Fernando was tellin' me about."

I'd taken the bar stool in the far corner, the one nearest the door. Wasn't feeling very talkative. I listened to him say, "You got a face like Iowa, so it's not much of a guess . . . and from that expression, I'd say you either just screwed the pooch or the Turk's been showing you some of his video toys."

It was a little before 7:00 P.M. and a jungle breeze came off the water carrying aromatic little pockets of open sea, of jasmine and frangipani blossom . . . and of the city, too. The Old Walled City was just across the bridge. Narrow alleys of cobblestone, little markets that hadn't missed a morning in three hundred years.

Even this far away, there was a hint of mangos plus crushed pineapple in the wind . . . and the odor of water on worn stone.

After my time aboard *Moon of Kiz Kulesi,* the breeze smelled pure, wonderfully uncontaminated. Can there be virtue in the fragrance of moving air?

"You're name's Ford, right, mate? Turns out we've got several mutual friends. Here—have a beer on me."

That was a surprise. Apparently, some of my former associates had been on the telephone.

He'd wrapped the ten ounce bottle of Aquila in a brown napkin to keep it cool. I took it, drank it half down, paused to look at the condensation dripping down the bottleneck, then finished it.

"Must be thirsty."

"Yeah."

"Another?"

"Make this one a Polar."

He used a church key to pop the top. No twist offs down here.

"After an hour or so with the Turk, it's too bad a man can't drink soap. Or get his soul pressure-washed. There's just no quick way to get clean."

"No. No, there's not."

"He try to sell you a membership to their freaky-deeky club?"

"That's not the way he put it, but, yeah. Sounds pretty nice. I'm going to buy. Sounds like a great place."

"Bullshit. You don't need to lie to me. Like I said, we've got mutual friends. If the beer's free, the least you can do is tell me the truth." The man winked. "Hell, I'd tell the bloody truth all night long for free beer!"

I looked at him a moment and thought, yes, more than likely . . . he had that look . . . he'd been some places, seen some things, so we probably did have a lot in common. Maybe it was the same thing when Tucker and Fernando saw each other, members of the same secret club.

The man wore fishing shorts and a white T-shirt. The breast pocket of the shirt read: Walker Wilderness Tours—Northern Territory—Australia.

His hair was cropped short; looked to be in his late thirties maybe early forties. He had a flat, Irish face, a brown push-broom mustache and a nose that had done some traveling. Currently, it was pushed over to the right, just beneath his eye.

When he put the beer in front of me, I said, "Thanks."

"Not a problem. Get five or six of those down you, I'll start charging you triple, you won't even notice."

"You're Garret, the guy who owns the place. I've heard about you, too."

He had a good, strong laugh. Actually, it was more like a roar. "Hah! From the bloody Turk, I bet! What'd that nasty little sand nigger say about me? It was a lie, whatever it was. The man wouldn't know the truth if it bit him on the arse!"

In Colombia it is always the cocktail hour. It was now also the dinner hour, so I was not alone in this open room with its ceiling fans and decorative flags hanging from the palm thatching.

Garret didn't care. He didn't care who heard.

"The Turk? Fuckin' Turk, I don't know if he wants me to put him in jail or adopt him!"

"He says you let him stay here because you want his vessel."

"Hah! That's a bloody good'un! The only thing worth a shit on that piece of garbage is the two or three hundred kilos of hashish he thinks the *federales* don't know about. Which is why I won't touch his boat, because I refuse to deal with the poisonous shit. Not everyone in Colombia runs drugs, you know. But I'll auction his tub off fast enough when the courts put his ass in jail!" Garret slapped the bar: Hah hah hah!

Down the bar was Raymond, a sixty-some-year-old Irishman I'd met earlier. He was a merchant seaman who'd missed his ship and was now stranded in Cartagena. Used his accent and his stories to charm drinks. Always had a cigarette and glass in his hand, a rummy. There were three or four tables of men and women eating dinner. A table of Brits and a table of Italians, judging from conversations. Nearby was also a German couple, men. They wore T-shirts over their jock-sized bathing suits. Homosexuals sailing the coast, nice people not bothering anybody. Also at the bar were a couple of American men, one middle-aged, the other in his twenties. Regular-looking, but they had some money. They belonged to an absolutely stunning forty-two-foot Hinkley moored just down from the Turk's ghost freighter. I'd met them earlier, too. Jim and Chris aboard the *Windelblo*. From New England, the kind of men you trust right away, the two of them in a customized million-dollar work of art but like it was no big deal.

Garret said, "So I'll ask you again: tell me you didn't buy into their freaky sex club."

I leaned forward. "I need to get to Panama. Right away. Tonight, if I can."

"Tonight? It'll be dark. Nothing'll be open, and you won't be able to see a damn thing."

"That's why I want to get there when it's still dark."

The man nodded. "You're goin' after the woman. The woman the fat man kept down here on his boat."

I leaned back and thought about it for a moment. Then I used my index finger to signal him closer. Into his ear I said a single word that implied the accomplishments of two men. Then I asked Garret to fill in the blanks, supply the missing names.

The men I described were two good Australians I'd worked with, both SAS, one from Perth, the other Darwin. If Garret could be trusted, he'd know exactly who I was speaking of.

He knew the names.

Good. It was a good connection to have. I relaxed a little. "That's right, I'm going after the lady. Damn right I'm going after the lady. How'd you know?"

"Simple. A woman like her throws a big wake. Class and style, it's worth . . . well, with a woman like that, let's just say men don't give love, they invest it. And there she is running around loose?" Garret's expression said he knew the ideal comparison. "You see that Hinkley sailboat out there? Finding the lady in this bar was like finding that Hinkley abandoned on the high seas. It just ain't gonna happen. The only mystery was how she got mixed up with the fat man. After I ran him outta here, I told my wife, 'Somebody's gonna show up looking for that woman. And they'd better hurry, before she's dead.'"

I didn't like the sound of that, nor the way he said it: Very matter-of-fact, not joking around. "You think he plans to kill her?"

"Naw. Someone doesn't get her soon, though, she'll probably do the job herself. Suicide, I mean. You can see it in her eyes. She's got these sad, sick eyes, but very bright. Beautiful eyes. You've met the lady. Or were you hired?"

"Neither. She was the wife of an old friend."

"Then you've missed something. With her face, a body like that, even at her age she could pass for some Latin American fashion model. A Yank accent, but her people are from the Equator, I'd bet on it. Plus she's got the most beautiful eyes you've ever seen. Almost like they're two different colors."

No doubt about it now, he'd definitely seen Gail.

Garret said, "The fat man, one night here in the bar, he was offering her out to the street people, the dock hands, whatever. Like he was proving to everybody he was such a big shot that a woman like her meant nothing to him. Sell her like a whore, what did he care? A big joke, but she wasn't laughin'. Because he meant it, damn right he did. He offered her to Fernando, ten pesos. About seven dollars U.S.

"It had nothin' to do with money—bastard's loaded with cash—the fat man's just an asshole. Vicious. He likes to hurt people, just like his bodyguard . . . or a boyfriend, whatever the hell he is. Merlot's giant boy-toy, a fella they call Acky. You know about him?"

"A little."

"Well, if you're goin' after the fat man, you'd better know more than just a little. Acky came close to killin' one of our local fellas. Got him down out there on the dock. Used his fists and his feet on him, damn near tore the man's face right off. He's a guy who likes to fight and likes to see people hurt. That's one of the reasons I ran them off. The other is, I caught Merlot trying to talk one of the local kids onto his boat. The cook's son, just a little shaver. And it weren't to teach the kid how to kick a bloody soccer ball!"

Garret didn't mind telling me about it. But first he wanted to know if I'd had supper. He was one of those you-have-to-eat-have-to-drink-guys. Probably a good father; a perfect person to own a restaurant.

I told him I had no appetite, not after the stench of being aboard the wind freighter from Istanbul. But maybe a glass of milk and some toast with Vegemite on it. If the kitchen had Vegemite.

That got a laugh.

"An Aussie without Vegemite? Gotta be kiddin', mate. Ever notice that every country's got its own perfect food? And it always tastes like shit to outsiders, but the locals are addicted. Colombia? We've got Amazona, the perfect pepper sauce. You know, *verde*. Blokes here eat the stuff on eggs, crackers, everything. It's gotten so I'm just as bad. I'll tell Fernando to bring you some toast."

Listening to Garret was a pleasure after enduring close quarters with the Turk. He wasn't a fan of either man's. Said that Merlot and the Turk were birds of a feather. They'd worked out a deal; the Turk had told him all about it. The Turk supplied Gamboa with women and drugs, for which Merlot paid cash, plus marketing rights to Gamboa. What did Panama care about women from Colombia? For Merlot and his new club, Colombian women were cheaper, plus there was less red tape.

It essentially confirmed the story that the Turk had told me.

The Aussie added, "I knew the woman was in trouble when I realized that the Turk was stopping in at least once a month to mail her postcards. Understand what I'm saying? They wanted to give someone back in the States the impression that the lady was still here. There's our little postbox. I peeked at the cards and I ain't bloody shy, so I asked him about it. Hah! The Turk, he just puts a finger to his lips and grins. 'Jealous husband,' he says, or some bullshit like that.

"The fat man musta had her write the cards out in advance, probably thinking the same thing: Someday someone would come looking for her."

As the Aussie spoke, I began to feel a nonspecific panic. What the hell had I dropped into?

I knew one thing: I had to find Gail Calloway and I had to find her quickly. From what I'd seen and heard, the woman was already so badly damaged that there might not be any way to save her . . . or any way to spare her good, good daughter, Amanda the sickening truth: Merlot had now violated and, perhaps, damaged beyond redemption the final two branches of a unit that had once been Bobby Richardson's family.

I said, "Do you think Merlot is in Panama? In his little village there."

"I know he is. Or was as of this morning. The Turk called him just before you blokes came in." The man glanced over his shoulder, "We've got a phone log and I make folks use it or kick their asses out. The Turk's got the *federales* out there waitin' on him, so he does what I say."

"Then that's where I'm going. Gamboa. I'll pay, I've got cash."

Garret looked at his restaurant—not too busy, everything going smoothly. Then he looked at the clock behind the bar. It'd just turned 7:00 P.M. A nice night with stars, the light of a quarter moon already showing on Cartagena Bay. He thought for a moment before saying, "You can't drive to Panama, I hope you're not planning on that."

No, I knew better. Not on the front end of the rainy season, anyway, which is precisely what April is. The jungled path between Colombia and Panama is an old silver transport foot route called the Darien Trail. This time of year, it would be all mud. There was no road.

"What is today, Friday? Saturdays, the first commercial flight doesn't leave till one tomorrow, get you into Panama City about one-thirty. Is that quick enough for you?"

"No. Not if I have a better choice."

"Well . . . there's one other way." His expression asked: Interested?

I nodded. Damn right I was interested.

He said, "I don't suppose you know how to fly a Cessna? Nice one, a one-eighty-two."

"Not well enough to make that trip, no. Not alone anyway."

"But you know how to steer? If I dozed off, got some shut-eye on the way, you'd know how to steer a course, do all the basics? I'm tired as hell. I was up all night last night."

I tried to remember if I'd ever met an Australian man who didn't know how to fly a small plane.

I said, "Sure, I can steer. They made us log enough air time to get a private license, but I've never really used it."

"I can have you at Paitilla Airport, classiest little airport in Panama, in just under two hours. There's a landing strip at Gamboa, but no lights. Can't land there at night."

"Panama City, that'll be okay."

"If you've got friends in the City, they can bring you a rental car or drive you, whatever. Gamboa's only half an hour away. I'll have to cut you loose, though, and fly back." He smiled. "My wife and son miss me if I'm gone too long."

I got the impression that Garret just wanted to get up in the air, get away from the lunacy of running a marina, dealing with the public.

Maybe have the chance to talk about things he didn't normally get a chance to talk about.

As the man had said: We knew some of the same people.

Surprise, surprise: I watched Tucker Gatrell lurch into the bar as I told the Aussie, "You finish up what you need to do. I've got to make some phone calls."

The man looked terrible. He'd lost his cowboy hat. His white sports coat had some kind of purple stain down the front, he'd apparently been sick.

I watched Tucker stumble and knock most the drinks off a nearby table, as I added, "The calls are long distance, but I'll use a charge card, if that's okay. The Vegemite, I'll take it with me. And I need to change clothes."

I had a light, long-sleeved black turtleneck and jeans that seemed like the thing to wear. I would, after all, be roaming around Gamboa at night. I might even compromise Merlot's house if I got the chance.

I watched Tucker turn, staggering, as if to acknowledge the mess he'd made, but his boot caught on the leg of one of the tables and he fell backwards, landing hard on his butt. It was pathetic to watch: a bow-legged caricature of an old-time Florida cowboy totally lost and out of control. I said, "And Garret? You mind if the old man bunks here? I'll pay cash in advance for any damage he does. And for his rack, his drinks, whatever he needs. I just don't want him with me."

Garret had watched the exhibition along with the rest of the bar. "Can't say as I blame you, mate."

✹

I'd been keeping track of the digital glow of the GPS, hoping Garret would wake up. Had a private little debate about it: Let the man sleep until we were closer to Panama City? Or make him take over the controls now?

Thoughtfulness won out. Let the man sleep. Yeah, I was paying him, but he was still doing me a gigantic favor. Plus, he'd be flying back to Cartagena alone and he'd need all the rest he could get.

I checked the GPS once again before I adjusted my headset, touched the transmit button and said, "Colón tower, this is Skylane four hundred Delta Hotel . . . I'm ten miles south-southeast at two-point-five with information Bravo."

GPS meaning Global Positioning System. Information Bravo meaning I'd just checked the weather, was completely under control. At least, that was the impression I wanted to give them.

I waited for what seemed a long time before I repeated my previous transmission, adding, "Copy, Colón tower? Do you read?"

Nope, apparently not. Garret had set the radio frequency, but I checked it again: 122.8. That seemed about right. Checked the GPS again. Yep, now nine miles out of Colón and closing.

I touched the transmit button once more and said for anyone to hear, "This is Skylane four hundred Delta Hotel and I'll be passing Colón to the south, bound for Panama City at two-point-five but climbing to four-point-five when I reach the mouth of the canal." Said it more for any other aircraft in the area rather than the sleeping tower in the nasty little port town of Colón. Felt like adding that everyone should stay the hell out of my way, because I wasn't much of a pilot and we were roaring into Panamanian airspace at 160 knots but at varying altitudes, and on a course that had more in common with a roller-coaster than with the normal patterns of a plane flown by someone who knew what he was doing.

Years ago, after my first required solo, our instructor had described my touchdown as, "More like a midair collision with earth than what you'd call a landing."

But I could steer okay. In fact, I was enjoying it, because it took my mind off things I preferred not to think about.

What I preferred not to think about was becoming quite a long list . . .

Things I preferred not to think about: hearing Amanda's voice through the telephone, but seeing her as a child again in that heart-breaking photo as she told me that the medical examiner had decided Frank had probably died from a heart attack that may have been catalyzed by slipping in the kitchen, cracking his head open on the counter.

Skipper, the young widow, was taking it pretty well. Maybe not so surprisingly well. She'd lost a soul mate, but gained three maybe four million in assets, not counting her beachfront home in Boca Grande.

Funeral was set for Monday.

Apparently, Frank had sprinted from the pool into the house—knocked the sliding door off its tracks, that's how fast he'd been going. Maybe hurrying to answer the phone, she guessed. But that didn't make sense because there was a phone near the pool. It was almost like he was in a panic. Running after something or running from something. How else could he generate that kind of force?

Part of what she said struck a chord: *In a panic, running from something.*

Scared to death, that's what the medical examiner was suggesting. But by what?

I asked, "There were two weird red lines on Frank's neck. Did the medical examiner say anything about that?"

No—and I could tell that Amanda did not enjoy having to again visualize her stepfather lying dead on the floor.

Something else was, she had a call in to the investigator Frank had hired, but no luck yet. She'd left a message.

I told her not to worry about it. I didn't need the information anymore. Told her that I had a good lead on her mom and that what she'd probably better do was call the airlines as soon as we hung up and book a flight for tomorrow morning. The earlier she could get here, the better.

That got her excited. "You're kidding me! Already? My dad was right, you really do have special talents."

I wondered if my lighthearted enthusiasm sounded as contrived as it felt. "We'll see," I told her, and that as soon as I knew more, I'd call. Sometime late tonight, probably.

Just before we hung up, she'd said in a shy voice, "I miss you."

A nice thing to hear, but she said it in a voice that told me she hoped to be more than a friend . . . which is probably why it hurt me so much.

Something else I preferred not to think about was Tuck. He'd made a big scene at Club Nautico when I told him I was leaving him behind. So drunk and drugged up that he could hardly speak, but still coherent enough to make himself the center of attention.

I'd told him that he'd find a way to embarrass me, and he had. Stood in the doorway of the marina weaving, trying to form words, and then—I couldn't believe it—he began to weep.

I'd never even heard the man's voice break before, but there he was sobbing, people in the bar hearing it all, but not understanding, when he yelled at me, "Why won't you give me a chance to make it up to you! You don't think it's damn near drove me crazy all these years? She was my sister, goddamn it! My only *sister!*"

It was the first time he'd ever mentioned the death of my mother or had even acknowledged that it had happened. That's how stoned he was. That's how old and broken, filled with regret, he'd become.

I felt some sympathy, but not enough to take him along.

Something I didn't mind remembering, though, was telephoning computer whiz Bernie Yager, timing it lucky enough so that he was at home.

After explaining to him where and what and why, I gave him the Internet address for Club Gamboa's Web page. I'd copied it onto a little piece of paper before I left the Turk's boat. To Bernie, I said, "I'll be forever in your debt if you destroy the son-of-a-bitch. The sooner the better."

Bernie had an evil little grin in his voice when he replied, "This whole terrible thing with Commander Richardson's wife, it's got the entire community talking."

"It does?"

"They're burning up the phone lines. Take it from me. And your fat friend? An hour from now, there won't be a data bit left standing of his Web page. All that money he paid? Down the drain. And every time he rebuilds it, I'll do it all over again."

※

Yeah, I was enjoying the flight, feeling the little plane beneath me. Concentrate: light touch of the wheel, foot-rudder controls and a nicety of trim all keyed to engine speed. Kept my eyes moving from horizon to altimeter, checking over and over to make certain that all gauges were in the green.

We'd been at forty-five hundred feet when Garret dozed off, but I'd dropped down to the deck, twenty-five hundred, to get a better view.

What I saw beyond the flare of my own running lights was the Caribbean Sea glittering in the moonlight. Off to the left was a black hedge of coastline, no lights, no life at all. Mangroves. Had to be mangroves. I repeated my transmission twice more, no reply. Had the feeling that I was alone in the world, suspended in darkness above a revolving earth.

What worried me was, I knew there were military bases nearby. The Jungle Operations Training Base at Fort Sherman was still operating. I'd done some training there years ago: tropical billets on a 30,000-acre preserve of untouched rain forest. Magnificent. There were Forts Gulick and Davis, too, but they'd already been turned over to the Panamanians. I remembered enough from my flight training that such bases generally have restricted areas associated with them called MOAs, or Military Operation Areas.

You can't fly through a restricted area without prior permission. To get that, I'd have to call the base's approach frequency before entering . . . a frequency I did not know. So, if I screwed up, I could expect to soon see a couple of Tomcats, war lights strobing, insisting that I land so that I could have a little talk with base security.

It's the sort of thing that inexperienced pilots want to avoid. . . .

Ahead now I could see an iridescent mushroom that had to be the big city glow of Colón. Separated from Colón by a panel of darkness was a galaxy of anchor lights at the Caribbean entrance to the Panama Canal. Lots of freighters and cruise ships waiting to transit.

It was still difficult for me to accept the reality that the Panamanian government had chosen the power brokers of Taiwan and Hong Kong as the canal's major concessionaires.

China?

It gave me something new to think about. Something to take my mind off the picture that kept re-forming behind my eyes . . .

Axiom: Whoever controls the ports of Panama controls the Panama Canal. Accept the premise and you have to also accept the fact that, as of December 1999, it will be China. To be exact: Panama Ports Corporation, subsidiary of a major Hong Kong conglomerate.

At first, I was shocked . . . but then, as I flew along gazing at the lights of ships at anchor, it began to make some sense . . . then it made perfect sense.

It wasn't just business, pure and simple; it was business *and* the politics of the coming millennium.

Most believe that the United Nations will provide scaffolding for the emerging "World Government" or "New World Order." That's what right-wing conspiracy kooks and leftist dilettantes preach, anyway.

Both are wrong. Unnoticed by the working public, a world government has been emerging strongly, steadily, for the last decade, and it is not the United Nations. It is a government made up of international conglomerates. These conglomerates have become the behind-the-scenes arbiters of power worldwide. Toughened by the economic expedient, they have become efficient and mobile administrators of legislation and policy. They have their own legislative and executive branches; they have their own sophisticated intelligence-gathering capabilities and their own loyal citizenry. Microsoft, British Petroleum, NEC, Canon, Toyota, Dow Chemical, Time Warner, Turner Broadcasting—of the world's largest one hundred economies, more than half of them are not countries, they are corporations.

So, yes, it made sense. Couriers of the New World Order were taking control of the earth's most important and profitable canal, and it had nothing to do with conspiracies. It was the Darwinian template acted upon by political dynamics. Yes, there were some Panamanian legislators who stoked and tended hard feelings toward the U.S. Maybe that was part of it. But Asia, booming on-the-move Asia, was a sound financial choice.

China now controlled the Panama Canal. . . .

It was a difficult truth to accept.

Some critics will say that, somewhere, a good man who was devoted to the well-being and security of his own great nation is rolling over in his grave; a hardened little Rough Rider who, to his credit, had nothing in common with New Age chief executives who lack what he most admired: courage, integrity and fidelity to the greater good.

And those critics will be correct.

There will also be advocates who point out that after years of manipulation, murder, ill-use and what amounts to political slavery administered by the United States, the small nation of Panama has not only a right but an obligation to do what is best for its own people.

They will be correct as well. But neither viewpoint carries an ounce of currency when applied to this new Darwinian template of world government. The dynamic is neither evil nor good, neither left-wing nor right-wing. It is pure. It is power. In such an environment, liars often prosper and cheaters usually win. Things are changing. The hubs of world authority are in a constant state of flux. Why did I find that surprising? Why would anyone find it surprising?

"We almost there yet?" Garret was stirring in the left seat. He glanced out the window, then he sat up quickly. Jammed his headset down over his ears and said, "Christ, that's Colón over there! We were supposed to cut inland way back."

"I know, I know, but I didn't want to wake you up and I didn't want to fly into any mountains, so I reset the GPS and it gave me a new route."

"I thought you said you didn't know how to fly."

"I'm a terrible pilot, but I'm a fair navigator. Some people feel safer over land, I happen to feel safer over water. Besides, I've never flown down the canal at night."

He said, "That's the first problem. We're not allowed to fly down the canal."

"Can we fly along it?"

"Yeah. Just don't buzz any cruise ships. We don't want a bunch of newlyweds and nearly-deads complain' to the Panamanian authorities about us."

I was banking southwest now over a vast darkness that was Gatun Lake, one of the largest manmade lakes in the world. The channel was lit up like a freeway. Open all the locks at once, and it would be like pulling the plug on a bathtub. The lake would drain almost dry, not enough water left to float a pontoon boat, let alone a thousand-foot-long container ship.

The mountains fed the lake, the lake fed the canal. Thus the necessity of the locking system on this highway between two seas.

Garret said, "Your friend who's picking you up at Paitilla Airport? He's gonna be sittin' on his hands twenty minutes or so longer than expected, 'cause that's how late we're gonna be."

"He's the friend of a friend, really. A real live Zonie, fourth generation. Born here, went to high school here, and now he's been temporarily stationed at the embassy. That's what I was told, anyway. He's a Company man."

Garret flew for a while before he said, "One of the Christians in Action fellas? One of the blue-shirt guys, is that the company you're talking about?"

I didn't reply to the question. "The best thing is, he says he lives near Gamboa. And he's got a car I can use. Some kind of transportation once I get there."

"Good on ya'," Garret said. "Seems like it's coming together bloody well."

"So far."

Panama City lay ahead, a void of the tangible insinuated by hills on the rim of horizon and moonlight. Gaillard Cut and the Continental Divide were out there. Gamboa and Gail Calloway were out there, too.

I was watching thunderheads to the southwest crackle with sulfurous light. The clouds vanished, then reappeared. The Aussie surprised me a little when, after a long silence, he replied, "No, that's not what I meant when I asked if he was CIA. What I meant was, if you're going to kill the fat man, it'll be handy to have a guy like that on your side. A spook, I mean."

18

The man driving the van from Paitilla Airport was probably in his mid-twenties, not more than a year or two out of some Ivy League college. He assumed a telltale variety of nasal wit that requires careful tending. Princeton, maybe Yale. The Company has always been big on recruiting from the Ivy Leagues.

But he was a Zonian, he said, the great-grandson of an engineer who'd come to the Zone back in the 1920s and stayed. Before the transfer, his mother and father both had had offices in the museumesque Canal Commission administration building with its red-tile roof up there on Ancon Hill. Now his great-grandparents and his grandparents were in the cemetery at Corozal, beneath the mango trees.

His name was Matt Davidson. Or so he claimed. Big rangy blond with a gawky, grinning Opie Taylor face. Had his aviator sunglasses in the pocket of his blue button-down shirt, sweat stains beneath both arms.

On the ground now, I was sweating, too. A hot night, like being immersed in bath water. So humid that when I first swung out of the plane I thought maybe that it'd just finished raining. But no. The tarmac was dry. Thunderheads were still strobing out there over the Pacific, sailing landward with the wind.

Davidson told me he'd just returned from a three-month assignment in Asia and man-oh-man was it good to get back to the Zone. "Couldn't wait to get here and go to the Tablita for a Sobe and choris."

I said, "Huh?"

He chuckled, "Sorry, forgot you're from the States. Or maybe I've still got a bad case of moonpongitis. What I said was . . . it's like Zonian Speak. Soberana's a beer. Chorizo, that's a kind of sausage. Really good sausage. Maybe we'll get you one while you're here."

Like I'd stopped in for the weekend, me in my black turtleneck with leather gloves and a navy watch cap I'd borrowed from Garret.

"Moonpongitis?"

From the look on his face, I got the impression that he'd misspoken. It was like: uh-oh. "Just an expression I picked up somewhere. It means like gone, you know, stir crazy. But those sausages I was telling you about, choris, the best place to get them is this car wash called Tablita. . . ."

No doubt, he'd said something he wasn't supposed to say. Not a big deal. I would have never asked him about Asia—professional courtesy prohibited it—but he's the one who offered up the familiar name. Moonpong? Phumi Moonpong, actually. It was a remote village in the Cambodian interior. The jungle was massive there, leaves the size of elephants' ears in the high tree canopy, and vines that snaked out the portals of Hindu temples that were eight hundred years old. Villagers lived in hootches with swept lawns on the banks of a river named by French missionaries: the River of Sin. I was supposed to forget a name or a place like that? It was said that the missionaries so named it because they were pissed off about something or because the river was black from rice paddies.

Davidson's small talk about the Zone didn't interest me. All I cared about was that he apparently worked for the CIA. There was something very odd about friends of my friends arranging for a Company man to meet me at the airport, provide me with a ride and probably a place to stay if I needed it.

Why? Why should they risk even peripheral involvement in a fray between private citizens?

I thought Davidson might give me a hint, let me know what was going on. But no, he played it straight as he drove through Panama City traffic, then into Balboa and out of town into the darkness of rain forest, headed for Gamboa.

Nothing but careful conversation that seemed designed to prove to me that he really had grown up in the Zone: "I understand the political reasoning behind transferring the canal, but it still doesn't seem right that they're making us leave. We had our own court system, fire departments, hospitals, schools, everything. It was our home. . . ."

Like it would be big news to me. Almost all Zonians felt that way. The man was filling up space, saying nothing.

He told me, "In the Zone, there was no crime, no unemployment, and if somebody got out of line, the company shipped their asses back to the states like *yesterday*."

Same thing. Nothing.

Matt said he'd attended Balboa High, surfed Tits Beach, played golf at Amador, got the shits drinking from the Chagres, took the train to Cristobal for football games and snuck beers all the way back. "It was a good place," he said. "Why else would our families choose to be buried here? Hey"—his tone brightened—"how can you tell if you're a Zonian?"

I had to listen to him play the little game: You know you're a Zonian if you've spray-painted your girlfriend's name on a bridge . . . if your boat has a better paint job than your car . . . if you can name the president who gave the canal away but can't name any presidents since . . .

We were on the narrow road that twisted through the foothills, nothing but trees and moon shadow. I could see his face in the dash lights. Finally, I said, "Matt, let's drop the bullshit, okay? I'm appreciative, I really am. But I'm also curious: Why are you people doing this?"

His tone was studied, concerned. "Pardon me? I'm giving you a ride to Gamboa. What's the big deal? Some friends of yours told me that's what you needed, so here I am."

I sat back. "Does that mean you can't say? Or are you just playing hard to get?"

We drove in silence for what seemed a long time. Finally: "Can we talk off the record?"

"Gee, is there any other way?"

The man was nodding, smiling. Then: "Bobby Richardson, he must have been quite a guy, huh?"

So that was it. Bobby.

"Yeah. A good man. He was very . . . reasonable. Very smart."

"I've heard some of the stories. You were there when he was hit."

"No. But in the general area. I helped ship home what was left."

"People still rave about the man. He's like a legend in certain circles, this All-American cover-boy type who also happened to be a serious shit-kicker. So let's put it this way: Your friends and my friends don't like the idea of some freak taking advantage of Commander Richardson's wife. I'm talking about certain people in the organization who believe your story. They trust your judgment in the matter. They are people who . . . people with a lot more juice than me and they think that the intelligence community needs to take care of its own."

"I'm flattered—and surprised. My impression is that the Company would never trust anyone who refused to work for them."

"Okay, so maybe I didn't say it right. That's the word on you, by the way: a details freak, precise wording. Know what else?"

I was enjoying this. Fitness reports from the past. "I'm all ears."

"That's the point: there is nothing else. People know who you are, but they don't know what you did. People know that you were part of it, probably a big part, maybe a main player, but no one seems to know who you worked for. A few, a very few, have met you and say they like you, but none of them can really explain why."

"I'm just an all-around swell guy, Matt. Get used to it."

"Yeah, you're being facetious, but that's what they say. And that you probably got out of the business because you like people. Maybe like them too much."

I said, *"What?"*

"That you're a nice guy, what's wrong with that? You care about people too much to fuck them over, so you got out of the business."

"I'm a marine biologist, that's all. It's what I do."

"Uh-huh, sure. We all know that story. The scientific types, they can go anywhere, ask anything and no one ever doubts them."

"It's not a story. I've got a lab. Ask me almost anything about fish."

"The rumor is that there is an intel organization in this country so black, so deep, that even the big-time politicos know nothing about it. Financing was set aside years ago, the whole group recruited during Nam. Really top hands. Name it: assassination, dissemination, political sabotage. The rumor also says, 'Hey, that's what Ford did.' Any of this sound familiar?"

I said, "No, but it's a great story. I'll look for it on HBO. You were telling me why the Company is being so helpful."

"I never said that the Company is being helpful. The Company's got nothing to do with this. It would be bad politically, plus it's illegal. But there's nothing wrong with our mutual friends asking me, a private American citizen, to help you."

"How far," I asked, "are you willing to take it?"

Suddenly, Matt was not the nice, easygoing Opie Taylor clone he pretended to be. "I don't want to hear a damn thing about any of it, that's exactly how far I'll take it. What you want to do, what you've got planned, it makes no difference to me. Maybe you're thinking about killing the piece of shit, which I wouldn't mind doing myself. But me, I don't want to hear about it."

He said, "Here's the drill. When we get to Gamboa, we've got a little safe house there, it's vacant. You can use it if you want. There's food in the refrigerator, not much, but it'll get you by if you need to stay for a few days. Stay there longer and I'll make a house call. In the garage is a motorcycle if you need transportation. All fueled up, ready to go."

A motorcycle? I hadn't ridden a motorcycle since Cambodia. It was the only thing we could count on because of the mud trails.

Davidson said, "After that, I'll show you where the Club Gamboa office is and where Merlot lives. It's the old golf clubhouse, a place called The Ridge. Then you're on your own. But be careful. His office and his house have first-rate security systems. The same security company that does our bid work did his place. That's how I know."

"They've got cops out here?"

I could see the look he gave me in the dash lights: I was joking, right? "If you get caught, the cops coming would be the luckiest thing that could happen to you. But they won't. His alarm system will notify Panama City police and they'll call and check to make sure he's okay. But it would take them an hour to get out here."

"You've seen Merlot."

"I know he's there. And I know Commander Richardson's widow is there. Which is why I'm now going to tell you something important: Play it very, very cool. Merlot really does have a lot of juice in this country. Why? Because he's got blackmail video of top-level Taiwanese honchos misbehaving. Take a guess at what they're doing. All Merlot has to do is make a phone call or two and he can have you arrested, shot, blown up, you name it. Welcome to the new Panama."

"You think I'll have any trouble getting the commander's wife out?"

"That's my point. If you piss him off, my advice is don't try to use public transportation out of here. I'm talking about the main airports." He handed me a slip of paper. "We have a boat all fueled and ready for you at the Balboa Yacht Club. You know where that is?"

I did.

"The name of the boat is *Double Haul,* in great big letters. Don't ask me why. It's one of the big ocean racer Scarab boats. The hull's canary yellow with red trim, easy to find down there with all those sailboats. It'll do seventy, eighty miles an hour. My advice is head southwest to the Azuero Peninsula. Do you know the area I'm talking about?"

"I know it. Not well. It's that big foot of jungle that sticks out into the Pacific."

He was nodding. "There's a little town there called Chitre. You'll be able to see it from the water. It has a pretty nice paved airstrip that our people built. We have a friend there, ask for Vern. Everyone knows him. He'll fly you to Costa Rica. By water, the trip should take you an hour, hour and a half tops. With your sea time, no big deal."

"What should I do with the boat?"

"I couldn't care less. The DEA confiscated it in some drug bust, so we truly don't give a shit what happens to it. When you get to Chitre, cut it loose, make some local happy. Or tell Vern where it is. If there's not a lot of heat on, someone will pick it up. One other thing: In the garage of the safe house, on the motorcycle's seat, someone's put a little bag of goodies there. Stuff you might need but don't have."

"Someone."

"That's right. And it's all nice and clean."

Davidson seemed to be telling me that if I wanted to kill Merlot, it was fine with them. They were happy to provide the tools if I was willing to provide the labor. "All I ask," he added, "is that you let me know in advance when you plan to take Merlot down."

That was easy. I said, "What time is it now?"

"Eleven-fifteen or so."

"Then give me an hour after we get there."

"You seem pretty sure of yourself."

"You want time to get out of the area, right? Plausible deniability, make sure you're seen by neutrals while I'm grabbing the woman. So I'm telling you, it's not going to take me long. If I'm in Gamboa for more than two hours, it was a bust. Merlot got me, I didn't get him."

Davidson seemed to be smiling a little as he said, "In that case, I'll make sure I'm long gone."

Something very odd about the way he said that. But why else would he want to know?

❋

There were lights of a village ahead, Paraiso. A little bend in the road with a grocery store that was still open. I told Davidson I wanted to stop in, use the phone.

When Amanda answered, I told her everything was set, to go ahead and take the Miami–to–Panama City flight.

She said, "I've got a confirmed seat on American at eight-fifty that will put me into Panama at twelve-forty-eight . . . no, eleven-forty-eight. I didn't figure in the time difference. Or I can try standby later in the afternoon if you want."

I told her the flight she had booked was fine, but come prepared to travel. Carry-on bag only, comfortable dress and boat shoes.

"Boat shoes?" she said.

"Yeah, I'm going to take you for a cruise, then we're going to tour the rain forest by small plane."

I described the yellow Scarab; told her that when she arrived in Panama, have her cab stop so she could buy food and drinks—some champagne to celebrate if she wanted—and to stow it aboard the boat when she got there. Her mother and I would meet her at the Balboa Yacht Club at one and absolutely no later than one-thirty, unless I called the bar and left word.

She was getting excited. "You've got my mom? Can I speak with her?"

I told her, "No. But I'm going to get her tonight."

That dropped her intensity down a notch, but she still sounded happy. "Doc, you know what I'm going to do right now? This friend of mine, Betty, she's big in the Unity Church up in Ohio and she's organized what they call a prayer chain for my mom. I'm going to write her the second I hang up and tell her our prayers have been answered."

A religious side—the first I'd seen of that. But nice. After what Amanda had gone through as a child, perhaps it explained her stability now.

I remember reminding myself that for every Jackie Merlot in the world, there were unnoticed thousands, tens of thousands, of genuinely decent and thoughtful people. These were people like Betty.

Nice, yeah, very nice.

※

Jackie Merlot had commandeered the old Gamboa golf clubhouse. No surprise there. A board-and-batten classic with a pitched copper roof that was barely visible through the trees from the road. The house was built on a hill, with a long screen porch looking out. Nothing but banana trees and ficus between it and the water. Because the lower level was enclosed with white trellis, the house looked even bigger than it actually was. For the last, what? seventy-some years, Zonian families had lived in this place. Lots of babies, school plays, graduations, retirements within those walls. Now Merlot had it.

A hydraulic lift, I noticed, had been installed next to the back stairs. I'd never seen anything like that in Central America. Apparently the fat man was too lazy to walk up and down the steps on his own. I could picture him waddling from the Mercedes diesel parked beneath the house to his own little elevator.

I'd made sure the motorcycle would start while still inside the sealed garage of the safe house. It was a Harley Sportster with a black teardrop fuel tank, saddlebags tossed over the rump as if the thing were a horse. No papers with it, no serial numbers that I could find.

Clearly, the boys in blue shirts didn't want to risk being linked to this business in any way.

I walked the Harley the half mile or so to The Ridge and the entrance of Merlot's drive. My second nocturnal tour of Gamboa. This time, though, the little village seemed deserted. No lights on in the houses, but lots of construction happening, lots of signs of remodeling. Something else: What I remembered best about Gamboa was that it sat within a cavern of shadows and dense forest.

Not now. The landscape around the houses was a pock-work of yellow stumps. A chainsaw's whine is the national anthem of every Third World country that still has rain forest standing. The loggers had been busy here. So check the price of rare tropical hardwood, multiply it by board feet and tally the small fortune that Merlot and company had already made. Developers and resource hogs are discovering what the sexual predators discovered long ago: Life is free and easy outside the U.S.

Or maybe the fat man was keeping it all for himself.

I was now standing in a thicket of bananas beside the house. It had begun to rain. Just rain, no lightning yet, although I could hear the distant rumble of thunder. A steady, soaking drizzle. I wore gloves and the navy watch cap; my face was darkened with the waxy tech paint I'd found in the goody bag left for me by Matt Davidson.

Not that I now believed that Davidson was his real name. No, he'd probably come up with it when getting the motorcycle ready. Harley Davidson. Matt Davidson. Clever.

Other useful articles in the bag: wire clippers, bolt cutters, two flashlights, a leather sap, a cheap stiletto, duct tape, a nautical chart showing the Panamanian coastline, a glass cutter, a drugstore first-aid kit.

No firearms. Maybe Bobby's old friends were reluctant to get their hands too dirty.

So I stood there in the rain, smelling the wet wool, watching water fauceting down the canoe-size leaves. In the moonlight, the Panama Canal looked to be more than a quarter mile wide here, jungle on the other side. An idea: I take Jackie Merlot by the collar and sidestroke him to the middle of the Canal. Say to him, "I just saw a photograph of you and my dear friend Amanda. It was one of the most disgusting things I've ever seen. So the good news is, you're only forty feet from land. The bad news is, it's straight down."

Say something clever to him and watch his face. Remind him of his tough guy *Darkrume* persona, say, Why aren't you acting tough now? Then nail him.

It would be nice, very nice . . . but it would also be very dumb. No, freeing Gail was my sole objective. And I planned to do it in the simplest, safest and most effective way.

A basic snatch-and-bag.

How many of those had I participated in during the early years? What could be simpler?

First things first, though. I took the knife and punctured three of the Mercedes's tires.

Let them try to chase me now. . . .

I found the telephone connection box at the base of Merlot's house. Underground cable entered from the road. Lights were still on upstairs and I could hear voices. Heard Merlot say something about the television, heard a much deeper, stronger voice with a Middle Eastern accent say, "Fuck you, do it yourself. All you do is sit at that computer. Or have this bitch of a whore do it. She never does anything around here!"

A grumpy night in paradise.

Then I heard Gail's voice for the first time. Heard her say, "I will do anything to make you two stop arguing. At least grant me the peace of silence. I should be allowed that."

Her voice was deeper than I had anticipated. It had a strength and a clarity that was unexpected, considering the circumstances. Class—Garret had described her that way. What I heard in her voice, though, was something I valued more highly. It was dignity. After what she'd been through, this was, indeed, someone special. Bobby had chosen well.

Kneeling in the rain, hearing her voice so close, it suddenly seemed hugely important to rescue her, to keep her safely within arm's reach until we were home in Florida.

I had the lid to the connecting box open. Merlot had three phone lines going into the house. His computers—that explained the additional lines. One phone line, and probably two Internet access lines. A couple of days before, he'd sat up there at his keyboard and communicated with me through one of these lines, baited me as *Darkrume*.

He'd written: "Find me, asshole."

I'd replied: *Exactly what I plan to do.*

Now I had.

A little-known fact: Most security systems work like incremental switches linked in a series that completes a low-amp, low-voltage electrical circuit. Cut the power and most good systems have a battery backup. Cut the phone line, however, and all but the very best systems are worthless.

I was counting on Matt Davidson having given me accurate intel: this was a very good system.

I loosened all six of the brass nuts onto which were attached three different pairs of red and green wires. I pulled the top pair of wires off first.

From upstairs, I heard: "Goddamn it! Now what's wrong with this fucking connection!" Merlot's voice with his limited vocabulary.

I'd apparently knocked him off line.

I reattached the top pair of wires, then disconnected the second. Nothing.

Maybe Merlot hadn't armed the alarm yet. Maybe they waited until bedtime, just before they turned the lights off.

After reconnecting the second pair, I yanked the final wires free . . . there was an immediate siren scream from above; an electronic tone so loud that it was numbing.

A terrible sound. Even so, I could hear the rumble of footsteps moving overhead. The fat man in a hurry, judging from the thump-thump-thump vibration. I gave him what I hoped was enough time to get to the alarm's keypad and punch in the shut-off code before I reattached the phone wires and shut the box.

There, that was done. Now all I had to do was wait.

I took the sap from my back pocket, held it comfortably in my right hand. It was a flexible weight, wrapped hard with black leather. Hit a man correctly, he would experience temporary paralysis even if he was conscious.

Hit a man incorrectly, and he would never regain consciousness again.

Seconds later, the siren stopped, its echoes faded. In the fresh silence of falling rain, I felt as if I could hear air molecules reasserting themselves around my eardrums.

Upstairs, Merlot said something. Couldn't make it out.

Then Acky's deeper voice: "Why is it I am always the one who must do these things? Why do you not go outside and look for yourself?"

This time, I had no trouble hearing Merlot's shrill reply: "I have my reasons, you fool! If I tell you to check, it's because I have my reasons!"

"But it's raining . . . and this happens so often. Why can't you take a turn?"

"Because . . . my slow-witted . . . darling . . . *you don't have the fucking brains to remember the fucking password when the cops call!*"

Dramatically patient and then furious: Merlot sounded even more like an overweight woman when he was mad.

Acky: "You have no right to yell at me in this way. One day you will raise your voice to me at the wrong time! I warn you!"

Merlot: "'*Duh-h-h-h, lightning set the fucking alarm off again!*' How many times have the cops called and you said that? '*Duh, the password, I don't remember any password.*'" Very abusive; his voice gradually getting louder: "I give the orders here! I give the fucking orders and if you don't like it, I'll contact my business associates in Panama City." Now the man sounded truly crazed.

Something else I could hear was Gail. She had begun to sob. It was a sound of absolute despair. She'd had enough—it was that sound, exhausted.

Merlot still wasn't done: "Remember the stinking beggar I saw snooping around her the other day? One phone call, one phone call to my friends, and guess what happened to him. Fucking disappeared, didn't he! Just like you'll disappear, Acky. Back to Lebanon if you give me any more of your shit! Or maybe . . . maybe I should tell the police where to find my safety deposit box. Let them read about the two men I watched you beat to death. Better yet, remember the poor little slum girl in Maracaibo?"

The phone rang.

Heard Acky yell, "Fuck it all! Fuck it all!" then nothing.

The phone continued to ring. The police or the security company were calling from Panama City, checking to see if Merlot actually had a security problem.

Seconds later, the door to the back stairs creaked open. Having been threatened, Acky was coming to investigate.

I waited just as long as I could . . . waited until I heard Merlot thumping around again—phone call done—before I snipped the line at the base of the telephone cable, then stepped back into the shadows. No more calls tonight.

Acky had a flashlight, coming down the stairs.

Something else Acky had was a pistol.

19

At one point, the beam of his flashlight swept across my legs, but I remained frozen, body pressed hard against the pilings of the house, trying to blend in.

Apparently, I did.

Acky paused, looked in my direction, then continued walking, checking downstairs doors. I got the impression that false alarms had become routine for him. When the siren sounded, it was usually the same: he grabbed a pistol and flashlight, made the obvious rounds outside, then returned to bed because no one was ever there. Power surges and failed telephone lines are not uncommon in Panama.

Still, Merlot had insisted that he search outside. He'd screamed at him, "I have my reasons! I have my reasons!"

Did that mean something? Or was it simply a coward's insistence on overprecaution?

I watched Acky intensely, barely breathing, trying to calculate the most effective point of intersection. He was a huge man; lots of weightlifter muscle. This would have to be done carefully and quickly.

I watched him disappear behind a hibiscus hedge at the back of the house, saw the beam of the flashlight sweep the hillside. It was still raining, coming down harder now. That was good. Rain provided cover. So did the occasional rumble of distant thunder.

I had the leather club in my hand, ready. Still watching Acky, I began to move.

There is rhythm to such a maneuver. It requires patience and a refusal to panic. Fortunately, it does not require great coordination—a gift I do not possess. I kept it simple. When he moved, I moved. When he slowed, I froze. . . .

The house was between us . . . then the hedge was between us . . . and then I was behind Acky, traveling quickly, quietly, because if he happened to turn while I was in the open, there was not much doubt that he would use the pistol in his right hand. . . .

Now he was plodding sideways down the hill toward the water. We were on the old golf course now. Was he checking to see if an uninvited visitor had arrived by boat?

Yes, that was it. He was shining the flashlight, painting the canal's bank with a yellow column of light as I continued to close, moving faster now because I had no cover at all. . . .

. . . Then, when I was only three or four strides away, it happened. He turned to face me, perhaps alerted by the sound of my feet on grass, or the air pressure of my bulk moving toward him, or possibly by some atavistic alarm that warned of predators—for that is certainly what I was in the instant, a predator; a predator locked so precisely on my target that all else vanished in a charge of adrenaline so pure, so potent, that the feeling surely mimicked elation.

I heard an unexpected sound: a thoracic growl. Could a human being make such a sound? Yes. It was the sound of terror, an inhuman reflex, and I could see the shock in Acky's eyes when he realized that I was on him, his mouth opening wide to scream as his pistol hand levered toward me.

I caught the pistol in the crook of my arm as I swung hard with the sap . . . was aiming at the delicate bone behind his ear, but his head dropped instinctively and I caught him high on the cranial globe. The pistol went flying from his hand, but he did not collapse in a heap as I had anticipated. Instead, he staggered drunkenly for a moment, then lunged hard toward me—a very big man who was now crazy with fear.

I caught his chin in the palm of my hand, locked his head against my chest as I threw my legs behind me, sprawling to avoid the reach of his arms . . . and then I gator-rolled with the full momentum of my weight, back arched off the ground, 360 degrees with Acky's head still locked tightly against me, two hundred and twenty–some pounds of torque.

That sound . . .

The sound that his body made was sickening. It was the sound of green wood snapping, sap exploding. It was the sound of a human spine twisting until severed.

When it happened, my head was tucked hard against his back, applying pressure. The noise, transmitted through the man's own viscera, seemed deafening. I could feel the trembling of his body as his muscles spasmed out of control . . . and then there were no more spasms, no movement, nothing.

I stood.

Acky was a dark mass at my feet. Dead. If Merlot really had filed away letters about the men and the Venezuelan girl that Acky had supposedly killed, they were useless now.

I didn't much care one way or the other. I'd been involved in the deaths of much better men than this, plus there was a feeling in me now . . . a feeling of terrible energy that was fueled by the most basic of elements: moon, moving water, wind, blood. . . .

Blood. Had I drawn blood? I fought the urge to check.

Yet the feeling remained, a kind of instinctual madness that ruled from the marrow; a feeling that I knew in my memory and despised in my soul because I'd drawn on it too often years before, and it drained from me that which I value most: my reason, my self-control.

Moon, wind, water, blood . . .

In that instant, those things were in me. Those elements *were* me.

I moved away from the body. Everything around me had been blurred by my intensity, but now I took a look at my surroundings. We were screened from the house by trees. Only a few yards behind me was the Panama Canal. The water was black in the moonlight. To the northwest was a transiting cruise ship. The newly wed and nearly dead. It was lit up like a floating city, moving toward Gamboa and the locks at Miraflores. It was far away. No one could have possibly seen me snap this man's neck. Flawless!

Now I had things to do.

Yes, things to do . . .

I used Acky's flashlight to hunt around until I found the pistol. A cheap little .38 special. But loaded.

I tossed it into the water.

I found the sap. I'd dropped it when I wrestled with the man. Now I jammed it into my back pocket. No clues, no man-spore. Didn't want to leave any sign of me.

From the direction of the porch, I then heard Merlot's voice. "Acky? Acky! Get your ass back in here! The computer's working again and I've got something to show you!"

I heard the back door slam. A petulant sound.

I didn't hesitate. I ran; ran hard along the hill and up the back stairs to the door where Acky would have reentered. As I reached for the knob, though, the door was suddenly flung open and Merlot thrust a revolver out. From the expression on his face—a mixture of expectation and terror—my first thought was: *He knew I was coming. . . .*

※

When he threw open the door, we each froze for a micro-second, both of us stunned to be standing nose to nose. So close I could smell him: a fried bacon odor, sweat, cigarettes. I could look through his eyes into him.

It was that moment of shock that saved me. He backpedaled slightly, me still coming hard through the door, and as he brought the pistol up, I knocked the barrel away from my face just as he pulled the trigger—ker-WHAP—the bullet's cone of percussion deafening me but missing.

Merlot's voice was shaking and he sounded near tears as he yelled, "Stay away from me or I'll kill you. I mean it! Stay back!"

I was still moving toward him; wanted to stay close as he brought the pistol down for another try. I caught his wrist in both hands, twisted counterclockwise as I used my knee to bang him hard beneath the ribs . . . and then I was holding the revolver as he stumbled backward and fell hard on his butt.

"*Oww-w-w!* You kicked me!"

Merlot was buckled over in pain as I pointed the revolver at his belly. I still felt the intensity, that appetite, but was fighting it. Shoot a man in cold blood? That was something I had never done. Yet the urge, the craving was there. I spoke to diffuse that feeling of want, of need. How could my voice sound so calm? I might have been joking around with a locker-room buddy. I said: "Know what? You really hurt my feelings, *Darkrume*. One fun night on the computer, then you never call, you never write. I feel downright used."

Something about the way I was smiling must have frightened him, because he began to cry now. *Boo-hoo-hoo,* actually making the distinctive noise, the skin on his face jiggling as the head bobbed. He had his hands out, palms toward me—*Please stop!*—as he said, "That was all a joke! You thought I was serious? I was *kidding.* It's one of those on-line E-mail things that everybody does. My God, if I thought you'd actually take the time to come looking for me, I'd have apologized right there!" Crying and shaking. His black eyes looked abandoned in the massive pink face; this gigantic baby with perfect hair and a baggy brown guayabera who had to weigh four hundred pounds but it was like Jell-O.

I turned to Gail. She wore jeans and a navy crewneck pullover. They were wrinkled and splotched as if she hadn't changed in a week. Her black Latina hair was combed back, heavy on her shoulders. She looked gaunt, badly used, but her face truly was lovely, haunting. That song, "The Twelfth of Never," it made sense now. For the first time, I understood. I said, "Are you okay?"

Her expression said she didn't know what to think. Scared, too. If I killed Merlot, was she next? She said, "Who are you?"

"I'm a friend of your husband's."

"My husband? You mean Frank sent you."

"No. Bobby's friend. A long time ago, I was Bobby's friend."

I watched her sag; watched her exhale, trembling as if just hearing that name had created within her an overwhelming surge of loneliness and regret. Very softly, she said, "Bobby's friend? My Bobby . . ."

I said, "Yes. Your Bobby."

She moved to stand near me, her hand touching my shoulder, saying Amanda? I knew Amanda? For God's sake, please tell her that Amanda was okay and didn't hate her, although she had every reason. . . .

I comforted her; dealt with the first concern of a good mother before I said, "You may not want to answer this, but I really have to ask: How'd you get hooked up with a freak like this?"

Merlot was on his feet again, following the conversation. Kept inching back. I knew the wheels were turning, trying to figure a way out.

She still seemed a little dazed. "I . . . I truly don't know." She was shaking her head slowly, as if trying to remember something. "I was so lost . . . so badly hurt that I must have lost touch with . . . reality? No. I must have lost touch with my sanity. I've spent the last month trying to figure it out, thinking of almost nothing else. How did it happen? Why did I end up with him? He was just always there, always . . . always right in front of me, no matter which way I turned. It got so I didn't even have to think because he did all the thinking for me, and I didn't have to cook or clean because he took care of that, too, and he was always saying the nicest things . . . and the next thing I knew, all my family and old friends were gone and he was selling me to men, to women and men, making me do things that I never thought . . . never thought—"

She couldn't continue. More tears, that sound of utter exhaustion.

Merlot didn't like the direction this was going, his shrill voice interrupting: "It was consensual, I'll swear to that! Everything this woman did with me or anyone else, it was always always consensual. I have her model release on file! I'll show you if you want. The pictures, the videos, she consented to everything—"

Merlot stopped abruptly. I was looking at him, looking into his face because he would not meet my eyes, and I could feel it in me stronger than I had ever felt it before, and he knew it. He knew. The voice that spoke did not sound like my own, as I said, "Did she consent to blackmail?"

Gail said, "What?" And then: "I was wondering about that. A second ago, why did you call him *Darkrume*? That's the only thing Jackie actually helped me with. I got mixed up with this person, this sick criminal from California. On the Internet, his name was *Dark-rume*. Not—"

I interrupted. Said to Merlot, "Do you want to tell her or should I?" I was still looking at him, wanting to do it, and he could see it in me, how badly I wanted to do it. I said, "A buddy of mine says that the way you worked it was with pin numbers. Lots of fake accounts and ATM machines. Was he right?"

When Merlot didn't answer, I cleared my throat and said in a much softer voice. "Last time I'm asking. Was he right?"

I got a quick nod, as he dropped slowly to one knee, then the other. Wanted to let me see the depth of his regret. Submissive, a primal gesture. Said, "Don't hurt me anymore. Please. I'll do anything. Anything you say, just tell me. I was wrong. Very wrong! But you have to understand that her husband—Frank I'm talking about—you have to realize that he treated me very badly years ago. I was angry. You don't think I have a reason? I'm a good person, normally. It was him, the way he treated me. The sonuvabitch had me put in jail and . . . and you don't know what they do to people like me in jail!"

In barely more than a whisper, I said, "Oh? I thought he treated you for pedophilia. He did, didn't he?"

The picture of Merlot and Amanda was there again, just behind my eyes. The revolver felt very light in my hand. Self-control, I was fighting to maintain it, as I heard myself say, "Don't want to talk about it? Okay, let's change the subject. Start by telling me how much cash you have in the house."

"Money? Not much. I really don't. Maybe a thousand dollars. You can have it all. I'm serious. I'll *give* it to you if it means no hard feelings. There's no reason why we all can't be friends!"

I used the pistol to motion at his face. "A thousand dollars? You'd better have a lot more than a thousand dollars. What you're doing here, fat man, is buying your life back. So dig deep."

The woman had moved close enough to me that our shoulders touched if I turned or gestured. She was watching, listening, maybe figuring things out. After I said, "So dig deep," she interrupted: "I don't care about the money. Just take me away from here. Let's go now. Please." She put long fingers to my elbow as if to stress her point. "But you need to have him arrested. Have him put away. Or you need to kill him, because he will never let me leave this country. I mean that. Not if he can get to a telephone."

I drew the hammer back on the revolver.

"Gail! You can leave. Honest! All I want is for you to be happy." His palms were pressed out again. "Did I say a thousand dollars? I have more. I forgot! Here, follow me. Follow me!"

He had more than $40,000 locked in a metal box behind a desk, plus some gems, some stock certificates and three nice Rolex watches.

I put it all in a pillowcase that I had stripped off the bed.

I said, "What about your video collection. And photographs?"

He was still very nervous, not convinced that I wasn't going to kill him. As if confused, he said, "Videos? Of who?"

"Of her, Gail . . . or pictures of anyone else I might know."

A light seemed to go on behind his eyes. Could see him thinking, Oh dear God, when he realized that I meant Amanda; that I had seen what Gail knew nothing about—the photo of him with her child daughter.

"I keep the pictures in my office," he said quickly. "I have a large safe there, humidity-controlled. Ask Gail, she's seen it. I'll take you there. Destroy them all, yes—I'll help! I've been meaning to do it, really. To look at them now, it makes me sick. It really does. Ask her!"

For a moment, only a moment, I let down my guard, as I turned to look at Gail for confirmation . . . and, too late, I heard her scream just before I felt the crushing impact of Merlot on me, his weight compressing my chest, one of his fat hands locked onto the revolver as he pushed me backward, backward toward the French doors of the little office we were in. . . .

I lost control of the pistol; heard it hit the floor.

When his big hand moved from my right wrist to my throat, I ducked under the mass of him and punched him hard in the kidneys . . . then slapped his face when he turned into me; slapped him with forehand, backhand, forehand, backhand . . . saw his big nose burst, the blood pouring . . . and then I hit him chin-high with a heavy right fist that knocked him through the French doors, where he tumbled backward over the railing and disappeared.

I picked up the revolver and went to the railing. He'd hit the ground hard, but was already on his feet. It is a distressing thing to watch fat people struggle to move quickly. They have been reduced by their own excesses, proof that suicide takes many forms. He was limping, but still trying to find cover as fast as he could move. The feverish determination reminded me of something . . . a wounded animal.

Gail was looking at him, too. What she said then surprised me, because she said it without pause or emotion: "I meant it. You should have killed him."

❈

I had my arm around Gail; had the money in the pillowcase as I led her down the steps to the driveway, where she waited while I straddled the Harley, got the kickstand up and ready to go.

"You really were a friend of Bobby's?"

"Ask your daughter. She can show you the letters."

"Then you're him. You're Doc. He wrote about you."

"Yeah. I'm Doc Ford."

She slid on behind me, huddled close in the rain. Had her hands meshed together over my stomach, her head resting against my back. As I throttled off, I had to remind myself: hand clutch on the left; the Harley's foot gearing was one down, four up.

There was something in the wind. Woodsmoke? Yes, I smelled smoke. . . .

It was the rainy season. Why?

Then I could see flames ahead, not far away on the village street.

I throttled toward the flames. Saw that it was one of the classic old Zonian houses ablaze . . . then I realized that I knew this place: Jackie Merlot's office and headquarters for Club Gamboa. No fire engines around as we rumbled past. No sirens in the distance . . . but a few people out now and watching, their silhouettes backdropped by flames as the place burned to the ground.

Matt Davidson had pointed out this building.

Matt Davidson had insisted on knowing when I was going to nail Merlot.

The man has videos of Taiwanese honchos misbehaving. . . .

Maybe because of that, or maybe something else. I would never be told because I had no need to know.

As I throttled off toward Panama City, Gail pressed her lips against my ear and said, "I was with Merlot for the same reason I was with Frank." I realized that she was still trying to answer my question: How had she ended up with such a freak? But that made no sense. Frank had been a good man; Merlot was a social anomaly. Or maybe it did make sense. Still talking into my ear, she added, "I was in love once. After that, other men are just a way of passing time."

20

It is difficult for me to write about what happened next because I remember so little about it. The events of that Saturday afternoon at the Balboa Yacht Club come back to me in little vignettes of memory, small intrusions of nightmare.

Once, weeks after I had been discharged from the hospital in Panama City, I awoke in the arms of a woman who was shaking me, then holding me. I sat bolt upright, looked around to find that I was safe in my little stilthouse on Dinkin's Bay.

That feeling, of being safe . . . it was such a relief.

"You were calling out again," the woman said. "I'm sorry. I couldn't bear it anymore." She touched her mouth to my cheek, then my lips. "It'll go away. It'll take time, but it will go away."

She meant Panama.

What I remember most consistently is a simple thing that Gail Richardson told me while still in Gamboa: *You should have killed him.*

My brain plays and replays that simple sentence. I can be jogging or preparing slides in the lab or sitting on the porch of my home looking at the lights of the marina, listening to liveaboards crack beers beneath Chinese party lanterns while Jimmy Buffett or Danny Morgan sing about their good, good lives on Captiva or in one particular harbor or Leadville or in Margaritaville.

That sentence will return: *You should have killed him.*

Here is what I remember: I remember checking into the Hotel Panama in downtown Panama City. A classic old hotel decorated with fiftyish chrome and marble and a good-sized pool beneath palms.

I remember Gail crying. The two of us talking, holding each other, as she buried her face in my shoulder and she sobbed and sobbed and sobbed.

We were in the bar? Yes, the bar. I had requested that the band play a song for her: "The Twelfth of Never."

Something else: the shower . . . she commented on the shower. About how good it was to be clean. The way she said it, it reminded me of an observation that Garret had made while I was in Colombia, something about the Turk. Something about the difficulties of getting clean. Or was that Tucker?

No . . . not Tucker. It was Tucker who had said, "You won't give me a chance to make it up to you!"

Tucker and Gail. Both right.

❋

The rest of it jumps ahead in time. It is all blurry, so jumbled that dredging it up plays through the memory like a badly framed home movie. Here are little snippets of video that remain with me:

Gail holding my hand as we walked down the yacht club's wooden steps to the bar on a verandah of worn gray marble. Seeing the big water, sailboats out there anchored with their wind fans spinning, the Panama Canal and the volcanic gloom of islands beyond . . .

Then hearing a familiar voice: "Hello!" Amanda standing topside aboard a large canary yellow racing boat, a Scarab. Waving at us from the cement pier, this huge grin on her face and maybe a little teary-eyed as she called, "I just got here! Haven't even put the groceries away yet!"

The boat's name in red letters, *Double Haul*, I remember reading that, plus a little surge of pleasure at seeing the lines of the Scarab, the implicit speed, and thinking it was going to be fun running a boat so fast and well designed up Panama's jungle coast.

Then . . . and then Gail is helped aboard and hugged by her much relieved daughter . . . the two of them disappearing below deck, each with a bag of groceries in hand . . . and suddenly, unexpectedly, I hear the shout of a man's voice: *"Get them off that boat!"*

I turn to see Tuck and the black bartender from Club Nautico charging down the steps toward me. Fernando? Yes, that was the man's name.

What the hell were they doing there?

Fernando and Tucker running, their expressions panicked, Tucker's feet going *clump-clump-clump* on sea-going wood that had probably never been fouled by a cowboy boot.

It made no sense seeing them. Tucker was in Colombia. I'd left him there at the little marina where his Freemason buddy worked as a bartender. How had they gotten to Panama? And how could Tucker possibly know where to find me?

"Marion! *Marion!* GET THEM OFF THAT BOAT!"

I was on the finger pier now, about to step aboard. From the galley below deck, I could hear Gail and Amanda laughing. Heard one of them say, "Where's the power switch?"

I stopped; looked at the open hatch, then looked at Tucker, who was still yelling: "The Turk, he was getting Amanda's E-mail! You understand?"

No. Nothing made sense. I stepped toward Tucker, my hands held out to stop him, but he charged right past me, almost knocked me into the water, as he jumped aboard the Scarab. Moved pretty good for a man that old. Was still yelling: "Amanda. Amanda! Don't touch a damn thing. They know you're here, that you're meeting your mama. You told 'em in your letter."

I couldn't hear her, but Amanda must have asked what or why, because Tucker said, "That Ohio woman. What the hell's her name, Betty? You've been writing to a church lady named Betty, but it's really the fat man!"

Which is when I was blinded by a light so devastatingly bright that it was as if a shard of ice had been driven through my brain. . . .

Then I was in the water. I was in the water and deaf, stone deaf, before a bright and busy inferno, from which tumbled the frantic shapes of people I had once known but could no longer recognize. . . .

The Mangrove Coast

A blazing cowboy hat worn by a flailing old man who had been long shadowed by the guilty memory of the very thing that now killed him . . .

A woman who might have been Gail, but it was difficult to be certain because she had no face . . .

A third person blasted from the flames who was so badly damaged that I refuse to attempt description. I will not do it.

The Panamanian police asked me about Amanda, saw the look in my eye and did not ask again.

※

Seventeen days later, when I awoke from what the good doctors described as a "life-threatening concussion," Fernando had recovered sufficiently to tell me what he had already learned.

Tucker had been shipped back to Florida and buried with full Masonic honors. But not until after word of some lingering trouble in Cartagena. Someone had beaten the Turk senseless, pissed on him (I didn't ask how that was verified), pick-axed his computer plus all its gear, stolen his hookah and then nosed the Turk's old junk wind freighter out into Cartagena Bay, where the *federales* did, indeed, impound the cache of hashish aboard, arrest the injured man and take him to a prison hospital.

"Your uncle was *mucho hombre,* much man, much man!" Fernando said. "But I would not return to Colombia for a while. Tucker Gatrell became famous there in a very short time. It will be remembered by some small and angry people that you are a relative."

Amanda, dear sensitive Amanda, was also killed instantly in the blast. Gail, however, though badly burned, had held on for many days before finally succumbing to pneumonia.

"One day I went to see her, but her bed was empty," Fernando said. "She was just gone. Disappeared. They told me that she had been flown back to Florida to be laid to rest next to the daughter and the first husband, the husband she loved."

Fernando gave me two more interesting tidbits of news. Our huge hospital bills had been paid in full by someone, they wouldn't tell Fernando who.

The men in the blue shirts, probably. Their generosity was unexpected, but not out of character. Matt Davidson had been right; the intelligence community tries to take care of its own.

Other news was that Panamanian authorities, working with the FBI and Interpol, were after Jackie Merlot and whomever he'd hired to rig the bomb in the boat.

So far, there was no sign of him.

It was as if he'd vanished from the earth.

Epilogue

For the next six months, I concentrated on my work and getting my health back. Physically, I recovered quickly. I was running and swimming as fast and as far as ever, but my mental health vacillated between depression and rage.

It worried my friends. I could see the concern on their faces when they thought that I wasn't looking.

It worried me, too. Something I did not tell them was this: I feared that I was slowly, inexorably, going insane.

That sentence, *You should have killed him,* came to haunt me in a way that I suspect Tucker Gatrell had been haunted by a mistake he had made many years before. To experience such a thing revealed to me much about why my uncle behaved as he did. To openly discuss what had happened would have invited a weight of despair that might have crushed him. So he locked the guilt away in a little room. He lived with the monster.

I was now living with my monster.

Much of my time alone was spent anticipating the day when I would corner Jackie Merlot and once again stand face to face with him. The authorities still had no leads on his whereabouts. Nor had my many contacts worldwide from the intelligence community been able to supply me with any hint of where the man was hiding.

I became so obsessed with finding him that I bought a superb computer and modem and spent my evenings trolling the chat rooms, asking people if they'd ever been contacted by *Merl* or *Darkrume* or *BettyofUnity*.

All of them the fat man.

I have never quit anything in my life.

Our day would come.

✳

Something helpful was that Maggie, my workout partner from Tampa, finally separated from her husband, and she took it upon herself to oversee my recovery. At first, the Dinkin's Bay women were less than friendly. I was THEIR patient and no long, leggy blonde from Hyde Park was going to come onto THEIR docks and take charge.

As JoAnn Smallwood said in a moment of pique, "What're you doing with this Maggie woman, Doc? She doesn't even like to fish."

No . . . but Maggie made me laugh. She could make faces like a sitcom comedienne. She was smart and kind and thoughtful and I liked the smell of her and I could crawl naked into bed beside her and, for ever longer periods of time, I felt at peace . . . at peace until I drifted off and the dreams returned. . . .

Black rain, banana leaves fauceting water, lunar halos, small precise breasts, a woman's eyes diminished by uncertainty, a mangrove shore. . . . Moon, wind, water, blood . . .

Those images and words came back to me in an endless, repetitive chorus that was maddening.

But it helped that Maggie was there. And because she is a kind and valuable person, the Dinkin's Bay women soon accepted her and she became a member of the community.

I was getting better.

✳

It was Maggie who brought me the hand-wrapped little package that arrived via UPS on a blustery December afternoon. The afternoon was cold enough for a fire in the little wood stove that I'd installed myself only weeks before.

Woodsmoke and turtlenecks and thick socks on Dinkin's Bay. It was a nice change.

I'd been drinking a mug of hot chocolate that the lady had provided me.

I should have put the mug safely on a table when I opened the package.

I did not.

When I opened the package and saw what was inside, I dropped the mug. Hot chocolate all over me and the floor, but I didn't even notice.

"Doc? *Doc?*" Maggie said hurrying toward me. "My God, you look like you're going to faint. What is it?"

I had my mouth open, forcing myself to breath. I took a few steps back and sat heavily in the reading chair beside my Celestron telescope near the north window. Finally, I had enough air to speak. "It's nothing. Don't worry about it. It's just a photograph of . . . of someone I knew."

"What'd you mean, don't worry about it? You're white as a ghost!"

She moved to put her arms around me, but I gently, very gently, nudged her away. I couldn't let her see this photograph.

Two photos, actually.

One was gruesome beyond imagination. It was a stock print of a sort that I recognized from my years working in the foreign service. It was clean—which is to say it was printed via a process that could not be traced.

It was a vertical shot, eight-by-ten color glossy. It had been taken early in the morning or late in the day in a mangrove swamp. The light was very rich: golds and iridescent greens beneath a peach-colored sky. It could have been taken anywhere. Florida, Central America, Asia. Anyplace that had been isolated by mangrove coast.

Mangroves were in the background. In the foreground was a stout pole that had been planted in the muck. Atop that pole was Jackie Merlot's pumpkin-sized head. His mouth was a round dark hole, a defining void, and his black eyes were opened wide but glazed with something. Flies?

I looked more closely.

Yes, flies.

Even so, those eyes seemed directed at the mound of flesh at the base of the pole.

Someone had positioned the head so that it faced its own body. Perhaps the Phmong were right. Perhaps Merlot's brain had fuctioned long enough. Perhaps the last thing he saw was his own decapitated corpse. . . .

"Doc . . . ? Doc, please! Tell me what's wrong. You're scaring me, Doc."

I was standing again. Kept the photos with me—no one could ever see them. Ever. I rushed to my dresser, opened the botton drawer, and pulled out the scarf with the raspberry red checks that I'd found the afternoon Frank Calloway died.

I was grinning at Maggie. I could see in her face that she thought that maybe, just maybe, I really had gone mad.

I told her, "I know what this is now. Finally! It's a traditional scarf that the mountain people wear. It's called a *kramas*. And the smell—the odor it had. It's this fermented fish sauce. Terrible stuff, but the locals get addicted to it. Like Vegemite in Australia, only this stuff is rotten. It's called *nuoc mam*."

The smell of it had tainted the air at Frank Calloway's house. But that is not what had frightened the man and caused him to panic.

I looked at the second photograph: There on the eight-by-ten glossy was the man who had frightened Calloway, caused Calloway to panic . . . and he was wearing a scarf like the one I had found.

I could hear Annie at the Temptation Restaurant telling me, "I just saw Crab Man hangin' around here."

I could hear Merlot reminding Acky of the beggar that he'd caught snooping.

I looked at the photograph and felt dizzy. I said to Maggie, "Would you mind bringing me a glass of water? Then giving me a few minutes alone?"

Her eyes were welling up. "Ford, please tell me you're okay. What is it?"

I said, "I'm fine. In fact . . . this is the best I've felt in a while. But give me a minute, okay?"

✳

There was a typed, unsigned note attached to the photograph. I read:

> The guy you know as Matt Davidson told me what I never doubted: You can be trusted. Over here we still operate on a need-to-know basis and here's what I think you need to know.
>
> After what you did, my friend, it's what you deserve to know, too.
>
> There are about forty of us still living here. Not because we have to but because we're all so screwed up we figured the only thing we could do back in the World is join the circus, maybe work as freaks. The POW camp my team was searching for? What it turned out to be was a collection of good guys who had too much pride to be a burden to their families. No one's really sure how it got started, but there wasn't any doubt in my mind that's where I wanted to go once I realized that mortar round had turned me into a monster.
>
> MIA guys who didn't want to return. That's something we never figured on, huh? It's hard to find men who don't want to be found.
>
> For the first six months, I thought I'd die. For the next year I hoped I would. Lots of us did. Those of us who didn't, realized something: We still had our brains and we had some of the best training in the world.
>
> I'm now a rich man, Doc. Rich beyond imagination. Every guy in our little company has made a bundle. Intelligence, weapons, brokered information to the CIA, NSA, Mossad, the big-money boys. We are the perfect middlemen because freaks are like clowns: we're invisible behind our

masks and we don't show pain. We've also started buying petroleum leases throughout Asia and investing in politicians. In terms of income, we are our own small country now. It's all we think about. It's all we do.

Once a year I come to Florida. I always stay in a little town called Gibsonton—I won't say why. It's too embarrassing. In previous years I always came with the hope of getting a couple of glimpses of my girls. I'd do it quick, from cab windows. Or late at night outside their house. I just wanted to make sure they were happy, didn't need anything.

Once, when Amanda was seven and alone in the backyard, she smiled at me. She actually said a few words to me. I didn't scare her. It is one of the treasured moments of my life. It means even more now that she's gone. And I thought I was beyond tears!

When I heard that Gail was in trouble, I was a step or two ahead of you. At first, anyway. Then I was always a step or two behind. Frankie Calloway's death was an accident. He panicked when he realized who I was and what I wanted. I sometimes forget how truly frightening I am.

Unfortunately, there is no way that either of us could have seen what was coming. And that's what this letter is about. Remember that idea we messed around with in the jungle, what we called the Perfect Law? In case you forgot, here it is: *In any conflict, the boundaries of behavior are defined by the party which cares least about morality.*

Merlot chose the boundaries. Check out the enclosed photo. He ended up with a whole different viewpoint, huh?

I thought you might enjoy this other picture, too. For the first time in many years, Doc, I am at peace.

It was another glossy photo and, in ways it was more shocking than the first. The extraordinarily handsome and vain man that I knew as Commander Bobby Richardson no longer existed. I wouldn't have recognized him. Ever.

He was so changed by his wounds and by the years, that I prefer not to describe the half-man in that photo, so I will not. What I noticed—and what I prefer to remember—is that he looked happy.

Bobby was smiling. Smiling a big, crooked country-boy grin as he posed with a tiny woman in Asian dress and black equatorial hair . . . a woman who could have passed for a Vietnamese burned, perhaps in a napalm attack. Yet there was a lovely expression of grace and acceptance on her ruined face; an expression elevated to devotion by the glow of her eyes as she looked at the man she loved: one eye the powder blue of turquoise, the other a deep jungle green.

She had drawn a heart on the photograph and signed it:

The Twelfth of Never!